WITHOUT MORAL LIMITS

*This book is one of the greats in women's health care literature.
Eloquent. Clear. The author has a talent for assembling volumes of
scientific research and condensing it for us all. She does not back
away from any important issue, however controversial. Abortion,
unnecessary cesareans and hysterectomies, the ethical implications
of live embryo research, the inefficacy of infertility diagnosis, test
tube babies, and the grandiose dreams of many of today's obstetri-
cian/gynecologists — the creation of artificial wombs where physicians can not only control conception and birth, but also gestation,
itself. Her insights on all these issues are invaluable. No hedging
on any topic do we find. Her answers are always backed by meticu-
lously researched facts.*

*All the questions I have had on these procedures she has answered.
And all my long-held suspicions have been confirmed. I shall be
quoting this book for a long time to come. Thank you, Debra Evans,
for your painstaking and tireless pursuit of the truth. May your
work lead many to freedom.*

David Stewart, Ph.D.
Executive Director, NAPSAC International

Also by Debra Evans

The Complete Book on Childbirth
The Mystery of Womanhood
Heart and Home
Fragrant Offerings
Beauty for Ashes
Preparing for Childbirth Pocket Guide

WITHOUT MORAL LIMITS

Women, Reproduction, and the New Medical Technology

DEBRA EVANS

CROSSWAY BOOKS • WESTCHESTER, ILLINOIS
A DIVISION OF GOOD NEWS PUBLISHERS

Cover design: Diane Fliehler
Cover photo: Four By Five, Inc
Photo/illustration: Karl and Diane Fliehler
Illustrations in Chapter 9 by Mark Marcuson.

First printing, 1989.

Printed in the United States of America.

Library of Congress Catalog Number 89-50319

ISBN 0-89107-472-4

To my daughters,
Joanna Elisabeth and
Katherine Laurel

Contents

Acknowledgments

*F*or their clear presentation of ideas about the interrelationships between human dignity, women's sexuality, and procreation, I wish to applaud the work of the following men and women: Leon Kass, M.D., Paul Ramsey, Nicholas Tonti-Filippini, Winnifred Egan, and Erwin Chargath (reproductive technology and embryo experimentation); Robert Mendelsohn, M.D., Herbert Ratner, M.D., Marian Tompson, David and Lee Stewart, Niles Newton, Ina May Gaskin, and Brigitte Jordan (women's health, childbearing, midwifery, and lactation); Janet Smith, John and Sheila Kippley (human sexuality and natural family planning); Sidney Callahan, Terry Selby, Bernard Nathanson, M.D., and Suzanne Rini (psychosocial consequences of abortion); Jean Vanier, Wolf Wolfensberger, and Jerome Lejeune (human rights advocacy for persons with genetic disorders); and C.S. Lewis, Francis Schaeffer, George Gilder, and Jacques Ellul (the spiritual and social effects of scientific utilitarianism).

I am also indebted to Lane Dennis, for his ongoing publishing support; to Lila Bishop, for her thorough editing of the manuscript; and to my *doula* team — Nancy Munger, Lori Marcuson, Nonie Nicklas, Sandy Kelley, Shawn Lohry, Carol Newsom, and Rogene Argue — for persevering.

To my husband Dave, with whom I've shared the pain and joy of writing/birthing *Without Moral Limits* chapter by chapter, I give my love and renewed appreciation. Thank you for daily accompanying me, shoulder to shoulder, through the past eighty seasons.

The endless cycle of idea and action,
Endless invention, endless experiment,
Brings knowledge of motion, but not of stillness;
Knowledge of speech, but not of silence;
Knowledge of words, and ignorance of the Word.
All our knowledge brings us nearer to our ignorance,
All our knowledge brings us nearer to death,
But nearness to death no nearer to God.
Where is the Life we have lost in living?
Where is the wisdom we have lost in knowledge?
Where is the knowledge we have lost in information?
The cycles of Heaven in twenty centuries
Bring us farther from God and nearer to the Dust.

T. S. Eliot,
from *The Rock, Chorus I* [1]

Preface

Strangely enough, the incident that sparked the desire to write this book was an appointment I had at a dental college in the spring of 1987—an odd place to start a research project on reproductive medicine, I must admit. As a volunteer in the University of Nebraska-Lincoln Dental School's board exams, I hadn't realized that in exchange for receiving a free gold filling I would end up spending two full days as a senior student's model mouth.

Needless to say, when a break arrived for lunch that first morning, I had little desire to head for the cafeteria and visited the campus library next door instead. While searching through rows of bookshelves in the human development stacks, I noticed a book curiously titled *Marriage and Family in the Year 2020*. One of the editors, Lester Kirkendall, was a name I had become familiar with while teaching sex education at the university. (Kirkendall had been a cofounder of the Sex Information Council of the United States, or SIECUS, the group responsible for introducing situation ethics and values clarification into sex education programs around the nation.) *Interesting,* I can remember thinking, *I wonder where Kirkendall hopes our culture will be thirty-five years from now.*

I checked the book out and immediately retreated to the lobby of the college to wait until the dental boards resumed. The contributors to the book, I discovered, had written their essays as if they were professors already living in the next century, reminiscing about how the American family had "progressed" beyond a traditional belief system to a more "fully human" philosophy of life. Looking up Kirkendall's piece, *The Transition from Sex to Sensuality and Intimacy,* I was greeted by these introductory statements:

> Explaining to persons living today, in 2020, how sensuality and intimacy were regarded in earlier centuries presents problems. To begin with, the language used in the past two centuries to

describe these qualities has changed. Over time, various words and phrases have become obsolete, forgotten, abandoned; new ones have taken their place. So we must begin our discussion by examining these language changes.

Even as recently as a century ago, the primary, and also the only morally acceptable use of the sensual organs, then known as the genitals, was to produce offspring . . . Since children came as a result of joining the female/male sensual organs, these were referred to as the "reproductive organs." But as children became economically less profitable and the reproductive emphasis diminished, penile-vaginal coupling was used less and less for procreation, and the term "reproductive organs" was almost completely dropped. It was then that the term "sex organs" came into being. But that term is now seldom heard. About the only time "sex" is used is when someone inquires as to the gender of a newly-lifed, or newly-delivered child (formerly said to be "newborn"), but for most of us even that information has relatively little significance. Female and male have become so similar in their life patterns that no one cares much about sex membership in the old-fashioned sense . . . We are all human beings first, female or male later.[2]

Kirkendall thereupon cites a note of warning (promise?) from someone whose name is immediately recollective of the not-so-distant sixties, Marshall McLuhan. A piece he had co-written with George Leonard, predictably titled *The Future of Sex,* had appeared in *Look* magazine nearly twenty years prior to my date with the dentist:

Sex as we think of it may soon be dead. Sexual concepts, ideals, and practices already are being altered almost beyond recognition . . . what it will mean to be a boy or a girl, man or woman, husband or wife, male or female, may come as one of the great surprises the future holds for us.[3]

Eliminating the biological differences through muting or obliterating the unique reproductive functions of men and women will mean the betrayal of marriage and the family, not *their future,* I thought. *What is happening to woman? What will happen to tomorrow's children? Where will we be if we head toward where today's attitudes are taking us?*

Glancing up at the clock, I noticed I had twenty minutes left before resuming my day-long adventure in dentistry. I read through

Kirkendall's list of the seven social trends he predicts will change the face of sexuality:

- Increased control over reproductive processes
- Increasing acceptance of sensuality and intimacy
- Harmonizing intimacy with other life experiences
- Acceptance of equalitarian ways of attaining gender identity
- A shift in behavior models
- A rounded life
- Emphasis on rationality in decision making

He then describes the cultural abandonment of all historic sexual taboos. Incest, the need for privacy, sanctions against public self-stimulation, and rules against sexual interaction between people of widely differing ages, he explains, have all been dropped. Sex education has been replaced with "sensual intimacy education." All of this is presented as desirable, normal, *wanted* . . . (By *whom?*) I could not help wondering what such a society would be like, knowing what our current level of sexual confusion has already unleashed upon us.

In his discussion of "The Process-Oriented Versus the Act-Oriented Value System," Kirkendall concludes:

The integration of sensuality and intimacy into the whole of life has moved us toward different moral/value concepts. A century ago the above heading would have been *The Existing Moral Code*. People were praised or condemned by their compliance with a rigid and limiting code of prescribed acts. At that time, the code centered heavily on sensual/intimacy activities. The intent was to ban any relating which might lead to pregnancy, to sexually transmitted diseases, or result in pleasure. This essentially barred any personal, private, or group sensual activity, except for a physical connection (i.e. intercourse) in which the possibility of procreation was fully accepted. Anything else was a perversion. But as the rigid code relaxed, new concepts evolved. At the same time vocabulary was altered: perversions became abnormalities, abnormalities became deviancies, deviancies became variations, variations became options, options became preferences, preferences became choices, and choices became life-enhancing experiences. With these developments came diversity and a growing concern with values geared toward building caring and responsible relationships.[4]

In one paragraph, this man dismisses centuries of cross-cultural wisdom as an "existing moral code!" Why is he so eager to sacrifice the covenant of marriage to a morality that has inflicted intense pain and suffering upon so many lives? What human toll does chastity reap in comparison to rampant sexual addiction? The burden of proof lies with men like Lester Kirkendall, not traditional moralists, to demonstrate that monogamy harms people. The tragedy is that Kirkendall's hoped-for future is approaching faster all the time.

With this, my lunch break ended. I spent the afternoon under the influence of Novocain, tilted back beneath the softly-filtered beams of an examining light, reflecting upon what the term sexual revolution actually means. I began thinking in larger terms about how current assumptions regarding sex and procreation, contraception and childbearing impact the dignity of woman.

Later, I read more of Kirkendall's book. I went on to learn of the mechanization of reproduction and mass-marketing of abortion, of artificial wombs and the cryopreservation of human embryos, of the "final liberation" of woman from her biological destiny and its complementary effect upon man. I have wept often at the picture that has emerged before me, not wanting to believe my eyes, as I have gathered over six thousand pages of documentation to substantiate my concerns about what is casually called the sexual revolution.

Concentrating on important journal articles written by physicians and scientists, I present to you the evidence that this revolution is being successfully manipulated and exploited by medicine, leading to an unprecedented explosion of surgery, human experimentation, and expansion of reproductive technology.

A new ethic now pervades what were formerly known as the healing arts. It is already affecting all of our lives.

Introduction

*I*n the Metropolitan Museum of Art hangs a little known Renaissance painting that is easy to miss unless you are specifically looking for it. Rarely pondered for its theme or composition, the subtly shaded canvas must vie for attention with dozens of world-famous pieces. Still, this unusual portrait makes a powerful statement. Time has not changed the beauty of the woman represented here, nor has it diminished the value of her message. She seems to be waiting to teach those willing to stop and look.

Clothed in a long, loosely gathered rose-toned dress, a beige shawl softly draped around her auburn hair and shoulders, she appears almost casual; she is elegant, relaxed, and open with her body. No harsh edges obscure the smooth contours of her features. Kindness glimmers in the radiance of her skin and smile.

But something more is going on in this picture. Next to the woman's heart reclines a naked toddler, calmly sucking at her breast, while another infant peacefully dozes in her lap. A third child at her right shoulder has captured his mother's attention. Their eyes meet as she seems to reassure him that he will be next to nurse. Her steady presence and ease of posture impart a transcendent dignity to the scene. The painting is titled *Charity*.

Charity? Surrounded by the needs of several infants, prepared to nurse two in rapid succession, this gentle matron affronts our modern notions of womanhood. Naturally, observers are prone to wonder: what happened to this woman's sense of self? Did she yearn for personal freedom? How could she have possibly cared for so many young children at the same time? Wasn't she aware of the necessity of finding a life for herself?

If such a picture were painted of this woman today, people would be offended. Critics would denounce the preposterous presentation of three nursing toddlers. Since breasts are no longer viewed as symbolic of comfort and commitment toward children in our culture, it would be virtually impossible to understand this woman in less than overtly sexual terms.

The meaning of women's breasts has been fundamentally altered since the 1930s, their reproductive role having been almost entirely exchanged for the erotic. Consequently, "boobs" are featured in advertisements for everything from deodorants to diet soda, but not in portraits of nursing babies. Visitors from Third-World countries even remark about the recreational fixation our country has with this part of the anatomy, perplexed at why so much national attention is geared toward certain sets and sizes of attractively displayed mammary glands.

Considering how quickly this aspect of women has been sexualized and subsequently exploited—all in the space of just one generation—it is not unreasonable to wonder what effects new reproductive technologies and attitudes about childbearing will have upon women in the next generation.

In the same way that bottle feeding made breastfeeding optional, widespread cultural acceptance of contraception, abortion, sterilization, and other counter-reproductive technologies render the womb optional as well. Unless a woman *chooses* to be pregnant, it is now fashionable to view fertility as merely a peripheral aspect of female sexuality, an accessory feature to be turned on and off at will, an oft-times irritating component of gender identity. In other words, it is no longer considered a central fact of a woman's existence.

In less than twenty years, sterility has become more acceptable than fertility, a vacant womb more valued than a pregnant one. Our social consciousness has moved much closer to the reproductive reality of Aldous Huxley's *Brave New World* than we might like to think. Not all women, however, accept this change as a step forward for humanity.

I, for one, am grieved that the "blessings of the breast and womb"[1] —nursing and childbearing—are no longer regarded as an integral part of women's experience, as cultural symbols of love and strength and generosity. I am grieved that a mother nursing her young children has become an antiquated metaphor for charity and compassion.

I am grieved that thousands of women each day elect to open up their wombs to the destructive invasion of physicians' cannulas and curettes rather than to the life-giving act of birth. I am grieved that millions of men and women have chosen surgical sterilization as the solution to living with the reality of procreation, accepting almost without question the prescribed number of "two children or less" per family.

I am grieved that our society has become increasingly captivated by sexual perversion and pornography, while growing hostile toward women's normal reproductive functions. I am grieved that more than 300,000 women will lose their fertility as a result of sexually transmitted diseases this year, victims of a hideous nationwide epidemic of infections called chlamydia and gonorrhea.

I am grieved that one in every four babies is now born by cesarean section, delivered by surgeons through incisions in their mother's abdomens instead of being birthed by the women themselves. And I am grieved at the transfer of lovemaking and conception to the medical clinic and the research laboratory, where woman's body becomes an apparatus and her eggs subject to search and seizure.

The question that keeps haunting me is this: If the biological integrity of woman continues to be invaded, altered, and separated from her soul, what will happen to the children? When the appointed guardians of new life depart, civilization becomes coolly efficient and calculated toward its weakest citizens. Social programs replace family nurture and traditional wisdom. Substitutes and surrogates are hired to fulfill maternal responsibilities. The betrayal of woman results in commercialization of the natural processes that create and maintain the basic bonds of life. Children are not commodities to be bought and sold—they are God's precious gifts, to be accepted, protected, and cared for without discrimination on the basis of sex or handicap.

We are rapidly becoming a nation that neglects this fundamental human truth. We no longer collectively value the uniqueness of man and woman and life created between them. We think we can buy anything for the right price, including children.

As a culture, we have not reached consensus on ethical issues surrounding conception and the prenatal period. Consequently, techniques that manipulate women's wombs, eggs, and offspring flourish. New reproductive technologies—based on a thirst for profit and the opportunity for research, discovery, and the pioneering of even better techniques—are developing at breakneck speed in a moral vacuum. Birth, death, and even conception itself are increasingly surrendered to the dominion of medical science, thus placing our faith, as Eliot noted, "farther from God and nearer to the Dust." The chemical, surgical, and cultural alteration of woman is symbolic of this process—advance warning of what could come.

It is as if someone had repeatedly stolen into the art museum and vandalized the painting of the charitable woman, one step at a time, erasing first her breasts, severing her physical connection to the children. The texture of her skin is subtly changed. A variety of interesting objects appear in the background, and then move to a position of prominence in the portrait. Infants begin to disappear from the surface of the canvas, eventually leaving only a solitary figure.

With a few more strokes of the brush, the transformation is complete: a new image has appeared, wholly representative of sexual autonomy, reproductive freedom, and personal success. The openhearted expression and sympathetic embodiment of charity have vanished. Without breasts or womb, a woman from the late twentieth century gazes with longing into the distance.

Part One

ASSAULTS ON THE WOMB

*. . . technological ventures into the space of woman,
though less cinematically spectacular, are both
more advanced and more portentous than any prospective
adventures of astronauts.*[1]

Chapter One

WOMEN AND REPRODUCTIVE SURGERY:
The Current Crisis

*Although medical and surgical overkill are routinely
inflicted on all Americans, its primary victims are women.* [2]

Robert S. Mendelsohn, M. D.,
Male Practice

*I*n the past fifteen years, women's reproductive systems have become the most surgically manipulated area of the human body. Of the fifteen most frequently performed operations in the United States, *seven are applied only to women.*[3] Of these surgeries, *three of the top four* — abortion, hysterectomy, and cesarean section — *focus solely on the womb.* [4]

The majority of these procedures are done by obstetrician-gyne-cologists. While most women view their "ob/gyns" as highly skilled specialists well qualified to recommend and perform these various operations, the threat of reproductive medicine is becoming clearly apparent — yet women continue to buy the belief that their doctors know what is best for them, either requesting or submitting to proce-dures that often have greater potential for harm than for benefit.

James L. Breen, M.D., past president of the prestigious American College of Obstetricians and Gynecologists (ACOG), admits that his field "is the only specialty that allows a physician to perform major surgery with only eighteen months of surgical training, much of that representing other than actual operating room experience."[5]

If obstetrician-gynecologists applied their surgical techniques with greater restraint, this lack of training would not seem so shock-ing. Women's attitudes toward their physicians would make more sense! But given current surgical statistics and the impact of rising health care costs upon society, it is every woman's right — *indeed, it is her moral responsibility* — to question the rationales used to justify these procedures. We must carefully evaluate technologies applied with increasing frequency to women's wombs.

In 1970, there were reportedly 18,876 practicing obstetrician-gynecologists in the United States; by 1985, this number had increased by *a full two-thirds* (67 percent) to 30,867.[6] Commenting on this phenomenon, Dr. Harry S. Jonas of the American Medical Association in Chicago predicts where coming years may lead:

> If professional liability has been the greatest threat to the pro-fession in the last decade, perhaps the next thundercloud on the horizon is the *intense competitiveness and marketplace aspect* of medicine. Alternative approaches to physician reimburse-ment seem inevitable. Physician income may have reached a plateau or experience a decline. . . .

The excitement of juggling the most ethical dilemmas in society, of mastering the appropriate use of each new technological breakthrough, and of functioning in a brave new world of competition and, at times, hucksterism — *all of which were essentially absent from the practices of earlier generations of obstetrician-gynecologists* — may provide the challenges that serve as attractions for tomorrow's young professionals.[7]

"Historians of birth have described what doctors and medical technology have done for women and children. . . . Too seldom have they described what birth has done for doctors," writes sociologist Dorothy C. Wertz. "Doctors owe much of their present social and economic status to the women whom they have delivered in the past two hundred years."[8] This statement particularly applies to the socioeconomic benefits reaped by ob/gyns during the past two decades alone. What began as a handful of specialists in the nineteenth century has become a medical megabusiness, supported by an oversupply of surgeons expanding their trade at the expense of women's wombs.

Consider these recent figures associated with the most common obstetric-gynecological procedures today:

- 953,000 cesarean sections were done in 1987, with the number having risen more than 400 percent since 1968;[9]
- American women currently have a 50 percent chance of having their uterus removed before they die, with over 650,000 hysterectomies performed annually;[10]
- More than 1.5 million surgical abortions are done in the United States every year, with an estimated cumulative total of 22 million having been performed since 1973.

The statistics are so staggering that it is difficult to grasp the number of lives and billions of dollars involved. Cesarean section, hysterectomy, and abortion are now experienced by over *3,000,000* women in America annually. Has this crisis been partially precipitated by too many physicians entering the field of obstetrics and gynecology since 1970?

Whatever the reason, the fact is that the past fifteen years have unleashed an unprecedented invasion of the womb, at tremendous cost, during which women's normal reproductive experience has been drastically altered by drugs and surgeons. It is no coincidence that also during this time, women's eggs, embryos, and fetuses have increasingly become the targets of a rapidly expanding field of diagnostic tools and scientific technology. None of these things would be happening if the medical profession had not succeeded in convincing women that all of this is necessary.

Throughout history, women traditionally have passed along their knowledge of the womb and its ways to their daughters, who in turn entrusted their granddaughters with these precious secrets. Childbirth was the exclusive domain of women, and midwifery was an art characterized by watching, waiting, helping, and heeding.

Women today have lost this folklore, these ancient traditions. We are the first generation in the history of the world to have been birthed under heavy anesthesia, fed almost exclusively with cow's milk via bottles, reared strictly according to schedule, and put on the potty before we had learned to talk. We were raised "scientifically," according to the experts. Our mothers no longer trusted the advice of their great-grandmothers and the old midwives. Doctors took the place of the women who had gone before, but at what cost?

Somewhere along the way, women lost a fundamental respect for their bodies that protected the integrity of their breasts and wombs. Even though we have witnessed the rise in popularity of "natural childbirth," how many births today can honestly be called natural? How many pregnancies succumb to the abortionist's tools? How many women reach the age of sixty with their reproductive systems intact?

Women are being drugged, suctioned, scraped, scanned, shaved, injected, and cut open *by the millions.* The domain of woman has become the domain of doctors. Our reproductive competency is being increasingly eroded and sabotaged by our faith in technology.

Before we can relearn the old truths, we must look at what we are in danger of becoming: women who cannot conceive, carry new life, or give birth without being plugged into machines, cut open with scalpels and hooked up to monitoring devices. We must unlearn what we may have come to believe about our bodies.

Chapter Two

CESAREAN SECTION: Surrendering Childbirth

When we become so confident as to believe that we can reproduce and design such a complex event as birth, we are assuming that we can, indeed, play God.[1]

Nancy Wainer Cohen and Lois J. Estner,
Silent Knife

This morning I attended the birth of a friend's third child by cesarean section. It was a paradoxically joyous and frightening moment as the surgery began and, moments later, her new son appeared through the incision. Standing close by, videotaping the event at the parents' request, I aimed the camera toward the sights and sounds of the first cry, the first touch, the first greetings. I was astonished once again at the apparent ease with which babies born by cesarean often enter the world.

Focusing the camera between oxygen tubes, I.V. poles, and the cardiac monitor, I tried to catch one of life's most mysterious and meaningful events: the arrival of a brand-new life into the circle of a family. My surgical mask covered my smile as I peered at the parents' beaming faces through the viewfinder.

Fast, professional, and technically accomplished, the surgical team was finished within half an hour. Because of the baby's birth and the uneventfulness of the operation, it was difficult to believe that major surgery had taken place. In fact, in many ways, the baby was born more efficiently than he might have been as a result of vigorous, natural labor—and that is precisely the threat cesarean section poses to the integrity of vaginal birth.

In 1940, well over half of all American babies were still born at home. Just one generation later, in 1970, hospitalization for childbirth had climbed to nearly 100 percent.[2] This constituted the first step toward the surrender of childbirth to the dominion of science. Since the early seventies, I have been an eyewitness to yet another revolutionary transformation in childbearing practices: the quadrupling of the cesarean birthrate.

Today, fewer and fewer of the women I teach are experiencing normal, vaginal childbirth. It is not unusual today for four or five mothers out of a class of nine couples to have their babies by cesarean. Health care professionals elsewhere around the United States confirm that my area of the country is not unique. What was once viewed as a medical emergency in obstetrics—a cesarean section—has become a commonplace event. In just twenty years, cesarean sections increased from just over *5 percent of births in 1970* to nearly *25 percent in 1988*.[3] This is an increase of more than *one percentage point per year.* The current cesarean rate is a prime example of our nation's naive fascination with high-tech obstetrics and reproductive medicine.

Who can possibly measure the impact of this trend on hundreds of thousands of mothers and babies each year? Where is documented proof that the costly cesarean epidemic has substantially improved birth outcomes? Why hasn't the American public demanded justification for the phenomenal rise in cesarean section rates?

What is especially appalling is that *at least half* of the cesareans now being done are medically unnecessary for women and their babies.[4] Could the the sky-high cesarean birthrate actually be benefiting physicians (and hospitals) *more* than their clients?

"The bottom line, I think, is that a cesarean is often much easier for an obstetrician," openly admits ob/gyn Dr. Stephen A. Myers of Mount Sinai Hospital in Chicago. "They don't have to stay up all night waiting."[5]

Unless doctors change their attitudes regarding long labors, common obstetrical challenges, and the practice of doing routine repeat cesareans soon, the National Center for Health Statistics predicts that the United States will reach a *40 percent cesarean section rate by the year 2000.*[6] In 1988, the rate had already climbed to a rate of 35 percent or higher at more than 100 American hospitals.[7]

Redefining the Meaning of Safety

"My cervix wouldn't dilate past seven centimeters."
"The baby was too big for my pelvis."
*"I was told the reason for the surgery was 'failure to
    progress.'"*
"Our first child was born by cesarean."
*"I pushed for two hours; then they decided to take the baby by
    c-section."*

Over the past fifteen years I have heard these comments from countless women who were convinced that a cesarean section was their only safe option for making it through labor and having a healthy baby. Only occasionally have I heard of a birth where a cesarean *without question* was necessary for the mother or her baby. Such cases make up a very small percentage (6-8 percent) of cesareans done today.

Isn't it just common sense that nearly one million American women per year wouldn't suddenly require major surgery in order to have a baby? The human race would have never survived such an onslaught of dangerous natural births! Over the past fifteen years, women have been coerced into believing that a cesarean is the *prima-*

ry way to solve childbirth difficulties. There is no real basis for this belief, however.

Dr. Helen Marieskind, in her study of cesarean birth for the National Institutes of Health, highlights physicians' lack of professional restraint in adopting cesarean section as a reason for this situation. She offers the following insightful comments:

> Cesarean section is a highly useful and essential part of modern obstetrical practice. The extent of its application and its benefits, however, should have been carefully evaluated and scientifically analyzed *before* it was widely adopted. It should not be necessary to come *later* and assess merits and consequences of a practice when it is already widespread, entrenched, and affecting over 600,000 [now over 950,000] women and babies every year.[8]

Dr. Marieskind found that the threat of malpractice suits, a strict policy of repeat cesarean section, physicians' overall training, an unsubstantiated belief in superior outcomes resulting from cesarean section, and new indications for the procedure to be the most significant reasons for this surgical explosion.[9] Studies conducted since her results were published solidly back these conclusions.[10] Notice that *none* of the major changes in c-section rates have involved life-threatening dangers. (Fig. 2.1) The greatest increases are associated with indications that *have never been proven to benefit* mothers and babies.

Since 1978, approximately half of all cesareans were performed only because the mothers had had previous surgical births — in other

---

Indications for Cesarean Section Showing Greatest Effects on the Increase in the U.S. Cesarean Birthrate, 1970-1978*

INDICATION	% OF ALL CESAREANS DONE FOR THIS INDICATION IN 1978	% CONTRIBUTION TO RISE IN RATE
Prolonged labor	31	30
Repeat Cesarean	31	25-30
Breech Presentation	12	10-25
Fetal Distress	5	10-15

*Source: NIH Development Task Force on Cesarean Childbirth

FIG. 2.1 CESAREAN RATE IN THE UNITED STATES, 1970-1978

words, *there was no actual medical indication for the operation.*[11] The widely accepted practice of "Once a cesarean, always a cesarean"[12] has determined the terms of birth for millions of mothers and their babies. Yet in recent years, this notion has been proven false.[13]

"For almost half a million women and babies [annually] to undergo the risk and pain of major abdominal surgery, with no apparent benefit," states C/SEC's Beth Shearer, "should be a national scandal."[14]

The rate of repeat cesarean section has continued to climb, year after year, as women have bought the belief that vaginal birth is a risky, hazardous process from which physicians dutifully rescue them.

A recent article appearing in the *American Journal of Public Health* based on a national survey of hospital records reveals that "except for the uterine scar from the previous cesarean, VBAC (vaginal birth after cesarean) mothers appear to have about the same history and frequency of complications as mothers with other vaginal deliveries."[15] Put simply, this means that a woman's ability to labor and give birth vaginally *is not affected in any significant way by a previous cesarean birth !*

The time has come for women to seriously question the motives of physicians who do not promote and encourage VBACs. Becoming familiar with the risks of cesarean birth is a key to changing this situation.

Considering the Risks and the Rationales: Who Benefits?

A Rhode Island study of maternal mortality associated with cesarean sections found the risk of death to be twenty-six times greater for cesarean delivery than for vaginal birth.[16] Even once allowances were made for co-existing factors, the researchers found a tenfold increase related to the surgical procedure itself. Currently accepted estimates state that there is a *two to four times* higher risk of death and *five to ten times* higher risk of illness for mothers who give birth by cesarean section compared to women having vaginal births.[17] In 1988 alone, there were 25,000 infections caused by cesarean births.[18]

Other risks and costs associated with cesarean section include:[19]

- A sevenfold to twentyfold increase in the rate of maternal infection
- Risks of anesthesia to the mother
- Surgical injuries to the mother's urinary tract and bowel

- Increased risk of maternal blood loss, blood clot formation, and blood vessel obstruction
- More respiratory distress syndrome in surgically delivered infants
- Higher risk of complications in newborns from reduced uterine blood flow, anesthesia, accidental surgical injury, aspiration, cold stress, and absence of labor
- Psychological and physical stress associated with having major surgery
- Substantially longer hospital stays
- Higher medical costs
- Longer recovery period

Cesarean section remains a major surgical procedure, with all the potential complications of any operation, even though its apparent ease might suggest otherwise.

"A growing body of research makes it alarmingly clear that every aspect of traditional American hospital care during labor and delivery must now be questioned as to its possible effect on the future well-being of both the obstetric patient and her unborn child," points out Doris Haire, president of the American Foundation for Maternal and Child Health.[20]

After having a cesarean section, women also have *greater difficulties conceiving and carrying subsequent pregnancies* to term.[21] Furthermore, the 1982 National Survey of Family Growth revealed that *sterilizations are more frequent and performed at a younger age among women who have had cesareans* than among women who have given birth vaginally. When both of these factors are combined, decreased fertility becomes an additional risk factor rarely mentioned to the public.

In spite of these concerns and a set of new guidelines issued by the American College of Obstetricians and Gynecologists aimed at reducing the repeat cesarean rate,[22] it may be some time before VBACs and lower cesarean rates become the norm — that is, unless health insurance companies stop covering payments for elective repeat cesareans. Is it only a coincidence that repeat cesareans and the need for VBAC are in the news? Insurance companies had *already announced their intent to discontinue reimbursement* for elective repeat cesareans well before the American College of Obstetricians and Gynecologists held a widely publicized press conference and announced that "repeat cesarean births should no longer be routine."[23] Does money talk louder to health care providers than documented cesarean-related death and illness rates?

Am I Having This Cesarean for You, Doctor, Or for Me?

Hospital reimbursement for vaginal births runs approximately $3,000 lower than for cesarean sections, and doctors' fees for vaginal deliveries may run as much as $500 less than for performing a cesarean.[24] The cost of cesareans totaled one billion dollars in 1988 and kept women in hospitals an extra 1.1 million days.[25]

Not surprisingly, three separate studies of the relation of payment source to cesarean birth rates showed that *private physicians perform significantly more cesareans* than house officers and attending physicians.[26] Additional surveys show that when insurance pays the bill, cesarean rates *double.* [27] (Fig. 2.2)

Cesarean Section Rates by Type of Insurance, 1983*

PAYMENT SOURCE	CESAREAN SECTION RATE, %
Blue Cross	22.5
Other private, commercial insurance	21.5
Medicaid	18.6
Self-pay	17.1
Other government sources	16.7
No charge	11.4

*Source: American Journal of Public Health

FIG. 2.2

Dr. Norman Gleicher, an ob/gyn at Mount Sinai Hospital Medical Center in downtown Chicago, comments on this controversy:

> The physician's clearest disincentive toward vaginal delivery is the currently accepted fee structure in which cesarean deliveries command higher rates than vaginal deliveries, despite the fact that cesarean section requires approximately one hour of physician's time, while protracted labor may require substantially more. A financial incentive for vaginal delivery should, therefore, be instituted by raising fees for vaginal deliveries above those for cesarean sections. . . .
>
> Hospital administrators' and physicians' incentives toward cesarean delivery may at times run parallel. . . . In our own community, the media reported cesarean section rates of higher than 25 percent in some suburban community hospitals with almost no high-risk population and at the same time cesarean

birthrates of 14 percent to 16 percent in some of the highest-risk areas of the nation (*Illinois SUN Journal*, March 5, 1983). It is worthwhile to mention that only the media noted the difference. Medical organizations never did.[28]

Beyond the economic incentives involved, fear of malpractice suits also promotes surgical intervention.[29] Seminars in the legal aspects of obstetrics (with titles such as "The Brain-Damaged Baby") are now offered nationwide to enable lawyers to better prepare malpractice cases. Since 1976, the number of lawsuits against ob/gyns has tripled: *nearly two out of three* have been sued at least once, and one in five has been taken to court three or more times.[30] In some areas of the country, obstetricians pay over $60,000 annually in malpractice insurance premiums.

"Taking the baby by cesarean," has unfortunately become a trademark of defensive medicine because it is viewed as rescuing the baby from the hazards of labor. "The climate is such that if the physician has done a cesarean, he has done everything he can," says Dr. Thomas Garite, a specialist at Long Beach Memorial Hospital Medical Center in California. "If he tolerates a long vaginal birth and gets a damaged baby, it is more likely to be attributed to the physician's not doing enough."[31]

Lawsuits involving million-dollar-plus settlements over "damaged" babies born vaginally are partially responsible for the increase in cesarean sections performed for long labor. Even though cesareans are in fact *more dangerous* to both mother and baby than vaginal births in the majority of cases (see notes 16-19), most malpractice claims center upon nonsurgical deliveries. *Doctors consider it legally safer to perform a cesarean section than to risk being sued for damages that might possibly arise during a challenging vaginal birth.* Also, it is difficult to prove that surgical intervention did not benefit the baby.

Nevertheless, nationally known physician Emanuel A. Friedman of Beth Israel Hospital in Boston reaches this conclusion about the relationship of labor management to birth outcome:

Most fetal death and damage is unpreventable, in that it is related to events or factors before delivery, over which the physician has no control. It is unrealistic, therefore, to expect every delivery to result in a living, healthy, unaffected infant. No amount of expertise, skill, or excellence of care can compensate for or undo existing damage. This is not meant to absolve providers of their responsibility for diligent attention and astute management, but rather to put the matter into a realistic perspective. The tools at the obstetrician's disposal for assessing fetal well-being during labor are inadequate. The promise of such major technological advances as continuous electronic monitoring of the fetal heart rate and fetal-scalp blood sampling has not been fulfilled.[32]

Additional Controversies in Obstetrics

In the late sixties and early seventies, longer labors were viewed as causing problems such as cerebral palsy, depression, and neurological impairment.[33] In spite of research that consistently fails to support this view,[34] the diagnosis of long labor, or what is formally termed *dystocia,* has made the largest contribution to the increase in cesareans.[35]

Dr. Randall Bloomfield of New York City's Kings County Hospital Center calls dystocia a "wastebasket term" doctors use to identify anything from weak labor contractions to difficulty the baby has in passing through the mother's pelvis.[36] Yet this catch-all diagnosis is responsible for at least a *30 percent share* of the increase in cesarean section rates over the past twenty years.[37] (See Figure 2.1.)

The Cesarean Birth Task Force, conducting a review for the National Institutes of Health in 1980, found *no evidence* that normal weight babies are healthier if delivered by cesarean in cases of long labor, recommending that doctors should work with this problem in other ways instead. Rest, fluids, walking, upright positions, emotional support, and nipple stimulation can help shorten labor. In spite of excellent research in the past eight years validating these alternatives, the high rate of cesarean sections performed for prolonged labor continues.

Also contributing to the changes in approach to long labors has been the introduction of a new medical technology: *continuous electronic fetal heart rate monitoring,* or EFM. This obstetrical assessment tool was originally developed in the late 1960s to improve detection of fetal distress in only those labors considered to be at-risk (5 percent) for developing complications. By 1972, however, an estimated 1,000 EFM systems were in use throughout the United States.[38] A standard feature of obstetrical departments today, EFM is now routinely applied to healthy women as well as those termed "high-risk" patients.

Seven randomized clinical trials have been conducted to determine whether EFM improves newborn mortality and morbidity rates.[39] Each study reached the same conclusion: compared to periodic checking of the baby's heart rate by amplified stethoscope or fetoscope, the additional data provided by EFM does not appear to improve infant outcomes when applied to healthy laboring women. In other words, *there is no evidence that the benefits of routine EFM exceed the risks.* For the baby, these risks include false identification of fetal distress and scalp abscesses, and for the mother, three times more vaginal exams, stress reactions to being connected by belts to a machine during labor, decreased ability to move about during labor, increased rate of pelvic infection, and up to *double t*he rate of cesarean section.[40]

Periodically checking the baby's heart rate externally with an amplified stethoscope or a fetoscope during labor *eliminates or lowers* all of these risks. In addition, listening to the baby's heartbeat in this manner (auscultation) offers one-to-one "hands-on" nursing care to women giving birth. According to Dr. Albert D. Haverkamp and his associates at Denver General Hospital:

> There are subtle, less obvious factors involved in the actual care of laboring patients which could influence infant outcome. Nursing attention . . . with respect to maternal comfort, emotional support, and "laying on of hands" could have a significant impact on the fetus. . . . [we] have the impression that the reassuring psychological atmosphere created by personal nurse interaction and the absence of the recording machine in auscultated patients contributed to the excellent infant outcome.[41]

Making the Abnormal Normal

It appears that most doctors are finding themselves caught in a classic Catch-22 situation: if physicians significantly reduce their cesarean rate, they may be taken to court when involved in a poor outcome associated with a vaginal birth; if they continue to protect themselves legally by performing cesareans for "borderline" situations, they may be held accountable for doing too many cesarean sections. *The very existence of obstetrical technology has created a legal mandate for its use, regardless of the unproven benefits and clear risks.*

By promoting the concept that childbirth is hazardous and that the specialty of obstetrics produces better babies (thereby making the physician's services seem all the more necessary), doctors have created a monopoly on maternity services and, at the same time, inadvertently have built their own impasse. American medicine has yet to provide the evidence to support a cesarean rate of much higher than 10 percent,[42] yet there were almost *two and a half times* that many surgical births in 1988. Is the availability of obstetric technology irresistible to those who control it?

"History teaches that what is introduced for the unusual, the infrequent, and the abnormal, with time, becomes the usual," explains physician and family advocate Dr. Herbert Ratner. "The litany is long: bottle-feeding, vitamins, miracle drugs, tonsillectomy, and in obstetrics, sedation, anaesthesia, episiotomy, low forceps, with cesarean in the offing and intravenous fluids given routinely."[43]

What was first introduced as the unusual, the infrequent, and the abnormal has indeed become the usual, the frequent, and the normal. Numbers alone cannot convey the far-reaching impact of this revolution in birth practices. Unless we see beyond the data and the demographics, our hearts and minds will remain numb to the tragic scope of the cesarean crisis. We may even convince ourselves that it does not matter.

But birth *does* matter. It is far more than a momentary medical emergency: it is a landmark event in the life of a woman. *Cesarean section is not just another type of abdominal surgery*—it is a bypass route around intensely intimate and sexually significant territory, a detour that completely changes the scenery of one of life's most significant passages. How long will American women continue to surrender their children's births to the whims of medical fashion?

Chapter Three

HYSTERECTOMY:
A Double Standard of a Different Kind

Some readers may feel a twinge of queasiness at a public disrobing of the medical priest. We have all made investments of trust in our doctors and hospitals. It isn't pleasant to be confronted with evidence of their inadequacies or to learn that the patient's welfare doesn't always top the list of priorities. We feel betrayed. But confronting the facts of this betrayal of trust is the necessary first step on the road to reform.[1]

Charles B. Inlander, *Medicine on Trial*

Do gynecologists in the United States perform too many hysterectomies? Are healthy wombs being removed without women's *informed* consent? Should it be considered unethical for a physician to perform a hysterectomy for elective sterilization?

Based on current knowledge of this procedure, the answer to all of these questions is an emphatic *yes*.

Hysterectomy, or surgical removal of the uterus, is a major operation that permanently affects a woman's mind, body, and sexuality in several significant ways. In addition, the risk of death from the procedure is one to two for every 1,000 operations.[2] Unless the uterus poses considerable risks to a woman's health, it is best to avoid both the short- and long-term complications related to hysterectomy by applying alternative solutions whenever possible.

Between 1970 and 1978, more than 3.5 million women of reproductive age (between fifteen and forty-four) underwent hysterectomy in the United States.[3] During this time, hysterectomies were performed in record-breaking numbers, at a rate higher than that associated with any other major operation.[4] Prior to the sixties and seventies, hysterectomies were more common only among older women. Today, two-thirds of the hysterectomies performed each year are done on women under forty-five.[5] By this age, one out of every five American women has undergone hysterectomy.

In his book *Women Under the Knife,* Dr. Herbert H. Keyser points out that "at most hospitals, any gynecologist who honestly evaluates the surgery taking place knows that unnecessary operations are being done. . . . Thus women who wish to avoid unnecessary surgery must become medically sophisticated and make use of second opinions."[6] In other words, *the high rate of hysterectomy is likely to continue as long as women are offered the procedure and think that major surgery is their best — or only — option.*

An indication that hysterectomies are being done according to medical fashion rather than as treatment for disease is reflected in the varying rates of different countries. In the United States, the national hysterectomy rate is *five times higher* than the current rate in six European countries (ours — 21 percent; theirs — 4 percent).[7] What accounts for the huge difference?

Dr. Philip Cole, of the Harvard School of Public Health, believes the answer lies in medicine's view of this reproductive organ:

I doubt that there have been different rates of increase in clinically important uterine diseases. Rather, the difference in the national rates is probably explained by a difference in the indications for the operation. . . . I suggest that the difference in national rates and the increase in the United States rates are due particularly to the growth of "prophylaxis" [preventative treatment] as an indication for surgery—based on the rationale that if a woman is thirty-five or forty years old and has an organ that is disease prone and of little or no further use, it might as well be removed.[8]

A recent nine-year study of hysterectomy rates in Switzerland supports Dr. Cole's point. Appearing under the headline "Effect of Information Campaign by the Mass Media on Hysterectomy Rates," a summary of the article states:

The annual frequency of hysterectomy was monitored in the Canton Ticino, Switzerland, from 1977 to 1986. From February to October, 1984, there was a public information campaign in the mass media about rates of and need for hysterectomy. *After the start of the campaign and during the following year the annual rate of operations per 100,000 women of all ages dropped by 25.8%, whereas in the reference area (Canton Bern), where no information was given to the public, hysterectomy rates increased by 1%.* In the same period the hysterectomy rate per 100,000 women [in Canton Ticino] aged 35-49 *declined by 33.2%,* and the number of hysterectomies performed annually per gynecologist *decreased 33.3%.* In Canton Bern, these rates were *unchanged.* The decline began two months after the start of the information campaign. The reduction in the number of hysterectomies was greater (p<0.001) in non-teaching hospitals (31.9%) than in teaching hospitals (18.1%). *Information on regional rates and on the need for hysterectomy given through the mass media to the general population can change professional practices.*[9]

Reproductive biologist and medical researcher Dr. Winnifred B. Cutler states that in America, "The population rates of hysterectomy are startlingly different."[10] Cutler has discovered that women living in the southern and central regions of the United States have hysterectomies *"two to three times more often* than women in the Northeast and on the West Coast."[11] Might this be because women in these parts of the country are better informed about the risks of hysterectomy and more knowledgeable concerning strategies for avoiding surgery?

Using alternatives to elective hysterectomy – such as stress management, pelvic floor exercises ("Kegels"), and vitamin therapy – enables many women to avoid the invasive "cure" advocated by many gynecologists. Gaining information about these alternatives ofte requires adjusting one's lifestyle to promote reproductive health, as well as ongoing determination to seek answers from a wide variety of sources: wellness centers, textbooks, health guides, magazines, support groups, medical journals, and self-help books.

Until recently, very few physicians presented women with alternatives to surgery; even today doctors often neglect to inform their client of the full range of options that are available. Unfortunately, women who repudiate this belief by making informed choices about ther health care are still the exception rather than the rule.

Changing Indications for Hysterectomy

In the past, the majority of hysterectomies were performed primarily due to life-threatening disease. This is no longer true today. Even though cancer of the uterus is the *only* diagnosis for which hysterecto-

---

A thirty-two-year-old woman visits her physician for an annual Pap smear. Mentioning that she had recently been experiencing involuntary leaking of urine upon sneezing or coughing, she is told excessive pelvic floor relaxation has occurred and is advised to have a hysterectomy.

Her doctor puts it this way. "If you've got a bad bag in there, you take it out."

---

my is automatically indicated, data collected in the United States between 1978 and 1981 revealed that this surgery was performed as a result of a malignant or precancerous condition in just 10.6 percent of the cases involving women between the ages of fifteen and forty-four.[12] When women of all ages are added to this total, only *one out of every five* hysterectomies is performed for a cancer diagnosis.

In 1969, an editorial appearing in *Obstetrics & Gynecology* strongly advocated a radical change in the criteria for hysterectomy. Dr. Ralph C. Wright revealed the opinion of many of his colleagues when he wrote:

If we bear in mind the logic of one basic principle, the future course seems clear. *The uterus has but one function: reproduc-*

tion. After the last planned pregnancy, the uterus becomes a useless, bleeding, symptom-producing, potentially cancer bearing organ and therefore should be removed. . . .

After completing her family at age thirty, why should a woman accept the nuisance, the inconvenience, or *the disability of menstruation* for another twenty years? . . .

In summary, elective hysterectomy is prophylactic and sterilizing and provides permanent symptomatic relief. The patient can now lead a happier more comfortable and more productive life, free from the anxieties and the monthly problems associated with *the useless and potentially lethal reproductive organs.* . . .

Will women in this modern era awaken to the fact that the monthly "curse" is no longer a necessary part of life? Will there arise a crusader like Margaret Sanger? Or will gynecologists take the lead and move to the logical conclusion? Perhaps both will occur. But regardless of the source of the final impetus, we will inevitably arrive. *Elective hysterectomy is just around the corner.*[13]

Note Wright's characterization of women's normal reproductive function and the "logical conclusion" he recommends: *elective hysterectomy* following the birth of the last baby! Admitting that some patients would not accept this approach, he warns that many will be "deterred by such factors" as their belief in the "need" for menstruation, fear of surgery and "misconceptions about the after effects of hysterectomy."[14]

The fact is, no one — including Wright — fully knows what the aftereffects of hysterectomy are. The benefits and risks of elective hysterectomy are as yet largely unknown. "For how many women the quality of life is improved after hysterectomy, and for how many it is made worse we simply do not have the data," explains Dr. John Bunker, a professor of Family Medicine at Stanford University."[15]

In a profession in which over 92 percent of its members were men, however, Wright's recommendation found wide acceptance across the nation when he described the uterus as "useless," "symptom-producing," "potentially cancer bearing," and "potentially lethal."[16] At a meeting of the American College of Obstetricians and Gynecologists two years after the editorial appeared, the desirability of elective hysterectomy was openly debated. Afterwards, proponents outclapped opponents on an audiometer by a substantial margin.[17] *The hysterectomy rate climbed every year thereafter,* reaching a record high of nearly 900,000 hysterectomies in 1978.

Weighing Risks and Benefits

In spite of insufficient information on the long-term effects of the procedure, elective hysterectomy as a solution to pelvic pain and bleeding problems remains common. As for the use of hysterectomy as an effective cancer-prevention measure, Dr. Robert S. Mendelsohn sees this approach as "akin to getting rid of mice by setting the house on fire."[18] He writes in his excellent book *Male Practice:*

> There is less chance that a woman will die from uterine cancer than that she will die when a hysterectomy is performed. . . . There is only one rational explanation for all of the needless hysterectomies that are being performed. Doctors, being dedicated to the most extreme forms of intervention and wanting the income that comes from intervening, fail their patients miserably by not giving them the information they need in order to make an informed choice.
>
> How many women would permit, much less seek, a hysterectomy for a reason that was not life-threatening if they knew that in 1975 more than 1,100 women died from the procedure? How many would welcome sharing the misery experienced by more than 30 percent of the patients who had some type of infection as a result of the surgery, or the one in six who required blood transfusions? How many women would relish being exposed to the additional danger of infectious hepatitis [and now AIDS] from the transfused blood or from the equipment used in delivering intravenous fluids?
>
> Would women deliberately choose hysterectomy as a means of sterilization if they were told that the procedure is twenty times more likely to kill them than a tubal ligation? Would they accept a hysterectomy as a means of preventing cancer if it were suggested that this was also a good reason to have both breasts removed?[19]

The answers to these questions seem obvious, yet more than *655,000* women underwent this surgery in 1987. In the United States, the average age at which hysterectomy is currently experienced is *thirty-five years.* Has our society bought the belief voiced by Dr. Wright that the womb has little anatomical, physiological, or psychological value beyond its childbearing function?

Dr. Malkah Notman, of Beth Israel Hospital in Boston, finds it absurd that the uterus of a woman past childbearing age "could be considered a nuisance or a foreign body." Says Notman, a psychiatrist, "It appears to me extreme to assert the uterus has no function and seems contrary to both common beliefs and psychologic realities."[20]

A thirty-four-year-old woman with a "tilted" uterus sees her physician for severe pain associated with her menstrual periods. She is told that a hysterectomy would solve the problem by removing excess pressure from within her pelvic area.

Why Is the Womb Treated Differently?

Picture the following situation involving a thirty-five-year-old woman. She has just been told she might need a hysterectomy to treat a stubborn pelvic infection. After returning home from the doctor's office, the woman asks her husband what he would have said to a physician who suggested removal of his testes upon a single recurrence of an infection in that area. Her husband laughs (not at his wife, but at the very idea that a physician would suggest such a thing) and says in no uncertain terms that he would never consider it unless the infection was life-threatening.

"But why should women's wombs be treated any differently?" she responds.

"Because men don't view a woman's uterus and ovaries the same way they view their testes," is his blunt, but honest, reply.

Testes are viewed by our culture as more essential to sexual health and identity than the uterus or ovaries. *But why are women's wombs (and ovaries) considered less valuable than men's testes? Why is hysterectomy the fourth most common surgery performed in the United States? Why do one out of every two women consent to having their wombs removed during their lifetime?*

The testes — like the ovaries — have two primary functions: the production of gametes, or sex cells, and the secretion of sex hormones. If a man does not wish to have children, he would obviously opt for a vasectomy over having his testes removed. But, until recently, hysterectomy was *the most common method of permanent contraception for women.*[21]

A number of physicians have gone on record saying that performing a hysterectomy primarily for sterilization can no longer be justified, citing the following reasons: the mortality and sickness rates for women having hysterectomies are *tenfold to one hundredfold greater* than for tubal ligation; the expense and recovery time associated with hysterectomy are much greater; and the long-term physical and psychological impact of this procedure appears to be greater as well.[22]

> *A woman in her early forties whose grandmother died of uterine cancer is told that the lining of her uterus has a tendency to develop excess tissue. Since this condition may lead to cancer, she is told it would be wise to have a hysterectomy in order to avoid that danger.*

When a family history of testicular cancer exists, men do not have their testes removed as a preventative measure. Furthermore, one never hears about men on "hormone replacement therapy" (HRT) due to the surgical loss of their testes. Yet HRT in women for the same reason — removal of the gonads — is widespread today. The testes are not considered simply an accessory to masculinity. *They are viewed as part and parcel of what it means to be a man.* To further illustrate, consider this brief but revealing report from the *Medical World News* :

> During a cancer conference last year, a discussion took place among surgeons on attitudes toward orchiectomy (removal of the testes) versus ovariectomy, and it was agreed that surgeons rarely hesitate to remove an ovary, but think twice about removing a testicle. The doctors readily admitted that such a sex-oriented viewpoint can and does arise from the fact that most surgeons are male. Said one of them, wryly, "No ovary is good enough to leave in, and no testicle is bad enough to take out."[23]

While it would be unfair to characterize all physicians by this statement, the bias undoubtedly exists. Dr. James C. Doyle's article "Unnecessary Ovariectomies: Study Based on the Removal of 704 Normal Ovaries from 546 Patients" speaks for itself.[24] In reviewing surgical reports of private hospitals in the Los Angeles area, Doyle discovered that in every case where normal ovaries had been removed, the procedure had accompanied hysterectomy.[25] "The routine removal of ovaries during other gynecologic operations as a prophylactic or preventive measure against future development of cancer of these organs has been advocated by certain physicians," writes Doyle. "Now and then a physician recommends that a prophylactic should not be done at any age."[26]

Now and then? Have physicians ever advocated the removal of the testes as a "prophylactic and preventive measure"? Yet testicular cancer accounts for *12 percent of all cancer deaths* in men fifteen to thirty-four years of age![27] Lest one think that Doyle's findings are in any way outdated, the *Ob. Gyn News* reported in 1980 that in the previous decade, ovariectomies had increased by 48 percent in women forty-five to sixty-four years old, and by 23 percent in younger women.[28] How many of these surgeries were unnecessary?

Counting the Costs

Not all gynecologists minimize the effects of reproductive surgery on women. Dr. Leroy Weeks, professor of obstetrics-gynecology at the University of Southern California School of Medicine, admits that "Complications of gynecological surgery are considerable and when reviewed in detail are almost frightening. . . ." Listing the ten most common errors made by doctors performing abdominal hysterectomies, Weeks concludes, "Every surgeon has his favorite operation, technique, maxims, and superstitions, and as long as they are being used in the best interest of the patient, all is well. The risk is that he may lose his flexibility, assume a posture of God, and become careless about the application of his expertise."[29]

Severe pelvic pain sends a thirty-six-year-old woman to her gynecologist, who informs her that she has endometriosis, a condition in which tissue lining the uterus attaches to the ovaries and other areas in the abdomen as well. The doctor informs her that a hysterectomy is necessary to resolve the condition.

The total complication rate associated with the hysterectomy procedure has been reported to be between 30 and 45 percent,[30] and includes the following health risks:[31]

- Death
- Life-threatening events, including cardiac arrest, severe allergic reaction, shock, and anesthesia-related accidents
- Profuse bleeding requiring transfusion
- Lung collapse
- Unintended major operative procedures related to bowel, bladder, or ureter trauma associated with surgery
- Urinary tract infection
- Bowel obstruction
- Nervous disorders
- Formation of blood clot and inflammation deep within a vein (thrombosis-thrombophlebitis)

- Abdominal incision infection
- Pneumonia
- Fever
- Infection in the bloodstream
- Rehospitalization for bleeding, infection
- Wound separation
- Urinary retention
- Sudden hormonal shock
- Loss of energy and slow recovery process

The price tag for a hysterectomy is alarming as well. Gynecologists receive a fee of $1,500 to $2,000 for performing this surgery; the total cost, including hospitalization, anesthesia, and other related expenses ranges from $6,000 to $8,000.

If women were *honestly informed* of all these possible complications, which even an experienced physician described as "considerable and . . . frightening," and if they had been *fully educated* as to possible alternatives to hysterectomy, would 655,000 wombs still have been lost in 1987?

Life After Hysterectomy

Dr. Winnifred B. Cutler asserts that in spite of many studies exposing the risks and debilitating side effects of hysterectomy, there remains among physicians "a lack of perception and awareness of the often serious physical and emotional problems experienced by women who undergo hysterectomy and ovariectomy."[32]

Basing her conclusion on some 3,000 articles taken from medical and scientific journals, Cutler states that problems after a hysterectomy can include: *a threefold to sevenfold increase in death from heart attack; increased risk of hardening of the arteries; 50 percent chance*

Symptoms of menopause begin to appear in a thirty-nine-year-old woman: hot flashes, night sweats, insomnia, nervousness. The hysterectomy she had three years earlier appears to be responsible for the discomfort she is experiencing.

---

of serious postoperative depression as much as two years after surgery; disruption and alteration of hormone levels; deterioration of bone health, often leading to osteoporosis; increased incidence of inability to contain urine (urinary stress incontinence); reductions in sexual functioning; and premature aging.[33] The woman who keeps her ovaries will not experience symptoms related to the loss of ovarian function, but she may experience retained ovary syndrome after undergoing hysterectomy surgery.[34] This condition appears to result from scar tissue forming around the ovaries. Large fluid-filled cysts can form on the ovaries as well. Cysts or no cysts, the condition can cause significant pain and require a second operation to remove the affected ovaries — an unnecessary event if the hysterectomy had not been done in the first place.

"While the overall outlook for health [without special treatments] after hysterectomy is not good, not every woman suffers every effect," says Cutler, "and the degree of difficulty from particular effects differs from woman to woman,"[35] adding

> What needs to be most strongly emphasized is that not all of the aftereffects of hysterectomy are obvious. Cardiovascular problems and osteoporosis progress silently, often making themselves known only when serious conditions have developed. . . . Hysterectomy frequently produces some predictable deficits in nervous system functioning, and these deficits, in turn, affect the whole person.[36]

More Than Just a "Baby Bag"

In recent years the womb has been found to directly affect the secretion of chemical substances from the brain through its influence on the hormone cycle.[37] Called endorphins, these natural secretions

---

A woman in her late forties, without complications after her hysterectomy, realizes eighteen months later that her desire for lovemaking has not returned: vaginal lubrication is almost nonexistent, intercourse is painful, and she rarely experiences orgasm. The doctor says there is no clinical basis for these problems, neglecting to tell her that as many as 60 percent of women who have had hysterectomies frequently abstain from having sex for these reasons.

---

are connected with feelings of euphoria, pain relief, and relaxation. In addition, glands within the lining of the uterus supply endorphins to the body as well.

The uterus also affects a woman's nervous system and sexuality from the area of the cervix. The cervix, located on the front wall of the vagina, is the only fixed portion of the uterus. It contains an abundant supply of nerve endings which are sensitive to the movement of the penis during intercourse. Capable of a phenomenal range of nerve impulse firings, studies have shown that this firing pattern actually stimulates areas of the brain to trigger the release of *additional* hormones. These in turn affect the reproductive cycle in numerous ways. From this evidence, it is very clear that the full range of physiological activities associated with the uterus are as yet unknown.

Hysterectomy can also affect a woman's sexual responsiveness in several other ways. By interrupting reflexes originating in the "G-Spot," a small sponge-like area behind the urethra located near the cervix, a woman may become less able to be aroused vaginally following this surgery. With the uterus missing, the vagina's capacity for expansion ("ballooning") in the moments preceding orgasm may change as well.

Perhaps most noticeable of all is the disappearance of uterine contractions which normally accompany climax after the womb's removal. While few women may realize what these sensations are or where they originate *before* hysterectomy, many indicate awareness that "something's changed" *afterwards*. Is it because physicians fail to discuss what "changes" to expect before obtaining a woman's consent to perform this surgery?

In spite of what we have been taught to believe, the role of the uterus is not limited solely to its reproductive function. The womb is intimately related to the way a woman experiences herself *as a woman*. It is a uniquely female organ, without counterpart in the male body. Respect for the extraordinary range of contributions the uterus makes to a woman's physical and emotional well-being is essential.

When surgery is not our best or only option, we can learn how to cope with the ups and downs of our reproductive systems without resorting to invasive "cures." Reserving radical surgery for when it's truly needed is just plain common sense — especially once the risks of hysterectomy and ovariectomy are fully considered.

Chapter Four

ABORTION:
Into the Heart of Woman

Abortion is an alternative to birth that is elected by women of all ages and marital and family statuses.[1]

Abortions, especially when performed early in pregnancy, are quite safe, simple, and inexpensive.[2]

Abortion is a surgical procedure. The American College of Obstetricians and Gynecologists affirms its support of unhindered access by women to safe abortion services, consistent with the conscientious beliefs of the women and physicians involved.[3]

Abortion is a surgical procedure in which a woman's body is forcibly entered and her pregnancy is forcibly "terminated." Because it is intrusive, and because it disrupts a natural process (pregnancy), abortion poses both short-term and long-term risks to the health and well-being of the aborted woman. Abortion is never without risks.[4]

Abortion is the rape of the womb.

*T*he woman undresses, changes into a cotton hospital gown, and goes over to a narrow table about half the length of her body. Two L-shaped stirrups, angled towards the walls, are fitted in place at the foot of the firmly padded bed. The room is stark, sparsely furnished; an exam light hangs obtrusively from the ceiling. The woman lies down on the table and shivers — whether from the air conditioner or the state of her nerves, she cannot tell — and without thinking, places her hand protectively over her abdomen. She is ambivalent about this baby, this silent crisis, and longs for relief from the questions bombarding her heart and mind.

"You're pregnant," the nurse had said simply. And with those two words, the whole world had shifted. The ground, so solid and substantial before, no longer seemed capable of bearing her weight. She did not want to be pregnant. She did not want to be an abortion statistic. She did not want to *be* at all.

It took several days for the see-saw effect of the news to stop. Still unsure, she had phoned for the appointment. That was almost a week ago.

"Now . . . now. . . ." she tells herself as she lies upon the table, "now it's going to be over. It's for the best — I'm not ready to bring a child into my life. I don't know if I'll ever be ready . . . but I'm not ready now."

She hears an abortion being done in an adjoining room. She closes her eyes and hums. The skin on her belly feels soft and warm. Suddenly, she wants to get up, put her clothes back on, and never think of this place again.

The door opens. A nurse comes in to do the "prep:" an I.V., legs placed wide apart in stirrups, soapy solution over her genitals, positioning of the overhead light. Naked from the waist down, the woman watches her doctor enter the room and assume his position at the foot of the table between her knees.

After performing a brief manual examination, the doctor inserts a speculum to visualize her cervix. A needle nearly six inches long, protected by a stainless steel sheath, slides into her vagina, aiming for its target. The nurse mumbles a warning about feeling a couple of pinches, but the injections into the neck of the womb cause the woman to gasp and grip the edges of the table. Momentarily, she is aware of a medicinal taste in her mouth.

"Breathe deeply and slowly," says the nurse calmly. "It will help you to relax."

Metallic sounds emanate from behind the doctor. Starting to work, he moves quickly. A suction machine, holding two cloth-covered bottles, sits alongside the table. In an obscene imitation of intercourse, the woman wills her body to open itself to the gynecologist's dilators, the transparent silicone tube, the aspirator's vibrations; her pelvis shakes violently with the force of the assault. Intense cramping pierces her pubic area, too strong a sensation to be masked by her dose of analgesia. She thinks she is going to vomit. For several minutes she is caught in a spasm of physical and emotional anguish. Tears run effortlessly down the sides of her face into her hair; she does not care to hide them.

Then the abortion is over. Feeling strangely empty and diminished, she lies quietly in recovery for an hour, is given instructions of warning signs to watch for, and returns home, cramping and bleeding.

She promises herself she will forget the experience, choosing to focus on the thought that she is no longer pregnant instead. The memory and the loss, however, will remain a part of her consciousness for the rest of her life.

Abortion is an alternative to birth that is elected by women of all ages and marital and family statuses. Abortion is the rape of the womb.

Defense of the Indefensible

In his book *1984,* George Orwell envisioned a time when political speech and writing had largely become the "defense of the indefensible." He described a future society where language was "designed to make lies sound truthful and murder respectable, and to give an appearance of solidity to pure wind." Nowhere is this language more widely used today than in the arena of abortion. What *"liberation"* is there in the destruction of one's own child? What *"victory"* for women's rights has been wrought doing such violence to the womb? What kind of *"choice"* is it really when a woman's life-giving, procreative power is betrayed for a mere $250?

Philosopher Mary R. Joyce compares this phenomenon to another form of sexual service suffered by women throughout the centuries:

> Women are still big business for men. Abortion now provides a new multimillion-dollar business in another kind of feminine prostitution. In the first form of prostitution women are paid by

men. But when women prostitute themselves to what is called the "baby scrambler," the suction machine for abortion, they give the money to men more often than not. In New York alone doctors and hospitals are reported to have made $139,061,000 [during the first year and a half of legalized abortion]. If women were not so intellectually passive, they would be able to see through this so-called liberation very clearly.[5]

Femininsts' claims that "there always has been and therefore always will be" the practice of abortion is the same argument used to sanction prostitution. But it is an empty argument as well as a lie. Both practices, by their very nature, prevent women from achieving true sexual strength, health, and wholeness.

Until 1970, abortion was largely illegal in the United States. Starting that year, however, states on both coasts passed legislation permitting abortion under a wide variety of circumstances. This occurred in response to pressure building from *within* the medical community to legitimize abortions performed by physicians, with additional backing from the world population and women's liberation movements.[6]

Testifying on behalf of abortion reform to the California legislature in 1963, the chairman of the state's Criminal Procedures Committee termed abortion an "extralegal" procedure, correctly identifying it as "the *present* practice of the medical profession."[7]

Earlier, psychiatrist and U.C.L.A. professor Dr. Jerome Kummer had pointed out that proposed legislation to change existing abortion laws "is merely codifying that which reputable physicians, and I'll use that word again —*reputable physicians* — in some of our leading hospitals have been practicing for a good many years."[8] These statements were made while abortions were still being performed by doctors largely on an *illegal* basis.

To further substantiate this statement, Stanford University professor Ralph J. Gampell submitted reports of a survey conducted at nonreligious hospitals throughout the San Francisco and Los Angeles metropolitan areas. The study revealed that all but two had been approving abortions that were illegal by state law.[9] Gampell also discovered that over 50 percent of "therapeutic" abortions in California were accomplished for reasons other than the physical health of the mother and that during the 1950s, the percentage of abortions performed for psychiatric reasons in New York State rose from *8.2 to 40 percent.*[10]

"Why do physicians reject guidelines on abortion?" asks Dr.

Myre Sim from British Columbia. "Surely it is not to be able to practice better medicine, but to be free from the constraints of medical
ethics. . . . Doctors have been the major culprits in this departure
from medical ethics. Some have, unashamedly, done it for money."[11]

Doctors gained substantially from decriminalizing procedures
which they had *already* been performing illegally in private offices,
clinics, and hospitals for many years. The notion of getting rid of the
"back alley abortionist" was really not the primary issue at all. *At
issue was legitimizing what had already become medical practice,
thereby enabling physicians to more easily obtain insurance reimbursement and legal coverage for surgical abortion procedures.*

The medical establishment, not a citizens' referendum, became
the powerful wedge that eventually forced open the door to legal
abortion. Physicians had been campaigning for a change in the law
for over two decades before abortion was sold to the public as a
women's rights issue.

Creation of a New Industry

In 1973, abortion was legalized throughout the United States. On
January 22, the Supreme Court decided two landmark cases — *Roe v.
Wade* [12] and *Doe v. Bolton* — that made it possible for a woman to
obtain an abortion during the entire nine months of pregnancy.[13] Of
this historic event Princeton University professor Paul Ramsey wrote:

> A shudder along the spine of every American is surely a fitting
> reaction to the Court's account of why Western medicine has
> always been concerned to protect unborn lives. This is to be
> accounted for, we are told, because Christianity happened to
> take on the views of the Pythagoreans, a small sect in the
> Graeco-Roman world, with its Hippocratic oath pledging physi-
> cians never to give abortifacients. In now overcoming that limi-
> tation, we are asked to recall that pagan outlooks in general and
> medicine in particular in pre-Christian ages opposed neither
> abortion nor suicide. Passed over in silence is the fact that
> approval of abortion was also associated with approval of infan-
> ticide. . . .
>
>   To say the least, the Court started . . . retrogressions into
> medical barbarism, from which we will not soon recover, when
> it exercised no judicial restraint, when it refused to trust the
> people's moral sensibility and legislative deliberation to achieve
> rough agreement about who belongs with us in the community
> of equal-rights bearers. That decision must be reversed and life-

and-death standard-setting must again be deprivatized. In doing this, the Court itself rolled back with one stroke of the pen steadily increasing respect for the unborn in the law itself—propelled onward and upward for decades by our increased knowledge of unborn life in the modern period.[14]

In summary, the two cases stated that during the first trimester (the first twelve weeks of pregnancy), abortion cannot be regulated by the state; during the second trimester (between thirteen and twenty-four weeks), the state may choose to regulate abortions for the purpose of promoting public health; and during the last trimester (following the twenty-fourth week), the state, if it chooses, may regulate and prohibit abortion except under certain medical circumstances to preserve the life or health of the mother. At no point is the child in the womb protected by law in these rulings.

As a result, *between three and four out of every ten pregnancies* have been surgically aborted since the late 1970s, with about 3 percent of all women between the ages of fifteen and forty-four experiencing abortion *each year.*[15] *Roe v. Wade* and *Doe v. Bolton* placed abortion beyond the reach of consumer protection laws, guarded by the Supreme Court's declaration against governmental intrusion into any procedure taking place during the first trimester. In so doing, the Court, while seeking to "privatize" abortion, blocked women from receiving adequate information about surgical treatments. *No laws govern first-trimester abortions,* including laws designed to *protect* consumers through requiring informed consent for surgery. Is this in the best interest of the patient—or her physician?

For this reason, the National Center for Health Statistics keeps no public records of abortions performed, nor does it review their outcomes. Statistics from the Centers for Disease Control rely on *voluntary* reporting by abortion providers who wish to participate in government studies. Like brothels, abortion clinics exploit women while simultaneously reaping huge profits in the process.

"All medical procedures should have proper medical indications, and when these indications are being abused, strict guidelines are laid down by the profession; those who ignore them are censured," asserts Dr. Myre Sim. "Such guidelines include a whole range of procedures, from the prescribing of certain drugs to laboratory investigations. Abortion [has been] specifically excluded from such guidelines, yet abortion carries certain death for the fetus as well as hazards for the pregnant woman."[16]

When abortion became available nationwide, most abortions took place in hospital settings. However, there has been a steady trend toward nonhospital abortions since that time.[17] *Today, almost 90 percent of the surgical abortions done in this country occur in nonhospital facilities.* As of mid-1986, charges for a nonhospital abortion performed during the first twelve weeks, or first trimester, of pregnancy ranged from just $75 to nearly $900.[18]

Abortion clinics, which make up only 15 percent of all abortion providers, were responsible for 60 percent of the procedures performed in 1985.[19] Of all abortions taking place in that year, *three-quarters* took place in clinics that aborted *over 1,000 women annually.*[20] The *2 percent* of abortion providers that had caseloads of *5,000 or more* in 1985 — the last year for which figures are currently available — were responsible for *one-fifth* of the more than 1.5 million abortions that took place that year.[21] In no way could this be termed the practice of safe, ethically sound medicine.

What Kind of Doctors . . .

Not surprising, of the doctors who staff such clinics, few are women. Given the nature of the work these physicians do and the astronomical numbers of abortions they perform, one wonders what draws these men to abort women hour after hour, week in and week out. For each abortion along the assembly line, there is a woman's body to be violently invaded, a suction machine to be employed, the baby's feet to be searched for and measured,[22] a bloody service to be rendered. What type of gynecology is this? What kind of men do such things for money?

"A fetus is nothing!" states Dr. Howard I. Diamond, later adding, "You won't get me to say I'm sorry for the fetus." A physician at Beth Israel Medical Center and assistant professor at New York University Medical School, Diamond also practiced abortion at a private clinic in New York City.

"Abortion is much more important than the life of a child that doesn't exist," Diamond declares.[23]

In the clinical opinion section of the prestigious *American Journal of Obstetrics and Gynecology,* Dr. Stephen Mumford, a public health specialist at the International Fertility Research Program, declares that abortion is no less than a major *national security issue.* Mumford claims that "the national security implications of abortion have not been addressed in a public forum but could come to be the single most important facet of the abortion debate."[24] He concludes with this statement:

The American College of Obstetricians and Gynecology is to be congratulated for its unyielding commitment to making abortion an available choice for all American women.[25]

How have these utilitarian attitudes come to exist in a profession founded upon the promise of fostering maternal well-being and protecting the health of the fetus?

Dr. Bernard N. Nathanson, a co-founder of the National Association for the Repeal of Abortion Laws (NARAL), discovered that he could *not* reconcile the practice of obstetrics and gynecology with abortion. Originally believing abortion was a medically sound solution to the dilemma of unplanned pregnancies, Nathanson fought long and hard for legalization of the procedure. He used his professional credentials in publicity campaigns, demonstrations, and political action groups.

Soon after the New York State abortion statute was passed and signed into law by Governor Nelson Rockefeller in 1970, Nathanson was appointed director at an abortion clinic. Under his supervision, 60,000 abortions were performed. Named in true Orwellian fashion, Nathanson's *Center for Reproductive and Sexual Health* became, in his own words, "the first — and largest — abortion clinic in the Western world." It was here that Nathanson finally implemented his ideal of making "low cost, safe, and humane abortions" available for women.[26] After a tenure of a year and a half, however, Dr. Nathanson left the job.

Two years after his resignation, Nathanson boldly admitted to his colleagues, "I am deeply troubled by my own increasing certainty that I had in fact presided over 60,000 deaths. There is no longer serious doubt in my mind that human life exists within the womb from the very onset of pregnancy."[27] Dr. Nathanson, an atheist, also offered these conclusions he had reached about the deeper human meaning of abortion:

> Life is an interdependent phenomenon for us all. It is a continuous spectrum that begins in utero and ends at death — the bands of the spectrum are designated by such words as fetus, infant, child, adolescent, and adult.
>
> We must courageously accept the fact — finally — that human life of a special order is being taken. And since the vast majority of pregnancies are carried successfully to term, abortion must be seen as the interruption of a process that would otherwise have produced a citizen of the world. Denial of this reality is the crassest kind of moral evasiveness. . . .

Somewhere in the vast philosophic plateau between the two implacably opposed camps — past the slogans, past the pamphlets, past even the demonstrations and the legislative threats — lies the infinitely agonizing truth. We are taking life, and the deliberate taking of life, even of a special order and under special circumstances, is an inexpressibly serious matter.[28]

When the doublespeak of abortion rhetoric is stripped away, the truth of Bernard Nathanson's words rings loudly and clearly. The surgical invasion of the womb for the sake of stealing its life speaks for itself: in an abortion, not only is a child destroyed, but *the very purpose of the womb itself — that of nourishing and protecting fetal life — is profoundly violated.*

A Closer Look

Understanding what an abortion involves completely refutes the idea that these are "safe and simple" procedures. From eight to fifteen weeks of pregnancy, suction D&C and its counterpart Dilation and Evacuation (D&E) are now the most common surgical techniques used to perform an abortion. Up to twelve weeks, nearly all abortions in the United States are done by suction D&C; after this time period, D&E is the most frequently performed technique.[29]

Suction D&C is often preceded by the insertion of laminaria tents (commercially prepared seaweed sticks that dilate the cervix) into the opening of the uterus. As many tents as the cervix will hold are applied. These are left in place for anywhere from two to twenty-four hours, and then removed. A bi-manual (two-fingered) exam is performed to determine the size of the uterus and angle of the cervix. The vagina is then stretched open with a speculum to allow visual and manual access to the uterus. An anesthetic called a paracervical block, requiring injections into the muscle of the cervix, is commonly administered. The woman may receive additional pain relief through a combination of drugs such as Valium (a tranquilizer) mixed with Demerol (a narcotic) administered by slow injection into a vein.

When the various medications have taken effect, the cervix is grasped by a sharp, hooklike instrument; metal rods with tapered ends are used to dilate the uterus further when necessary. A spoon-shaped instrument at the end of a clear tube, attached to an aspiration machine, is introduced into the cervix. Suction and scraping are then performed. The amount of suction applied through the "vacurette" is reportedly twenty-nine times more powerful than a household vacuum cleaner.[30] With this device, the physician dismembers and removes the developing child in pieces along with the placenta, membranes and amniotic fluid, followed by scraping of the uterine lining.

Dilation and Evacuation is performed at thirteen to twenty-four weeks of gestation and beyond. It requires more extensive cervical dilation, higher doses of pain relief medication, larger vacurettes and heavier crushing instruments than a D&C. The baby's skull must be collapsed and the body dismembered. If the brain or other vital organs are to be used for experimental purposes, care is taken to preserve these tissues.

Although the baby being destroyed is "unwanted," he or she is clearly more than mere tissue to the people conducting the abortion. "D&E is less expensive and emotionally and physically easier to handle for the patient [than other second-trimester abortion techniques]; however, the emotional trauma is transferred to the clinician and operating room staff," admits abortion provider Dr. Robert G. Castadot of Johns Hopkins Medical Center.[31]

It is no wonder that many women request to be put to sleep while having a D&E, even though general anesthesia is more expensive and places them at significantly greater risk of developing anesthesia-related complications.[32]

Physicians are not required by law to discuss the complications associated with abortion procedures. But risks and complications include:[33]

- Death
- Perforation of the uterus
- Bleeding requiring transfusion
- Tearing of the cervix, with unknown impact upon cervical competence during subsequent pregnancies
- Anesthesia-related accidents, including convulsions, shock, and cardiac arrest from toxic reaction to the anesthetic used
- Pelvic inflammatory disease and possible associated infertility
- Unintended surgery, including laparotomy, hysterotomy, and hysterectomy
- Bladder perforation
- Bowel perforation
- Persistent bleeding
- Tissue retention
- Anemia
- Peritonitis (a serious infection of the membranous coat lining the abdominal cavity)

- Minor infections and fever of unknown origin
- Undetected tubal pregnancy
- Pulmonary emboli (obstruction of the pulmonary artery)
- Venous thrombophlebitis (inflammation of a vein developing before a blood clot)
- Depression
- Psychosis
- Suicide

"At best, abortion clinics avoid telling women the truth in order to minimize the natural feelings of fear, doubt, and guilt associated with abortion," points out Nancyjo Mann, founder of Women Exploited by Abortion (WEBA). "They may want to create a comfortable 'safe and easy' view of abortion to minimize stress and, hopefully, to accelerate recovery. At worst, they avoid explanation for fe r of losing a paying customer.

"This type of deceit only serves to aggravate the psychological and emotional aftereffects of abortion," explains Mann. "When some physical complication develops, or when unexpected feelings of loss and guilt develop, or when a popular magazine article on the marvels of modern medicine shows the pictures of a fetus which is seen to be the baby rather than a 'blob of cells,' the aborted woman is caught unprepared. She feels betrayed, manipulated and deceived. Or when she learns that there were alternatives and support groups available of which she had not been informed, she is quite right to complain, 'Why didn't anyone tell me of this before?'"[34]

What Kind of Choice for Women?

Who are the women who abort their pregnancies? The majority are less than twenty-five years of age (62 percent), white (70 percent), and unmarried (81 percent).[35] Among nonwhite women, *40 percent* of all pregnancies are currently being surgically aborted.[36] For those women who are single and become pregnant, nearly *two-thirds* choose abortion.[37]

More than half of the women forty years of age or older at the time of conception abort their pregnancies. And *just under one-half of all pregnant teens* are surgically aborted every year.[38]

In an extensive survey of almost two thousand abortion patients, researchers from the Alan Guttmacher Institute found that most respondents have several reasons for their decision. Listed in order of importance — interference with work, school, or other responsibilities; the inability to afford a child; various relationship problems; and the

Why Women Abort Their Babies

(Survey participants could give more than one answer.)

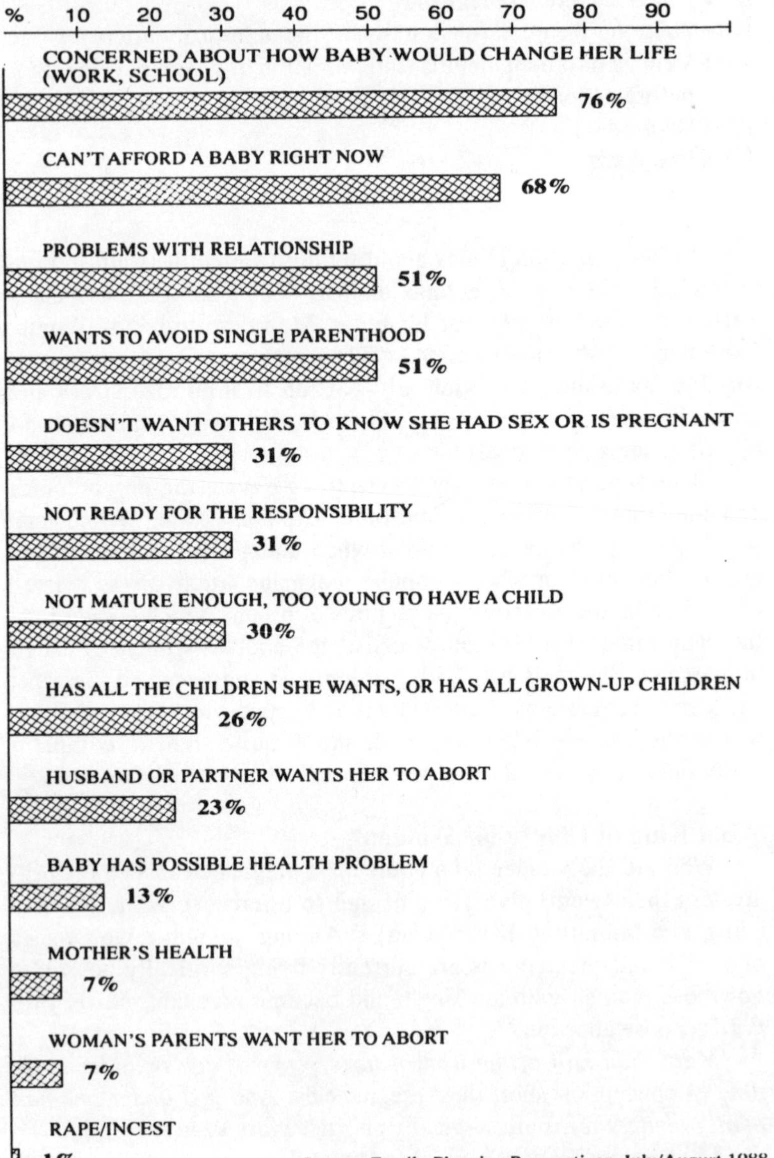

%   10   20   30   40   50   60   70   80   90

CONCERNED ABOUT HOW BABY WOULD CHANGE HER LIFE
(WORK, SCHOOL)
76%

CAN'T AFFORD A BABY RIGHT NOW
68%

PROBLEMS WITH RELATIONSHIP
51%

WANTS TO AVOID SINGLE PARENTHOOD
51%

DOESN'T WANT OTHERS TO KNOW SHE HAD SEX OR IS PREGNANT
31%

NOT READY FOR THE RESPONSIBILITY
31%

NOT MATURE ENOUGH, TOO YOUNG TO HAVE A CHILD
30%

HAS ALL THE CHILDREN SHE WANTS, OR HAS ALL GROWN-UP CHILDREN
26%

HUSBAND OR PARTNER WANTS HER TO ABORT
23%

BABY HAS POSSIBLE HEALTH PROBLEM
13%

MOTHER'S HEALTH
7%

WOMAN'S PARENTS WANT HER TO ABORT
7%

RAPE/INCEST
1%

Source: Family Planning Perspectives, July/August 1988

FIG 4.1

desire to avoid single parenthood were the reasons most women gave.[39] (Figure 4.1) Given these replies, one feels compelled to ask: Is abortion the way women are accommodating to living in a man's world?

"Abortion helps a woman's body be more like a man's," affirms pro-life feminist, author, and social psychologist Ms. Sidney Callahan, adding:

> Instead of being empowered by their abortion choices, young women having abortions are confronting the debilitating reality of *not* bringing a baby into the world; *not* being able to count on a committed male partner; *not* accounting oneself strong enough, or the master of enough resources, to avoid killing the fetus. Young women are hardly going to develop the self-esteem, self-discipline, and self-confidence necessary to confront a male-dominated society through abortion.
>
> The male-oriented sexual orientation has been harmful to women and children. It has helped bring us epidemics of venereal disease, infertility, pornography, sexual abuse, adolescent pregnancy, divorced, displaced older women, and abortion. Will these signals of something amiss stimulate pro-choice feminists to rethink what kind of sex ideal really serves women's best interests?
>
> . . . While the ideal has never been universally obtained, a culturally dominant demand for monogamy, self-control, and emotionally bonded and committed sex works well for women at every stage of their life cycles. When love, chastity, fidelity, and commitment for better or worse are the ascendant cultural prerequisites for sexual functioning, young girls and women expect protection from rape and seduction; adult women justifiably demand male support in childrearing; and older women are more protected from abandonment as their biological attractions wane.[40]

Once, not many years ago, abortion was considered a desperate choice for women. It was certainly never considered to be just another "option." Now we have arrived at a time when close to half of all pregnancies are ended by women who have learned to see death as better than life, abortion as better than birth, an empty womb as better than an expectant one. The transformation of *Charity* is nearly complete.

How many women realize only after it is too late that they have lost something of inestimable value?

Part Two

THE NEW MEDICINE

Ten years ago, the world marveled at the birth of Louise Brown, the first 'test-tube' baby. In the past decade, the infertility industry has mushroomed; this year alone, an estimated $1 billion will be spent on treatments in the United States.[1]

Chapter Five

EGG HARVESTING AND EMBRYO EXPERIMENTATION: Lab-Oriented Conceptions

The greatest evil is not now done in those sordid "dens of crime" that Dickens loved to paint. It is not even done in concentration camps and labor camps. In those we see its final result. But it is conceived and ordered (moved, seconded, carried and minuted) in clean, carpeted and well-lighted offices, by quiet men with white collars and cut fingernails and smooth-shaven cheeks who do not need to raise their voice.[2]

C. S. Lewis, *The Screwtape Letters*

These are not perverted men in white coats doing nasty experiments on human beings, but reasonable scientists carrying out perfectly justifiable research.[3]

*I*n the earliest weeks of prenatal development, each tiny female embryo contains stem cells that later organize into two small clumps of tissue high in the fetal abdomen near the kidneys. At the time of birth a complete supply of about one-half million immature eggs will have formed in these twin, almond-shaped clusters. By puberty, all but approximately ten thousand ova degenerate. By the age of fifty, most will have disappeared.

Over a span of about thirty-five years, from menarche until menopause, only four to five hundred eggs are stimulated by hormones to develop within a woman's ovaries.

During the preovulatory phase of the menstrual cycle, fifteen to twenty ova are brought to the brink of ripening. In most cases, only a single egg bursts forth each month from its fluid-filled sac lying within one of the ovaries. A mature egg, once released from this ripened follicle, is actually quite fragile, requiring continual nourishment and protection as it enters the Fallopian tube and begins its long journey toward the womb. This is provided by a billowy, heaped-up mass of "nurse cells," called cumulus cells, that escape from the follicle along with the egg. After its departure from the ovary, an ovum is receptive to fertilization for only twelve to twenty-four hours.

As it passes into the pelvic cavity, the liberated egg is then literally picked up by the fringed fimbria ("fingers") at the entry way of the Fallopian tube. Here it is greeted by thousands of continuously beating hairlike filaments called cilia which create a constant current toward the womb. The egg is thus propelled forward and cleansed of its cumulus cells; rhythmic muscular contractions within the oviduct's wall contribute to the one-way path the ovum is compelled to travel.

Until recently it was only here, in the distant portion of an oviduct, that the fate of a miniscule egg could be decided. Deep within the warmth of a woman's Fallopian tube, sheltered protectively under layers of skin and fat and muscle, the ovum undergoing fertilization merges with a singular sperm, one of several million released during an episode of lovemaking. The transmission of life from one generation to another had never happened in any other way: a woman's body held all the wonders and mysteries of her child's conception.

In the history of science, the twentieth century will be remembered for many things, but among the most significant, the disconnection of life's beginnings from the intense intimacy of sexual love will be ranked right along with the Manhattan Project, mass-produced antibiotics, and the discovery of DNA.

Two Historic Hunts for Human Eggs

The transfer of conception from the center of human sexuality to the control of third-party producers is built upon a forty-year legacy of clandestine egg hunts and extralegal embryo experimentation. By the time the first "test-tube baby" was born by cesarean section in 1978, countless eggs had been surgically removed from women's ovaries and reproductive tracts, inseminated in petri dishes, and examined in excruciating detail under microscopes. Without this fundamental research, the generation of human life in the laboratory would never have been possible.

Of all the scientific searches for human ova conducted to date, two stand out from among all the rest: the fifteen-year egg hunt performed by obstetrician-gynecologists John Rock and Arthur Hertig in the United States, and the studies of geneticist Robert Edwards and ob/gyn Patrick Steptoe in England. Many more experiments using human ova have been (and are still being) conducted,[4] but only these four researchers have been bold enough to go public with detailed accounts of their work thus far.[5]

Before 1938, the year the Rock-Hertig project began, very little was known about the intricate mechanisms involved in sexual reproduction. It was not until 1827 that the existence of a human egg was discovered. Another sixteen years went by before it was clearly demonstrated in 1843 that a sperm actually enters an ovum during conception. Only in 1875 was it shown that fertilization takes place when the nucleus of the sperm joins with that of the ovum. The two sex hormones produced by the ovaries, estrogen and progesterone, were not discovered until 1929 and 1934. It was at this point in history that Dr. Rock and Dr. Hertig entered the race to discover additional secrets about early human development.

The site of the team's exploration of fertility and embryology was the privately endowed Free Hospital for Women in Brookline, Massachusetts, an affiliate of Harvard Medical School. Founded in 1875, only poor women were entitled to use its services. They could not be charged for their medical care, nor were the physicians who worked there allowed to be paid a fee. Charitable contributions covered all the costs of the elective gynecological surgery performed at the Free Hospital. The medical services were offered in quiet, elegant surroundings in a French-style estate house located in a beautiful riverside glen on four acres of land outside the city of Boston. The "Free" was quite large and well-equipped for that era, with fifty in-patient beds, three operating rooms, modern X-ray equipment, fully equipped laboratories and the first intensive care recovery room in the country.

In exchange for their professional services, the Free Hospital for Women offered almost absolute research freedom to the physicians and medical students who worked there. John Rock's biographer explains the situation this way:

> During Rock's scientifically bountiful years there, the Free became something of a private research preserve for its princi-pal staffers, a cultured as well as competent clique of men also well versed in Harvard academic politics and content to remain aloof on their own protected turf. While medical insiders knew more or less what was going on in the research programs at the Free, the general public knew little of it.[6]

What exactly did some of the Free's little-known research entail? The harvesting of some 1,000 eggs from the dissected wombs, tubes, and ovaries of hundreds of hysterectomized patients. The artificial insem-ination of ova extracted from these organs with the sperm of medical students without the consent of the eggs' "donors." And strategically timed surgery scheduled to coincide with prospective patients' love lives and ovulatory cycles for the purpose of obtaining fresh, *fertil-ized* ova.

During this project, nearly three dozen human beings in their ear-liest stages of life, found in women's tubes and uteri that had been removed by Dr. Rock, were painstakingly prepared and proudly mounted for framing by Dr. Hertig and his dedicated coterie of labo-ratory technicians.

Conceptuses, Abortuses, or Human Waste?

The ethical implications involved in this research—lack of informed consent from participants, the performance of early abor-tions, human experimentation, and the exploitation of impoverished women—appear to have been outweighed by the importance of studying embryonic growth. "Induced abortions were illegal in Massachusetts and the Free Hospital for Women was not running an abortion clinic," Hertig points out, "however, we and others were vitally interested in early human development."[7]

Potential ovum donors, most of whom were Catholic, had to meet very specific criteria in order to be considered for admission to the program. In addition to their need to have a hysterectomy, they were required to be "married and living with their husbands, intelligent, and to have demonstrated prior fertility by delivering at least three full-term pregnancies, and they had to be willing to record menstrual cycles and coitus without contraception."[8] This information was carefully recorded from postcards mailed to Dr. Rock's assistant, Miriam Menkin, in order to determine the scheduling of each operation.

The Pill, John Rock and the Church contains the following comments concerning the attitudes of the physicians regarding their work:

> It unquestionably was a delicate ethical maneuver. Both Rock and Hertig thought about the ethical implications long and hard. Eventually, for both, it came down to "a necessary scientific endeavor using material that would have gone to waste but would not have been put to the use for which the Lord intended it." Neither Rock nor Hertig considered the conceptuses they hoped to find to be abortuses. At the few days to two or so weeks of development of the fertilized eggs, Hertig and Rock considered them undifferentiated bits of protoplasm, tiny gelatinous packets of human protein, destined to end up, undetected, in a surgical waste bin. . . .
>
> But the question hangs in the air. Couldn't the women have been instructed to refrain from marital intercourse and thereby eliminate any possibility of pregnancy at the time of surgery? Hertig vehemently maintained that they were not instructed *to* have intercourse, or *not* to, but only to record it if they did.[9]

Clearly, by their own admission the doctors were looking for "conceptuses": conceived human beings undergoing their initial phases of embryonic development. "We were not doing abortions," Hertig insists, "but we hoped we would find [a fertilized] ovum."[10] By walking the fine line made possible by a lack of reliable means to detect pregnancy in its earliest stages, this approach was completely defensible and morally justified in the minds of these physicians.

But what about the mothers of the "conceptuses"—the aborted babies? Since the pregnancies were never "confirmed" and none of the women had missed a period, Hertig stresses, "There was no way in God's world at that time of knowing whether they were pregnant or not. There were literally no tests."[11] Apparently, according to his way of thinking, what the women didn't know certainly wasn't going to hurt them, and it would help the cause of science, not to mention the team of Rock and Hertig, one heck of a lot.

Another question that remains is, How much of the surgery performed on these women was unnecessary? An article appearing in the *Journal of the American Medical Association* in 1952 reported the removal of 704 normal ovaries from 546 patients in the Los Angeles area.[12] "Our patients' faith and trust will be justified so long as we are professionally and intellectually honest with them and ourselves," wrote Dr. James C. Doyle.[13] Yet he admitted that the "unwarranted sacrifice of normal ovaries" was "not at all unusual" as demonstrated by the statistics he had carefully collected.[14] The report is especially significant because it is from exactly the same period of time that the hunt for human ova at the Free Hospital for Women was being conducted.

In 1948, John Rock and Arthur Hertig were presented the coveted American Gynecological Society Award for their ground-breaking work. At the award banquet the dynamic duo was affectionately dubbed "the ham and the egg."[15]

A Morula Named Dominic

Rock and Hertig's active search for women's unborn offspring during the first two weeks of prenatal life lasted from 1938 until 1953. During this time, Dr. Hertig managed to take thirty-four early embryos from Dr. Rock's unknowingly pregnant patients.

Inspecting the "specimens," as Hertig refers to the extracted organs, was accomplished by examining ovaries, flushing Fallopian tubes, cutting over two hundred wombs in half and carefully incising the uterine tissue while it was immersed at room temperature under a specially prepared fluid. "By tubal washing and this uterine technique," claims Hertig, "we obtained all the significant preimplanting stages of human development."[16]

Following this procedure, Dr. Hertig would then look over each uterus twice, both before and after applying a special fixative called Bouin's fluid to clarify the womb's surface. By this method, Hertig was able to find embryos *up to seventeen days of age* nesting in the womb's lining. "Surprisingly, all the normal conceptuses were found implanted on the posterior wall of the uterus, whereas all those considered abnormal were located on the anterior wall," Dr. Hertig drily reports in the *American Journal of Obstetrics and Gynecology.*[17] Surprising, indeed.

Hertig recounts a favorite story from his work in a recent article:

The following anecdote illustrates the interest in the project on the part of my house staff, the clinical house staff, and the visiting staff and faculty. During the 1946 World Series between the Boston Red Sox and the St. Louis Cardinals, in the eighth inning, Dominic DiMaggio (Red Sox center fielder) hit a double that tied the game and the series. Of course, we (the Red Sox) went on to lose the series (and game) when Enos Slaughter stole home on his single owing to Johnny Pesky's moment of indecision in throwing to home plate. Of importance to this tale is the fact that I found, at the moment of Dominic's double, an unimplanted nine-cell ovum that proved, like the series, to be a pathological one! As was the custom in those days, when early human ova (i. e., embryos) were rarely found, illustrated, and published, the finder's name was affixed to the specimen he or she discovered. Thus, this pathological nine-cell morula-ovum was appropriately named "Dominic." I found it the minute he hit his famous double against the left field wall of Fenway Park.[18]

The named embryo was preserved for posterity and may be found today in Plate #47 in the Carnegie human embryology collection in Baltimore.

"I have been told by experts in in vitro fertilization that this series of naturally occurring human ova laid the foundation for their pioneering work in solving developmental aspects of human infertility," Dr. Hertig explains.[19]

It is from this inauspicious beginning, then, that the new medicine of laboratory-oriented conception was born.

"Nearly 800 Human Follicular Eggs Have Been Isolated"

Whereas Arthur Hertig has the distinction of being the first to find and photograph a series of early human embryos, his partner John Rock is better known for other outstanding accomplishments in medicine. A famous actor as a Harvard undergraduate, Rock eventually became one of the most undeniably colorful figures in the history of obstetrics and gynecology.

It is indeed ironic, however, that Dr. Rock was a practicing member of the Catholic Church. He was the only Catholic among fifteen eminent Boston physicians to sign a petition circulated by Margaret Sanger's Birth Control League to repeal Massachusetts' birth control law. In 1936, soon after the "Rhythm Method" was propounded, he became the first in the United States to open a clinic teaching women of his denomination how to determine their monthly fertile period for the purpose of both attempting and avoiding pregnancy.

Apparently undeterred by the doctrines of his faith concerning human sexuality, Rock pursued his scientific interest in gynecology with passion. Throughout his entire career he remained at the forefront of medical bioengineering and infertility research: designing the now widely-used vacuum aspirator/curettes to collect hundreds of uterine tissue samples for biopsy studies; spending several years measuring the electrical potential of women's vaginas in attempts to determine the timing of ovulation; testing the first synthetic materials to be used as replacements for damaged Fallopian tubes; performing the earliest experiments with fertility drugs and sex hormones; and pioneering techniques now used in artificial insemination — the collection, freezing, and storage of sperm.

Dr. Rock was also a renowned speaker and writer. Among his most memorable contributions was a landmark article on human ovulation for the prestigious *New England Journal of Medicine* in 1941. In 1949, in the same journal, another of his remarkable papers was published: "The Physiology of Human Conception." Rock's greatest achievement came just over a decade after this article was printed, on May 11, 1960. It was on this date that his work with biologist Gregory Pincus regarding the influence of sex hormones on women's fertility resulted in the federal government's final approval of the first oral contraceptive pill.

To this long list of obstetrical and gynecological "firsts," John Rock hoped to establish himself as the first physician to accomplish the extraordinary feat of test-tube conception. In 1944, along with his assistant Miriam Menkin, he wrote:

> First stages of cleavage [cell division] of the fertilized human egg have, as far as we know, never been reported, and while *in vitro* fertilization of tubal eggs of the rabbit has been described, we have found no record of such experiments with higher mammals. . . . Utilizing surgical material [i. e., *women's ovaries*] available at the Free Hospital for Women, we have, during the past six years, made numerous attempts to achieve *in vitro* fertilization and cleavage of human eggs obtained from ovarian tissue just prior to the expected time of ovulation.[20]

The process worked this way: Rock and Menkin would prepare hysterectomy patients at the Free by counselling them on how how to keep an accurate record of their menstrual cycles prior to hospital admission. By operating close to the time of ovulation, they were able to maintain a supply of nearly ripe eggs for their trials of test-tube conception.

Throughout the research, Miriam Menkin would stand outside the operating room every Tuesday, holding a jar of sterile solution as she waited to collect ovaries, oviducts, and wombs. After carrying the excised organs to a small laboratory, Menkin would then flush the ovaries with a sterile solution and drain the contents of each organ into a dish. Any eggs that she found were gently washed several times, transferred to a glass flask, and placed in blood taken from the egg "donor" prior to surgery. The ova would then be incubated in the blood at body temperature for twenty-four hours. When ripe eggs became available, a man who was willing to sell sperm to the hospital would be notified that his semen was needed.

John Rock coordinated and oversaw the semen collection portion of the program. By compiling a list of young interns from Harvard Medical School, Dr. Rock put together a group of men who were particularly eager to fulfill his requests. In exchange for a small fee, they were asked to masturbate and ejaculate semen samples into sterile containers. A special, nonclinical atmosphere was created expressly for this purpose: a private cubicle lined with large posters of seductively posed nude women that Dr. Rock had brought back from Sweden to help "inspire the young men to action."[21] The job was quite simple in comparison to the role the women played in the project.

Between 1938 and 1944, nearly 800 human follicular eggs were isolated from ovaries during the course of the Menkin-Rock investigation in this way.[22] Of these, 138 were painstakingly observed for signs of prenatal development after exposure to medical students' fresh spermatozoa. The research was made possible by a grant from the Carnegie Corporation of New York.[23]

Mouse, Sheep, Cow, Pig, Rhesus Monkey . . . and Human Ovarian Oocytes

Without question, no one has contributed more to today's practice of in vitro fertilization (IVF) than Robert G. Edwards, a British scientist with a doctorate in animal genetics. In spite of reports published by John Rock and Miriam Menkin claiming that they had accomplished human fertilization in a test tube in 1944, it was Edwards who was the first to definitively accomplish external human fertilization twenty-five years later.[24]

Nine years of intense research using human ova preceded this historic event. Edwards's story reveals the irresistible power science holds over researchers, nudging them step by step along the path of discovery. "If it can be done, it must be done," was clearly the principle that propelled Edward's research inexorably forward; the ethical implications of his work were simply unimportant in comparison to the knowledge to be gained by producing human life for examination in the laboratory.

In *A Matter of Life,* a book Edwards wrote with Patrick Steptoe, we hear the voice of a man who had spent his entire career working with lab animals describe his initial shock at the harsh realities involved in hunting down human ova:

> Dissecting mice and rats, that was one thing. This was utterly different. Here, in the operating theater, I felt myself to be exactly what I was—a novice. I stood at the back, wearing a mask, careful not to touch anything. I obeyed all instructions to the letter. "Come forward now," directed Molly and I came forward clutching my glass sterile pot—the receptacle for the precious bit of superfluous ovarian tissue.
>
> Two or three times a month I would be summoned to Edgware General Hospital. I was always impressed by Molly Rose's surgery. And, as I waited for her to call me forward, as I glimpsed the naked skin of another human being being cut and human blood spurting, the clamps applied, I sometimes questioned my right to be there. "What am I doing?" I asked myself. "Do I really have a place in this theater?" There on the operating table, was a woman who had been ill whom Molly hoped to make well again. . . . And I? I was there merely for some spare eggs, for a piece of ovary that had to be removed anyway and which I would take back to my safe laboratory bench in Mill Hill. . . .
>
> Now that I had a small but regular supply of human ova from Edgware—and elsewhere, for I had persuaded other gynecologists to bequeath me ovarian tissue also—I could plan my work.[25]

Unfortunately, Edwards's initial encounter with feelings of awe and shame while invading the privacy of gynecological patients quickly wore off. After just five years, he had tracked down enough eggs to accumulate the necessary data to publish the details of human egg development in laboratory apparatus.[26] In his article titled "Maturation *In Vitro* of Mouse, Sheep, Cow, Pig, Rhesus Monkey, and Human Ovarian Oocytes," he identifies the major stumbling block imposed upon his work:

> The investigation of early development in many mammalian species is restricted by the difficulty of obtaining sufficient numbers of oocytes [eggs] and embryos at particular stages of development. . . .
>
> Only small pieces of ovary from patients undergoing surgery for various disorders were available, and the number of oocytes from any one piece were seldom sufficient to provide samples for examination after different periods of time. [27]

Nevertheless, Edwards's single-minded pursuit of human eggs and in vitro fertilization continued. His hunt for human eggs took him from the British National Institute for Medical Research to researchers Howard and Georgeanna Jones at the renowned Johns Hopkins Hospital in Baltimore, to a small group of gynecologists in North Carolina, and finally, to a permanent academic post in the physiology department at Cambridge University in England.

From Surgical Patients to Infertile Couples

Robert Edwards's breakthrough arrived upon meeting a British gynecologist named Patrick Steptoe. To overcome difficulties in obtaining fresh human ova at exactly the right moment of maturation, Edwards realized it was essential that he work with a physician who could combine regimens of hormone treatments with a simpler means of egg retrieval. Steptoe offered both. In his work with a large volume of patients at a branch of the National Health Service, Patrick Steptoe was the first physician in Great Britain to perfect the clinical use of a technique called laparoscopy.

By means of inserting a special stainless steel scope with its own light source into a woman's pelvic cavity, he found access to the reproductive organs could be obtained without major surgery. Through an inch-long incision made near the navel, and by expanding the abdominal cavity with carbon dioxide gas, diagnostic examinations and delicate surgery could be accomplished at a minimum of risk to the patient. The rate of postoperative discomfort and infection with laparoscopy was significantly less than with laparotomy, which involves a much larger incision, more extensive surgical repair and a longer hospital stay.

After reading an article written by Steptoe about the new procedure, Edwards phoned him and told the gynecologist about his hopes of achieving in vitro fertilization. Steptoe was very receptive to the idea, having worked with the dilemma of infertility for a number of years, and agreed to lend his expertise to Edwards's project. It was in this manner that the focus of IVF shifted from ovariectomy as a human egg source to the infertile women who willingly gave up their ova in hopes of becoming pregnant through in vitro fertilization.

Child Breeding in the Laboratory

As an animal geneticist, Edwards was not only interested in IVF's application to human infertility. Even though he knew infertile couples might eventually benefit from IVF, he was equally interested in its eugenic (selective breeding) potential and related population control issues.

Edwards clearly understood that fertilizing human eggs in a laboratory setting does much more than bypass a pair of blocked Fallopian tubes: examination of chromosomes at the earliest stages of prenatal development permits an IVF technician to view an embryo's basic genetic make-up very soon after conception. Robert Edwards recognized this from the onset of his research. Virtually everything he has written on the subject describes the direct interrelationship between IVF and early genetic diagnosis. In addition, his studies were financed by the Ford Foundation, a major backer of world population and eugenics-related research. It is highly doubtful that Edwards's grant source was primarily interested in the application of his work to the problem of human infertility.

Four years before he had succeeded in accomplishing the feat of the world's first test-tube conception he remarked:

> It had occurred to me that, once the problem of human *in vitro* fertilization was solved, the sex of the embryos could be identified at a very early stage by examination of their chromosomes, and that it would be possible therefore to choose whether the mother gave birth to a girl or a boy. At first, animal husbandry would benefit. Farm animals could be induced to superovulate, their fertilized eggs removed, examined to see what sex they were, and only the ova of one or the other sex replaced into the womb of the mother animal. In man, certain diseases could perhaps be reduced.[28]

Today superovulation is regularly practiced in women as well as sheep and pigs and cattle. It is the standard practice of IVF clinics all over the world to synthetically induce multiple ovulation in women via hormone injections and medications prior to oocyte removal. The chromosome analysis of IVF embryos that Edwards predicted is already being utilized.[29] It is now possible, in fact, to use highly specific DNA "probes" to determine the sex of an eight-cell embryo and diagnose a variety of genetic disorders before selective transfer to a woman's womb.[30]

Shortly after Robert Edwards had obtained large numbers of human eggs through his collaboration with infertility specialists at Johns Hopkins University, he concluded an article for *Scientific American* with these words on child breeding:

> We intend to continue these experiments; the ability to observe cleaving eggs could be of great medical and scientific value . . . oocytes and embryos showing anomalies [defects] could be eliminated in favor of those developing normally. This achievement might one day permit some choice to be made in the type of offspring born to particular parents.[31]

In the first paper to announce Edwards's success with IVF, he begins by hailing the embryo's usefulness to science rather than the progeny's intrinsic value or desirability to his or her parents. The message here is very clear about the importance of IVF to reproductive research:

> The technique of maturing human oocytes *in vitro* after their removal from follicles provides many eggs for studies on fertilization. Their fertilization *in vitro* would yield a supply of embryos for research or clinical use, but in previous attempts the incidence was too low to be useful.[32]

Furthermore, Edwards proposes several novel ideas on how human embryos might specifically be used for the research and clinical use he alluded to: growing human life in the laboratory for the purpose of tissue harvesting and organ farming. On this subject he says:

> Will we be able to extract the stem cells of various organs from the embryo, the precious foundation cells of all the body's organs and then use them therapeutically? Will it ever be possible to use these cells to correct deficiencies in other human beings — to replace one deficient tissue with another that functions normally? For instance, will we be able to use the blood-forming tissue of an embryo to re-colonize defective blood-forming tissue in an adult or child? And will these notions be met with pursed lips and frowning faces?
>
> Perhaps the whole concept will fall to the ground and be proved to be a mistaken one in medical treatment. I doubt it, so

much is on our side — the very foundation cells have been and will be again seen in our cultures and we know they are capable of displaying the initial signs of tissue differentiation. These same embryonic cells may offer us one further therapeutic advantage. They may one day be used [by cloning an embryo from a host "parent"] without having to worry about graft rejection such as we all know is associated with kidney, heart, and liver transplantations.

Perhaps this whole approach may seem heartless to those who feel the embryo is a human being. . . . To grow fetuses to later stages of growth when they take a recognizable human shape and then extract their organs would be an utterly repugnant concept; but to obtain cell colonies from minute embryos useful in medicine for the alleviation of certain human disorders — is that not a legitimate target to aim at? It is a target that may be reached, should be reached, if we can understand the priceless secrets of those embryonic cells growing in our cultures.[33]

Are these simply the far-out fantasies of a Cambridge genetics professor — or the accurate predictions of the world's foremost expert on human ectogenesis? What in fact did Robert Edwards do with the dozens of embryos he created in the lab before the first was transferred to a mother's womb? Were women who gave their eggs to Edwards accurately informed of the experimentation their offspring were involved in? Is similar research still going on today with spare embryos obtained from the artificial insemination of women's eggs? This final story gives some of the answers to these questions.

Bob's and Barry's Babies: Success at Last

Unbeknownst to their mother, the first children to be conceived by in vitro fertilization were fathered by Robert G. Edwards and his Cambridge associate, Barry D. Bavister.

In March 1968, Edwards was able to get one final batch of fresh ova from a patient operated on by Dr. Rose. "This was the last piece of ovarian tissue that I was to obtain from Edgware General hospital," recalls Edwards. "It yielded me twelve human eggs."[34]

After ripening the eggs for thirty-six hours in a culture concocted by Bavister, the two men ejaculated their semen into collection bottles, washed their sperm mildly by spinning them in a centrifuge, and poured the precious fluid into the culture medium where the eggs awaited. Ten hours later, this is what Edwards found as he peered at the culture through a high-powered microscope:

I held my breath. A spermatozoon was just passing into the first egg. We examined and re-examined it and there was no doubt. Marvelous. An hour later, we looked at the second egg. Yes, there it was, the early stages of fertilization. A spermatozoon had entered the egg without any doubt — *we had done it.*

"Yes," I said softly.[35]

We can be quite certain that the woman from whom these eggs were taken had absolutely no idea that her ovary would be carried from the operating room, inspected for oocytes by a researcher at Cambridge University and inseminated with the sperm of scientists. Nor did she know that her twelve ova would make history as the first human beings to be to be generated in a laboratory. The embryos created without her permission were methodically analyzed and painstakingly photographed by Edwards and Bavister for international publication.[36]

How many other ova have been extracted for use in research laboratories? Or inseminated with the sperm of strangers? How many more embryos have been created without their mother's knowledge? Mounted and framed for museum collections? Photographed in phase-contrast for scientific journals?

Some hospitals bury women's ovaries.[37] Considering what can happen to reproductive tissue these days, it seems a reasonable way to dispose of a woman's eggs, doesn't it?

Chapter Six

INFERTILITY DIAGNOSIS AND TREATMENT: To Catch a Falling Star

Many doctors and lay people think that the great technical advances in the past twenty years in treating infertility have led to high success rates in treatment, but this is a myth. Subspecialists often do not appreciate the limited therapeutic impact of the many diagnostic tests, and many couples achieve pregnancy independently of medical intervention.[1]

Dr. Richard J. Lilford and Maureen E. Dalton

Go, and catch a falling star,
Get with child a mandrake root,
Tell me, where all past years are,
Or who cleft the Devil's foot.

John Donne

Vicki and Bill Eckhardt of Annandale, Virginia, have spent over $35,000 on infertility treatments since 1981. This amount does not include medical costs reimbursed by their health insurance company. Vicki's infertility was caused by a devastating pelvic infection brought on by an intrauterine contraceptive device (IUCD) called a Dalkon shield.[2]

"Because of the damage it did," explains Vicki, "my tubes were completely blocked. Bill and I finally realized that we couldn't have children unless we tried some kind of special treatment."[3]

The Eckhardts' dream of having a baby remains unfulfilled in spite of the thousands of dollars they have spent.

Deborah Gerrity and her husband Kevin have also paid more than $35,000 for infertility services. They, too, have been trying to bear a child for eight years without success. This is Debbie's description of her "workup" to determine the cause of their infertility:

> I have taken my basal body temperature approximately 1,260 times or for forty-five consecutive months. Now to most of you, that probably doesn't sound tough, but imagine not being able to move a muscle in the morning until you reach for a thermometer. . . . And that is the easy part. During the diagnostic phase, I had three endometrial biopsies—which consist of taking tissue from the inside of the uterine wall to determine hormone levels—and two postcoital tests—removal of the cervical mucus to analyze sperm activity. . . . I have also had two diagnostic laparoscopies—the navel surgery done with general anesthesia to look at the ovaries, tubes, and uterus. The second of these surgeries included a hysteroscopy—examination of the inside of the uterus—and a D&C. . . . All of that comprised the diagnostic workup.
>
> My diagnosis was unexplained infertility.[4]

For Debbie Gerrity, the quest for pregnancy isn't over. She and Kevin have tried everything their infertility specialist has recommended: artificial insemination, hormone therapy, surgery, in vitro fertilization (IVF), and gamete intrafallopian transfer (GIFT). They are now trying sperm washing.

Surprisingly, Debbie has no regrets about all the stress and pain she has endured. "To not go through this," she says, "would have made me feel like it was my fault, because I wasn't willing to try. No one, not even I, can look at me today and say, 'If you really wanted a biological child you could have one.'"[5]

Nancy and Jonathan Carlson of Minneapolis spent nearly $30,000 in just two and a half years on attempts at conception. Unlike most couples, however, the Carlsons decided to seek help from an infertility specialist soon after they got married. Nancy was thirty-eight and was understandably concerned that her capacity for child-bearing was waning.

In spite of extensive testing, antibiotic therapy, and three operations — one for Jonathan and two for Nancy — doctors have been unable to determine the cause of the Carlsons' infertility. Nancy, who is now forty, is satisfied with her decision to seek medical assistance. "Whatever the outcome, we will have no regrets about the money we've spent."[6]

Was the $30,000 to $35,000 these couples paid for the battery of unsuccessful tests and therapies really justified? Who has benefited more from the infertility services they have received so far — the three couples or their physicians? What did they get in exchange for such a large sum of money? At what point does reproductive medicine become medical exploitation of the infertile couple?

The Rapid Expansion of Reproductive Medicine

Couples in search of parenthood are often willing to try anything, at any cost, to achieve conception. Rachel's cry to her husband Jacob — "Give me children, or else I'll die!"[7] — is expressed by women in a different way today. Rachel bargained for mandrake roots. Now, medical technology is believed to possess the power to cure infertility. Convinced that modern treatments are highly effective, couples often naively submit to the humiliation and risks of extensive "therapies." They assume that if they just try hard enough and long enough, something will finally work. In fact, this "hard enough/long enough" attitude becomes *a way of coping* with the loss of control couples feel after an infertility diagnosis. The news that having a child may not be possible often creates a "we'll try anything" approach.

Dr. Allen DeCherney, an infertility specialist at Yale-New Haven Hospital, believes infertile couples suffer "a life crisis as devastating as any disease known to man" if they think they may be unable to become parents. He adds: "Telling a couple they can never have children is worse than telling a seventy-year-old he is dying of cancer."[8]

Compassionate physicians such as Dr. DeCherney are frequently quoted in popular magazine articles on infertility. But the commercialization of human reproduction has not been based on sympathy alone. With the declining birth rate, ob/gyns profit substantially from the business infertile couples bring to their practices. "Normal" low-risk, nonsurgical obstetrics just isn't a very big money maker these days. Whereas OB packages (including ten to sixteen prenatal visits, the birth, and a post-partum check-up) are worth about $1,000 to a physician, a one-hour diagnostic procedure such as a laparoscopy yields about $800.[9]

Consider a recent want-ad appearing in the yellow pages of the *Wisconsin Medical Journal* :

> OB/GYN, board-certified or eligible, to join highly progressive, rapidly growing practice. Normal and high-risk obstetrics emphasized along with highest levels of infertility care (microsurgery, GIFT, IVF, Laparoscopic Laser Surgery) as well as extensive gynecology and surgery practice. Easy lake country or Milwaukee suburban living. Salary and guarantees to meet your needs with opportunity for partnership within one year. Available July 1988, or earlier.
> Contact. . . .[10]

To boost the business and expertise of infertility diagnosis and treatment, an entire subspecialty — *endocrinology/infertility* — has been created within the field of obstetrics and gynecology. Physicians who practice this specialty are called *reproductive endocrinologists.*

Endocrinology/infertility was not recognized as a certifiable subspecialty of obstetrics and gynecology until 1974. By 1978, 64 physicians had received board certification in this field; in 1982 the number had more than doubled to 135.[11] As of December 31, 1987, there were 287 board-certified reproductive endocrinologists in the United States.[12] Given this rate of growth, the total is likely to hit 400 by the end of 1990.

Another measure of physicians' interest in infertility is membership in the American Fertility Society (AFS). The AFS grew from 3,600 in 1974 to over *12,000 members* in 1988.

This explosion in infertility specialization has fueled related research, which in turn has promoted the rampant development — and mass marketing — of new reproductive technologies. An article in the *Journal of the American Medical Association* offers the following insights on this phenomenon:

> From the mid-1960s to the mid-1970s, the number of births declined rapidly, creating a "baby bust" situation. During this interval, *the annual number of births fell from more than four million per year to just above three million per year.* Thus, medical specialists with a primary interest in women's health care [i.e., ob/gyns] were faced with a decreasing volume of patients requesting obstetric services. *In part to fill this void, many obstetricians expanded their sphere of interest. . . .*
>
> The increased physician interest in infertility problems, while initially stimulated by the technical improvements in diagnosis/treatment and the consultations of higher-income populations with infertility problems, itself *stimulated further scientific research and patient consultations.* Thus, the interactive process between health care providers and consumers, once set into motion, actually became an important factor reinforcing the growth and public visibility of the infertility field. . . .
>
> Recent advances in treating infertile couples have generated wide-spread publicity. The "test tube babies" resulting from in vitro fertilization have raised hopes of barren couples that these advanced methods might be applicable to them. In addition, techniques and use of microsurgery have increased in recent years. Finally, the advantages of new drugs to enhance fertility have also gained media attention. Continuously hit by press statements highlighting successes in treating infertility, infertile American couples have had their hopes raised of possibly overcoming their inability to conceive. Because of heightened expectations, an increasing proportion seek medical advice to correct their infertility.[13]

"Technology has given people unreasonably high expectations," says Shulamit Reinharz, a sociologist at Brandeis University. "Couples delay marriage and pregnancy, use contraceptives and stop, and then expect to conceive."[14]

The first generation with the ability to prevent the births they *do not want,* couples today have difficulty coping when they can't have the children they *do* want. Fertility is now viewed as a controllable aspect of life. Physicians act as the mediators of this process.

Modern medicine induces infertility through the Pill, vasectomy, and tubal ligation; now it is also expected to *undo* infertility via techniques such as IVF, embryo transfer, and artificial insemination.

Laying It out on the Table

A standard infertility work-up is a costly, time-consuming, and emotionally draining process. What's more, determining the cause of infertility is often difficult. For a large percentage of infertile couples — up to 20 percent — the cause remains unknown.[15]

Treatments prescribed vary greatly in their effectiveness. Even the results of various tests, such as semen analysis and the post-coitus test, can show considerably different results when done at different times. Although the procedures performed depend upon the situation of each particular couple, the list below describes the types and costs of common diagnostic measures used today:[16]

Couple's history and physical exam: A complete health history may be the single most important diagnostic tool a physician can employ. It should include information on the couple's education, employment, personality, stimulant and substance use, medications and treatments, nutrition and diet, exercise, immunizations, surgical history, family health history, psychological history, and sexual history. The physical exam seeks possible physiological and anatomical causes of infertility. Average cost: $125 ($50-415).

Semen analysis: Basic characteristics of sperm and seminal fluid are examined, including the quantity and activity of the sperm. Average cost: $45 ($15-108).

Resting body temperature and other menstrual cycle mapping: Since the resting, or "basal," body temperature changes during the menstrual cycle, charting these changes may help to pinpoint ovulation. The woman performs this procedure herself, so the cost involves only the price of the thermometer.

Cervical mucus evaluation: Another method of ovulation prediction relies upon examination of cervical mucus. Microscopic analysis of these secretions reveals hormone-related changes in the mucus. Average cost: $40 ($25-200).

Measurements of hormone levels: A patient's blood and urine are tested for levels of hormones related to ovulation. Average cost per test: $50 ($25-85).

Post-coital test: One to two days before ovulation, the couple has intercourse two to four hours before arriving at their physician's office; one to three samples of the deposited discharge is then taken from different areas along the length of the cervical canal and analyzed. Average cost: $40 ($25-100).

Infection screen: Tests for sexually transmitted diseases are included to determine whether reproductive loss may be associated with infection. Average cost per person: $40 ($18-75).

Sperm antibody test: Antibodies to sperm may be present in a woman's vaginal secretions; this test examines the sperm-mucus interaction. Average cost: $75 ($35-300).

Ultrasonography: High-frequency sound waves are used to obtain detailed outlines of the reproductive system, especially changes in the ovaries related to ovulation. Average cost per exam: $100 ($40-186).

Endometrial biopsy: A hollow tube is passed through the cervix for removing a small amount of the uterine lining for microscopic examination. This is used to date the menstrual cycle. Average cost: $85 ($50-350).

Hysterosalpingogram: Radio-opaque dyes are slowly, and painfully, injected into the uterus while X-rays are taken to determine the condition of the Fallopian tubes. Average cost: $150 ($50-1,500).

Laparoscopy: Direct visualization of the female reproductive tract through an illuminated long, narrow instrument. Minor surgery can also be done during this procedure. Average cost: $800 ($400-2,500).

Hysteroscopy: Direct visualization of the interior of the uterus through a long, narrow, illuminated instrument inserted through the cervix; also allows minor surgery to be conducted. Average cost: $400 ($130-1,100).

Hamster-egg penetration assay: The husband's sperm are incubated with hamster eggs and watched for signs of fertilization. While penetration of the ova by a sperm is a sign of normal sperm, the reliability and significance of the test is controversial. Food for thought: conception between an animal and a man takes place during this laboratory procedure. Average cost: $275 ($35-390).

These diagnostic procedures are aimed at identifying many possible causes of infertility, such as tubal obstructions, hormone imbalances, low sperm counts, and reproductive diseases. Some conditions correct themselves over time without treatment, whereas others directly benefit from medical intervention.

Nevertheless, infertility specialists should be very clear about success rates *before* recommending or performing any treatment. Many physicians fail to do this. Citing studies and figures that will support their practices, they lay possible options out on the table for couples to pick and choose from. This, in effect, discounts available data on infertility treatment and prevents couples from making informed choices. Infertile couples often do not refuse offered treatments, even when paying for medical bills at their own expense.

Different Kinds of Customers

Since 1968, the number of office visits to physicians for infertility-related services rose from about 600,000 to 1.6 million in 1984.[17] Estimates place the number of office visits in recent years at over two million annually. Yet this quest leads many couples down a complex and emotionally rocky path where their hoped-for destination — parenthood — frequently remains out of reach.

Infertility specialists help to raise couples' expectations. "There is always another therapy that I can try and never a point at which I tell of husband and wife that they have done everything that there is to do," explains Dr. George Tagatz, director of the infertility clinic at the University of Minnesota Medical Center. "Even when we know the chances are slim, it's not up to us to tell someone when to quit."[18]

Dr. Wayne Decker, director of New York's Fertility Research Foundation, holds the same philosophy. One of his clients had *133* artificial inseminations and two operations before giving birth. "Should I have told her to stop trying?" Decker asks.[19]

On the other hand, couples like John and Joanne Smith of Maryland wish one of their three physicians *had* recommended quitting. Joanne has endometriosis, a disease diagnosed in nearly one-third of all women with infertility problems. In endometriosis, the tissue that lines the inside of the uterus begins growing outside the womb, often preventing the sperm from meeting the egg in the

Fallopian tubes. Joanne's situation was further complicated by cysts on her ovaries. She had four operations in five years in attempts to remove them.

"Each time, they'd take a piece of my ovary. So I was down to maybe a half an ovary left," explains Joanne. At that point, a physician recommended in vitro fertilization — even though his clinic had *never produced a baby* by IVF. Because their insurance company refused to cover the $7,000 in vitro procedure, the Smiths turned down his proposal. "That's when we finally said, 'Enough's enough. Let's try the adoption route.'"[20]

Infertile couples who can afford to pursue treatment may falsely assume that their physicians *will* tell them at what point they should stop trying. "There's no question that some couples are exploited," says Dr. Robert Rebar of Northwestern University School of Medicine. "But you have to ask, 'Are they intentionally exploited?' When the couple says they'll do anything to have a baby, it's very difficult for them to stop."[21] (Note: infertility specialists see it as their duty to offer and perform all available and appropriate treatments. *They are not neutral partners in a couple's medical treatment* — they are paid providers who sell professional health care on a fee-per-service basis.)

Rebar and eleven other leading infertility specialists say "there are many forces driving the development of this problem," including:

- *The malpractice crisis,* which is forcing obstetricians into the subspecialty areas of gynecology without adequate training;
- *The development of new technology,* which often occurs in an ethical and regulatory vacuum;
- *The entrance of for-profit organizations* into the infertility arena.[22]

William Winslade, professor of medical humanities at the University of Texas, comments on the potential for exploitation. "With infertile couples, we're dealing with different kinds of customers, people who are in stress and vulnerable and thus often spend too much money without thought," he asserts.[23] In his book *Choosing Life or Death*, Winslade and co-author Judith Wilson Ross point out:

Infertility treatment, like much plastic surgery, is *elective* treatment, undergone at the patients' request to alter their lives but not, in any ordinary sense, to improve their health. As a result, despite the fact that most physicians who specialize in infertility treatment sincerely desire to help the couples who come to them, *the field is ripe for commercialization.* Economic interests may cross over and affect medical interests. Infertility physicians frequently use the word desperate to refer to their patients. *An economically motivated physician faced with a desperate patient may go to extraordinary lengths to provide assistance.* [24]

There is no doubt that today's fertility drugs, techniques, and therapies have given hope to thousands of couples who would have been childless a generation ago. Until the 1960s, for example, women who had stopped ovulating simply stopped trying to become pregnant. Now, two powerful drugs — known commercially as Clomid and Pergonal — have been used successfully in many of these women.

Fertility drugs don't come cheap, however. For a month of treatment, clomiphene citrate (known commonly as Clomid) costs up to $277 and Pergonal can run as high as $1,500.[25] In addition to being very expensive, these medications are associated with a number of adverse reactions:

- Death
- Significantly increased rate of multiple pregnancy, associated with a higher risk of premature birth and neonatal mortality and morbidity
- Increased incidence of ectopic pregnancy
- Ovarian hyperstimulation syndrome, characterized by severe pelvic pain and ovarian enlargement, requiring hospitalization
- Rupture of ovarian cysts and internal bleeding which may require surgery to remove the affected ovarian tissue
- Increased incidence of ectopic pregnancy
- Bloating, stomach and pelvic pain
- Ovarian enlargement and formation of ovarian cysts
- Blurred or double vision
- Jaundice (yellowing of eyes and skin)
- Shortness of breath caused by a thromboembolism
- Nausea and vomiting
- Abnormal uterine bleeding
- Headaches, dizziness, lightheadedness
- Nervousness and insomnia
- Breast tenderness[26]

Clomiphene has been reported to cause vaginal tissue changes in mice while undergoing prenatal development, similar to those produced by DES (diethylstilbestrol).[27] What this will mean to the daughters of women who inadvertently were taking clomiphene during early pregnancy is not yet known.

Even the most effective drugs and treatments can only go so far in helping a couple to have a baby. American couples spent more than *one billion dollars* in 1987 seeking pregnancy.[28] But how many couples went home without a baby after spending thousands of dollars trying?

According to a study by the United States Office of Technology Assessment, therapeutic success rates vary tremendously and, as a whole, remain disappointingly low. "As many as half the infertile couples seeking treatment remain unsuccessful, despite trying various avenues of treatment," claims Dr. Gary Ellis, the project's director. "For as many as one in five couples, the cause is never found."[29]

Of the couples who do become pregnant, many conceive independently of their treatment. For the couples who will fail, how do they know when to stop?

Writer Katherine Bouton expresses the dilemma this way: "When you absolutely cannot have children, it's called sterility. When it seems to be taking an awfully long time but you still hope, it's called infertility. Infertility is worse."[30]

Dr. Eileen Aicardi, a pediatrician, and her husband Dennis spent four years enduring what she refers to as their "dehumanizing" bout with infertility tests and diagnosis. Making love according to a strict schedule and then "getting on a table and having sperm taken out of me" is one of the reasons why Eileen considers her experience dehumanizing.

She comments that her physician offered little comfort during this time. He once remarked: "All infertile women are depressed. See this box of Kleenex? I go through three boxes a day."

When Eileen's doctor gave her a prescription for medication that can cause low blood pressure and dizziness, she decided to seek a second opinion. Just after her new physician removed tissue that had been "acting like an IUD" inside her uterus, the doctor's office received a timely phone call: would the obstetrician be willing to provide services to a pregnant teenager? The Aicardis made arrangements to adopt the baby. A few months later, Eileen became pregnant.

Since being diagnosed as infertile, Eileen has given birth to four children. The Aicardis received a double blessing in June of 1987. "After all those years of putting your bottom on a pillow for a half-hour, to think I had twins!" she exclaims.

"It proves it was totally out of control."[31]

Has There Actually Been an Infertility Crisis?

In spite of all the publicity about infertility, not everyone is convinced that the infertility rate is rising as rapidly as some say. In fact, the Office of Technology Assessment found that the overall incidence of infertility in the United States remained relatively *unchanged* between 1965 and 1982.[32]

Jane Menken, associate director of the Office of Population Research, and her colleagues at Princeton University point out that *age-related infertility does not rise significantly until after a woman reaches thirty-five.* "Fertility, compared with that of women twenty to twenty-four, is reduced on average by 6 percent for women twenty-five to twenty-nine, 14 percent for those thirty to thirty-four, and 31 percent for women thirty-five to thirty-nine, with much greater decline thereafter," they point out. Also, their research indicates that *women do not become infertile instantaneously.* Instead, there is a period of declining ability to bear a child before sterility occurs.[33]

Under current medical practice, infertility is generally defined as "the inability of a couple to conceive after twelve months of intercourse without contraception."[34] Even for fertile women, however, Menken's group estimates that *the mean time to conception is more than eight months* and that at least 14 percent of those couples trying to have a baby take *at least* a year to conceive.[35]

This evidence is further supported by a two- to seven-year follow-up study of 1,145 infertile couples appearing in the *New England Journal of Medicine*. In this group, 41 percent of the treated couples conceived, but so did 35 percent of the *untreated* couples![36] Based on these findings, the researchers concluded that:

- The spontaneous cure rate of infertility is high
- Pregnancy occurs frequently in couples diagnosed as infertile, but who have received no treatment or have stopped all treatment
- For many infertile couples, the potential for conception *without* treatment is at least as high as *with* treatment[37]

Do infertility specialists share this information with their clients? If not, why not? Obviously, it would be counterproductive to business, to say the least. Compassion is not what motivates the infertility industry in the United States today.

"Clearly, the use of the one-year criterion as a measure of infertility confounds inability *ever* to conceive with difficulty in conceiving *quickly*," state Menken and her associates. "As a diagnostic tool, its advantage is that those with infertility problems have the opportunity to *start treatment* early. Nevertheless, because a substantial fraction of nonsterile couples takes more than a year to conceive, *use of this criterion may generate needless anxiety in couples who hope to become parents and leads to unnecessary and costly medical treatment in a substantial proportion of cases.*"[38]

Other reasons for today's focus on infertility:

Couples expect to be able to control fertility and plan parenthood according to schedule. After expending a great deal of effort turning off their reproductive ability, Americans think that controlling fertility is the main challenge, that getting pregnant is easy. It's hardly surprising, then, that many couples believe there are problems when a *wanted* child is not conceived *quickly*. Since there are fewer unintended pregnancies today, more couples are finally finding out how long it actually takes to achieve conception.

The birth rate is lower. With fewer women having fewer babies, and more couples controlling fertility more effectively, not as many women need obstetrical services. Consequently, a larger proportion of women are coming in to doctors' offices to have abortions or obtain help with conception, not to get prenatal care. The situation appears even worse because many women are delaying childbearing.

The contraceptive revolution and the legalization of abortion, combined with the increased tendency for single mothers to raise their own babies, has drastically reduced the availability of adoptive children. Attention now focuses on the problems of disappointed couples instead.

Sexually transmitted infertility is on the rise. An overall increase in pelvic inflammatory disease, or PID, is the main indirect evidence of this problem. PID can lead to extensive scarring of the Fallopian tubes. It represents the greatest known threat — and also the *most preventable* danger — to women's fertility. The primary causes of PID are gonorrhea and chlamydia, sexually transmitted diseases that have reached epidemic levels during the past twenty years.[39] Sexually transmitted diseases account for *an estimated 20 percent of all infertility* in the United States today.[40]

Intrauterine contraceptive devices have also caused PID-related fertility loss in thousands of American women.[41] Up to 88,000 women are currently estimated to be infertile due to using IUCDs as a birth control method.[42]

Temporary loss of fertility following use of oral contraceptives is common. Hormonal treatments may alleviate post-Pill infertility, but involve diagnosis and expensive medication.[43] *Oral contracep-*

tive use also enhances the risk of infection with chlamydia, the leading cause of PID in the United States today.[44]

Pelvic infections after abortion, surgery or invasive diagnostic testing contribute to infertility by provoking tubal damage and scarring of reproductive tissue.

D&C (vacuum aspiration) abortion during the late first trimester of pregnancy—and all abortions during the second trimester—pose a risk to women's fertility.[45] Therefore, increasing use of D&C's and D&E's may be expected to contribute to the infertility in the United States.

Smoking and drinking caffeine beverages—habits practiced by many women of childbearing age—have been linked to infertility.[46] Doctors in Boston studied more than 900 infertile women and found that smokers had more growths blocking their Fallopian tubes and more changes in the cervical mucus that prevented sperm from reaching the uterus.[47] Compared to non-smokers, women who smoke are *three to four times more likely* to take longer than one year to conceive.[48] Another recent study found that women who consumed more than one cup of coffee per day were *half as likely* to become pregnant, per cycle, as women who drank less.[49]

Other lifestyle factors related to infertility include regular strenuous exercise, poor nutrition, obesity, and stress. Women run an increased risk of reproductive impairment when repeated dieting, chronic stress, rapid weight loss, low body fat levels, or excessive weight create hormonal imbalances.[50] All are common among women today.

Infertility is overdiagnosed due to the medical definition of infertility. The standard one-year criterion has not been thoroughly researched; conflicting studies demonstrate that the length of time required for conception varies substantially from couple to couple. It is questionable whether the benefits of using so nonspecific a test outweigh the financial and emotional costs. Remember—for as many as one in five couples, the cause of infertility is never found.[51]

Excessive testing and diagnosis benefits our current health care system. Medical interventions for infertility generate business for doctors and hospitals. While physicians may provide infertility services partially out of compassion for their clients, their area of specialization also provides them with the challenge of mastering new skills and opportunities to boost their professional status.

New reproductive technologies—test tube babies, surrogate mothers, surgical interventions for infertility, and reversal of sterilizing operations—have brought public attention to fertility problems, but have failed to adequately address causes of reproductive impairment. Also, these expensive procedures are far from foolproof. Of the one billion dollars spent on infertility in 1987, some $66 million was spent on in vitro fertilization.[52] Yet the overall failure rate for this procedure is still more than *94 percent!* [53]

The picture of infertility being sold to the public is distorted by an overemphasis on treatment and too little focus on prevention. Infertility "is a problem requiring attention, *but that attention should be directed toward disease* and not distorted by an exaggerated impression of the effects of normal biological aging," concludes Menken's team. "The evidence indicates that *the woman who deliberately postpones childbearing and either abstains from sex or participates in a monogamous relationship does not face great risks*" of infertility.[54]

A letter appearing in the *Journal of the American Medical Association* sums up the issue well:

> Worldwide, approximately 5,000 children have been born as the result of in vitro fertilization (IVF). In the United States alone, there are about one million cases of pelvic inflammatory disease each year. If we assume that 130,000 to 500,000 of these cases lead to tubal occlusion [blockage], then in the United States alone *in one month or less,* pelvic inflammatory disease creates more new cases of infertility than have been successfully treated by all IVF programs in the world since Louise Brown was born in 1978.[55]

Okay. Why, then, is so little attention being paid to infertility prevention and so much to in vitro fertilization? Why so little emphasis on the relationship between contraceptive methods and permanent reproductive impairment? To the role of monogamy in protecting women's reproductive competency?

Why are millions of dollars being spent on medical "miracle" treatments such as IVF when up to 50 percent of the infertility occurring in this country might be *completely avoided* through healthier lifestyles and earlier childbearing? When the effectiveness of infertility treatments *have yet to be proven*? When treatment-independent pregnancies *are almost as common* as pregnancies in women treated for infertility?

Chapter Seven:

IN VITRO FERTILIZATION AND EMBRYO TRANSFER: Sex in a Dish?

Destruction of the natural means destruction of life. Knowledge and the will to live fall into disorder and confusion and are directed toward the wrong objects. The unnatural is the enemy of life.[1]

Dietrich Bonhoeffer, *Ethics*

*I*n recent years, stories of test-tube babies have been popular news items. But few Americans remember the names of John and Doris Del Zio, the first couple to attempt in vitro fertilization in the United States—and make national headlines in the process. Reflecting on this years later, Mrs. Del Zio explains, "I didn't do it to be the first; I did it because I wanted desperately to have our baby."[2] As the following story shows, it is this very desperation that made Doris the perfect target for experimental infertility treatment.

In writing about her experience with IVF for *Good Housekeeping* magazine, Doris shares the reasons behind her intense desire for a child:

> . . . I found it difficult to understand the wide interest in my case. Who cares about me? I'm a nobody from Plattsburgh, N.Y. My father worked in a paper mill; my mother was a saleslady in a jewelry store and I never went to college. I went to airline-stewardess school, married for the first time at eighteen, had a baby girl at nineteen and separated from my husband at twenty.
>
> After my divorce, I worked at two jobs: as a receptionist for a doctor in the daytime and as a clerk in a grocery store at night. It was hard, but my daughter, Tammy, and I made it on our own.
>
> Then I met my present husband, Dr. John Del Zio, a dentist. Twenty-five years older than I, he had been separated from his wife for nine years. His compassion was immediately evident and all enveloping. He invited me out and, although divorced women are fair game, I didn't have to fight him off. I felt comfortable with him and two years later we were married.
>
> We had discussed having a large family and, from the moment I said "I do" in 1968, I couldn't wait to have another baby.[3]

Sadly, Doris Del Zio suffered a ruptured ovarian cyst on her honeymoon, requiring immediate surgery. The Del Zios then spent a full year trying to conceive. When it was discovered she wasn't ovulating regularly, Doris's physician put her on Clomid, a fertility drug he told her would greatly increase the likelihood of multiple pregnancy. Instead of producing twins or triplets, the drug brought on nausea, weight gain, and more painful cysts on her ovaries.

In February 1970, a diagnostic test called a hysterosalpingogram turned up a more serious problem: Doris's Fallopian tubes were blocked. Her physician referred her to an infertility specialist, Dr. William J. Sweeney III, a professor of obstetrics and gynecology at Cornell University-New York Hospital. Further tests confirmed the tubal diagnosis. A procedure could be performed which might open her oviducts, Dr. Sweeney said, even though he could not guarantee success. Doris consented to the operation.

Like many infertile women, Doris had complete confidence in medicine's ability to come up with a solution to her problem. "I am a very simple person," she confesses. "If a faucet were broken, I'd have it fixed. If my tubes were blocked, I'd have them opened. I knew it wasn't that easy but, because I'd conquered polio when I was a little girl, I have great faith in science and medicine."4

In 1970, Dr. Sweeney performed a laparoscopy. But because of a childhood appendix operation and earlier surgery to remove her ruptured ovarian cyst, excessive scar tissue had developed inside Doris's abdomen. This made the tubal repair impossible. If her tubes could be opened at all, Dr. Sweeney told his client that a much more extensive and painful operation would be necessary.

For Doris, there was no doubt that the surgery was needed. She describes herself as a "fighter" and didn't mind undergoing additional surgery in order to become pregnant. From previous operations, she knew she was allergic to painkillers, yet remained positive about the operation. The reason, she said, was because "when I have hope, I can stand pain."5 At this point, Doris had already made a substantial emotional and financial investment in her battle against infertility. She was not about to give up the struggle as long as she had another option.

False Hopes and Unethical Human Experimentation

The operation was performed, and Doris conceived several months later in the autumn of 1970. Tragically, the pregnancy she had longed for ended in heartbreak. The baby was lost through miscarriage at Christmastime.

By the following spring, Doris had not become pregnant and was anxious to resume medical treatment. She and John decided to fly to New York from their new home in Fort Lauderdale, Florida, to meet with Dr. Sweeney. When he could offer no other therapy than attempting a second tubal reconstruction, Doris insisted on trying it.

In spite of the additional surgery and ongoing infertility treatment, pregnancy continued to elude the Del Zios. They attempted artificial insemination, with no results. In the meantime, additional cysts and adhesions had formed on Doris's reproductive system. The likelihood that she would ever be pregnant again diminished.

When her gall bladder acted up in the fall of 1971, Doris faced yet another medical crisis. "I was utterly miserable," she remembers. "My abdomen now looked like a road map, and my insides were a mass of adhesions. Sometimes they were so painful that I just couldn't straighten up. John felt that I had gone through enough, mentally and physically. I knew that, financially, he'd been through enough too."6

As with so many infertile couples today, the Del Zios continued to seek their physician's help in spite of the toll infertility treatment was taking. Doris traveled to see Dr. Sweeney again in April 1972. This time, however, he finally told her that she would not be able to conceive another child.

After two and a half painful years, countless office visits and exams, dozens of diagnostic procedures, risky hormone therapy, a laparoscopy, two tubal surgeries, the removal of her gall bladder, and a miscarriage, Doris was almost ready to give up. Facing Dr. Sweeney across his desk, she clearly remembers her reaction to hearing she couldn't become pregnant and to the strange piece of news that followed:

> Although his office was full of patients, he took the time to show me stacks of charts of women who had problems similar to mine. I cried all over his office. I was angry at medicine and science in general. "If they can get a man on the moon, why can't they let me get pregnant by bypassing my dumb little Fallopian tubes?" I asked.
>
> It was a long time ago but I can still see him sitting behind his desk, his white coat all starched, his telephone with its innumerable buttons silent. He must have told his secretary to hold his calls.
>
> After my outburst he asked, "Have you read any articles about *in vitro* fertilization?"
>
> I hadn't. It was the first time I had heard the expression.
>
> "It's a way of getting pregnant without using the Fallopian tubes," he explained. "But it has only been done with animals."7

A way of getting pregnant. . . . Perhaps there still is a chance after all. One can easily imagine how Dr. Sweeney's words must have sounded to a woman who had endured so much in hope of giving birth to her new husband's child. Across the Atlantic, Patrick Steptoe and Robert Edwards had already discovered that infertile women with damaged oviducts were ideal candidates for experiments with in vitro fertilization. Now Doris Del Zio was about to become the first American woman to test the procedure. By her own account, Doris apparently believed IVF might produce a viable embryo capable of implanting in her uterus. The technique, however, had not even been thoroughly studied in animals.

In June 1972, Doris had her third — and last — surgery in a final attempt to repair her Fallopian tubes. During the operation, Dr. Sweeney removed some of Doris's eggs, and sent them along with a sample of John's sperm for a trial run at in vitro fertilization.

The man pioneering the procedure was Dr. Landrum Shettles, a physician-researcher at New York City's Columbia-Presbyterian Hospital. Like Robert Edwards, Shettles had been conducting research on IVF since the 1950s.[8] But there was a big difference between the two technicians: Shettles's work on external fertilization in humans had never been fully accepted by the international scientific community. Claiming that he had achieved IVF as early as 1955, Shettles had failed to sufficiently document his success through detailed photographs and descriptions of his research.

Nevertheless, the Del Zios's trial of IVF apparently worked; Dr. Sweeney informed the Del Zios there had been a "take." He told them they could try external fertilization if Doris couldn't conceive in the months following her third tubal operation. By December 1972, she still wasn't pregnant. The Del Zios were ready to go ahead with IVF.

"John supported me, but I was the driving force," admits Doris. "It took a year of mental, physical, and financial planning. We would have begged, borrowed, and mortgaged everything for a June hospitalization."[9]

The Del Zios flew to New York City in September 1973. Doris was in the operating room for over ten hours while her eggs were harvested. When she awoke from her anesthetic in the recovery room, she saw Dr. Sweeney standing at her bedside.

"We did well. We got the eggs," Doris remembers him telling her. She also adds:

> I was in great pain, but he was giving me hope.
>
> When I came down to my room, John had told me that he had taken the eggs to Dr. Shettles and all was well.
>
> The next day, although I still had a tube in my nose and an IV in my arm, I was happy. We talked about names for the baby.

Later that afternoon, a nurse came in and told John that there was a call for him at the nurses' station. When John came back, he acted sort of funny. He didn't look at me in the eye when he said, "Dr. Shettles called Dr. Sweeney and told him that the eggs weren't fertilizing."

But I *knew* that the eggs had fertilized; there was something inside me that was sure.[10]

Later that evening, Dr. Shettles phoned Doris, saying over and over again, "I'm so sorry. I'm so sorry." It was the first time she had spoken to him.

Alone in her room, she listened to Landrum Shettles explain what had happened to her ova. When Shettles's supervisor, Dr. Raymond Vande Wiele, found out what had taken place, he stopped the IVF procedure by destroying the sterility of the eggs. The Del Zios later sued Vande Wiele, the hospital, and Columbia University for $1.5 million.

Defense attorneys argued that the procedure was dangerous and experimental — a fair and accurate portrayal considering the evidence. After hearing Doris recount her tragic story, however, the jury decided in favor of the Del Zios and their ill-fated offspring, awarding them $50,000. (The case is particularly interesting in light of the Supreme Court's earlier devaluation of the human embryo in abortion rulings.) The case continues to influence public policy, putting a halt to all federal research grants for human in vitro fertilization of humans beginning in 1975. The moratorium on IVF research funding has yet to be lifted.

Was Doris Del Zio given false hope when she was offered IVF as a solution to her infertility? Why did she believe her eggs could be successfully cultured and transferred to her uterus? Doris willingly submitted to a lengthy and painful operation and spent thousands of dollars on medical bills and travel expenses. She fought a long, drawn-out court battle because she thought her embryo had a good chance of survival. Why? Was it only her hope and desperation that fostered this belief, or was it also because IVF was presented to her by Sweeney and Shettles as a "possible therapeutic option"?

If Doris was in fact experimentally exploited, which man acted properly: Vande Wiele, who stopped the experiment because he believed it constituted unsafe and unethical experimentation on human lives? Or Shettles, who was willing to go ahead with IVF and embryo transfer to please the Del Zios regardless of the experiment's effects on both mother and child? Since IVF hadn't yet been analyzed in higher mammals, why did Shettles consider it safe to try with humans? Why was Mrs. Del Zio given the impression her embryo might grow in her womb even though international researchers were *years* away from the first viable embryo transfer?

It wasn't until 1981 that the first cattle were conceived by IVF and grew successfully in a cow's uterus.[11] Elizabeth Carr, America's first test-tube baby, arrived the same year. This is a staggering fact. After reading it, one can't help but wonder—do scientists think sex in a dish means the same thing to women as it does to cows (i.e., an appropriate and acceptable alternative to sexual reproduction)? After all, IVF is a *breeding technique*, not a *medical therapy*. A woman who uses it isn't *"cured"* of anything—she is *"made pregnant"* by a team of IVF technicians.

In 1971, two years before the Del Zio tragedy, a physician at the National Research Council clearly foresaw the dilemma that would be imposed on infertile women—and society—as a result of new reproductive technologies. In an article appearing in the *New England Journal of Medicine*, Dr. Leon Kass warned:

> To consider infertility solely in terms of the traditional medical model of disease (or in terms of a so-called right of an individual to have a child) can only help to undermine, both in thought and in practice, the bond between childbearing and the covenant of marriage. In a technological age, viewing infertility as a disease demanding treatment by physicians fosters the development and encourages the use of all the new technologies [superovulation, egg harvesting, IVF, laboratory testing of embryos, and embryo transfer].
>
> Just as infertility is not a disease, so providing a child by artificial means to a woman with blocked oviducts is not treatment (as surgical reconstruction of her oviducts would be). *She remains as infertile as before.* What is being "treated" is her desire—a perfectly normal and unobjectionable desire—to bear a child. There is no clear medical therapeutic purpose that requires or demands the use of the new and untested technologies for initiating human life and that might possibly justify the unconsented-to use of a human subject [the mother and/or embryo] for the benefit of others and at risk to [her or] himself. . . .
>
> It is altogether too easy to exploit, even unwittingly, the desire of a childless couple. It would be cruel to generate for them false hopes (e.g., by exaggerated publicity). It would be both cruel *and* unethical to generate hope falsely (e.g., by telling

women that they themselves, rather than future infertile women, might be helped to have a child) to obtain their participation in experiments.[12]

What Do I Tell My Patients?

In Oldham, England, long before Doris Del Zio had ever heard of the term *in vitro fertilization*, dozens of other infertile women had also been told they had one last chance of bearing a child. Women with blocked tubes. Women who had tried every possible means to overcome their infertility. Women willing to endure repeated trials of ovarian stimulation and reproductive surgery in the hope of producing a baby.

After Robert Edwards and Barry Bavister successfully fertilized those twelve human eggs in a petri dish at Cambridge University, the next question was how to get embryos to grow following the procedure. In order to accomplish this, Edwards knew he would have a better chance of success if he obtained *mature* eggs. Up until then, he had ripened ova in culture fluid using eggs removed from women during gynecological surgery.

By joining forces with ob/gyn Patrick Steptoe, Edwards gained access to living ovaries at precisely the right moment of the menstrual cycle. Of this, Edwards says:

> It was a question then of Patrick obtaining the ripened eggs directly from women by laparoscopy—to withdraw eggs from the ovary without damaging them in any way. No one had ever done that before. But already I had evidence of Patrick's extraordinary surgical skill and his ability to use the laparoscope superbly.
>
> "Yes," said Patrick. "If we can find a way to aspirate [suction out] the eggs, laparoscopy should be invaluable for this purpose. It makes few demands on the patient, permits many manipulations in the abdominal cavity, and *can be used repeatedly in the same patient.*"[13]

Before long, Edwards and his research associate, Ms. Jean Purdy, had invented an apparatus to be used during Steptoe's laparoscopies. Basically, its design allowed eggs to be vacuumed directly from mature ovarian follicles. Prior to surgery, volunteer subjects were given high doses of hormones to control their menstrual cycles and stimulate the ripening of the eggs—just as Edwards had done in mice a decade earlier. Then, at what he hoped would be the perfect time, laparoscopies were performed to collect the ova and begin culturing them in glass dishes. Unlike his earlier trials with IVF, Edwards carefully obtained the semen of patients' husbands to fertilize the eggs removed from Steptoe's patients.

In a limited way, the women operated upon were aware of Edwards's research. "We had to ask Patrick's infertile patients, those desperate for help and willing to undergo many trials in the hope of one day having their own babies, to cooperate in a project that was still in its stumbling early stages," he writes, adding, "We soon discovered that patients *needed to be restrained from volunteering too much.* Patients would offer themselves for a second laparoscopy or even come to Oldham General Hospital twelve times a year if necessary!"[14]

On March 3, 1970, the *Washington Post* carried an announcement about the research. Of particular interest is the statement made by the woman from whom an egg was taken:

> Dr. Patrick Steptoe, who heads the team of doctors working on the [IVF] experiment, disclosed on television that he had extracted an ovum from a thirty-four-year-old housewife and fertilized it with her husband's sperm. The woman, Mrs. Sylvia Allen, . . . *said she hoped the fertilized ovum would be implanted in her womb in the next two to six weeks,* meaning that the world's first baby conceived in a test-tube *could be born by the end of 1970.*[15]

Mrs. Allen's embryo was never placed inside her body. *The first embryo transfer at Oldham General Hospital did not take place until right before Christmas in 1971.*[16]

Needless to say, Edwards finally had plenty of eggs and embryos to study. Human ova, once fertilized, were tested for growth in different culture mediums, including the reproductive tracts of rabbits:

> The rabbit enjoyed the reputation of being a good embryo to grow, and also of being a good mother to support the embryos of other species; cow and sheep eggs will grow happily within the rabbit, and can even be flown around the world within it to establish herds in distant countries. We transferred some fertilized human eggs into rabbits to see if they would grow there, but they wouldn't.[17]

Environmental factors, such as incubation temperature, light exposure, and the chemicals used in culturing the embryos, were tested by observing embryos for their reactions to different substances. ("We had to test the fertilized human eggs in several different culture solutions to find which was best for their growth.")[18] Embryos that appeared to be growing normally were laboriously examined for signs of damage or abnormality. Inspired by these experiments, Edwards writes:

> To observe a living, vibrant embryo beginning its earliest steps of development is a most stimulating sight for an embryologist, whether it be a mouse, rabbit, sea urchin, or human. . . .
>
> I am still thrilled as an egg divides and develops for, in addition to the beauty of its growth, the embryo is passing through a critical period of life of great exploration. It becomes magnificently organized, switching on its own biochemistry, increasing in size, and preparing itself quickly for implantation inside the womb. After that its organs form—the cells gradually become capable of development into heart, lung, brain, eye. What a unique and wonderful process it is, as the increasing number of cells diverge and specialize in a delicate, integrated, and coordinated manner.[19]

Why is it a man like Robert Edwards can justify venturing where even angels fear to tread?

While Edwards was marveling at these events in the laboratory, infertile women were being told they had a chance at motherhood. They were experimentally injected with hormones, hospitalized, placed under general anesthesia, operated upon, and then sent home—without their embryos. *Nine years of intensive research passed before the first embryo was implanted successfully and survived until birth.*

The first time the Steptoe and Edwards partnership produced several healthy-looking embryos, the event provoked an immediate confrontation. Steptoe, a physician, was confused about what his associate planned to do with the embryos and what to tell his patient if they were destroyed. For Edwards, an animal geneticist, there was no question about what had to be done or how his partner should explain it:

> . . . the temptation to replace the blastocysts [five-day-old embryos] into the mother on the spot was very strong, and I have often wondered what might have happened had we succumbed. They belonged not to us but to the wife and husband who had donated their eggs and spermatozoa.
>
> "What are we going to do with them?" asked Patrick.
>
> "We're going to flatten them for chromosomes," I replied.

"What do I tell my patients?" Patrick insisted.

Patrick knew, as I did, that there would always be some embryos that could not be replaced inside their mothers. Instead, they would have to be examined; they would have to be fixed and stained for microscopic examination, and, as a result, their growth ended. Was it justifiable to use these blastocysts so that we could investigate early human growth? Did they have any rights? . . . The embryos cleaving in our culture fluids were minute and immature without the vestige of an organ or even a tissue compared with those aborted under the law. . . .

"What do I tell my patients?" Patrick had asked.

"I've got to see that the cell nuclei and the chromosomes are good," I had replied. "You'll be able to explain to them that we've taken another step forward."[20]

Beginning with his first IVF success in October 1968,[21] it had been Edwards's practice to "flatten" the embryos he manufactured after observing them for signs of development. He did this in order to study their genetic makeup. "This was a heartbreaking procedure considering all the efforts we had made to obtain and nurture them," Edwards says. "But it had to be done to make sure they were growing normally."[22]

Until December 1971, Edwards claims he had no intention of returning these brand-new lives to their mothers.[23] *The incident mentioned above occurred in 1969*, more than *two years* before the first embryo was transferred to a woman's womb in Steptoe and Edwards's program.[24]

The first four embryos — and several dozen afterwards — were squashed, stained, and mounted on glass slides for examination. The question is, what *did* Patrick Steptoe tell his patients during those years? Why would women keep coming back to endure the experiments voluntarily if they believed there was no chance whatsoever of their offspring surviving in their wombs?

"Our patients were childless couples who hoped our research might enable them to have children," said Edwards of his subjects in 1970.[25] This, and nothing else, is what must have led these women to surrender their eggs to Cambridge's IVF technicians.

Outside the Law: The Truth About Noncoital Reproduction in America Today

Surprisingly, IVF techniques, frequently portrayed as "no longer experimental" to potential customers by physicians, today have still not been accomplished in many mammals, including primates.

In an article he wrote with his wife, Ruth Fowler, Robert Edwards admits to achieving human in vitro fertilization "with confirmatory observations on a few cow oocytes."[26] What exactly does this mean? *It means that the safety and efficacy of IVF was never proven by adequate trials in animals before being applied to humans.* Doris Del Zio's story and Robert Edwards's experiments also demonstrate that *IVF research has taken place without the fully informed and voluntary consent of the human subjects involved.*[27] Furthermore, there is reason to believe that the IVF industry is continuing to exploit infertile couples by applying ineffective and often lethal techniques to human embryos without adequate regulation.

Of the more than 170 American IVF clinics now in business, *over half* had not produced a single baby as of May 1988.[28] *Yet at least $30 to $40 million were spent on in vitro fertilization by infertile couples in 1987* — representing 7 percent of the total amount spent on infertility.[29] The Office of Technology Assessment estimates less than 1 percent of all infertile couples in the country who sought treatment that year are responsible for these figures.[30]

While the exact number of IVF babies born in 1987 may forever remain a mystery, the U.S. Registry of IVF/ET and related practices reported the live birth rate at ninety-six clinics to be 1,858 babies.[31] Add it up: $30 to $40 million plus 14,647 reported IVF attempts= 1,858 much-wanted babies.[32] This in a country where babies are dying daily because their mothers can't afford basic prenatal care and more than 1.6 *million* unwanted babies were intentionally aborted surgically last year. As a society, Americans all pay, in one way or another, for these realities of current reproductive fashion.

Just ten years after the first IVF baby was born, IVF/ET research and related clinical programs are booming.[33] Who's footing the bill? Have researchers continued to exploit infertile couples as Leon Kass predicted? Are infertile women being adequately protected from unethical medical experimentation?

Consider: the widespread application of external fertilization procedures today is taking place without governmental oversight regarding:

- IVF's *proven safety and effectiveness;*
- *Licensing requirements* for practitioners;
- *Regulation* of embryo laboratories;
- *Governmental guidelines* for training;
- *Uniform reporting* of treatments and outcomes;
- *Standards* for IVF/ET laboratory equipment;

● *Recommendations* for use of advanced reproductive technologies.[34]

Yet anyone who *donates blood* or *submits a urine sample* to any licensed medical facility in the United States is protected by *all* of these safeguards! At a congressional hearing conducted by the Subcommittee on Regulation and Business Opportunities last year, IVF expert Dr. Richard Marrs was asked whether there were fewer regulations for embryo laboratories than for laboratories doing blood tests. Marrs replied:

> *There are absolutely no regulations.* The IVF [embryo] culture laboratories are not even a state recognized laboratory; they don't even exist in the minds of State regulatory agencies as far as licensing. We have to provide for our own hormonal laboratory in our center. We do our own hormonal measurement in blood and other plasma products; we have to give the State agency an updated monthly and quarterly analysis of our quality control, our variation of sampling, and we can be tested at any time by unknown samples that are sent from the State to be tested against our facility.
>
> Yet, in the embryo laboratory *we have made hundreds of babies* from our embryo laboratory and it has yet to be put into any kind of quality control oversight . . . when you see the number of clinics springing up from ten to almost two hundred in the last five years and the quality of outcome coming from over half of these clinics, I would have to say regulations need to take place because there is a lot of exploitation going on and I don't think the medical societies have the authority or power to do that. [Without government monitoring] I think we are going to self-destruct. I think with rampant use, and the uncontrolled use of these technologies, it would not be long before there would be major problems that would occur from the use of these technologies, and I think the public will then lose faith in the ability of the physicians in this area to provide safe and optimistic treatment form.[35]

Doesn't this mean infertile couples are being financially and medically exploited *right now*? But when Dr. Marrs presented guidelines on advanced reproductive technologies to members of the American Fertility Society in 1985, he says "there was open hostility about requiring any type of reporting or credentialing."[36] Discussion was tabled for a year, says Marrs, because "I was fearful of my life."[37]

Finally, in 1986, Marrs helped to found the Society for Assisted Reproductive Technology (SART), a credentialling process for IVF programs. Membership is open to IVF practitioners who conduct a minimum of forty treatment cycles yearly (in vitro fertilization cycles) and have had a minimum of three live births. SART also demands compliance with minimal standards for personnel and facilities as well as anonymous reporting of results to a central registry for annual publication. Even these minimum standards were met with "extreme hostility," says Marrs. Only 41 of the nation's IVF programs belonged to SART when it published its first report in January 1987.[38] By January 1989, membership had increased to 119 clinics; *more than 50 of these enrolled in 1988.*[39]

In an article titled "Easier Than Selling Soap," *Forbes* magazine claims that in vitro programs represent a potential market worth over $460 million annually due to the rise in pelvic inflammatory disease and age-related infertility.[40] Citing additional evidence for this phenomenon, *Forbes* states:

- One in every four IVF programs is operated on a for-profit basis and is owned by venture capitalists;
- IVF franchises are springing up coast to coast;
- Where insurance coverage for infertility treatment is mandated by state government, the high cost of IVF is no longer a barrier.

"These clinics, although operating as businesses, may be better described as ongoing, privately funded research projects with no overseeing regulatory body," points out Carol Peters, president of the de Miranda Institute for Infertility and Modern Parenting. "The medical community, which enjoys a special status in society, is not regulating itself."[41]

In Massachusetts, where infertility treatments are covered by insurance,[42] an IVF franchise called *In Vitro Care, Inc.* raised over $4 million in a public stock offering. That was in October 1985. They had yet to open a single clinic — let alone produce a baby — by February 1987.

"Buffeted by the pressures of commercial interests and near-desperate patients searching for a technological miracle, the [IVF] technique has become a major player in an increasingly lucrative infertility market," points out a news report in the *Journal of the*

American Medical Association: "In vitro fertilization has the potential to be a profit-making proposition because the pool of candidates is large."[43]

IVF/ET: A High-Risk, Low-Yield Business

In a rush to attract business, it is not uncommon for IVF clinics to minimize the risks of the procedure to potential clients, quote success rates from other programs, and give confusing statistics that don't tell how many live births have resulted.

"In the peculiar jargon of IVF/ET, 'success' is not a baby but a 'pregnancy.' And reported pregnancy rates are *not* pregnancies per number of women enrolled, nor women hormonally stimulated to superovulate, nor women from whom oocytes are retrieved," writes *Birth's* editor Madeleine H. Shearer. "Women whose flesh does not pass these hurdles simply disappear from the clinics' statistics like ghosts."[44] If doctors must ask one another to define pregnancy and are questioning the efficacy of high-tech infertility treatments already in use, something has gone terribly wrong with the practice of medicine.[45] It's called *the commercialization of reproduction*.

When the top journals in reproductive medicine begin carrying articles questioning the honesty and integrity of IVF practitioners, it's clear that women's health is in jeopardy.[46] Even leading IVF technicians, recognizing that deceit and greed have crept into their profession, are wondering what to do about this crisis.

"Some new IVF clinics seem more interested in selling stock than in actually serving customers," concludes *Forbes*. "Such facilities are mushrooming throughout the country. In vitro programs have multiplied from 4 in 1981 to over 150 currently [in February 1987], part of a burgeoning world of infertility specialists, research labs, and infertility drugs—all targeted at the growing number of infertile couples' quest for conception."[47]

Dr. Arthur Caplan, director of the Center for Biomedical Ethics at the University of Minnesota, describes the lengths some clinics will go to to achieve "success:"

> Fertility consumers are especially fragile customers. They are seeking any means to have a baby. They will go anywhere, spend any amount, to have a baby. They can be preyed upon. Centers often give average data. To me that is simply unethical in the area of informed consent.
>
> When one goes to a clinic, one does not care about pooled

or averaged data. One wants to know what is the success rate in this clinic at this time. That must be provided, or informed consent is a charade. . . .

IVF success rates are so discouraging that there are some centers trying to do better in terms of creating babies by using multiple [embryo] implants. It shows at the forty-one [leading] centers there were an average of three embryos used. Some centers use more than that. When they do, they sometimes create multiple pregnancies, three, four, five, or six babies.

Then they use fetal reduction, which is killing some fetuses to preserve the health of the mother and to help the other fetuses survive. That is a serious procedure. But because of the lack of pressure to standardize, routinize, and assure quality in the centers out there, we have this kind of dubious activity going on out there.[48]

It is incredible that physicians, going to such great lengths to produce babies by IVF, later intentionally destroy them in utero. Yet what Dr. Caplan is describing is now considered an acceptable means of achieving "success" among an increasing number of infertility specialists. By transplanting four to six embryos from the lab to the womb, the pregnancy rate significantly rises.[49]

In 1978 a leading British medical journal, *The Lancet*, carried the first published article on "selective reduction" of multiple pregnancy.[50] The paper describes a woman who voluntarily underwent amniocentesis for genetic diagnosis while carrying twins. Only one of her babies was found to have a genetically transmitted disorder. Both parents wished to avoid having the affected child and asked if the baby could be selectively aborted. The authors of the paper explain:

During these discussions the possibility of trying to pierce the heart of the affected fetus was mentioned, but we emphasized this procedure had not been done before and probably carried the risk of spontaneous abortion of the other fetus. After careful deliberation the parents decided to take this risk.[51]

The baby with Hurler's disease was killed in the twenty-fourth week of pregnancy after two attempts to puncture the child's heart with a needle. The second twin was born nine weeks later by cesarean section. "Mother and child are in perfect health," concluded the physicians who performed the puncture — yet they offer no follow-up study on the social and emotional effects of the abortion on the survivors and their family.[52]

Unbelievably, this killing technique is gaining popularity among physicians. The practice of inducing multiple pregnancies in infertile women through the use of fertility drugs (gonadotropins) and in vitro fertilization/embryo transfer are the reasons why.[53] IVF technician Rene Frydman and his colleagues state:

> Ovarian stimulation for ovulation induction and in vitro fertilization (IVF) have increased the multiple pregnancy rate from less than 1 percent to about 20 percent. The pathology of multiple pregnancy is well documented and involves high perinatal morbidity and mortality associated with immaturity and prematurity.[54]

While claiming that the multiple pregnancy rate can be controlled "to some extent" by reducing the degree of ovarian stimulation or reducing the number of embryos transferred to the uterus, Frydman's team points out that multiple pregnancy will continue to remain the major complication related to fertility drugs and IVF. Therefore, they conclude that "the development of *a means by which the number of developing embryos can be controlled is of primary clinical importance.*"[55] Here is the description of the means they advocate:

> At ten weeks gestation, a reduction in the number of embryos was performed at the Clamart Clinic in Paris. Guided by real-time ultrasonography and under abdominal local anesthesia (lidocaine 1 percent), ten milliliters of amniotic fluid from each of the two sacs was aspirated [drawn out] through a ten centimeter long, 21 gauge needle. The tip of the needle was then directed into the thoracic [chest] cavity of the fetus and a mixture of 1 milliliter of dolosal and 3 milliliters of xylocaine was injected. *The needle was left in place for up to ten minutes until cessation of cardiac activity was seen. If the initial injection was unsuccessful, it was repeated after ten minutes.* [56]

Two babies were killed through the mother's abdomen with this barbaric procedure. *For at least twenty minutes*, the woman had to lie with a needle piercing her womb as it slowly dispensed poison into her embryos' hearts. To recommend, let alone subject, a mother to this practice after inducing the multiple pregnancy to begin with is unconscionable.

Dr. Seymour Romney at the Albert Einstein College of Medicine in New York City suggests the term selective reduction be abandoned in favor of a "more positive" description. He recommends selective embryocide be called the *"enhanced survival of multifetal pregnancies."*[57] Dr. Jerome Lejeune, the French geneticist who discovered the chromosome for Down's syndrome, is appalled by such descriptions of fetal deathmaking. "When medicine is used to reinforce natural selection," he says, "it is not any longer medicine; it is eugenics. It doesn't matter if the word is palatable or not; that is what it is."[58]

Manufacturing babies without making love is a high-risk, low-yield proposition for women and children.[59] Stopping selective embryocide still won't solve the real problem with artificially induced conception and its dangers for women. When the new technologies shift lifemaking from the heart of marriage to the realm of the laboratory, they assault nature, *not* "assist" it.

A third party—the IVF/ET technician—initiates and conducts the process instead of the mother's body. Embryo manipulation and experimentation are part and parcel of this process.[60] Consequently, the entire context of reproduction changes. Instead of life spontaneously arising from the beauty of sexual love, sperm and ova are mixed together in a petri dish under the scrutiny of scientists. *The connection between intercourse and procreation is completely severed.* In IVF/ET, a *technique* replaces the function and purpose of *lovemaking*—but at what price? And what difference will this make to our society and our nation's parents and children?

"What precisely is new about these new beginnings?" asks Dr. Leon Kass. Looking beyond the sadness of infertility, he reminds us to think about what it means to produce children in new ways:

> What is new is nothing more radical than the divorce of the generation of new human life from human sexuality and ultimately from the confines of the human body, a separation which began with artificial insemination and which will finish with ectogenesis, the full laboratory growth of a baby from sperm to term. What is new is that sexual intercourse will no longer be needed for generating new life. This novelty leads to two others: there is a new co-progenitor (or several such), the embryologist-geneticist-physician, and there is a new home for generation, the laboratory. The mysterious and intimate processes of generation are to be moved from the darkness of the womb to the bright (fluorescent) light of the laboratory, and beyond the shadow of a single doubt.
>
> . . . We are considering not merely new ways of beginning individual lives, but also—and this is far more important—new

ways of life and new ways of viewing human life and the nature of man. A man is partly where he comes from, and the character of his life and his community will no doubt be influenced by (and will of course influence) the manner in which he comes to be.

Human procreation not only issues in new human beings, it is itself a human activity (an activity of embodied men and women). . . . Moreover, the techniques that at first serve merely to provide a child to a childless couple will soon be used to exert control over the quality of the child. A new image of human procreation has been conceived, and a new "scientific" obstetrics will usher it into existence. As an obstetrician put it at a recent conference: "The business of obstetrics is to produce *optimum* babies." The price to be paid for the optimum baby is the transfer of procreation from the home to the laboratory and its coincident transfer into manufacture.

Is there possibly some wisdom in the mystery of nature which joins the pleasure of sex, the communication of love, and the desire for children in the very activity by which we continue the chain of human existence?

To lay one's hands on human generation is to take a major step toward making man himself simply another of the man-made things.[61]

Women are not machines of reproduction, but are each unique, *individual persons* in body, mind, and spirit. IVF technicians manipulate the physical aspects of maternity as if there were no psychological or spiritual costs to high-tech intervention in conception. Yet in IVF, the bond between intercourse and life is broken: lifemaking is displaced, disembodied, and disconnected from the center of a woman's sexual experience. The joy of conception becomes a grueling battle against infertility in an expensive, painful procedure with a high-failure rate. Doctors sell this service to women who are willing to buy into the ordeal. But how many women really understand the terms of the contract?

Lovemaking, conception, pregnancy, and childbirth were made by God to be profoundly significant and deeply spiritual experiences. Human procreativity is drawn from these depths as new life arises from the life of man and woman and springs forth into being. Dehumanized attempts to subvert or circumvent this process will only harm us — and our children — in the long run. If that is the price for motherhood, then it is too high a price for any woman to pay.

Chapter Eight

EMBRYO TRANSPLANTS: The By-products of Manufactured Conception

Although the proof of a baby—unlike that of a pudding—does not rest on its consumability, and in the case of man not even on its being born, efforts towards proving what is good for vegetables is also good for human beings are being continued in many places. The life of man is, however, an unrepeatable experiment: no controls, no placebos. Although the expectations facing, and also checking, a breeder of men must be much higher than those restraining the animal breeder, there will be no one around to do the reckoning and to settle the accounts when the time has come. Human husbandry is so new a profession that society has not yet learned how to protect itself.[1]

Dr. Erwin Chargaff

*T*oday industry-related protocols govern the storage of frozen semen and viable embryos. These precious "commodities" are already being donated, sold, advertised, and traded.² As a result, a child may now be intentionally produced with the prearranged consent of five separate "parents": a *genetic mother* who produces the egg, a *genetic father* who provides the sperm, a *gestational mother* who carries the baby during pregnancy, and two *nurturing parents*— the *adoptive mother and father*—who will raise the child after s/he is born. But don't forget: if the *nurturing parents* get divorced and subsequently remarry, two more people—the *stepparents*—will be added to this confusing scenario.

Think of it. Can you imagine what it would be like to be born into such a "family"? Barbara Katz Rothman, professor of sociology at the City University of New York, points out the implications:

> Women never before were able to think about genetic motherhood without pregnancy, or pregnancy without genetic motherhood; if we were biological mothers (carrying babies), then we were genetic mothers. *But making the inseparable separate is what the technology of reproduction is all about.* And it is this issue that we are now facing; women, for the first time, have the potential for genetic parenthood without physiologic motherhood. At all. No pregnancy. No birth. No suckling. Women are about to become fathers.³

In the high-tech realm of laboratory reproduction, the wonder of conception is desexualized, disembodied, and divorced from the design of natural procreation. Consequently, the words *mother* and *father* take on entirely new and different meanings.⁴ Definitions of parenthood dissolve and are refashioned through experimental study and barely-tested scientific methods. Assorted couplings, tangled destinies, and genetically disenfranchised offspring are the result.

"In the average situation, two parents with equal genetic investment in the child are unified by their mutual relationship to their child," explains Ms. Sidney Callahan, professor of social psychology at Mercy College in New York. "They are irreversibly connected and made kin through the biological child they have procreated."⁵ She adds:

With third-party or gestational donors, however, the exclusive marital unity and equal biological bond is divided. One parent will be related biologically to the child; the other parent will not. True, the bypassed parent may have given consent, but consent, even if truly informed and uncoerced can hardly equalize the imbalance. While there is certainly no real question of adultery in such a bypassing situation, nevertheless, the intruding third-party donor, as in adultery, will inevitably be a psychological reality in the couple's life. Even if there is no jealousy or envy, the reproductive inadequacy of one partner has been reified, and superceded by an outsider's potency, genetic heritage, and superior reproductive capacity. Fertility and reproduction have been given an overiding priority in the couple's life.

. . . Fantasies about a child's past and future do make a difference, as all students of child development or family dynamics will attest. Third-party donors and surrogates cannot be counted on to disappear from family consciousness, even if legal contracts could control other ramifications or forbid actual interventions. . . .

It should be clear that adoption, which is a rescue of a child already in existence, is very different ethically from planning ahead of time to involve third-party donors in procuring a child. The adopted child, while perhaps harboring resentment against its birth parents, must look at its adopters differently from parents who have had him or her made to order. The "commodification of the child," drafting a child definitively into the service of parental will, is an infringement upon the child's dignity.[6]

Essentially, what Callahan is saying is that adopting a child who already exists is an act of *self-giving and compassion*, whereas the prearranged splicing of genetic bonds to obtain reproductive fulfillment is *child-tampering*. It is a well-known fact that adopted children often desire to meet their birth parents in order to better answer the question "Who am I?" What will happen when the children created by the new techniques are told that they were conceived with computer-selected gametes in a dish or rinsed out of an anonymous donor mother's womb after she was artificially inseminated at the doctor's office? *No one knows the answer to this question; we have no studies to tell us what genetic disenfranchisement will mean to these youth.* Sperm, ova, and embryos have become commodities in the medical marketplace. What is this going to mean to the child who was "bought" from anonymous donors?

On Making the Inseparable Separate

The researchers who have made commercial reproduction possible say it isn't their job to investigate the human implications of their discoveries. If a given technique produces results, it is deemed acceptable — at least by a small minority of daring technicians bold enough to try it. Claiming the ethical and spiritual questions are for philosophers and theologians, their work continues without consensus. Those who attempt to regulate new reproductive technologies are accused of placing "arbitrary limits" on valuable research. Scientists protect their turf by appointing likeminded ethicists to the groups that monitor their area of specialization. (The American Fertility Society's Board of Ethics, for example, is primarily made up of practitioners of advanced infertility techniques. It is hardly what one could call a consumer-oriented association.)

"Medical ethics does not grow out of medical roots," bioethicist Dr. Leon Kass reminds us. "Therefore, medicine cannot be self-governing . . . the sciences of the workings of the body do not yield moral knowledge."[7]

The people, then, must govern medical science; it is up to *us* to decide what we will and will not allow. Princeton University professor Paul Ramsey believes that as a society, however, we have become more protective of our planetary environment than of our own species. In a two-part series written for the *Journal of the American Medical Association* he explains:

> While the leopard, the great whale, and the forests are to be protected by restoring in mankind a proper sense of things, man as a natural being is to be given no such protection. There are aspects of the cheetah's existence which ought not to be violated, but none of man's. Other species are to be protected in their natural habitat and in their natural functions, but man is not. . . .
>
> So today we have the oddity that men are preparing to play God over the human species while many among us are denying themselves that role over other species in nature. There is a renewed sense of the sacredness of groves, of the fact that the air and streams should not be violated. At the same time there is no abatement of acceptance of the view that human parenthood can be taken apart in Oxford, England, New York, and Washington, DC; and, of course, it follows that thereafter human nature has to be wrought by Predestinators in the Decanting and Conditioning Rooms of the East London

Hatchery and in commercial firms bearing the name "Genetic Laboratories, Inc." in all our metropolitan centers.

I have no explanation of why there is not among medical scientists an upsurge of protest against turning the profession of medical care into a technological function. . . . Still there seems to be an evident, simple explanation of why people generally in all the advanced industrial countries of the world are apt to raise no serious objection, or apt at least to yield, to what the manipulation of embryos will surely do to ourselves and our progeny. It is a final irony to realize why invasions will now be done on man that we are slowly learning not to do on other natural objects; why natural human "courses of action" will be disassembled in an age in which we have learned to deplore strip mining. In actual practice minerals and vegetables may be more respected than human parenthood, and mankind may be ushered happily into *Brave New World*.[8]

The reason for the acceptance of this new technology, Ramsey asserts, is because it is being accomplished by doctors, figures of authority whom we are taught to trust without question.

Is Ramsey's indictment of medicalized reproduction too extreme? If you find yourself doubting his analysis, then consider the story of a company called Fertility and Genetics Research (FGR) Inc., founded in 1978.

Bargaining Over Babies

Founded by Richard G. Seed, a nuclear physicist turned biomedical engineer, and Dr. Randolph W. Seed, a surgeon, FGR plans on becoming a for-profit chain of nationwide fertility clinics by the end of this century. Using a cattle breeding technique they developed in the 1970s,[9] the Seeds' company offers embryo transplants through franchised medical clinics now in operation.[10]

The owners of Fertility and Genetics Research seem to think their network of independent technicians will eventually provide embryos to 30,000 to 50,000 women each year. In 1980, Richard Seed said the procedure would cost couples about "as much as a new car," adding, "It should be painful to them, otherwise it isn't worth our effort to work with them for a year or two."[11]

What price did FGR consider to be the going rate for human embryos? Seed estimated the final cost will be about $10,000 per child.[12] Others place the price a little lower.

Ob/gyns Dr. John E. Buster and Dr. Mark V. Sauer, who have worked with Richard and Randolph Seed to develop the technique, conclude an article on the procedure with the following statement:

> During 1986, nonsurgical donor ovum transfer [i. e., embryo transplants] will become clinically available through a publicly held medical technology company (Fertility and Genetics Research, Inc., Chicago, IL). *The first clinic will open in Los Angeles, and the company expects to open other centers throughout the United States shortly thereafter.* The cost is expected to be approximately $6,000 to $7,000 for four donor insemination attempts. [Additional information can be obtained by writing to: Fertility and Genetics Research, Inc., 624 South Grand Avenue, Suite 2900, Los Angeles, CA. 90017.][13]

FGR Chairman Lawrence G. Sucsy, an investment banker, believes the business has the potential to make revenues of more than $50 million annually. Sucsy, who also owns a firm specializing in medical technology and computer-related companies, was intrigued by the idea when first approached by Richard Seed in 1977. It took nearly a year for him to commit to the project. He says that what finally persuaded him to become involved was reading a poll stating that 75 percent of the women surveyed approved of in vitro fertilization. "That convinced me that women would also accept embryo transfers," says Sucsy.[14]

What exactly is the technique that FGR is selling? Basically, it's a new type of surrogate motherhood arrangement in which an artificially inseminated woman gives up her embryo after just five to seven days of pregnancy. Another term for the procedure is *surrogate embryo transfer*, or SET for short.

In what is commonly known as "surrogate pregnancy," a woman is artificially inseminated with sperm from the husband of a woman unable to bear a child. If a pregnancy results, this woman — the baby's natural or "genetic" mother — *carries the child until birth*. She then relinquishes her son or daughter to the child's father and his wife. However, surrogate motherhood isn't *real* surrogacy in the true sense of the word. It is a *third-party contract* between the people who will raise the child — the baby's genetic father and the adoptive mother — and the genetic/gestational mother. The woman who carries the baby is not simply a "stand-in" for the adoptive mother; she *is* the child's mother, a woman who has chosen to give up her maternal rights according to the terms of a contractual agreement.

Embryo transplantation is surrogate motherhood with a twist. In this procedure, a woman is artificially inseminated with sperm from another woman's husband, but carries the embryo *less than a week* instead of waiting a full nine months to deliver the baby. The idea is for the woman — the "egg donor" — to conceive an embryo that can be flushed from her reproductive tract before it has a chance to implant in her uterus. Her embryo is then transferred to the womb of an adoptive mother to carry and give birth to the child.

Since it appears that any woman can carry another woman's baby, embryo flushing (or *uterine lavage*) and transplantation make it possible for a wide variety of women to become pregnant. Women who are past menopause, who have no ovaries, who are carriers of a genetic disease, or whose tubes are impaired by disease or surgical sterilization are all possible candidates for this procedure.

Uterine lavage can also be used to transplant embryos into the wombs of women who wish to function as "gestational surrogates." In this procedure the flushed-out embryo is placed inside the womb of a woman who carries the baby during pregnancy, but gives the child to another woman after birth. The embryo comes from the *genetic mother* rather than the surrogate. Embryos produced by in vitro fertilization can be used this way as well.

As with other third-party pregnancy contracts, a pre-conception agreement requires the surrogate mother (who carries the baby) to relinquish the child at birth to the genetic father (from whose sperm the baby came) and his wife, the adoptive mother. *However, if the baby was conceived using sperm provided by a donor, then both of the nurturing parents are adoptive parents.* (Remember the five-parent scenario mentioned earlier? This is it.)[15]

"$50 a Flush with a $200 Bonus If We Recover a Fertilized Egg"

On April 14, 1977, Richard and Randolph Seed presented their idea about embryo transplantation at an international infertility conference.[16] But their research was completely based on their experience with cattle, not humans. An abstract of their session printed in the American Fertility Society's professional journal, *Fertility and Sterility,* reads:

Bovine embryo transplant is a technically and commercially viable proposition — we have transplanted from over 100 donors into over 300 recipients. On the most recent 11 consecutive fertile donors, an average of 10.4 viable eggs were actually transferred. The donor is superovulated with [hormones]. Commercial cattlemen purchase the services on a per-pregnancy basis as a means of rapidly multiplying the offspring of superior genetic material. The donor embryos are recovered at five to eight days of age by a transcervical (nonsurgical) flushing, using modified tissue culture medium. . . . Liquid nitrogen freezing and long-term storage with normal live calves (but low yield) have also been reported. . . . Application to humans of these experimental animal techniques (immunologic, genetic, hormonal, transcervical) is straightforward. No adverse effects are expected.

Technology outpaces ethics. There exists neither political law nor theological law governing any aspect of human embryo transplants. It is perhaps time.[17]

The panel consisted of the Seeds and a veterinarian named Donald Baker. The three cattle breeding specialists listed their address as the Embryo Transplant Corporation, Elgin, Illinois.

A year later, Richard and Randolph Seed, along with Lawrence Sucsy, opened the first Fertility and Genetics Research program in commercial space located in Chicago's elite Water Tower Place. By locating the Reproduction and Fertility Clinic in a fashionable retail area rather than a university medical center or private hospital, they successfully avoided publicity concerning the controversial techniques they planned to use.

"Our reception by and large has been quite favorable, but we structured it in such a way that there wasn't much negative that could be said about it," explains Richard Seed.[18]

"We expected we'd have pickets. We planned for pickets," he says. "It didn't happen."[19]

By 1980, the Seeds had a dozen interested couples with corresponding donors lined up to try their procedure.[20] Expecting to use the same donors over and over again, Richard Seed said they would pay all those who weren't volunteers, "$50 a flush, with a $200 bonus if we recover a fertilized egg."[21]

Only two unfertilized eggs and one embryo had been recovered after two years.[22] The procedure, they discovered, turned out to be much more difficult to perform on women than it had been with cows. *Yet, they offered the program not as an experimental procedure, but a professional service!*

"The interval which traditionally separates a scientific discovery and its application in everyday life has been progressively shortened. As soon as a discovery is made, a concrete application is sought," writes French sociologist Jacques Ellul in *The Technological Society*. "The scientist might act more prudently; he might even be afraid to launch his carefully calculated laboratory findings into the world. But how can he resist the pressure of facts? How can he resist the pressure of money? How is he to resist success, publicity, public acclaim? Or the general state of mind which makes technical application the last word? How is he to resist the desire to pursue his research?"[23]

With determination, Richard and Randolph Seed pursued additional avenues of testing their cattle breeding techniques. They began working with a team of physicians led by a professor of obstetrics and gynecology named Dr. John E. Buster. The team spent four years and went through over fifty catheter designs before finally succeeding with the technique of embryo transplantation in humans.[24] The experiments were conducted at the Harbor-UCLA Medical Center in Torrance, California.

"The uterus is a leaky organ," explains Buster, in an article appearing in *Fortune* magazine. "And the problem was to design an instrument that could recover the [fertilized] egg without flushing it out the cervix or into a Fallopian tube, where it could cause a tubal pregnancy."[25] Considering that nature never intended the uterus to have embryos flushed out of it, it isn't surprising that Buster's team ran into a few problems.

With the catheter design solved, the technique began to improve —slightly—on its previous 100 percent failure rate. Calling it *nonsurgical ovum transfer* instead of embryo transplantation, Buster's technique consists of five steps:

STEP 1 HORMONAL STIMULATION: An infertile patient is matched with a fertile donor according to genetic characteristics and blood type. Ovulation dates between the two women are synchronized by matching their menstrual cycles or administering fertility drugs. This is so the womb of the recipient is at the same point of the menstrual cycle as that of the donor at the time of the transplant.

STEP 2 ARTIFICIAL INSEMINATION: When the cycles of the two women become closely matched, the donor is artificially inseminated at the clinic with sperm from the infertile recipient's husband or an anonymous donor.

STEP 3 EMBRYO FLUSHING: On the fifth day after insemination, a plastic tube called a catheter is inserted into the donor's uterus. The physician then attempts to flush out the embryo with lavage fluid. The flushes, or lavages, are scheduled to allow the fertilized egg time to pass through the Fallopian tube toward the uterus. The flushing is repeated on the sixth or seventh day after insemination, if necessary.

STEP 4 EMBRYO SEARCH AND EXAMINATION: If an embryo is captured by the catheter, it must be located under a microscope and recovered from the lavage fluid. The embryo, if found, is then checked for signs of normal development. With recent improvements in embryo freezing techniques, the embryo can now be chemically treated and quick-frozen after retrieval. The embryo is then kept in cold storage until the recipient's womb is ready to receive the embryo. Or, the embryo may also be adopted by a suitable couple at a later date.[26]

STEP 5 EMBRYO TRANSFER: As in in vitro fertilization, if the embryo is judged to be suitable for transfer it is placed directly into the recipient's uterus via a plastic tube inserted through the vagina and cervix.[27]

Egg donors for the Harbor-UCLA research project were primarily located through newspaper ads which read *"Help an Infertile Woman Have a Baby."*[28] Of the 380 women who responded, forty-six were initially selected as potential candidates for the procedure. Psychological screening was then administered by the team's psychologists.[29] They found that abnormal psychological traits were *threefold to sixfold more common* among prospective donors than would have been expected within the general population.[30] Many of the women suffered from low self-esteem, while nearly one-third of the candidates had a history of abusive and/or alcoholic parents or other childhood problems.[31]

When classified ads turned up very few acceptable donors, John Buster and Richard and Randolph Seed came up with new ideas for locating subjects. These included encouraging infertile couples to find their own donors from among friends and relatives, placing brochures in doctors' waiting rooms, setting up a system similar to a blood bank where every embryo recipient would be required to recruit one or two donors, and hiring a public relations firm to send out press releases with a telephone listing for women interested in providing or receiving embryos. (The last four digits of the phone number spelled B-A-B-Y.)[32]

The UCLA donors were paid $5 to $10 for blood samples, $50 for inseminations, and $50 for uterine lavage. The team finally flushed an embryo out of one woman and placed it into the womb of another in March 1983, *three years after the project began.*[33] By July, two pregnancies were announced in a medical journal report.[34] Six months later, in January 1984, one of the pregnancies resulted in the birth of a baby boy by cesarean section.[35]

The Five-Day Pregnancy: New Methods of Abortion

Between July 30, 1982, and February 5, 1987, twenty-seven women were inseminated 115 times in this experimental study at the Harbor-UCLA Medical Center.[36] The research was funded by Richard and Randolph Seed's company, Fertility and Genetics Research, Inc.

Prior to insemination, all donors, recipients, and their respective husbands were asked to sign consent forms. Donor women and their husbands agreed to abstain from sexual intercourse near the time of ovulation. Subjects also were required to chemically or surgically abort their baby if the embryo implanted in the uterus.[37]

"The donors simply have to agree to an abortion," says Michael Eberhard of Memorial Health Technologies about the procedure. "If they won't, if that would not be emotionally or ethically acceptable to them, then we've got to screen them out. They don't belong as part of the donor program."[38]

During the study, 265 uterine lavages were performed on the twenty-seven women. Eight of the donors experienced more than twelve flushes each; one experienced fifty-three lavages.[39] A total of forty-three embryos were flushed out of their mothers' wombs and recovered from lavage fluid after undergoing microscopic scanning.[40] Clearly, most of the embryos did not survive. The number of births that resulted from the experiment is conspicuously missing from the article summarizing this research.

One of the donors experienced two retained pregnancies while participating in the experiment.[41] One of her embryos was lost through miscarriage, the other deliberately destroyed by abortion.

Physicians who performed the research concluded the incidence of retained pregnancy "may be further lessened through the use of short-term, high-dose oral contraceptives (morning-after pill) or progesterone antagonists (RU486) taken immediately after a lavage sequence."[42] In other words, one way or the other, pregnancies induced by this method must be guaranteed to be aborted—by lavage, by an abortifacient drug, or by vacuum aspiration.

In a later related experiment, six women underwent seven cycles of insemination and twenty-eight lavages after being "superovulated" with fertility drugs. (This is similar to what Randolph and Richard Seed had reported doing to cattle.) Doctors administered the high-risk drugs to donors in an attempt to stimulate the women's ovaries to produce more embryos.[43]

In a recent journal, the research team reported:

> Embryos were recovered from three of the women between 96 and 144 hours after ovulation. However, *no ova were recovered from the other three donors, two of whom were later noted to be pregnant.* Retained pregnancies occurred despite *postlavage administration of high-dose oral contraceptive pills, endometrial aspiration, and, in one case, RU486.* None of the infertile women became pregnant as a result of the trial. The authors conclude that although superovulation may increase ovum production, without reliable contragestion (i.e. abortifacients), such practice is unsafe for ovum donors undergoing uterine lavage.[44]

Since *none* of the infertile women became pregnant and *both* the women who retained embryos aborted, the abortion rate for this experiment was *100 percent. In other words, all five embryos conceived during the experiment died.* What's more, every donor endured treatments to ensure their embryos would not implant in their wombs. Yet even menstrual extraction, high doses of hormones, and RU486 failed to abort the two "retained pregnancies."

An article appearing in an issue of *Contemporary OB/GYN* announced "OT [ovum transfer/embryo transplantation] may be repeated as many times as required to produce a pregnancy, with what appear to be *negligible cumulative risks.*"[45]

What kind of medicine is this? Who and what is being treated by these procedures? This is not the practice of a healing art, the tending of the sick, the ministration of a cure: *it is medically induced, man-manipulated pregnancy* — initiated and ended by drugs and machines. Why are physicians practicing and endorsing such dangerous and dehumanizing procedures?

Paul Ramsey offers an excellent answer to this question. The reason the public will buy what reproductive technology offers, he says:

> will be not only [because] the agents of these vast changes are authority figures in white coats promising the benefits of applied knowledge. That, in other areas, we have learned to doubt in

some degree. The deeper reason is that the agents of these vast changes, defendable step by defendable step, are deemed by the public to be not researchers mainly but members of the healing profession, those who care for us, who tend the human condition. Before it is realized that the objective has ceased to be the treatment of a *medical* condition, it will be too late; and Huxley will have been proved true.[46]

Since 1978, Fertility and Genetics Research has promoted embryo transplantation as a viable solution to infertility and genetic diseases. Founded by cattle breeding experts, the company's clearly stated goal is to establish embryo transplant centers throughout the United States. Physicians may be the ones who apply Richard and Randolph Seed's methods to women, but it isn't the practice of medicine they're performing—it's human breeding.

"Anonymous donors become breeders," explains John T. Noonan, a professor of law at the University of California, Berkeley. "Its acceptance brings us to the worlds of Huxley and Orwell in which the final trick is played on the champions of procreation as a private choice. . . ."[47]

Testing the Products of Conception

By calling embryo transplants "ovum transfers" and women who are artificially inseminated and flushed "egg donors," medical technicians use inaccurate words to disguise the true meaning of their activities. It is no coincidence that the terminology of reproductive technology closely resembles the doublespeak of abortion.

Lawrence Sucsy, FGR's chairman and chief executive officer, predicts that the technique developed by the Seeds will eventually be a big money-maker. The name of Sucsy and the Seeds' company— Fertility and *Genetics* Research, Inc.—points to the eventual application of this technology to selective breeding through prenatal (that is, *preimplantation*) diagnosis. *Fortune* magazine, in discussing future possibilities related to Sucsy's venture, states:

> The technique could replace amniocentesis, the prenatal test for Down's syndrome and some other diseases; *an embryo removed from its mother's womb could be tested for as many as 2,000 diseases and safely returned to her.*
>
> Beyond that, Sucsy estimates that about 40 percent of the women who are waiting for FGR embryo transplants want to avoid passing on genetically transferred diseases such as

hemophilia and cystic fibrosis. Eventually, with the development of new gene altering techniques, doctors could remove an embryo from a woman with such a disease, alter the defective chromosomes, and return the embryo to the mother.[48]

Physicians John E. Buster and Mark V. Sauer affirm the natural link between embryo transplantation and applied genetics. Speaking with the authority of those who pioneered the procedure, they say:

> Although first introduced for ovum [embryo] donation, the catheter may ultimately be used as a diagnostic tool in both infertility and genetics. *Collection of preimplantation embryos allows diagnosis and treatment before implantation.*[49]

Robert Edwards, the world's foremost embryo technician, has *always* advocated examining the embryos from the perspective of a geneticist. In nearly everything he has published, he extols the virtues of identifying the genetic makeup of embryos for the purpose of preimplantation diagnosis.

"There is a wealth of information to be gained on the exact incidence and type of chromosome disorders in early human embryos conceived in various circumstances," claims Edwards.[50] During the early stages of his work with Patrick Steptoe, he wrote:

> The procedures leading to replacement and implantation open the way to further work on human embryos in the laboratory. . . . The basic procedure of embryo transfer will probably be combined with the identification of the sex of the embryo. Sexing can now be done with complete accuracy in the rabbit. The eugenic reason for sexing is that many genetic disorders are sex-linked; hence they usually occur in males.
>
> . . . the opportunity to give the mother a healthy embryo seems fundamentally humane. Sex-linked defects are only one sort of problem that might be avoided by the procedure; chromosome examination may one day prevent the birth of individuals with genetic anomalies such as mongolism. . . .
>
> Further developments that also depend on the growth of human embryos perhaps contain the most controversial issues. These developments involve not simply identifying sex or genetic defects, but rather modifying or adding to the embryo itself.[51]

As a featured speaker at the annual meeting of the American Gynecological Society at Colorado Springs in 1973, Edwards declared:

> The purpose of [my] work is to gain information about human conception, to use this information for the alleviation of certain forms of human infertility, and to obtain a deeper awareness of the physiologic events important to the development of new methods in contraception, human genetics, and other aspects of reproduction.
>
> . . . the availability of cleaving human embryos could also lead to the identification of those carrying specific genetic [mutations] and provide *a preferable alternative to the current methods of aborting fetuses with anomalies.* The preimplantation embryo can tolerate a considerable degree of interference; pieces of [embryonic tissue] have been removed from rabbit, mouse, and sheep blastocysts, and many of these embryos develop to term despite the loss of tissue. If human embryos are to be examined in this way for specific enzyme deficiencies, the number of cells available for analysis would have to be increased by culture or fusing them with other cells, and the embryo would have to be maintained by frozen storage until typing was completed. This possibility may be distant but perhaps not as far fetched as it may sound, especially since mouse blastocysts have been stored frozen at almost absolute zero. . . .[52]

It is now possible to freeze human embryos as well.

"To undertake *in vitro* fertilization without guarding as far as possible against the birth of a handicapped child is indefensible," says Edwards. "The clinical application of *in vitro* fertilization in all its forms demands research on embryos . . . the embryo produced *in vitro* is not a life which demands the protection of the law."[53]

"Preimplantation diagnosis" of human embryos is now possible through the use of specially designed and patented genetic markers called DNA "probes." Made of a particular sequence of DNA bases, a specifically labeled gene probe is inserted into a cell's genetic material and will bind to an identical sequence, thus showing up a "match." *Probes can detect extra or missing chromosomes, including male Y-chromosomes in embryos four to eight days old.*[54]

"It certainly wouldn't be ethical to use the method to choose the sex of a baby," says Dr. John West of the University of Edinburgh's IVF team, who developed the test. "But we wouldn't prevent the technique from being used that way."[55]

Gene probes are already being marketed and used to detect hereditary diseases and genetic disorders in human embryos in international IVF and embryo transplant clinics.[56] Down's syndrome, cystic fibrosis, hemophilia, and muscular dystrophy are among the conditions already being successfully identified.

British embryologist Anne McLaren, a long-time proponent of prenatal diagnosis, eugenic abortion, and embryo experimentation, asserts, "Every pregnant woman wants to produce a normal healthy baby." Consequently, she says, prenatal diagnosis is much in demand these days:

> Many older women avail themselves of amniocentesis, a procedure in which clinicians examine some of the cells shed by the fetus into the amniotic fluid. In Denmark, where such screening is widely available, *the incidence of Down's among babies born to women over thirty-five has fallen threefold since the 1970s.* . . .
>
> The termination of a wanted pregnancy, even in the first trimester after chorionic villus sampling, is distressing. It means that a woman who seeks to have a child has to go through the first two months of pregnancy (often the worst part) to no avail. . . .
>
> If it were possible to diagnose genetic or chromosomal defects during the interval between fertilization and implantation — so-called "preimplantation diagnosis" — women "at risk" of producing a fetus with a severe genetic disease would indeed be able to start a pregnancy "in the knowledge that it would not be affected." One way for clinicians to carry out such diagnoses at this early stage would be to use *in vitro* fertilization (IVF) and then check the pre-embryos before replacing them in a woman's uterus. . . .[57]

McLaren then explains how embryos can be biopsied (have cells removed) for diagnosis and then suggests "the development of the biopsied embryos could be halted, while the tests were underway, by freezing them in nitrogen. Then doctors could select the unaffected ones for replacement in the uterus."[58]

Biopsy of embryos "might be the preferred strategy," suggests McLaren, for *fertile couples* who desire diagnosis before their embryo implants.[59] She explains that this can be accomplished by either using in vitro fertilization or, more preferably, by uterine lavage. Claiming "the flushing procedure is no more stressful for the woman than an insertion of an IUD," McLaren points out that the women can return to the clinic a month after the removal of their embryos "for the replacement of those blastocysts (embryos) found to be unaffected by the gene in question."[60]

"John Buster and his colleagues at the University of California at Los Angeles have found that recovering blastocysts in this way and replacing them," says McLaren, "gives a good pregnancy rate."[61]

A Biologist's Vision

The clarion call for the application of reproductive technology to selective breeding and the modification of human embryos was sounded in 1959. During that year, a small but significant book titled *Can Man Be Modified?* was received with much enthusiasm. Written by a French biologist named Jean Rostand, the book very likely directly influenced men such as Robert Edwards. In it, Rostand details the responsibility of embryologists around the world to "direct the course of human evolution."

Praising the visionary book *Brave New World*, Rostand contemplates the application of Aldous Huxley's vision:

> *This vision of the future is based upon precise knowledge of the present.* To be sure, we cannot, for the moment, cultivate human embryos in test tubes, but already we can keep the embryos of rats, mice, rabbits, or guinea pigs alive for several days outside the womb; and the culture of embryos has indeed made considerable progress since Aldous Huxley wrote his *Brave New World*. (Etienne Wolff has succeeded with chickens in cultivating most of the embryonic organs—bones, eyes, the syrinx, the sexual glands, etc.). . . .
>
> An intermediary solution of the problem of pregnancy is, indeed, conceivable. Delivery could be stimulated artificially and the embryo placed in culture at the age of two or three months. In short, a woman would reproduce like a kangaroo.
>
> *If ever partial or total "test tube pregnancy" came to be applied to our species, various operations would become possible, resulting in a more or less profound modification of the human being in the course of formation.* It would then be no more than a game for the "man-farming biologist" to change the subject's sex, the color of its eyes, the general proportions of body and limbs, and perhaps the facial features. . . .
>
> Can we, then, not hope to modify a whole stock, not just

human individuals, in order to create a race or species of human beings superior to the present day? Even though we do not know exactly what is responsible for the intellectual power of different individuals, and if we merely start from the very probable postulate that it depends in part on hereditary conditions, it would be logical to try to reinforce it by using the method of *artificial selection*. This is a classic method, constantly used with success in plants and domestic animals. Every time it is proposed to accentuate this or that characteristic in a living stock, we choose as sires and dams the individuals that display this characteristic in the most marked degree. . . . If it were possible to apply similar methods to our own species, we should have no difficulty in creating stocks of men who would be taller or shorter, stronger or weaker, handsomer or uglier, etc. When we come to intellectual qualities the thing is less certain, but is still extremely probable.[62]

Just thirty years have passed since Jean Rostand's treatise on human embryology was published. *It is no longer a vision, but reality.* Human embryos have been tested for growth in the wombs of rabbits — not kangaroos — and test tube conception is practiced at over two hundred clinics across the nation; embryo transplant franchises not only exist, but are now conducting business; DNA probes are being advertised in *Nature* magazine with full-page announcements in decorator colors.

It is time to begin letting medicine know that this is not what we want for the future of our children.

Some Landmark Events in Reproductive Technology

IN ANIMALS		IN HUMANS
Use of artifical insemination in dogs	1782	
	1799	Pregnancy reported from artificial insemination
Birth from embryo transplantation in rabbits	1890's	
Use of cryoprotectant to successfully freeze and thaw animal sperm	1949	
First calf born after embryo transplantation	1951	
Live calf born after insemination with frozen sperm	1952	
	1953	First reported pregnancy after insemination with frozen sperm
Live rabbit offspring produced from in vitro fertilization (IVF)	1959	
Live offspring from frozen mouse embryos	1972	
	1976	First commercial surrogate motherhood arrangement reported in the United States
Transplantation of ovaries from one female to another in cattle	1978	Baby born after IVF in United Kingdom
	1980	Baby born after IVF in Australia
Calf born after IVF	1981	Baby born after IVF in United States
Sexing of embryos in rabbits Cattle embryos split to produce identical twins	1982	
	1983	Embryo transfer after uterine lavage (embryo flushing)
	1984	Baby born in Australia from embryo that was frozen and thawed
	1985	Baby born after gamete intra-fallopian transfer (GIFT)
		First gestational surrogate arrangement reported in the United States
	1986	Baby born in the United States from embryo that was frozen and thawed

SOURCE: Office of Technology Assesment, 1988

FIG. 8.1

Chapter Nine

ARTIFICIAL WOMBS:
The Final Separation

*Apart from medical uses, there is the great convenience
for the mother of not having to undergo pregnancy at all,
of skipping the morning sickness, the heavy step, the kick-
ing fetus, the labor pains. Of course, there will remain
staunch old-fashioned types who consider this more a
deprivation than a convenience. Many people feel it
would require a thorough-going revolution in ethics and
morals to make this whole idea acceptable. Yet sex as
recreation as opposed to sex as procreation has long since
gained popular acceptance. And how many women have
ever turned down labor-saving devices? Who would have
predicted that so many millions of women would be so
eager to interfere with their natural cycle of ovulation by
dosing themselves with birth-control pills every day?*[1]

> Albert Rosenfeld, *The Second Genesis:*
> *The Coming Control of Life*

A s a child, I remember seeing a movie in elementary school foretelling the wonders of twenty-first-century technology. What stands out in my mind most clearly is a section of the film on the weather. Hurricanes, tornadoes, drought, and thunderstorms would all eventually be controlled by chemicals someday, the narrator said. A cartoon depicted clouds appearing and disappearing at the flick of a switch.

Several months later, *Life* magazine published a four-part series titled "On the Frontiers of Medicine: Control of Life." What astonished me most about the articles was a colorful picture of a stainless-steel womb containing a living human fetus.[2] The accompanying text reads:

> Like something out of *Brave New World*, the tiny human fetus in the porthole window at right is being kept alive in an artificial womb. Separated from its mother as a result of a miscarriage when it was just ten weeks old, it is still connected, via the umbilical cord, to the placenta, and it floats in fluid just as it would if it were preceding a normal birth. But nothing else is the same. This womb-with-a-view is made of thick steel because the highly oxygenated saline solution it contains is held under very high pressure — 200 pounds per square inch, the same pressure a diver would encounter 450 feet down. At this pressure oxygen is literally forced through the skin of the fetus. Getting oxygen this way is called cutaneous respiration. But respiration also requires exhaling — getting rid of the waste carbon dioxide gas — and so far, the experimenter, Dr. Robert Goodlin, of the Stanford University School of Medicine, has found no way to force out the poisonous carbon dioxide. Thus the fetus can only survive . . . for no more than forty-eight hours. . . .[3]

The strange photograph fit all my youthful expectations regarding future scientific achievement. If space colonies and man-made weather would someday be a reality, why not this?

Years later, after giving birth to my own children, I returned to the picture in *Life* with an entirely different perspective. My immediate gut-level reaction was: *That's some woman's baby slowly being poisoned inside an artificial womb. Did they tell the mother her child had been born alive? Was parental permission obtained to use this still kicking/sucking/swallowing baby as a guinea pig? Didn't women back in 1965 wonder what this experimentation would eventually lead to – or were most people enthralled, as I once was, with the expanding use of medical technology?*

It was amazing to realize the *Life* magazine article is nearly twenty-five years old. If experiments on artificial placentation were this advanced in 1965, then what is happening *now*? Why is the public no longer being informed about this research? Are babies still being slowly suffocated in similar experiments today? Could this be one of the many ways aborted "fetal tissue" is being used?[4]

I stared for a long time at the photograph of the perfectly formed child floating silently in the colorless fluid. I noticed the picture had been taken by Lennart Nilsson. His awe-inspiring book, *A Child is Born*, had always fascinated me. Now that I knew how many of the pictures were obtained, I can no longer look at the book without my stomach turning.

While hopes of controlling weather have fallen flat in recent years, efforts to perfect artificial placentation continue unabated. "In San Francisco, researchers think we're only ten or fifteen years away from growing babies outside the womb," declared this morning's edition of *USA Today*.[5] I am convinced that the technology I first saw in *Life* magazine is nearing implementation.

Artificial Placentation Today

On December 1, 1968, the *American Journal of Obstetrics and Gynecology* printed an unusual article for a journal devoted to women's reproductive care. In "Maintenance of Sheep Fetuses by an Extracorporeal Circuit for Periods Up to 24 Hours," three British researchers report using sheep fetuses to test an artificial placenta.[6] Also called an *artificial perfusion unit*, the paper describes the mechanical exchange of blood through the umbilical vessels of the lambs and various ways to improve outcomes of the technique.

Nearly a year later, a similar article appeared in *Science* magazine: "Artificial Placenta: Two Days of Total Extrauterine Support of the Isolated Premature Lamb Fetus."[7] This time, the experiments had taken place at the National Heart Institute just outside Washington, DC. Reporting from the Laboratory of Technical Development, the authors explain:

> During perfusion, the fetus rested quietly in the artificial amniotic bath. About once each hour it moved its head or legs spon-

taneously. It exhibited a strong sucking reflex as well as a with-drawal reflex when pinched. After fifty-five hours of perfusion, the fetus abruptly underwent cardiac arrest [heart failure] and stopped extracting oxygen from the umbilical arterial blood. . . . Fetuses in four of the eight experiments survived for periods exceeding twenty hours, and we now have two apparently nor-mal long-term surviving lambs after four and ten hours of extrauterine support.[8]

An illustration of a fetal lamb lying in a basin of fluid — with a circu-lar tube leading away from and back to its umbilicus — appears on the first page of the article. A circuit containing two "pressure transduc-ers," a "membrane oxygenator," pump, and IV bottle dispensing nutrients and a drug to prevent blood clotting make up the artificial placentation system (APS) (Figure 9.1).

Last year, a five-minute segment on a local news broadcast immediately caught my attention. I saw a human baby hooked up to a system *almost identical* to the one used for the lamb fetus. I knew it had to be the same device.

Afterwards, I obtained a booklet describing the machine from the University of Nebraska Medical Center (UNMC), where the special news report had been taped. I wasn't surprised to see it included an illustration that matched the one in *Science* magazine.[9] The drawings were dissimilar in only two respects. The human fetus was attached to the artificial placenta through the neck instead of at the umbilicus, and the synthetic amniotic fluid was missing (Figure 9.2).

Researchers who developed this unit apparently chose not to call it by its original name. It is now called an *extracorporeal membrane oxygenation (ECMO) unit*, rather than an artificial placentation sys-tem.[10] Is this to impress parents with high-tech terminology (difficult to pronounce and easy to abbreviate) or to deflect controversy? Perhaps both.

Though early clinical trials began in 1975, ECMO has been in use around the country since 1980 — primarily at university-affiliated neonatal intensive care units (NICU's).[11] ECMO, however, remains a scarce technology. Its cost is exorbitant (in 1988, UNMC charged $1700 for setup and $1500 per day for a maximum of two weeks), and it must be administered by highly-trained personnel. Predictably, health care providers maintain their skills by practicing the technique on sheep.

Robert T. Francoeur, professor of embryology at Farleigh-Dickinson University, tells of showing a film to teach students about

Artificial Placentation System
(or Arteriovenous Pumping Perfusion)

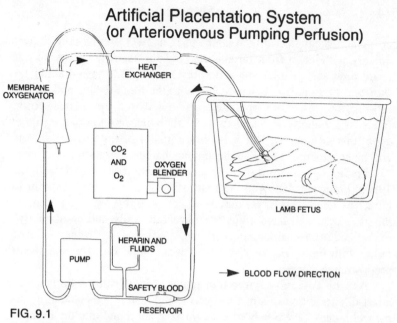

MEMBRANE OXYGENATOR

HEAT EXCHANGER

CO_2 AND O_2

OXYGEN BLENDER

PUMP

HEPARIN AND FLUIDS

SAFETY BLOOD RESERVOIR

LAMB FETUS

➤ BLOOD FLOW DIRECTION

FIG. 9.1
Adapted from *Science.* (See footnote 7.)

Extracorporeal Membrane Oxygenation
Circuit (or ECMO Circuit)

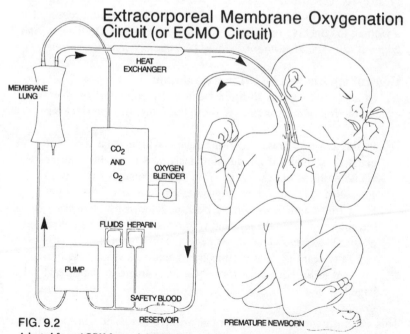

MEMBRANE LUNG

HEAT EXCHANGER

CO_2 AND O_2

OXYGEN BLENDER

FLUIDS HEPARIN

PUMP

SAFETY BLOOD RESERVOIR

PREMATURE NEWBORN

FIG. 9.2
Adapted from *AORN Journal, ECMO Parent Information.* (See footnotes 9 and 10.)

artificial placentation in fetal lambs back in 1973. But he says, "it was quickly withdrawn from circulation, and for about ten years no one heard anything definite about this research. People talked about the 'horrors' of an APS pregnancy, but with the film recalled and no one talking, there was no open 'enemy' on whom opposition could focus."[12] Evidently, researchers have their reasons for staying quiet about this technology. But it is only a matter of time before society will be considered "ready" to accept mechanical gestation.

Predicting that word of artificial placentation will resurface in the 1980s, Francoeur believes the first artificial womb (from "sperm to term," as Leon Kass says) may be functioning by 1995. By then, he thinks people will have adjusted "psychologically and emotionally" to the idea of mechanical motherhood.[13] After nearly twenty years of living with the reality of test-tube babies, the artificial womb won't seem strange any more.

As with IVF and embryo transplants, APS is being introduced as a last-ditch solution to a medical crisis. But history tells us that medical techniques have a way of changing the abnormal into the normal. The fact is, techniques are currently being used to produce human life extracorporeally (outside the body) and to maintain it extracorporeally at early gestational ages. *The womb is slowly being rendered nonessential to nurturing nascent life.* It will soon be unnecessary for a woman to conceive or carry a child inside her body. On the day that happens, *biological motherhood will become technically obsolete.*

Controlling Birth: The Ultimate Solution

In 1923, Margaret Sanger's book *Motherhood in Bondage* offered the following statements about the future of reproduction:

> In this era of standardization, during which most lives are planned externally if not autonomously, it is inevitable that the whole problem of rearing children will become as ordered, as controlled, as planned, as any other phase of life. Just as our finest fruits and flowers have been developed by choice and selection from wild flowers and wild trees, and our finest breeds of livestock have been developed by conscious control, so is humanity learning that the old traditional folkways, based on trial and error, have been too expensively tragic to the race at large.[14]

This current generation of American women is the first in history to collectively view the control of reproduction as a civic duty and personal right. To this end, millions have ingested mind-altering hormone drugs, used potent chemicals to create a "hostile vaginal environment" against live sperm, had their Fallopian tubes surgically mutilated, had foreign objects implanted inside their wombs, and — if all else failed or was accidentally forgotten — submitted to the gross invasion of suction abortions. What's more, some physicians are now advising us to kill our *wanted* babies if they are the wrong sex, wrong genetic type, or wrong size.

Margaret Sanger, the founder of Planned Parenthood, was correct in predicting the eventual control of childbearing in a highly technological society. What Sanger didn't make clear, however, was that it would be *women* who would sacrifice their sexual integrity for standardized conception. Many have paid the price with their hearts as well as their minds and bodies.

Curiously, men are not expected to alter the expression of their sexuality through invasive chemical treatments or killing. Women, not men, have been given the "choice" to repress and subvert their normal reproductive functions. Oral contraceptives, vaginal spermicides, tubal ligation, intrauterine devices, vacuum aspiration, and dilatation/evacuation have been sold to us as the medical means to "sexual liberation."

Rather than being freed to live in harmony with the natural rhythms of womanhood, women have been taught to fear what their wombs might produce: an unplanned pregnancy, a "defective" child, an untimely miscarriage. Some even say fertile women are "at-risk" of developing pregnancy — as if having a baby were a kind of cancer. But is it ever said that fertile men are "at-risk" of *producing* a pregnancy?

How many women in our nation are at peace with the natural state of their wombs, whether fertile or barren? We are pressured from every direction to live in a continual state of denial and apprehension regarding our bodies' sexual capabilities, and to use medicine to mask, bypass, or excise our nature.

"Pregnancy is the temporary deformation of the body of the individual for the sake of the species," according to feminist Shulamith Firestone. "Moreover childbirth *hurts*. And it isn't good for you."[15] In other words, the message here is: *pregnancy is unhealthy, childbirth is abnormal, and normal reproductive behavior hurts women.* If even women come to view their bodies' capabilities from such a negative anti-woman perspective, we can expect the practices of cesarean section, hysterectomy, abortion, and reproductive technology to continue flourishing in our culture.

"Artificial reproduction is not inherently dehumanizing," says

Firestone. "At the very least, development of an option should make possible an honest reexamination of the ancient value of motherhood."

She adds, "Until the taboo is lifted, until the decision to have children or not to have them 'naturally' is at least as legitimate as traditional [i. e., biological] childbearing, women are being forced into their female roles."[16]

Yet how can mechanical reproduction *not* be inherently dehumanizing? It is a hideous type of "freedom" that would suggest women surrender pregnancy and the nurture of unborn children to machines. *When this happens, children become the subject of scientific determination. Only the "best" and the "brightest" will be deemed worthy to survive.*

"One need only look at a tiny [human] fetus through the viewing porthole of Dr. Robert Goodlin's steel chamber at Stanford; — or at a similar primate fetus, in this case still attached to its mother via the umbilical cord, at the University of Nevada — to see how convenient observation and treatment would be," explains Albert Rosenfeld. "Faults could be detected much more readily. . . ."[17]

As a woman, I find it incredible that members of my sex advocate the elimination of unborn children purely on the basis of gender or genetic makeup. It is a perspective of human life I associate with militaristic-minded men and scientists motivated by utilitarian principles, *not* mothers. *Yet it is already being done.*[18] The ultimate solution to unwanted children, once conceived, is to kill them.

If babies are already being killed following prenatal diagnosis — at as late as twenty-six weeks of pregnancy — what is going to happen when eight-celled embryos the size of a pinhead are found to be the wrong genetic type? When a four-week-old fetus floating in an artificial womb shows signs of physical deformation?

In *The Abolition of Man*, C. S. Lewis warns that "the man-moulders of the new age will be armed with the powers of an omnicompetent state and an irresistible scientific technique: we shall get at last a race of conditioners who really can cut out all posterity in what shape they please."[19]

Make no mistake: children developing in a petri dish or an artificial womb will increasingly be judged according to their genetic value. Those found to be "substandard" will not pass quality control. Reproductive technology is a two-edged sword; its uses extend beyond the treatment of infertility and infants born too early.

* * *

At dinner he sat next to Filostrato. There were no other members of the inner circle within earshot. The Italian was in good spirits and talkative. He had just been given orders for the cutting down of some fine beech trees in the grounds.

"Why have you done that, Professor?" said a Mr. Winter who sat opposite. "I shouldn't have thought they did much harm at that distance from the house. I'm rather fond of the trees myself."

"Oh, yes, yes," replied Filostrato. "The pretty trees, the garden trees. But not the savages. I put the rose in the garden, but not the brier. The forest tree is a weed. But I tell you I have seen the civilized tree in Persia. It was a French attache who had it because he was in a place where trees do not grow. It was made of metal. A poor, crude thing. But how if it were perfected? Light, made of aluminum. So natural, it would even deceive."

"It would hardly be the same as a real tree," said Winter.

"But consider the advantages! You get tired of him in one place: two workmen carry him somewhere else. It never dies. No leaves to fall, no twigs, no birds building nests, no muck and mess."

"I suppose one or two, as curiosities, might be rather amusing."

"Why one or two? At present, I allow, we must have forests, for the atmosphere. Presently we find a chemical substitute. And then, why any natural trees? I foresee nothing but the art tree all over the earth. In fact, we clean the planet."

"Do you mean," put in a man called Gould, "that we are to have no vegetation at all?"

"Exactly. You shave your face: even, in the English fashion, you shave him every day. One day we shave the planet."

"I wonder what the birds will make of it?"

"I would not have any birds either. On the art tree I would have the art birds all singing when you press a switch inside the house. When you are tired of the singing, you switch them off. Consider again the improvement. No feathers dropped about, no nests, no eggs, no dirt."

"It sounds," said Mark, "like abolishing pretty well all organic life."

"And why not? It is simple hygiene. Listen, my friends. If you pick up some rotten thing and find this organic life crawling over it, do you not say, 'Oh, the horrid thing. It is alive,' and then drop it?"

"Go on," said Winter.

"And you, especially you English, are you not hostile to any organic life except your own on your own body? Rather than permit it, you have invented the daily bath."

"That's true."

"And what do you call dirty dirt? Is it not precisely the organic?

Minerals are clean dirt. But the real filth is what comes from organisms — sweat, spittles, excretions. Is not your whole idea of purity one huge example? The impure and the organic are interchangeable conceptions."

"What are you driving at, Professor?" said Gould. "After all we are organisms ourselves."

"I grant it. That is the point. In us organic life has produced Mind. It has done its work. After that we want no more of it. We do not want the world any longer furred over with organic life, like what you call the blue mould — all sprouting and budding and breeding and decaying. We must get rid of it. By little and little, of course. Slowly we learn how. Learn to make our brains live with less and less body: learn to build our bodies directly with chemicals, no longer have to stuff them full of dead brutes and weeds. Learn how to reproduce ourselves without copulation."

"I don't think that would be much fun," said Winter.

"My friend, you have already separated the Fun, as you call it, from fertility. The Fun itself begins to pass away. Bah! I know that is not what you think. But look at your English women. Six out of ten are frigid, are they not? You see? Nature herself begins to throw away the anachronism. When she has thrown it away, then real civilization becomes possible. You would understand if you were peasants. Who would try to work with stallions and bulls? No, no; we want geldings and oxen. There will never be peace and order and discipline so long as there is sex. When man has thrown it away, he will become finally governable." [20]

This book was written as a testimony about what is happening to one of nature's greatest masterpieces — the beauty and wonder of natural womanhood. Its intent is to provide documented evidence to demonstrate the extent of today's crisis in obstetrics and gynecology. As a result, this book's witness is meant to stimulate discussion and promote change through education about current practices in reproductive medicine. How the facts presented here will be used, however, is up to us. We *can* make a difference in reducing the number of annual surgeries performed upon the womb and techniques aimed at commercializing procreation. If it is not too late, I believe there are many people willing to speak out who have not yet done so. Perhaps *Without Moral Limits* will encourage you to become involved.

I am not a physician or a philosopher who brings to this discussion advanced skills in the art of diagnosis or debate. I have written about these topics as a woman, in a voice strengthened by my conviction that the God-given design of normal reproductive experience is worth guarding, protecting, and preserving. It is my hope that many other "ordinary" men and women will start speaking out on these issues as well.

Citizens of Great Britain and Australia have been engaged in heated public discussion and drafting legislation concerning reproductive technologies and embryo experimentation since 1985.[3] Commercial surrogacy has already been outlawed in England.[4] West Germany recently placed a strict ban on IVF-related embryo research.[5] *There is every reason to believe that we can accomplish the same protection for women and children here in the United States if we make our opinions known.* But there is no time to lose.

Congressional hearings concerning federal funding for IVF and fetal research (to be held in 1989 or 1990[6]) will provide an excellent opportunity to influence what happens in Washington. *Petition drives* and *public information campaigns* could further underscore our intent. An appendix at the end of this book has been included to encourage you to *target local agencies, clinics, and businesses with phone calls, letters, and boycotts* to express your opinions regarding their impact upon your community. A post office box is listed on the last page of Chapter 10 for those interested in receiving updates on value-centered reproductive health and alternative approaches to ob/gyn related treatments.

In Defense of Life's Creation

As a Christian, I understand the harm reproductive medicine produces when it counterfeits the natural processes of reproduction and devalues human life. As a woman, I have also experienced conception, pregnancy, birth, and breastfeeding according to the amazing design of my body — all activities from which most physicians are excluded, and thus cannot fully comprehend or understand. When I read the Psalms, I am particularly struck with the majesty and vulnerability of what it means to be created in God's image:

> *O LORD, our Lord,*
> > *how majestic is your name in all the earth!*
>
> *You have set your glory*
> > *above the heavens.*
> *From the lips of children and infants*
> > *you have ordained praise*
> *because of your enemies,*
> > *to silence the foe and the avenger.*
>
> *When I consider your heavens,*
> > *the work of your fingers,*
> *the moon and the stars,*
> > *which you have set in place,*
> *what is man that you are mindful of*
> > *him,*
> *the son of man that you care for*
> > *him?*
> *You made him a little lower than the*
> > *heavenly beings*
> *and crowned him with glory and*
> > *honor.*[7]

Technology often drowns out the sound of this symphony.

"A science-based culture, such as the present one, of necessity erodes and makes nonsense out of all sorts of bonds and connections which a Christian sees to be the case," says Princeton University theologian Paul Ramsey.[8] The reason for this, Ramsey explains, is directly related to our created identity:

Men and women are created in covenant, to covenant, and for covenant. Creation is *toward* the love of Christ. Christians, therefore, will not readily admit that the energies of sex, for example, have any other primary *telos*, any other final end, than Jesus Christ. Rather, they will find in the strength of human sexual passion (beyond the obvious needs of procreation) an evident *telos* of acts of sexual love toward making real the meaning of man-womanhood, nurturing covenant-love between the parties, fostering their care for one another, prefiguring Christ's love for the Church. . . . *And in human procreativity out of the depths of human sexual love is prefigured God's own act of creation out of the profound mystery of his love revealed in Christ.* To put radically asunder what God joined together in parenthood when he made love procreative, to procreate beyond the sphere of love (artificial insemination by donor, for example or making human life in a test-tube), or to posit acts of sexual love beyond the sphere of responsible procreation (by definition, marriage), means a refusal of the image of God's creation in our own.[9]

The current level of reproductive surgery performed on women in this country is attempting to redesign women's natural identity according to medical ideals. But instead of improving our health, many ob/gyn techniques sabotage the physiological integrity of our bodies. Advanced reproductive technologies are opening the way for an ever-widening invasion of God's design for procreation and parenthood.

In previous chapters, the role physicians have played in contributing to the current crisis in reproductive medicine was described in detail. This is not because I am so naive as to believe that all ob/gyns are equally responsible for the high rate of uterine surgery, nor do I see all infertility specialists as "technodocs"[10] who offer couples every available technique to produce a baby. On the contrary — it is *because I am no longer naive* that I can evaluate these practices and stand up for alternatives to high-tech trends in obstetrics and gynecology.

Shattering the Silence

It is with a certain amount of fear and trembling that I and others like myself seek to shatter the conspiracy of silence that shelters physicians from public accountability in our country. Doctors, after all, wield a great deal of power in this part of the world. But we must realize it is those who pay for medical care who will most influence change, *not* those who provide it. *You and I can decide where and how to spend our health care dollars* — what hospitals to utilize, which health care providers to use, and which preventative strategies to invest in — and thus make a direct impact on ob/gyn services in our local communities. *By educating ourselves about our bodies and becoming responsible about the health care choices we make,* we can avoid unnecessary surgery and high-risk, low-yield medical treatments.[11]

For normal childbirth and well-woman gynecological care, for example, we can select midwives in order to receive care from highly skilled providers trained in the art of nurturing healthy laboring women.[12] For breastfeeding assistance, we can contact lactation consultants to give us the advice and support we need for nursing our babies.[13] For family planning, we can learn how to live in harmony with the natural rhythms and patterns of our bodies during each menstrual cycle.[14] For fertility promotion, we can avoid stress, harmful contraceptive drugs and devices, sexually transmitted diseases, and delayed childbearing by the lifestyles we lead.

For healing in the aftermath of abortion, we can turn to women called to minister to those who have suffered this loss.[15]

When the services of an obstetrician-gynecologist are necessary, we can compare available physicians and select providers who best suit our needs.[16] *The selection of a reproductive specialist is one of the most important health care decisions a woman will ever make, so it is essential to shop carefully.* I cannot emphasize strongly enough how important this is. Physicians' skills, training, attitudes, and routines vary tremendously between local practices and, often, within the same group of doctors. Wouldn't it be wonderful if ob/gyns were required to post their episiotomy, cesarean, abortion, and hysterectomy rates along with the criteria they used to perform each surgery? Since that isn't likely to happen soon, we'll be left to do the investigating on our own.

Many women assume doctors are experts on normal childbirth. In reality, they know very little of what actually promotes natural, or physiological, labor. Few have seen the birth process take place — from start to finish — without medical intervention or within a woman's home environment. Ob/gyns are indeed experts — in the *abnormal*, the *unusual*, and the *infrequent complications*. There is a place for them, just as for any other type of expensive medical specialist when an indication for their use exists. It is very difficult for surgical specialists (which all ob/gyns are) *not* to use their skills to intervene or interfere with natural labor, even in the best of circumstances.

The greatest contributions to lowering the maternal death rate have had more to do with the discovery of antibiotics and use of hand-washing than with heroic medical procedures. Yet our belief in science leads us to view obstetricians as the ones who save us from the dire consequences of childbirth. From 5 to 10 percent of the time, their expert services are unquestionably needed. In another 5 to 10 percent of cases, their training may prove very useful. *But at least 70 to 80 percent of the time, a domiciliary midwife skilled in supporting natural labor will do more to help the mother than any ob/gyn can, or will. Midwives,* not *doctors, are the guardians of the normal, the usual, and the safe when it comes to healthy birthing women.*[17]

"Without the presence and acceptance of the midwife, obstetrics becomes aggressive, technological, and inhuman," declares Dutch physician G. J. Kloosterman, a former professor of obstetrics and gynecology.[18] If this is true, then why are ob/gyns used by women so much more than midwives in this country? In Denmark, Sweden, and the Netherlands, midwives enjoy an excellent reputation and remain the popular norm. In the five countries of the world with the lowest perinatal mortality rates, midwives attend *70 percent of all births.*[19] But in the United States — which currently ranks *sixteenth* in perinatal mortality worldwide — midwives today attend only *5 percent* of births. Why?[20]

I have often wondered how natural bowel function would be affected if men and women were hospitalized, undressed, checked with monitors, intubated with I.V.s, surrounded by masked health care providers, placed on their backs with their legs in stirrups, cleansed around the rectum, draped with sterile sheets, and told to *"Push."* Yet this is what women are frequently asked to do to have a baby. *It is dehumanizing, undignified, and physiologically harmful.* If the men who created these techniques had ever been able — or forced — to experience them, American obstetrics would not be the overrated conquest of nature it is today.

We may have "birthing rooms," but we still have a national episiotomy rate of at least 75 percent. We may have "father-attended" childbirth, but in one out of every four cases, Dad's standing beside an operating table observing a cesarean section, not holding his wife as she actively brings forth their child. We may have "natural" childbirth, but how many women leave the hospital without being drugged, shaved, and sutured? Is this what women truly want for the births of their babies?

In Whom — or What — Do We Trust?

Infertility medicine presents its own set of unique challenges and dilemmas. *If a woman is having difficulty becoming pregnant, she should take time to assess her lifestyle and learn how to observe signs of fertility* before *resorting to medical therapy—if there are no unusual symptoms of reproductive disease or disability.*

Stress, diet, weight, age, exercise, and a woman's current health status all contribute to the ability to carry a baby. In addition, it is important to remember that many women have at least one or two anovulatory cycles per year (cycles in which menstruation occurs, but not ovulation) and that the average length of time it takes to conceive is eight months. Because infertility diagnosis and treatment often involves expensive procedures without guarantees of success, it is essential to proceed carefully when selecting a health care provider or making decisions about infertility therapy.

A couple of weeks ago, I was phoned by a woman who has spent over $7,000 on infertility treatment in the last five months. She told me about being put on a fertility drug (Clomid) and the diagnostic tests she and her husband have endured. What angered me the most about this woman's story is that her physician had put her on this medication and performed a battery of diagnostic procedures, but hadn't even asked basic questions about her stress level, diet, and exercise habits, or attitudes about marriage and family life. Neither had she been adequately taught to observe her body's signs of fertility — cervical mucus, cervical dilation, and basal body temperature — to determine when, and if, she was ovulating. In fact, *the physician had not yet determined if ovulation was taking place!*

As we talked, I discovered this woman holds three jobs, travels out of town extensively, eats erratically, and describes herself as constantly under an incredible amount of stress. Nutritional therapy, ovulation awareness, and stress management had not occurred to her as possible resolutions to her difficulty in getting pregnant. Think about it: doesn't it make sense to try this approach *before* bombarding one's body with hormones and surgery?

Another woman — a labor and delivery nurse — told me that at her first infertility appointment, her gynecologist had automatically prescribed Clomid when she told him she wasn't conceiving. Other than taking her history, he made no attempt to determine whether she was ovulating. She then told me of a friend whose ob/gyn immediately decided to perform a laparoscopy when she asked for help in conceiving. Clearly, the expense and risks of these procedures should provoke couples to consider in advance how much they are willing to spend or endure at the hands of an infertility specialist, as well as to find out the appropriate indications for specific procedures.

"We live in an age when science has become God and technology is the Holy Spirit," says childbirth educator Lynn Baptisti Richards.

"We should perhaps have coins upon which are stamped, 'In Technology We Trust.'"[21]

But consider the Old Testament proverb which says:

> *Trust in the Lord with all your heart*
> *   and lean not on your own understanding;*
> *In all your ways acknowledge him,*
> *   and he will make your paths straight.*
> *Do not be wise in your own eyes;*
> *   fear the Lord and shun evil.*
> *This will bring health to your body*
> *   and nourishment to your bones.*[22]

When it comes to bearing a child, in whom will we place our highest trust—in God or modern medicine? For Christians, prayer and discernment concerning God's leading and timing in this area of life are more valuable than automatic reliance upon physicians who perform costly invasive treatments.

The Bible contains numerous stories of infertile women—Sarah, Rebekah, Rachel, Samson's mother, Hannah, a Shunammite woman, and Elizabeth—who were blessed with children due to God's direct intervention in their lives.[23] In each of these stories, infertility plays an important role in the overall context of history.

Of the two women who used handmaidens to satisfy their desire for a child, family turmoil soon followed.[24] Sarah's command that a substitute be used to bypass her infertility resulted in the spiritual bondage of an entire nation.[25] Rachel's intense desire for a second pregnancy ended in death.[26] The Bible's unfavorable portrayal of surrogacy provides a strong warning to steer clear of similar arrangements today. Artificial insemination by donor, third-party (surrogate motherhood) pregnancy contracts, egg donation, and surrogate embryo transfer, for example, all utilize the reproductive potential and genetic heritage of someone outside the marriage covenant to produce offspring.

John T. Noonan gives the solution to this problem when he states that "to avoid reaching that condition of society where . . . breeding of human beings as objects becomes routine, *the Christian insistence that procreation is indissolubly linked to conjugal love is the first and most significant safeguard.*"[27]

In contrast to Sarah and Rachel, Hannah's story presents an entirely different picture of a woman coping with the hidden despair of barrenness:

In bitterness of soul, Hannah wept much and prayed to the Lord. And she made a vow, saying, "O Lord Almighty, if you will only look upon your servant's misery and remember me, and forget not your servant but give her a son, then I will give him to the Lord for all the days of his life, and no razor will ever be used on his head."

As she kept praying to the Lord, Eli observed her mouth. Hannah was praying in her heart, and her lips were moving but her voice was not heard. Eli thought she was drunk and said to her, "How long will you keep getting drunk? Get rid of your wine."

"Not so, my lord," Hannah replied, "I am a woman who is deeply troubled. I have not been drinking wine or beer; I was pouring out my soul to the Lord. Do not take your servant for a wicked woman; I have been praying here out of my great anguish and grief."

Eli answered, "Go in peace, and may the God of Israel grant you what you have asked of him."

She said, "May your servant find favor in your eyes." Then she went her way and ate something, and her face was no longer downcast.[28]

Hannah's prolonged infertility brought her to a place of complete brokenness and humility before God. Rather than seeking to bear a child through using someone else, she poured out her anguish in prayer and fasting. She trusted God instead of devising her own solutions to the despair she encountered. God met Hannah at her point of need and provided her with a child she named Samuel. In response, Hannah wisely proclaimed, "The Lord brings death and makes alive; he brings down to the grave and raises up. . . . It is not by strength that one prevails."[29]

As many as one in five infertile couples receive no explanation for their condition by their physicians. Rather than viewing this situation as a dead-end diagnosis, however, couples might seize this new opportunity to deepen their faith and develop trust in God.

For some, this will mean rescuing children from abortion or abandonment through adoption.[30] For others, it may mean greater freedom to serve Christ in full-time ministry. For still others, it means God's direct, sovereign intervention will be provided according to the Lord's purposes and timing. The births of children to infertile women in the Bible are a powerful reminder of our Creator's role in procreation. *Such miracles still happen today.* Consider these recent examples:

- Linda and Bill, both personal friends of my family, conceived a child last year after a *fourteen-year* experience with infertility. They had long since given up "trying" to get pregnant, having reached the limit to what medicine could do for them years ago. There is no scientific explanation whatsoever for the birth of their son, Zachary, in January 1989.

- Last month, I met woman named Josie at a television station in Kansas City. When she heard I was a childbirth educator, she proceeded to tell me the wonderful story of her youngest daughter's conception.

  Josie's babies had all been born by cesarean section, and her physician warned her that a fourth pregnancy might cause her uterus to rupture. He recommended that she have her tubes tied after her third child was born while undergoing a surgical delivery. Some time later, however, Josie realized that she had gone ahead with the sterilization without really praying about it. She decided to pray and ask the Lord to reopen her womb if the tubal ligation had not been His will. The next month, Josie was pregnant. When the physician performed her fourth cesarean nine months later, he was amazed to find *a third Fallopian tube* had grown from Josie's uterus! *Her original oviducts were still tightly sealed.* The ob/gyn could offer no medical reason for this phenomenon. Josie's fourth daughter is now four years old.

- Karen was infertile for six years before she conceived her first child, and then miscarried her second baby sixteen weeks later. Several years went by, leading Karen to start a group for infertile couples at her small church. Participants committed themselves to prayer and Bible study as well as to providing mutual support to one another. Some relied on natural means to promote fertility while others chose to seek medical treatment. Within just a few years, *all six had borne children.*

- Bev and Randy recently became parents in direct answer to their prayers for a child. Unable to conceive due to chemotherapy treatments for cancer, Bev continued to believe God wanted her to become a mother. Last year, she was led to a single woman looking for a Christian couple to adopt her baby. Bev and Randy turned out to be the couple God had in mind, and they brought Joseph home just before Christmas in December 1988. They have found great joy in taking him into their home to share the love they have long been waiting to give a child.

The Giver of Life

While writing this book, I took time out to visit the Rocky Mountains and climb to the top of a mountain. The path was lined by alpine tundra. After spending countless hours in medical libraries, I enjoyed being surrounded with the nonsynthetic reality of glacier-fed streams and ancient rock formations.

The panoramic view surrounding me was thoroughly refreshing as I feasted on the beauty of snowy peaks rimming the horizon. As I reflected on the spectacular landscape, I was reminded of the following verses:

> *For you created my inmost being;*
> *you knit me together in my mother's womb.*
> *I praise you because I am fearfully and wonderfully made;*
> *your works are wonderful,*
> *I know that full well.*[31]

It was awe-inspiring to realize that the God who created the sky and mountains made me too.

Several weeks later, I ran into an article describing the nation's first IVF program in Norfolk, Virginia.[32] In it, the author describes a sign with a subtle but significant message hanging on the clinic's waiting room wall. It arrogantly declares:

> *They say babies are made in heaven,*
> *but we know better.*

Yet the Bible says:

> *Know that the Lord Himself is God;*
> *It is He who has made us,*
> *and not we ourselves.*[33]

Children are gifts of God, not laboratory designed creations. What reproductive technology delivers, in cleverly designed packages, is selective breeding, genetic diagnosis, embryo experimentation, and the medical control of life from the earliest moments — not babies. *No amount of technology can produce life.* That alone belongs to God to give.

Not surprisingly, one of the experimental projects recently conducted by a researcher from the Norfolk clinic (now called the Jones Institute for Reproductive Medicine) is a study of the abortion pill,

RU486.[34] Why is an *infertility* clinic also investigating contraception and abortion techniques? To say this is a conflict of interests is putting it mildly, unless one clearly understands that the "miraculous" results of infertility treatments are all the public is often allowed to see of these programs.

"We want to be able to develop to the fullest extent the research potential which lies in our program," says Dr. Howard Jones, Jr., the director of the clinic.[35] In the case of the Jones Clinic, this apparently means much more than providing infertile couples with children.

In vitro fertilization, embryo transplants, and artificial wombs dehumanize conception. Commercialized programs further destroy the inherent design of procreation. The ends simply do not justify the means when it comes to attempts to make human beings. Says attorney Joseph J. Piccone:

> In vitro techniques are grossly careless toward human life. In addition to the risks to children born through such intervention, in vitro techniques also require the destruction of human embryos. . . .
>
> We should rejoice in the real progress of science, but must evaluate advances so that science truly serves humanity. The technical ability to do something does not itself justify the action. We've got to be able to reflect on our technology or we will become victims of our short-term "success" and long-term failures.
>
> Poet e.e. cummings wrote that "a world of made is not a world of born." We have the ability to follow two different roads: one of respecting and enhancing human life, the other of reshaping and redefining it. This second choice is for the world of "made" in which life itself is mechanistic and impersonal. What is produced in the lab goes on to the courthouse, where it is just another issue in contract or property law.[36]

Which road will we choose to take? For Christians, there can be no doubt about the right path to follow. May our voices ring out loud and clear that the majesty of God's good creation is worth guarding, protecting, and preserving.

If you wish to keep up with future developments, write:

National Reproductive Health Project
P.O. Box 2018
Lincoln, NE 68502

Please enclose with your questions a self-addressed, stamped business envelope for reply. I look forward to receiving your ideas and comments.

Afterword

*T*he practices described in this book constitute a trend within the field of obstetrics and gynecology characterized by:

- Reliance upon drugs and medical technology
- The use of invasive techniques to redirect and control natural life processes related to human reproduction
- A hedonistic value system which places self-interest above the needs of society.

The surrender of fertility and reproduction to medical technology, rather than improving women's health, has in fact resulted in an unprecedented level of reproductive incompetency in our culture. The very people who benefit most from this crisis are those who also have a vested interest in selling these medical treatments and procedures.[1] The more expensive, more extensive, and more extreme the technology is, the greater the benefit to the practitioner. But this is not necessarily true for the woman being treated. Where treatments are physician-referred and physician-monitored at the client's expense, it is the client and not the physician who pays the physical, emotional, and economic price of the technique or procedure involved.

In addition, these technologies foster a disregard for the dignity of women and the value of prenatal life. Therefore, this type of medicine may be more appropriately called *gynetech* instead of obstetrics and gynecology. It is a new term for a new kind of medicine *that does not treat or heal but seeks to redefine the terms of fertility and reproduction.* Oral contraceptives, after all, do not *treat* anything — unless one considers fertility or pregnancy a disease. In vitro fertilization, surrogate embryo transfer, and artificial insemination do not *heal* infertility; they are simply animal breeding techniques applied to human beings. Prenatal diagnosis and eugenic abortion of children with Down's syndrome are neither *preventative* nor *therapeutic*, but are strategies used to kill humans judged unworthy of life. *Gynetech*, not traditional medicine, is the spirit and philosophy behind these examples.

The spirit of gynetech can grow only if we feed it with fear and ignorance, surrendering our wombs to techniques that can neither help nor heal. By identifying the new medicine for what it actually is, we can effectively resist and restrict its influence as we warn others of its dangers.

Our help is in the name of the Lord,
who made heaven and earth.[2]

Appendix A

VATICAN STATEMENT
Instruction on Respect for Human Life and the Dignity of Procreation

*The complete document issued by the Vatican on repro-
ductive technology in February 1987 is presented here as
a Christian rebuttal to the gynetech philosophy. Since
most Protestants and evangelicals like myself were only
informed of the Vatican's position through news headlines
blaring "VATICAN CONDEMNS NEW INFERTILITY
TREATMENTS," it seemed worthwhile to let people
judge for themselves. What follows here is a profoundly
beautiful statement about the meaning of procreation and
human life—a model for all Christians to consider
thoughtfully and prayerfully.*

D. Evans

This is the official Vatican English Language text of the "Instruction on Respect for Human Life in Its Origin and on the Dignity of Procreation: Replies to Certain Questions of the Day" issued by the Congregation for the Doctrine of the Faith dated 2/22/87 and published 3/10/87. [Reprinted by permission of CRUX, Clarity Publishing, Inc., Albany, NY.]

FOREWORD

The Congregation for the Doctrine of the Faith has been approached by various episcopal conferences or individual bishops, by theologians, doctors and scientists, concerning biomedical techniques which make it possible to intervene in the initial phase of the life of a human being and in the very processes of procreation and their conformity with the principles of Catholic morality. The present Instruction, which is the result of wide consultation and in particular of a careful evaluation of the declarations made by episcopates, does not intend to repeat all the Church's teaching on the dignity of human life as it originates and on procreation, but to offer, in the light of the previous teaching of the Magisterium, some specific replies to the main questions being asked in this regard.

The exposition is arranged as follows: An introduction will recall the fundamental principles of an anthropological and moral character which are necessary for a proper evaluation of the problems and for working out replies to those questions; the first part will have as its subject respect for the human being from the first moment of his or her existence; the second part will deal with the moral questions raised by technical interventions on human procreation; the third part will offer some orientations on the relationships between moral law and civil law in terms of the respect due to human embryos and fetuses (see note) and as regards the legitimacy of techniques of artificial procreation.

Note: The terms "zygote," "pre-embryo," "embryo" and "fetus" can indicate in the vocabulary of biology successive stages of the development of a human being. The present Instruction makes free use of these terms attributing to them an identical ethical relevance in order to designate the result (whether visible or not) of human generation from the first moment of its existence until birth. The reason for this usage is clarified by the text (cf. I 1).

INTRODUCTION

1. Biomedical Research and the Teaching of the Church

The gift of life which God the Creator and Father has entrusted to man calls him to appreciate the inestimable value of what he has been given and to take responsibility for it: this fundamental principle must be placed at the center of one's reflection in order to clarify and solve the moral problems raised by artificial interventions on life as it originates and on the processes of procreation.

Thanks to the progress of the biological and medical sciences man has at his disposal ever more effective therapeutic resources; but he can also acquire new powers with unforeseeable consequences over human life at its very beginning and in its first stages. Various procedures now make it possible to intervene not only in order to assist but also to dominate the processes of procreation. These techniques can enable man to "take in hand his own destiny" but they also expose him "to the temptation to go beyond the limits of a reasonable dominion over nature."[1] They might constitute progress in the service of man but they also involve serious risks. Many people are therefore expressing an urgent appeal that in interventions on procreation the values and rights of the human person be safeguarded. Requests for clarification and guidance are coming not only from the faithful, but also from those who recognize the Church as "an expert in humanity"[2] with a mission to serve the "civilization of love"[3] and of life.

The Church's Magisterium does not intervene on the basis of a particular competence in the area of the experimental sciences; but having taken account of the data of research and technology, it intends to put forward, by virtue of its evangelical mission and apostolic duty, the moral teaching corresponding to the dignity of the person and to his or her integral vocation. It intends to do so by expounding the criteria of moral judgment as regards the applications of scientific research and technology, especially in relation to human life and its beginnings. These criteria are the respect, defense and promotion of man, his "primary and fundamental right" to life,[4] his dignity as a person who is endowed with a spiritual soul and with moral responsibility[5] and who is called to beatific communion with God.

The Church's intervention in this field is inspired also by the love which she owes to man, helping him to recognize and respect his rights and duties. This love draws from the fount of Christ's love: As she contemplates the mystery of the incarnate word, the Church also comes to understand the "mystery of man;"[6] by proclaiming the Gospel of salvation, she reveals to man his dignity and invites him to discover fully the truth of his own being. Thus the Church once more puts forward the divine law in order to accomplish the work of truth and liberation.

For it is out of goodness — in order to indicate the path of life — that God gives human beings his commandments and the grace to observe them; and it is likewise out of goodness — in order to help them persevere along the same path — that God always offers to everyone his forgiveness. Christ has compassion on our weaknesses: he is our Creator and Redeemer. May his Spirit open men's hearts to the gift of God's peace and to an understanding of his precepts.

2. Science and Technology at the Service of the Human Person

God created man in his own image and likeness: "Male and female he created them" (Gn 1:27), entrusting to them the task of "having dominion over the earth" (Gn 1:28). Basic scientific research and applied research constitute a significant expression of this dominion of man over creation. Science and technology are valuable resources for man when placed at his service and when they promote his integral development for the benefit of all; but they cannot of themselves show the meaning of existence and of human progress. Being ordered to man, who initiates and develops them, they draw from the person and his moral values the indication of their purpose and the awareness of their limits.

It would on the one hand be illusory to claim that scientific research and its applications are morally neutral; on the other hand one cannot derive criteria for guidance from mere technical efficiency, from research's possible usefulness to some at the expense of others or, worse still, from prevailing ideologies. Thus science and technology require for their own intrinsic meaning an unconditional respect for the fundamental criteria of the moral law: That is to say, they must be at the service of the human person, of his inalienable rights and his true and integral good according to the design and will of God.[7]

The rapid development of technological discoveries gives greater urgency to this need to respect the criteria just mentioned: Science without conscience can only lead to man's ruin. "Our era needs such wisdom more than bygone ages if the discoveries made by man are to be further humanized. For the future of the world stands in peril unless wiser people are forthcoming."[8]

3. Anthropology and Procedures in the Biomedical Field

Which moral criteria must be applied in order to clarify the problems posed today in the field of biomedicine? The answer to this question presupposes a proper idea of the nature of the human person in his bodily dimension.

For it is only in keeping with his true nature that the human person can achieve self-realization as a "unified totality;"[9] and this nature is at the same time corporal and spiritual. By virtue of its substantial union with a spiritual soul, the human body cannot be considered as a mere complex of tissues, organs and functions, nor can it be evaluated in the same way as the body of animals; rather it is a constitutive part of the person, who manifests and expresses himself through it.

The natural moral law expresses and lays down the purposes, rights and duties which are based upon the bodily and spiritual nature of the human person. Therefore this law cannot be thought of as simply a set of norms on the biological level; rather it must be defined as the rational order whereby man is called by the Creator to direct and regulate his life and actions and in particular to make use of his own body.[10]

A first consequence can be deduced from these principles: an intervention on the human body affects not only the tissues, the organs and their functions, but also involves the person himself on different levels. It involves, therefore, perhaps in an implicit but nonetheless real way, a moral significance and responsibility. Pope John Paul II forcefully reaffirmed this to the World Medical Association when he said: "Each human person, in his absolutely unique singularity, is constituted not only by his spirit, but by his body as well. Thus, in the body and through the body, one touches the person himself in his concrete reality. To respect the dignity of man consequently amounts to safeguarding this identity of the man '*corpore et anima unus*,' as the Second Vatican Council says (*Gaudium et Spes*, 14.1). It is on the basis of this anthropological vision that one is to find the fundamental criteria for decision making in the case of procedures which are not strictly therapeutic, as, for example, those aimed at the improvement of the human biological condition."[11]

Applied biology and medicine work together for the integral good of human life when they come to the aid of a person stricken by illness and infirmity and when they respect his or her dignity as a creature of God. No biologist or doctor can reasonably claim, by virtue of his scientific competence, to be able to decide on people's origin and destiny. This norm must be applied in a particular way in the field of sexuality and procreation, in which man and woman actualize the fundamental values of love and life.

God, who is love and life, has inscribed in man and woman the vocation to share in a special way in his mystery of personal communion and in his work as Creator and Father.[12] For this reason marriage possesses specific goods and values in its union and in procreation which cannot be likened to those existing in lower forms of life. Such values and meanings are of the personal order and determine from the moral point of view the meaning and limits of artificial interventions on procreation and on the origin of human life. These interventions are not to be rejected on the grounds that they are artificial. As such, they bear witness to the possibilities of the art of medicine. But they must be given a moral evaluation in reference to the dignity of the human person, who is called to realize his vocation from God to the gift of love and the gift of life.

4. Fundamental Criteria for a Moral Judgment

The fundamental values connected with the techniques of artificial human procreation are two: the life of the human being called into existence and the special nature of the transmission of human life in marriage. The moral judgment on such methods of artificial procreation must therefore be formulated in reference to these values.

Physical life, with which the course of human life in the world begins, certainly does not itself contain the whole of a person's value nor does it represent the supreme good of man, who is called to eternal life. However it does constitute in a certain way the "fundamental value of life" precisely because upon this physical life all the other values of the person are based and developed.[13] The inviolability of the innocent human being's right to life "from the moment of conception until death"[14] is a sign and requirement of the very inviolability of the person to whom the Creator has given the gift of life.

By comparison with the transmission of other forms of life in the universe, the transmission of human life has a special character of its own, which derives from the special nature of the human person. "The transmission of human life is entrusted by nature to a personal and conscious act and as such is subject to the all-holy laws of God: immutable and inviolable laws which must be recognized and observed. For this reason one cannot use means and follow methods which could be licit in the transmission of the life of plants and animals."[15]

Advances in technology have now made it possible to procreate apart from sexual relations through the meeting "in vitro" of the germ cells previously taken from the man and the woman. But what is technically possible is not for that very reason morally admissible. Rational reflection on the fundamental values of life and of human procreation is therefore indispensable for formulating a moral evaluation of such technological interventions on a human being from the first stages of his development.

5. Teachings of the Magisterium

On its part, the magisterium of the Church offers to human reason in this field too the light of revelation: The doctrine concerning man taught by the magisterium contains many elements which throw light on the problems being faced here.

From the moment of conception, the life of every human being is to be respected in an absolute way because man is the only creature on earth that God has "wished for himself"[16] and the spiritual soul of each man is "immediately created" by God;[17] his whole being bears the image of the Creator. Human life is sacred because from its beginning it involves "the creative action of God,"[18] and it remains forever in a special relationship with the Creator, who is its sole end.[19] God alone is the Lord of life from its beginning until its end: no one can, in any circumstance, claim for himself the right to destroy directly an innocent human being.[20]

Human procreation requires on the part of the spouses responsible collaboration with the fruitful love of God;[21] the gift of human life must be actualized in marriage through the specific and exclusive acts of husband and wife, in accordance with the laws inscribed in their persons and in their union.[22]

I. RESPECT FOR HUMAN EMBRYOS

Careful reflection on this teaching of the Magisterium and on the evidence of reason, as mentioned above, enables us to respond to the numerous moral problems posed by technical interventions upon the human being in the first phases of his life and upon the processes of his conception.

1. What respect is due to the human embryo, taking into account his nature and identity?

The human being must be respected — as a person — from the very first instant of his existence. The implementation of procedures of artificial fertilization has made possible various interventions upon embryos and human fetuses. The aims pursued are of various kinds: diagnostic and therapeutic, scientific and commercial. From all of this, serious problems arise. Can one speak of a right to experimentation upon human embryos for the purpose of scientific research? What norms or laws should be worked out with regard to this matter? The response to these problems presupposes a detailed reflection on the nature and specific identity — the word "status" is used — of the human embryo itself.

At the Second Vatican Council, the Church for her part presented once again to modern man her constant and certain doctrine according to which: "Life once conceived, must be protected with the utmost care; abortion and infanticide are abominable crimes."[23] More recently, the Charter of the Rights of the Family, published by the Holy See, confirmed that "human life must be absolutely respected and protected from the moment of conception."[24]

This congregation is aware of the current debates concerning the beginning of human life, concerning the individuality of the human being, and concerning the identity of the human person. The congregation recalls the teachings found in the Declaration on Procured Abortion:

"From the time that the ovum is fertilized, a new life is begun which is neither that of the father nor of the mother; it is rather the life of a new human being with his own growth. It would never be made human if it were not human already. To this perpetual evidence . . . modern genetic science brings valuable confirmation. It has demonstrated that, from the first instant, the program is fixed as to what this living being will be: a man, this individual man with his characteristic aspects already well determined. Right from fertilization is begun the adventure of a human life, and each of its great capacities requires time . . . to find its place and to be in a position to act."[25]

This teaching remains valid and is further confirmed, if confirmation were needed, by recent findings of human biological science which recognize that in the zygote (the cell produced when the nuclei of the two gametes have fused) resulting from fertilization the biological identity of a new human individual is already constituted.

Certainly no experimental datum can be in itself sufficient to bring us to the recognition of a spiritual soul; nevertheless, the conclusions of science regarding the human embryo provide a valuable indication for discerning by the use of reason a personal presence at the moment of this first appearance of a human life: How could a human individual not be a human person? The magisterium has not expressly committed itself to an affirmation of a philosophical nature, but it constantly reaffirms the moral condemnation of any kind of procured abortion. This teaching has not been changed and is unchangeable.[26]

Thus the fruit of human generation from the first moment of its existence, that is to say, from the moment the zygote has formed, demands the unconditional respect that is morally due to the human being in his bodily and spiritual totality. The human being is to be respected and treated as a person from the moment of conception, and therefore from that same moment his rights as a person must be recognized, among which in the first place is the inviolable right of every innocent human being to life.

This doctrinal reminder provides the fundamental criterion for the solution of the various problems posed by the development of the biomedical sciences in this field: Since the embryo must be treated as a person, it must also be defended in its integrity, tended and cared for, to the extent possible, in the same way as any other human being as far as medical assistance is concerned.

2. Is prenatal diagnosis morally licit?

If prenatal diagnosis respects the life and integrity of the embryo and the human fetus and is directed toward its safeguarding or healing as an individual, then the answer is affirmative.

For prenatal diagnosis makes it possible to know the condition of the embryo and of the fetus when still in the mother's womb. It permits or makes it possible to anticipate earlier and more effectively, certain therapeutic, medical or surgical procedures.

Such diagnosis is permissible, with the consent of the parents after they have been adequately informed, if the methods employed safeguard the life and integrity of the embryo and the mother, without subjecting them to disproportionate risks.[27] But this diagnosis is gravely opposed to the moral law when it is done with the thought of possibly inducing an abortion depending upon the results: A diagnosis which shows the existence of a malformation or a hereditary illness must not be the equivalent of a death sentence. Thus a woman would be committing a gravely illicit act if she were to request such a diagnosis with the deliberate intention of having an abortion should the results confirm the existence of a malformation or abnormality. The spouse or relatives or anyone else would similarly be acting in a manner contrary to the moral law if they were to counsel or impose such a diagnostic procedure on the expectant mother with the same intention of possibly proceeding to an abortion. So too the specialist would be guilty of illicit collaboration if, in conducting the diagnosis and in communicating its results, he were deliberately to contribute to establishing or favoring a link between prenatal diagnosis and abortion.

In conclusion, any directive or program of the civil and health authorities or of scientific organizations which in any way were to favor a link between prenatal diagnosis and abortion, or which were to go as far as directly to induce expectant mothers to submit to prenatal diagnosis planned for the purpose of eliminating fetuses which are affected by malformations or which are carriers of hereditary illness, is to be condemned as a violation of the unborn child's right to life and as an abuse of the prior rights and duties of the spouses.

3. Are therapeutic procedures carried out on the human embryo licit?

As with all medical interventions on patients, one must uphold as licit procedures carried out on the human embryo which respect the life and integrity of the embryo and do not involve disproportionate risks for it, but are directed toward its healing, the improvement of its condition of health or its individual survival.

Whatever the type of medical, surgical or other therapy, the free and informed consent of the parents is required, according to the deontological rules followed in the case of children. The application of this moral principle may call for delicate and particular precautions in the case of embryonic or fetal life.

The legitimacy and criteria of such procedures have been clearly stated by Pope John Paul II: "A strictly therapeutic intervention whose explicit objective is the healing of various maladies such as those stemming from chromosomal defects will, in principle, be considered desirable, provided it is directed to the true promotion of the personal well-being of the individual without doing harm to his integrity or worsening his conditions of life. Such an intervention would indeed fall within the logic of the Christian moral tradition."[28]

4. How is one to evaluate morally research and experimentation (see note) on human embryos and fetuses?

Medical research must refrain from operations on live embryos, unless there is a moral certainty of not causing harm to the life or integrity of the unborn child and the mother, and on condition that the parents have given their free and informed consent to the procedure. It follows that all research, even when limited to the simple observation of the embryo, would become illicit were it to involve risk to the embryo's physical integrity or life by reason of the methods used or the effects induced.

As regards experimentation, and presupposing the general distinction between experimentation for purposes which are not directly therapeutic and experimentation which is clearly therapeutic for the subject himself, in the case in point one must also distinguish between experimentation carried out on embryos which are still alive and experimentation carried out on embryos which are dead. If the embryos are living, whether viable or not, they must be respected just like any other human person; experimentation on embryos which is not directly therapeutic is illicit.[29]

No objective, even though noble in itself such as a foreseeable advantage to science, to other human beings or to society, can in any way justify experimentation on living human embryos or fetuses, whether viable or not, either inside or outside the mother's womb. The informed consent ordinarily required for clinical experimentation on adults cannot be granted by the parents, who may not freely dispose of the physical integrity or life of the unborn child. Moreover, experimentation on embryos and fetuses always involves risk, and indeed in most cases it involves the certain expectation of harm to their physical integrity or even their death.

To use human embryos or fetuses as the object or instrument of experimentation constitutes a crime against their dignity as human beings having a right to the same respect that is due to the child already born and to every human person.

The Charter of the Rights of the Family published by the Holy See affirms: "Respect for the dignity of the human being excludes all experimental manipulation or exploitation of the human embryo."[30] The practice of keeping alive human embryos "in vivo" or "in vitro" for experimental or commercial purposes is totally opposed to human dignity.

In the case of experimentation that is clearly therapeutic, namely, when it is a matter of experimental forms of therapy used for the benefit of the embryo itself in a final attempt to save its life and in the absence of other reliable forms of therapy, recourse to drugs or procedures not yet fully tested can be licit.[31]

The corpses of human embryos and fetuses, whether they have been deliberately aborted or not, must be respected just as the remains of other human beings. In particular, they cannot be subjected to mutilation or to autopsies if their death has not yet been verified and without the consent of the parents or of the mother. Furthermore, the moral requirements must be safeguarded that there be no complicity in deliberate abortion and that the risk of scandal be avoided. Also, in the case of dead fetuses, as for the corpses of adult persons, all commercial trafficking must be considered illicit and should be prohibited.

Note: Since the terms "research" and "experimentation" are often used equivalently and ambiguously, it is deemed necessary to specify the exact meaning given them in this document.

1) By "research" is meant any inductive-deductive process which aims at promoting the systematic observation of a given phenomenon in the human field or at verifying a hypothesis arising from previous observations.

2) By "experimentation" is meant any research in which the human being (in the various stages of his existence: embryo, fetus, child or adult) represents the object through which or upon which one intends to verify the effect, at present unknown or not sufficiently known, of a given treatment (e.g., pharmacological, teratogenic, surgical, etc.).

5. How is one to evaluate morally the use for research purposes of embryos obtained by fertilization "in vitro?"

Human embryos obtained "in vitro" are human beings and subjects with rights: Their dignity and right to life must be respected from the first moment of their existence. It is immoral to produce human embryos destined to be exploited as disposable "biological material."

In the usual practice of "in vitro" fertilization, not all of the embryos are transferred to the woman's body; some are destroyed. Just as the Church condemns induced abortion, so she also forbids acts against the life of these human beings. It is a duty to condemn the particular gravity of the voluntary destruction of human embryos obtained "in vitro" for the sole purpose of research, either by means of artificial insemination or by means of "twin fission." By acting in this way the researcher usurps the place of God; and, even though he may be unaware of this, he sets himself up as the master of the destiny of others inasmuch as he arbitrarily chooses whom he will allow to live and whom he will send to death and kills defenseless human beings.

Methods of observation or experimentation which damage or impose grave and disproportionate risks upon embryos obtained "in vitro" are morally illicit for the same reasons. Every human being is to be respected for himself and cannot be reduced in worth to a pure and simple instrument for the advantage of others. It is therefore not in conformity with the moral law deliberately to expose to death human embryos obtained "in vitro." In consequence of the fact that they have been produced "in vitro," those embryos which are not transferred into the body of the mother and are called "spare" are exposed to an absurd fate, with no possibility of their being offered safe means of survival which can be licitly pursued.

6. What judgment should be made on other procedures of manipulating embryos connected with the "techniques of human reproduction?"

Techniques of fertilization "in vitro" can open the way to other forms of biological and genetic manipulation of human embryos, such as attempts or plans for fertilization between human and animal gametes and the gestation of human embryos in the uterus of animals, or the hypothesis or project of constructing artificial uteruses for the human embryo. These procedures are contrary to the human dignity proper to the embryo, and at the same time they are contrary to the right of every person to be conceived and to be born within marriage and from marriage.[32] Also, attempts or hypotheses for obtaining a human being without any connection with sexuality through "twin fission," cloning or parthenogenesis are to be considered contrary to the moral law, since they are in opposition to the dignity both of human procreation and of the conjugal union.

The freezing of embryos, even when carried out in order to preserve the life of an embryo — cryopreservation — constitutes an offense against the respect due to human beings by exposing them to grave risks of death or harm to their physical integrity and depriving them, at least temporarily, of maternal shelter and gestation, thus placing them in a situation in which further offenses and manipulation are possible.

Certain attempts to influence chromosomic or genetic inheritance are not therapeutic, but are aimed at producing human beings selected according to sex or other predetermined qualities. These manipulations are contrary to the personal dignity of the human being and his or her integrity and identity. Therefore in no way can they be justified on the grounds of possible beneficial consequences for future humanity.[33] Every person must be respected for himself. In this consists the dignity and right of every human being from his or her beginning.

II. INTERVENTIONS UPON HUMAN PROCREATION

By "artificial procreation" or "artificial fertilization" are understood here the different technical procedures directed toward obtaining a human conception in a manner other than the sexual union of man and woman. This Instruction deals with fertilization of an ovum in a test tube ("in vitro" fertilization) and artificial insemination through transfer into the woman's genital tracts of previously collected sperm.

A preliminary point for the moral evaluation of such technical procedures is constituted by the consideration of the circumstances and consequences which those procedures involve in relation to the respect due the human embryo. Development of the practice of "in vitro" fertilization has required innumerable fertilizations and destructions of human embryos. Even today, the usual practice presupposes a hyperovulation on the part of the woman: A number of ova are withdrawn, fertilized and then cultivated "in vitro" for some days. Usually not all are transferred into the genital tracts of the woman; some embryos, generally called "spare," are destroyed or frozen. On occasion, some of the implanted embryos are sacrificed for various eugenic, economic or psychological reasons Such deliberate destruction of human beings or their utilization for different purposes to the detriment of their integrity and life is contrary to the doctrine on procured abortion already recalled.

The connection between "in vitro" fertilization and the voluntary destruction of human embryos occurs too often. This is significant:

Through these procedures, with apparently contrary purposes, life and death are subjected to the decision of man, who thus sets himself up as the giver of life and death by decree. This dynamic of violence and domination may remain unnoticed by those very individuals who, in wishing to utilize this procedure, become subject to it themselves. The facts recorded and the cold logic which links them must be taken into consideration for a moral judgment on "in vitro" fertilization and embryo transfer: The abortion mentality which has made this procedure possible thus leads, whether one wants it or not, to man's domination over the life and death of his fellow human beings and can lead to a system of radical eugenics.

Nevertheless, such abuses do not exempt one from a further and thorough ethical study of the techniques of artificial procreation considered in themselves, abstracting as far as possible from the destruction of embryos produced "in vitro."

The present Instruction will therefore take into consideration in the first place the problems posed by heterologous artificial fertilization (II, 1-3) (see Note I), and subsequently those linked with homologous artificial fertilization (II, 4-6) (see Note 2).

Note 1: By the term "heterologous artificial fertilization" or "procreation," the Instruction means techniques used to obtain a human conception artificially by the use of gametes coming from at least one donor other than the spouses who are joined in marriage. Such techniques can be of two types:

a) Heterologous "in vitro" fertilization and embryo transfer: the technique used to obtain a human conception through the meeting "in vitro" of gametes taken from at least one donor other than the two spouses joined in marriage.

b) Heterologous artificial insemination: the technique used to obtain a human conception through the transfer into the genital tracts of the woman of the sperm previously collected from a donor other than the husband.

Note 2: By "artificial homologous fertilization" or "procreation," the Instruction means the technique used to obtain a human conception using the gametes of the two spouses joined in marriage. Homologous artificial fertilization can be carried out by two different methods:

a) Homologous "in vitro" fertilization and embryo transfer: the technique used to obtain a human conception through the meeting "in vitro" of the gametes of the spouses joined in marriage.

b) Homologous artificial insemination: the technique used to obtain a human conception through the transfer into the genital tracts of a married woman of the sperm previously collected from her husband.

Before formulating an ethical judgment on each of these procedures the principles and values which determine the moral evaluation of each of them will be considered.

A. HETEROLOGOUS ARTIFICIAL FERTILIZATION

1. Why must human procreation take place in marriage?

Every human being is always to be accepted as a gift and blessing of God. However, from the moral point of view a truly responsible procreation vis a vis the unborn child must be the fruit of marriage.

For human procreation has specific characteristics by virtue of the personal dignity of the parents and of the children: The procreation of a new person, whereby the man and the woman collaborate with the power of the Creator, must be the fruit and the sign of the mutual self-giving of the spouses, of their love and of their fidelity.[34] The fidelity of the spouses in the unity of marriage involves reciprocal respect of their right to become a father and a mother only through each other.

The child has the right to be conceived, carried in the womb, brought into the world and brought up within marriage: It is through the secure and recognized relationship to his own parents that the child can discover his own identity and achieve his own proper human development.

The parents find in their child a confirmation and completion of their reciprocal self-giving: The child is the living image of their love, the permanent sign of their conjugal union, the living and indissoluble concrete expression of their paternity and maternity.[35]

By reason of the vocation and social responsibilities of the person, the good of the children and of the parents contributes to the good of civil society; the vitality and stability of society require that children come into the world within a family and that the family be firmly based on marriage.

The tradition of the Church and anthropological reflection recognize in marriage and in its indissoluble unity the only setting worthy of truly responsible procreation.

2. Does heterologous artificial fertilization conform to the dignity of the couple and to the truth of marriage?

Through "in vitro" fertilization and embryo transfer and heterologous artificial insemination human conception is achieved through the fusion of gametes of at least one donor other than the spouses who are united in marriage. Heterologous artificial fertilization is contrary to the unity of marriage, to the dignity of the spouses, to the vocation proper to parents, and to the child's right to be conceived and brought into the world in marriage and from marriage.[36]

Respect for the unity of marriage and for conjugal fidelity demands that the child be conceived in marriage; the bond existing between husband and wife accords the spouses, in an objective and inalienable manner, the exclusive right to become father and mother solely through each other.[37]

Recourse to the gametes of a third person in order to have sperm or ovum available constitutes a violation of the reciprocal commitment of the spouses and a grave lack in regard to that essential property of marriage which is its unity.

Heterologous artificial fertilization violates the rights of the child: It deprives him of his filial relationship with his parental origins and can hinder the maturing of his personal identity. Furthermore it offends the common vocation of the spouses who are called to fatherhood and motherhood. It objectively deprives conjugal fruitfulness of its unity and integrity; it brings about and manifests a rupture between genetic parenthood, gestational parenthood and responsibility for upbringing. Such damage to the personal relationships within the family has repercussions on civil society: What threatens the unity and stability of the family is a source of dissension, disorder and injustice in the whole of social life.

These reasons lead to a negative moral judgment concerning heterologous artificial fertilization: Consequently, fertilization of a married woman with the sperm of a donor different from her husband and fertilization with the husband's sperm of an ovum not coming from his wife are morally illicit. Furthermore, the artificial fertilization of a woman who is unmarried or a widow, whoever the donor may be, cannot be morally justified.

The desire to have a child and the love between spouses who long to obviate a sterility which cannot be overcome in any other way constitute understandable motivations; but subjectively good intentions do not render heterologous artificial fertilization conformable to the objective and inalienable properties of marriage or respectful of the rights of the child and of the spouses.

3. Is "surrogate" (see note) motherhood morally licit?

No, for the same reasons which lead one to reject heterologous artificial fertilization: For it is contrary to the unity of marriage and to the dignity of the procreation of the human person.

Surrogate motherhood represents an objective failure to meet the obligations of maternal love, of conjugal fidelity and of responsible motherhood; it offends the dignity and the right of the child to be conceived, carried in the womb, brought into the world and brought up by his own parents; it sets up, to the detriment of families, a division between the physical, psychological and moral elements which constitute those families.

Note: By "surrogate mother" the Instruction means:

a) The woman who carries in pregnancy an embryo implanted in her uterus and who is genetically a stranger to the embryo because it has been obtained through the union of the gametes of "donors." She carries the pregnancy with a pledge to surrender the baby once it is born to the party who commissioned or made the agreement for the pregnancy.

b) The woman who carries in pregnancy an embryo to whose procreation she has contributed the donation of her own ovum, fertilized through insemination with the sperm of a man other than her husband. She carries the pregnancy with a pledge to surrender the child once it is born to the party who commissioned or made the agreement for the pregnancy.

B. HOMOLOGOUS ARTIFICIAL FERTILIZATION

Since heterologous artificial fertilization has been declared unacceptable, the question arises of how to evaluate morally the process of homologous artificial fertilization: "in vitro" fertilization and embryo transfer and artificial insemination between husband and wife. First a question of principle must be clarified.

4. What connection is required from the moral point of view between procreation and the conjugal act?

a) The Church's teaching on marriage and human procreation affirms the "inseparable connection, willed by God and unable to be broken by man on his own initiative, between the two meanings of the conjugal act: the unitive meaning and the procreative meaning. Indeed, by its intimate structure the conjugal act, while most closely uniting husband and wife, capacitates them for the generation of new lives according to laws inscribed in the very being of man and of woman."[38] This principle, which is based upon the nature of marriage and the intimate connection of the goods of marriage, has well-known consequences on the level of responsible fatherhood and motherhood. "By safeguarding both these essential aspects, the unitive and the procreative, the conjugal act preserves in its fullness the sense of true mutual love and its ordination toward man's exalted vocation to parenthood."[39]

The same doctrine concerning the link between the meanings of the conjugal act and between the goods of marriage throws light on the moral problem of homologous artificial fertilization, since "it is never permitted to separate these different aspects to such a degree as positively to exclude either the procreative intention or the conjugal relation."[40]

Contraception deliberately deprives the conjugal act of its openness to procreation and in this way brings about a voluntary dissociation of the ends of marriage. Homologous artificial fertilization, in seeking a procreation which is not the fruit of a specific act of conjugal union, objectively effects an analogous separation between the goods and the meanings of marriage.

Thus, fertilization is licitly sought when it is the result of a "conjugal act which is per se suitable for the generation of children, to which marriage is ordered by its nature and by which the spouses become one flesh."[41] But from the moral point of view procreation is deprived of its proper perfection when it is not desired as the fruit of the conjugal act, that is to say, of the specific act of the spouses' union.

b) The moral value of the intimate link between the goods of marriage and between the meanings of the conjugal act is based upon the unity of the human being, a unity involving body and spiritual soul.[42] Spouses mutually express their personal love in the "language of the body," which clearly involves both "spousal meanings" and parental ones.[43] The conjugal act by which the couple mutually express their self-gift at the same time expresses openness to the gift of life. It is an act that is inseparably corporal and spiritual. It is in their bodies and through their bodies that the spouses consummate their marriage and are able to become father and mother. In order to respect the language of their bodies and their natural generosity, the conjugal union must take place with respect for its openness to procreation; and the procreation of a person must be the fruit and the result of married love. The origin of the human being thus follows from a procreation that is "linked to the union, not only biological but also spiritual, of the parents, made one by the bond of marriage."[44] Fertilization achieved outside the bodies of the couple remains by this very fact deprived of the meanings and the values which are expressed in the language of the body and in the union of human persons.

c) Only respect for the link between the meanings of the conjugal act and respect for the unity of the human being make possible procreation in conformity with the dignity of the person. In his unique and irrepeatable origin, the child must be respected and recognized as equal in personal dignity to those who give him life. The human person must be accepted in his parents' act of union and love; the generation of a child must therefore be the fruit of that mutual giving[45] which is realized in the conjugal act wherein the spouses cooperate as servants and not as masters in the work of the Creator, who is love.[46]

In reality, the origin of a human person is the result of an act of giving. The one conceived must be the fruit of his parents' love. He cannot be desired or conceived as the product of an intervention of medical or biological techniques; that would be equivalent to reducing him to an object of scientific technology. No one may subject the coming of a child into the world to conditions of technical efficiency which are to be evaluated according to standards of control and dominion.

The moral relevance of the link between the meanings of the conjugal act and between the goods of marriage, as well as the unity of the human being and the dignity of his origin, demand that the procreation of a human person be brought about as the fruit of the conjugal act specific to the love between spouses. The link between procreation and the conjugal act is thus shown to be of great importance on the anthropological and moral planes, and it throws light on the positions of the Magisterium with regard to homologous artificial fertilization.

5. Is homologous "in vitro" fertilization morally licit?

The answer to this question is strictly dependent on the principles just mentioned. Certainly one cannot ignore the legitimate aspirations of sterile couples. For some, recourse to homologous "in vitro" fertilization and embryo transfer appears to be the only way of fulfilling their sincere desire for a child. The question is asked whether the totality of conjugal life in such situations is not sufficient to ensure the dignity proper to human procreation. It is acknowledged that "in vitro" fertilization and embryo transfer certainly cannot supply for the absence of sexual relations[47] and cannot be preferred to the specific acts of conjugal union, given the risks involved for the child and the difficulties of the procedure. But it is asked whether, when there is no other way of overcoming the sterility which is a source of suffering, homologous "in vitro" fertilization may not constitute an aid, if not a form of therapy, whereby its moral licitness could be admitted.

The desire for a child — or at the very least an openness to the transmission of life — is a necessary prerequisite from the moral point of view for responsible human procreation. But this good intention is not sufficient for making a positive moral evaluation of "in vitro" fertilization between spouses. The process of "in vitro" fertilization and embryo transfer must be judged in itself and cannot borrow its definitive moral quality from the totality of conjugal life of which it becomes part nor from the conjugal acts which may precede or follow it.[48]

It has already been recalled that in the circumstances in which it is regularly practiced "in vitro" fertilization and embryo transfer involves the destruction of human beings, which is something contrary to the doctrine on the illicitness of abortion previously mentioned.[49] But even in a situation in which every precaution were taken to avoid the death of human embryos, homologous "in vitro" fertilization and embryo transfer dissociates from the conjugal act the actions which are directed to human fertilization. For this reason the very nature of homologous "in vitro" fertilization and embryo transfer also must be taken into account, even abstracting from the link with procured abortion.

Homologous "in vitro" fertilization and embryo transfer is brought about outside the bodies of the couple through actions of third parties whose competence and technical activity determine the success of the procedure. Such fertilization entrusts the life and identity of the embryo into the power of doctors and biologists and establishes the domination of technology over the origin and destiny of the human person. Such a relationship of domination is in itself contrary to the dignity and equality that must be common to parents and children.

Conception "in vitro" is the result of the technical action which presides over fertilization. Such fertilization is neither in fact achieved nor positively willed as the expression and fruit of a specific act of the conjugal union. In homologous "in vitro" fertilization and embryo transfer, therefore, even if it is considered in the context of de facto existing sexual relations, the generation of the human person is objectively deprived of its proper perfection: namely, that of being the result and fruit of a conjugal act in which the spouses can become "cooperators with God for giving life to a new person."[50]

These reasons enable us to understand why the act of conjugal love is considered in the teaching of the Church as the only setting worthy of human procreation. For the same reasons the so-called "simple case," i.e., a homologous "in vitro" fertilization and embryo transfer procedure that is free of any compromise with the abortive practice of destroying embryos and with masturbation, remains a technique which is morally illicit because it deprives human procreation of the dignity which is proper and connatural to it.

Certainly, homologous "in vitro" fertilization and embryo transfer fertilization is not marked by all that ethical negativity found in extraconjugal procreation; the family and marriage continue to constitute the setting for the birth and upbringing of the children. Nevertheless, in conformity with the traditional doctrine relating to the goods of marriage and the dignity of the person, the Church remains opposed from the moral point of view to homologous "in vitro" fertilization. Such fertilization is in itself illicit and in opposition to the dignity of procreation and of the conjugal union, even when everything is done to avoid the death of the human embryo.

Although the manner in which human conception is achieved with "in vitro" fertilization and embryo transfer cannot be approved, every child which comes into the world must in any case be accepted as a living gift of the divine Goodness and must be brought up with love.

6. How is homologous artificial insemination to be evaluated from the moral point of view?

Homologous artificial insemination within marriage cannot be admitted except for those cases in which the technical means is not a substitute for the conjugal act but serves to facilitate and to help so that the act attains its natural purpose.

The teaching of the Magisterium on this point has already been stated.[51] This teaching is not just an expression of particular historical circumstances, but is based on the Church's doctrine concerning the connection between the conjugal union and procreation and on a consideration of the personal nature of the conjugal act and of human procreation. "In its natural structure, the conjugal act is a personal action, a simultaneous and immediate cooperation on the part of the husband and wife, which by the very nature of the agents and the proper nature of the act is the expression of the mutual gift which, according to the words of Scripture, brings about union 'in one flesh.'"[52] Thus moral conscience "does not necessarily proscribe the use of certain artificial means destined solely either to the facilitating of the natural act or to ensuring that the natural act normally performed achieves its proper end."[53] If the technical means facilitates the conjugal act or helps it to reach its natural objectives, it can be morally acceptable. If, on the other hand, the procedure were to replace the conjugal act, it is morally illicit.

Artificial insemination as a substitute for the conjugal act is prohibited by reason of the voluntarily achieved dissociation of the two meanings of the conjugal act. Masturbation, through which the sperm is normally obtained, is another sign of this dissociation: Even when it is done for the purpose of procreation the act remains deprived of its ultimate meaning: "It lacks the sexual relationship called for by the moral order, namely the relationship which realizes 'the full sense of mutual self-giving and human procreation in the context of true love.'"[54]

7. What moral criterion can be proposed with regard to medical intervention in human procreation?

The medical act must be evaluated not only with reference to its technical dimension, but also and above all in relation to its goal, which is the good of persons and their bodily and psychological health. The moral criteria for medical intervention in procreation are deduced from the dignity of human persons, of their sexuality and of their origin.

Medicine which seeks to be ordered to the integral good of the person must respect the specifically human values of sexuality.[55] The doctor is at the service of persons and of human procreation. He does not have the authority to dispose of them or to decide their fate. A medical intervention respects the dignity of persons when it seeks to assist the conjugal act either in order to facilitate its performance or in order to enable it to achieve its objective once it has been normally performed.[56]

On the other hand, it sometimes happens that a medical procedure technologically replaces the conjugal act in order to obtain a procreation which is neither its result nor its fruit. In this case the medical act is not, as it should be, at the service of conjugal union, but rather appropriates to itself the procreative function and thus contradicts the dignity and the inalienable rights of the spouses and of the child to be born.

The humanization of medicine, which is insisted upon today by everyone, requires respect for the integral dignity of the human person first of all in the act and at the moment in which the spouses transmit life to a new person. It is only logical therefore to address an urgent appeal to Catholic doctors and scientists that they bear exemplary witness to the respect due to the human embryo and to the dignity of procreation. The medical and nursing staff of Catholic hospitals and clinics are in a special way urged to do justice to the moral obligations which they have assumed, frequently also, as part of their contract. Those who are in charge of Catholic hospitals and clinics and who are often Religious will take special care to safeguard and promote a diligent observance of the moral norms recalled in the present Instruction.

8. The suffering caused by infertility in marriage.

The suffering of spouses who cannot have children or who are afraid of bringing a handicapped child into the world is a suffering that everyone must understand and properly evaluate.

On the part of the spouses, the desire for a child is natural: It expresses the vocation to fatherhood and motherhood inscribed in conjugal love. This desire can be even stronger if the couple is affected by sterility which appears incurable. Nevertheless, marriage does not confer upon the spouses the right to have a child, but only the right to perform those natural acts which are per se ordered to procreation.[57]

A true and proper right to a child would be contrary to the child's dignity and nature. The child is not an object to which one has a right nor can he be considered as an object of ownership: Rather, a child is a gift, "the supreme gift"[58] and the most gratuitous gift of marriage, and is a living testimony of the mutual giving of his parents. For this reason, the child has the right as already mentioned, to be the fruit of the specific act of the conjugal love of his parents; and he also has the right to be respected as a person from the moment of his conception. Nevertheless, whatever its cause or prognosis, sterility is certainly a difficult trial. The community of believers is called to shed light upon and support the suffering of those who are unable to fulfill their legitimate aspiration to motherhood and fatherhood. Spouses who find themselves in this sad situation are called to find in it an opportunity for sharing in a particular way in the Lord's cross, the source of spiritual fruitfulness. Sterile couples must not forget that "even when procreation is not possible, conjugal life does not for this reason lose its value. Physical sterility in fact can be for spouses the occasion for other important services to the life of the human person, for example, adoption, various forms of educational work and assistance to other families and to poor or handicapped children."[59]

Many researchers are engaged in the fight against sterility. While fully safeguarding the dignity of human procreation, some have achieved results which previously seemed unattainable. Scientists therefore are to be encouraged to continue their research with the aim of preventing the causes of sterility and of being able to remedy them so that sterile couples will be able to procreate in full respect for their own personal dignity and that of the child to be born.

III. MORAL AND CIVIL LAW

The Values and Moral Obligations That Civil Legislation Must Respect and Sanction in This Matter

The inviolable right to life of every innocent human individual and the rights of the family and of the institution of marriage constitute fundamental moral values because they concern the natural condition and integral vocation of the human person; at the same time they are constitutive elements of civil society and its order. For this reason the new technological possibilities which have opened up in the field of biomedicine require the intervention of the political authorities and of the legislator, since an uncontrolled application of such techniques could lead to unforeseeable and damaging consequences for civil society. Recourse to the conscience of each individual and to the self-regulation of researchers cannot be sufficient for ensuring respect for personal rights and public order. If the legislator responsible for the common good were not watchful, he could be deprived of his prerogatives by researchers claiming to govern humanity in the name of the biological discoveries and the alleged "improvement" processes which they would draw from those discoveries. "Eugenism" and forms of discrimination between human beings could come to be legitimized: This would constitute an act of violence and a serious offense to the equality, dignity and fundamental rights of the human person.

The intervention of the public authority must be inspired by the rational principles which regulate the relationships between civil law and moral law. The task of the civil law is to ensure the common good of people through the recognition of and the defense of fundamental rights and through the promotion of peace and of public morality.[60] In no sphere of life can the civil law take the place of conscience or dictate norms concerning things which are outside its competence. It must sometimes tolerate, for the sake of public order, things which it cannot forbid without a greater evil resulting. However, the inalienable rights of the person must be recognized and respected by civil society and the political authority. These human rights depend neither on single individuals nor on parents; nor do they represent a concession made by society and the state: They pertain to human nature and are inherent in the person by virtue of the creative act from which the person took his or her origin.

Among such fundamental rights one should mention in this regard:

a) every human being's right to life and physical integrity from the moment of conception until death;

b) the rights of the family and of marriage as an institution and, in this area, the child's right to be conceived, brought into the world and brought up by his parents. To each of these two themes it is necessary here to give some further consideration.

In various States (Nations) certain laws have authorized the direct suppression of innocents: The moment a positive law deprives a category of human beings of the protection which civil legislation must accord them, the state is denying the equality of all before the law. When the state does not place its power at the service of the rights of each citizen, and in particular of the more vulnerable, the very foundations of a state based on law are undermined. The political authority consequently cannot give approval to the calling of human beings into existence through procedures which would expose them to those very grave risks noted previously. The possible recognition by positive law and the political authorities of techniques of artificial transmission of life and the experimentation connected with it would widen the breach already opened by the legalization of abortion.

As a consequence of the respect and protection which must be ensured for the unborn child from the moment of his conception, the law must provide appropriate penal sanctions for every deliberate violation of the child's rights. The law cannot tolerate—indeed it must expressly forbid—that human beings, even at the embryonic stage, should be treated as objects of experimentation, be mutilated or destroyed with the excuse that they are superfluous or incapable of developing normally.

The political authority is bound to guarantee to the institution of the family, upon which society is based, the juridical protection to which it has a right. From the very fact that it is at the service of people, the political authority must also be at the service of the family. Civil law cannot grant approval to techniques of artificial procreation which, for the benefit of third parties (doctors, biologists, economic or governmental powers), take away what is a right inherent in the relationship between spouses; and therefore civil law cannot legalize the donation of gametes between persons who are not legitimately united in marriage.

Legislation must also prohibit, by virtue of the support which is due to the family, embryo banks, post-mortem insemination and "surrogate motherhood."

It is part of the duty of the public authority to ensure that the civil law is regulated according to the fundamental norms of the moral law in matters concerning human rights, human life and the institution of the family. Politicians must commit themselves, through their interventions upon public opinion, to securing in society the widest possible consensus on such essential points and to consolidating this consensus wherever it risks being weakened or is in danger of collapse.

In many countries the legalization of abortion and juridical tolerance of unmarried couples makes it more difficult to secure respect for the fundamental rights recalled by this Instruction. It is to be hoped that states will not become responsible for aggravating these socially damaging situations of injustice. It is rather to be hoped that nations and states will realize all the cultural, ideological and political implications connected with the techniques of artificial procreation and will find the wisdom and courage necessary for issuing laws which are more just and more respectful of human life and the institution of the family.

The civil legislation of many states confers an undue legitimation upon certain practices in the eyes of many today; it is seen to be incapable of guaranteeing that morality which is in conformity with the natural exigencies of the human person and with the "unwritten laws" etched by the Creator upon the human heart. All men of good will must commit themselves, particularly within their professional field and in the exercise of their civil rights, to ensuring the reform of morally unacceptable civil laws and the correction of illicit practices. In addition, "conscientious objection" vis a vis such laws must be supported and recognized. A movement of passive resistance to the legitimation of practices contrary to human life and dignity is beginning to make an ever sharper impression upon the moral conscience of many, especially among specialists in the biomedical sciences.

CONCLUSION

The spread of technologies of intervention in the processes of human procreation raises very serious moral problems in relation to the respect due to the human being from the moment of conception, to the dignity of the person, of his or her sexuality and of the transmission of life.

With this Instruction the Congregation for the Doctrine of the Faith, in fulfilling its responsibility to promote and defend the Church's teaching in so serious a matter, addresses a new and heartfelt invitation to all those who, by reason of their role and their commitment, can exercise a positive influence and ensure that in the family and in society due respect is accorded to life and love. It addresses this invitation to those responsible for the formation of consciences and of public opinion, to scientists and medical professionals, to jurists and politicians. It hopes that all will understand the incompatibility between recognition of the dignity of the human person and contempt for life and love, between faith in the living God and the claim to decide arbitrarily the origin and fate of a human being.

In particular, the Congregation for the Doctrine of the Faith addresses an invitation with confidence and encouragement to theologians, and above all to moralists, that they study more deeply and make ever more accessible to the faithful the contents of the teaching of the Church's Magisterium in the light of a valid anthropology in the matter of sexuality and marriage and in the context of the necessary interdisciplinary approach. Thus they will make it possible to understand ever more clearly the reasons for and the validity of this teaching. By defending man against the excesses of his own power, the Church of God reminds him of the reasons for his true nobility; only in this way can the possibility of living and loving with that dignity and liberty which derive from respect for the truth be ensured for the men and women of tomorrow. The precise indications which are offered in the present Instruction therefore are not meant to halt the effort of reflection, but rather to give it a renewed impulse in unrenounceable fidelity to the teaching of the Church.

In the light of the truth about the gift of human life and in the light of the moral principles which flow from that truth, everyone is invited to act in the area of responsibility proper to each and, like the Good Samaritan, to recognize as a neighbor even the littlest among the children of men (cf. Lk 10:29-37). Here Christ's words find a new and particular echo: "What you do to one of the least of my brethren, you do unto me" (Mt 25:40).

During an audience granted to the undersigned prefect after the plenary session of the Congregation for the Doctrine of the Faith, the Supreme Pontiff, John Paul II, approved this Instruction and ordered it to be published.

Given at Rome, from the Congregation for the Doctrine of the Faith, Feb. 22, 1987, the Feast of the Chair of St. Peter, the Apostle.

Cardinal Joseph Ratzinger,
Prefect
Archbishop Alberto Bovone,
Secretary

GYNETECH DIRECTORY: Programs and Services

*T*he following directory has been included to increase public awareness of the current extent of gynetech-oriented programs and to encourage people to actively oppose the promotion of dehumanizing procedures and techniques, and to join others in standing against the medical crisis facing women today.

TARGET ORGANIZATIONS

Abortion Rights Mobilization (ARM), 175 Fifth Ave., New York, NY 10010. (212) 677-0412. Organization formed to implement and promote Supreme Court's 1973 decisions on abortion; focuses on litigation and lobbying.

Alan Guttmacher Institute, 111 Fifth Ave., New York, NY 10022. Founded by one of the early proponents of Planned Parenthood, Dr. Alan Guttmacher; studies trends in human population groups.

American Association of Tissue Banks, 12111 Parklawn Dr., Rockland, MD 20852. (301) 738-0600. Sets standards for sperm banks and, will eventually, for egg and embryo banks.

American Civil Liberties Union's (ACLU's), Foundation Reproductive Freedom Project, 132 West 43rd St., New York, NY 10036. (212) 944-9800. Handles lawsuits related to abortion and publishes a variety of pamphlets promoting abortion on demand as a constitutional issue.

American College of Obstetricians and Gynecologists, 600 Maryland Ave., S.E., Suite 300, Washington, DC 20024. Key organization involved in promoting high-tech, expensive solutions to birth, infertility, family planning, and other women's health issues.

American Fertility Society, 1608 Thirteenth Ave. South, Suite 101, Birmingham, AL 35205. Offers referrals to infertility specialists and reproductive endocrinologists; promotes assisted conception techniques; publishes the journal *Fertility and Sterility*.

Biogenetics Corporation, 950 Sanford Ave., Irvington, NJ 07111. Toll free number: (800) 942-4646. Sperm bank.

Catholics for a Free Choice, 2008 Seventeenth St. N.W., Washington, DC. (202) 638-1706. Trains counselors to process Catholic women for abortion.

Center for Reproductive Alternatives, 3333 Vincent Rd., Suite 222, Pleasant Hill, CA 94523. (415) 930-6220. Donor insemination program.

Committee to Defend Reproductive Rights (CDRR), 2845 24th St., San Francisco, CA 94110. (415) 826-4401. Educates groups to organize within their communities and to use the media effectively to promote abortion.

Fenway Community Health Center Insemination Project, 16 Haviland St., Boston, MA 02115. (617) 267-7573. Sponsors insemination service; provides related information.

Fertility & Genetics Research, Inc., 624 South Grand Ave., Suite 2900, Los Angeles, CA 90017. Corporation promoting franchised embryo flushing and transplantation as a solution to infertility and genetic problems; founded by Richard and Randolph Seed in 1978.

Fertility Center of California, 1125 East Seventeenth St., #120, Santa Ana, CA 92701. (714) 953-4683. Offers insemination service and information for single and married women; support groups.

Fertility Selections, 4639 Main St., Bridgeport, CT 06606. Performs Ericsson serum albumin technique to favor conception of a male child; is researching techniques to enhance female conception.

Gametrin, Ltd., 475 Gates Rd., P.O. Box 1507, Sausalito, CA 94966. (415) 332-3141. Performs albumin gradient selection on semen.

Idant Laboratories, 645 Madison Ave., New York, NY 10022 (212) 935-1430. The nation's largest sperm bank; infertility clinic.

Lesbian Mother National Defense Fund, P.O. Box 21567, Seattle, WA 98111. Sells artificial insemination packet for ten dollars with articles supporting the reproductive right of lesbians; donor insemination consent forms.

Lesbian Rights Project, 1370 Mission St., San Francisco, CA 94103. Advocates reproductive rights for lesbians, especially donor insemination.

Lesbians Choosing Children Network, 46 Pleasant St., Cambridge, MA 02139. (617) 354-8807. Offers information and support for lesbians choosing donor insemination.

Los Angeles Fertility Institute, 435 North Bedford Dr., Beverly Hills, CA 90210. Gives information and assistance to couples considering reproductive alternatives.

March of Dimes Birth Defects Foundation, 1275 Mamaronek Ave., White Plains, NY 10605. Provides grant money to eugenic projects; makes referrals for genetic diagnosis.

National Abortion Federation (NAF), 900 Pennsylvania Ave. S.E., Washington, DC 20003. *National Abortion Federation Hotline*, 1-800-772-9100 (in Washington, DC, 202-546-9060). Provides information on abortion clinics and doctors who perform abortions; geared toward networking among members (physicians, clinics, Planned Parenthood); holds training seminars to ease medical professionals' entrance into the abortion industry and gives "public action" seminars to promote abortion among nonprofessionals; publishes newsletter.

National Abortion Rights Action League (NARAL), 1424 K St. N.W., Washington, DC 20005. (202) 347-2279. Single-issue political lobbying organization which publishes legislative updates on pro-abortion topics, a newsletter and pamphlets, raises funds for pro-abortion political candidates; connects with media to influence public opinion related to the abortion industry; persuades women to view abortion as a sane solution to an unwanted pregnancy rather than to see it as the invasive medical procedure and unforgettable womb assault it actually is.

National Genetics Foundation, 555 West 57th St., New York, NY 10019. Provides list of genetic counseling centers, promotes the concept of eugenic abortion by publicizing the availability and desirability of genetic diagnosis; emphasizes mother's responsibility to make an informed decision regarding her child's fate.

National Organization for Women (NOW) Action Center, 425 Thirteenth St. N.W., Suite 723, Washington, DC 20004. (202) 347-2279. Mobilizes community level support for reproductive choice as a major priority; offers Reproductive Rights Resource Kit and a variety of pamphlets, thereby ironically dehumanizing and betraying woman's biological integrity. Promotes the devaluation of uterine capability and the desecration of life within the womb through abortion on demand.

National Research Foundation for Fertility, 53 East 96th St., New York, NY 10128.

National Women's Health Network (NWHN), 224 Seventh St., S.E., Washington, DC 20003. (202) 543-9222. Offers an Abortion Rights Organizers Kit, publishes a newsletter, maintains national network of communications regarding abortion-related issues and legislation, and assists groups with local organizing through the NWHN Abortion Rights Project.

Oakland Feminists' Women's Health Center, 2930 McClure St., Oakland, CA 94609. (415) 444-5676. Offers woman-controlled donor insemination; sperm bank.

Planned Parenthood Federation of America, 810 Seventh Ave., New York, NY 10019. Now known for its sex education and birth control programs, PP was founded upon eugenic (selective breeding) principles; promotes abortion, sterilization, and genetic diagnosis.

Religious Coalition for Abortion Rights (RCAR), 100 Maryland Ave. N.E., Suite 307, Washington, DC 20002. (202) 543-7032. Organization of thirty-one denominations promoting abortion; gives mixed messages on the value of the womb and the reality of abortion trauma and its effects on reproductive integrity; promotes uterine desecration by popularizing contemporary myths related to the concept of reproductive choice.

Repository for Germinal Choice, 450 Escondido Blvd., Escondido, CA 92025. (619) 743-0772. "Super-baby" sperm bank started by millionaire follower of eugenics proponent Hermann J. Muller; uses elite donors only.

Reproductive Rights National Network (R2N2), 17 Murray St., Fifth Floor, New York, NY 10007. (212) 267-0412. Joins reproductive rights groups from around the country through distribution of a national newsletter, bumper stickers, pamphlets, and buttons; seventy groups currently are active members of R2N2.

Southern California Cryobank, Inc., 2080 Century Park East, Suite 308, Los Angeles, CA 90067. (213) 553-9828. Sperm bank.

Xytex Corporation, 1519-A Laney-Walker Blvd., Augusta, GA 30904. Toll free number: (800) 241-9722. Sperm bank.

IVF/ET CLINICS

ALABAMA

IVF Australia at Birmingham
Women's Medical Plaza, Suite 508
2006 Brookwood Medical Center Dr.
Birmingham, AL 35209
(205) 870-9784

University of Alabama-Birmingham Medical Center
Laboratory for IVF-ET
547 Old Hillman Building, University Station
Birmingham, AL 35294
(205) 934-5631

IVF/GIFT Program
University of South Alabama
Room 326
Mobile, AL 36688
(205) 460-7173

ARIZONA

Arizona Center for Fertility Studies
IVF Program
4614 East Shea Blvd., D-260
Phoenix, AZ 85028
(602) 996-7896

Arizona Fertility Institute
2850 North 24th St., Suite 500A
Phoenix, AZ 85008
(602) 468-3840

Phoenix Fertility Institute
Good Samaritan Hospital
1300 North Twelfth St., Suite 522
Phoenix, AZ 85006
(602) 252-8628

The Reproductive Institute of Tucson
El Dorado Medical Center
Tucson Medical Center, Building 800
5200 East Grant Rd.
Tucson, AZ 85712
(602) 325-0802

CALIFORNIA

Alta Bates Hospital
IVF Program
3001 Colby St.
Berkeley, CA 94705
(415) 540-1416

*Berkeley-East Bay Advanced
Reproductive Service*
2999 Regent St., Suite 201
Berkeley, CA 94705
(415) 841-5510

*Central California In Vitro
Fertilization Program*
Fresno Community Hospital
P. O. Box 1232
Fresno, CA 93715
(202) 439-1914

Fertility Institute of San Diego
Sharp/Children's Medical Center
9834 Genessee Ave., Suite 300
La Jolla, CA 92037
(619) 457-8680

*Scripps Clinic and Research
Foundation*
10666 North Torrey Pines Rd.
La Jolla, CA 92037
(619) 457-8680

*University of California at Irvine
Memorial Hospital*
2880 Atlantic Ave., Suite 220
Long Beach, CA 90806
(213) 595-2229

Beverly Hills Medical Center*
Department of Ob/Gyn
1177 South Beverly Dr.
Los Angeles, CA 90024

*California Reproductive Health
Institute*
Division of IVF
California Medical Hospital
1338 South Hope St.
Los Angeles, CA 90015
(213) 742-5970

Cedars-Sinai Medical Center
444 San Vicente Blvd., Suite 1101
Los Angeles, CA 90045
(213) 855-2150

Century City Hospital
2070 Century Park East
Los Angeles, CA 90067
(213) 201-6604

Southern California Fertility Institute
California Institute for In Vitro
Fertilization, Inc.
Right to Parenthood
12301 Wilshire Blvd., Suite 415
Los Angeles, CA 90025
(213) 820-3723

Tyler Medical Clinic
921 Westwood Blvd.
Los Angeles, CA 90024
(213) 208-6765

University of California — Los Angeles
School of Medicine
Department of Ob/Gyn: IVF Program
Los Angeles, CA 90024
(213) 825-7755

*Northridge Hospital Medical Center**
IVF Program
18300 Roscoe Blvd.
Northridge, CA 91328

University of California — Irvine
Department of Ob/Gyn
101 The City Dr.
Orange, CA 92668
(714) 638-1500

South Bay-AMI Hospital
IVF Center
415 North Prospect Ave.
Redondo Beach, CA 95825
(213) 318-4741

Northern California Fertility Center
87 Scripps Dr., Suite 202
Sacramento, CA 95825
(916) 929-3596

Pacific Fertility Center
2100 Webster St., Suite 220
San Francisco, CA 94120
(415) 923-3344

University of California, San
Francisco IVF Program
Department of Ob/Gyn and
Reproductive Sciences

Room M 1480
San Francisco, CA 94143
(415) 666-1824

Stanford University
Department of Ob/Gyn
S-385 Medical Center
Stanford, CA 94305
(415) 723-5251

Fertility Medical Group in the Valley
IVF Program-Northridge Hospital
18370 Burbank Blvd., Suite 301
Tarzana, CA 91356
(818) 946-2289

*UCLA-Harbor**
Department of Ob/Gyn
1000 West Carson D-3
Torrance, CA 905089

John Muir Memorial Hospital
Department of Ob/Gyn: IVF Program
1601 Ygnacio Valley Rd.
Walnut Creek, CA 94598
(415) 937-6166

Whittier Hospital Medical Center
The Genesis Program for In Vitro
Fertilization
Center for Human Development
15151 Janine Dr.
Whittier, CA 90605
(213) 945-3561, ext. 549

CANADA

University of Calgary
IVF Program
3330 Hospital Dr. N.W.
Calgary, Alberta
Canada T2N 4N1

University of British Columbia
Grace Hospital
Department of Ob/Gyn
4490 Oak St.
Vancouver, British Columbia
Canada V6H 3V5

Dalhousie University
IVF Programme
c/o Endocrine and Infertility Centre
5821 University Ave.
Halifax, Nova Scotia
Canada B3H 1W3

University Hospital
University of Western Ontario
IVF Program
339 Windemere Rd.
London, Ontario
Canada N6A 5A5

Toronto East General Hospital
LIFE Program
825 Coxwell Ave.
Toronto, Ontario
Canada M4C 3G2

*Le Centre Hospitalier de l'Universite
Laval*
La consultation de Fertilite, F. East C.
2705 Blvd. Lauirier
Ste. Foy, Quebec
Canada G1V 4G2

COLORADO

Reproductive Genetics In Vitro PC
455 South Hudson St.
Level Three
Denver, CO 80222
(303) 399-1464

*University of Colorado Health
Sciences Center*
IVF Program
4200 East Ninth Ave.
Box B198
Denver, CO 80262
(303) 394-8365

CONNECTICUT

*University of Connecticut Health
Center*
Division of Reproductive
Endocrinology & Infertility
Farmington, CT 06790
(203) 674-2110

Mount Sinai Hospital
Department of Ob/Gyn
Division of Reproductive
Endocrinology and Infertility
675 Tower Ave.
Hartford, CT 06112
(203) 242-6201

Yale University Medical Center
Department of Ob/Gyn: IVF Program
333 Cedar St.
New Haven, CT 06510
(203) 785-4019, 785-4792

DELAWARE

The Medical Center of Delaware
Reproductive Endocrinology and
Infertility Center
P. O. Box 6001
4755 Stanton-Ogletown Rd.
Newark, DE 19718
(302) 733-2318

DISTRICT OF COLUMBIA

Columbia Hospital for Women
Medical Center
IVF Program
2425 L St., N.W.
Washington, DC 20037
(202) 293-6500

George Washington University
Medical Center
Department of Ob/Gyn: IVF Program
901 23rd St., N.W.
Washington, DC 20037
(202) 994-4614

FLORIDA

Shands Hospital
University of Florida
IVF Center
Gainesville, FL 32610
(904) 395-0454

Fertility Institute of Northwest Florida
Gulf Breeze Hospital
1110 Gulf Breeze Parkway, Suite 202
Gulf Breeze, FL 32561
(904) 934-3900

Memorial Medical Center of
Jacksonville
IVF Program
3343 University Blvd. South
Jacksonville, FL 32216
(904) 391-1149

IVF Florida
HCA Northwest Regional Hospital
5801 Colonial Dr.
Margate, FL 33063
(305) 972-5001

Mount Sinai Medical Center
University of Miami
4300 Alton Rd.
Miami Beach, FL 33140
(305) 674-2139

University of Miami
Department of Ob/Gyn: D-5
P. O. Box 016960
Miami, FL 33101
(305) 547-5818

Naples Life Program
775 First Ave. North
Naples, FL 33940
(813) 262-1653

Orlando Regional Medical Center
Sand Lake Hospital
9400 Turkey Lake Rd.
Orlando, FL 32819-8001
(305) 351-8537

Florida Fertility Institute
Palms of Pasadena Hospital
3451 66th St., North
St. Petersburg, FL 33710
(813) 872-2988

Humana Women's Hospital
University of South Florida
3030 West Buffalo Ave.
Tampa, FL 33607
(813) 872-2988

GEORGIA

Atlanta Center for Fertility and
*Endocrinology**
Northside Hospital
5675 Peachtree-Dunwoody Rd. N. E.
Atlanta, GA 30342

*Atlanta Fertility Institute**
Georgia Baptist Medical Center
300 Boulevard N.E.
Atlanta, GA 30312

Reproductive Biology Associates
993F Johnson Ferry Rd., N.E.,
Suite 330
Atlanta, GA 30342
(404) 843-3064

*Augusta Reproductive Biology
Associates*
810-812 Chafee
Augusta, GA 30904
(404) 724-0228

Humana Hospital
In Vitro Fertilization Section
2 East, 3651 Wheeler Rd.
Augusta, GA 30910
(404) 863-6234

HAWAII

Pacific IVF Hospital
Kapiolani Women's and Children's
Hospital
1319 Punahou St., Suite 1040
Honolulu, HI 96826
(808) 946-2226

Kauai Medical Group, Inc.
University of Hawaii
G. N. Wilcox Memorial Hospital
Department of Ob/Gyn
3420-B Kuhio Highway
Lihue, HI 96766

ILLINOIS

Michael Reese Medical Center
IVF-ET Program

31st St. at Lakeshore Dr.
Chicago, IL 60616
(312) 791-4000

Mount Sinai Hospital Medical Center
Department of Ob/Gyn: IVF Program
California Ave. at Fifteenth St.
Chicago, IL 60608
(312) 650-6727

Northwestern Memorial Hospital
Prentice Women's Hospital: IVF
Program
333 East Superior St., Suite 454
Chicago, IL 60611
(312) 908-1364

Rush Medical College
Department of Ob/Gyn: IVF Program
600 South Paulina St.
Chicago, IL 60616
(312) 942-6609

*University of Illinois College of
Medicine*
Department of Ob/Gyn
840 South Wood St.
Chicago, IL 60612
(312) 996-7430

The Glenbrook Hospital
Northwestern University
IVF Program
2100 Pfingsten Rd.
Glenview, IL 60025
(312) 729-6450

INDIANA

Indiana University Medical Center
Department of Ob/Gyn
Section of Reproductive
Endocrinology

926 West Michigan St., N. 262
Indianapolis, IN 46223
(317) 264-4057

Pregnancy Initiation Center
Humana Women's Hospital
8091 Township Line Rd., Suite 110
Indianapolis, IN 46260
(317) 872-5103

IOWA

University of Iowa Hospitals and
Clinics
IVF-ET GIFT Program
Iowa City, IA 52242
(319) 356-1767

KANSAS

University of Kansas College of
Health Sciences
Ob/Gyn Foundation
39th St. and Rainbow Blvd.
Kansas City, KS 66103
(913) 588-6246

KENTUCKY

University of Kentucky Medical
College
Department of Ob/Gyn
Kentucky Center for Reproductive
Medicine
Lexington, KY 40536
(606) 233-5410

Norton Hospital
IVF Program
610 South Floyd St.
Louisville, KY 40202
(502) 562-8154

LOUISIANA

Fertility Center of Louisiana
St. Jude Medical Center
200 West Esplande Dr.
Kenner, LA 70065
(504) 464-8622

Omega Institute
Elmwood Medical Center
4425 Conlin Dr., Suite 101
Metairie, LA 70006
(800) 535-4177

The Fertility Institute of New Orleans
Humana Women's Hospital
6020 Bullard Ave.
New Orleans, LA 70128
(504) 246-8971

Tulane University
Department of Ob/Gyn: IVF Program
1415 Tulane Ave.
New Orleans, LA 70112
(504) 587-2147

MARYLAND

Baltimore IVF Program
2435 West Belvedere Ave. #41
Baltimore, MD 21215
(301) 542-5115

Greater Baltimore Medical Center
IVF Program of the Women's Fertility
Center
6701 North Charles St.
Baltimore, MD 21204
(301) 828-2484

The Johns Hopkins Hospital
Division of Reproductive
Endocrinology: IVF Program

600 North Wolfe St.
Baltimore, MD 21205
(301) 955-2016

Union Memorial Hospital
IVF Program: Department of Ob/Gyn
201 East University Parkway
Baltimore, MD 21218
(301) 235-5255

Genetic Consultants
Washington Adventist Hospital
5616 Shields Dr.
Bethesda, MD 20817
(301) 530-6900

Montgomery Fertility Institute
10215 Fernwood Rd., Suite 303
Bethesda, MD 20817
(301) 897-8850

MASSACHUSETTS

Beth Israel Hospital
Department of Ob/Gyn: IVF Program
330 Brookline Ave.
Boston, MA 02215
(617) 732-5923

Brigham and Women's Hospital
IVF Program
75 Francis St.
Boston, MA 02115
(617) 732-4239

IVF Center of Boston
Boston University Medical Center
75 East Newton St.
Boston, MA 02118
(617) 247-5928

*New England Medical Center
Hospitals*

Division of Reproductive
Endocrinology
260 Tremont St.
Boston, MA 02111
(617) 956-6066

Tufts-New England Medical Center*
Department of Ob/Gyn: IVF Program
171 Harrison Ave.
Boston, MA 02111

Boston IVF
25 Boylston St.
Chestnut Hill, MA 02167
(617) 735-9000

Greater Boston In Vitro Associates
Newton-Wellesley Hospital
2000 Washington St., Suite 342
Newton, MA 02161
(617) 965-7270

MICHIGAN

*University of Michigan Medical
Center**
L-2120 Women's Hospital
Department of Ob/Gyn
Ann Arbor, MI 48109
(313) 936-4000

*Hutzel Hospital/Wayne State
University*
IVF Program
4707 St. Antoine St.
Detroit, MI 48201
(313) 494-7547

Blodgett Memorial Medical Center
IVF Program
1900 Wealthy St. S. E., Suite 330
Grand Rapids, MI 49506
(616) 774-0700

William Beaumont Hospital
In Vitro Fertilization Program
33601 West 13 Mile Rd.
Royal Oak, MI 48072
(313) 288-2380

Saginaw General Hospital
IVF Program
Saginaw, MI 48603
(517) 771-4562

MINNESOTA

University of Minnesota VIP Program
Department of Ob/Gyn
Mayo Memorial Building, Box 395
420 Delaware St., S. E.
Minneapolis, MN 55455
(612) 373-7693

Mayo Clinic
Department of Reproductive
Endocrinology and Infertility
200 First St. S. W., W-10
Rochester, MN 55905
(507) 284-7367

MISSISSIPPI

*University of Mississippi Medical
Center*
Department of Ob/Gyn: IVF Program
Jackson, MS 39216
(601) 984-5300

MISSOURI

St. Luke's Hospital
IVF-GIFT Program
44th and Wornall Rd.
Kansas City, MO 64111
(816) 756-0277

Jewish Hospital
Department of Ob/Gyn: IVF Program
216 South Kings Highway
St. Louis, MO 63110
(314) 454-7834

Missouri Baptist Hospital
IVF Program
3015 North Ballas Rd., Room 301
St. Louis, MO 63131
(314) 432-1212, ext. 5295

Silber and Cohen
224 South Woods Mill Rd., Suite 730
St. Louis, MO 63017
(314) 576-1400

NEBRASKA

*University of Nebraska Medical
Center*
Department of Ob/Gyn
42nd St. and Dewey Ave.
Omaha, NE 68105
(402) 559-4212

NEVADA

Northern Nevada Fertility Clinic
350 West Sixth St.
Reno, NV 89503
(702) 322-4521

NEW JERSEY

*UMDNJ-School of Osteopathic
Medicine*
IVF Program
401 Hadden Ave.
Camden, NJ 08103
(609) 757-7730

*New Jersey School of Osteopathic
Medicine**
JFK-Cherry Hill Division
Department of Ob/Gyn
Cherry Hill, NJ 08034

*UMDNJ-Robert Wood Johnson
Medical School*
Department of Ob/Gyn: IVF Program
1 Robert Wood Johnson Place, CN19
New Brunswick, NJ 08903
(201) 937-7627

*Rutgers Medical School**
Department of Ob/Gyn
Academic Health Science Center,
CN19
New Brunswick, NJ 08903

UMDNJ-University Hospital
Center for Reproductive Medicine
100 Bergen St.
Newark, NJ 07103
(201) 456-6029

NEW MEXICO

Presbyterian Hospital
IVF Program
Cedar St. S.W.
Albuquerque, NM 87106
(505) 841-4214

NEW YORK

Children's Hospital of Buffalo
Reproduction Endocrinology Unit
140 Hodge Ave.
Buffalo, NY 14222
(716) 878-7232

Albert Einstein College of Medicine
IVF Center at Women's Medical
Pavilion

88 Ashford Ave.
Dobbs Ferry, NY 10522
(914) 693-8820

North Shore University Hospital
Division of Human Reproduction: IVF
300 Community Dr.
Manhasset, NY 11030
(516) 562-4470

Advanced Fertility Services, PC
1624 Third Ave.
New York, NY 10028
(212) 369-8700

*Columbia-Presbyterian Medical
Center*
Presbyterian Hospital IVF Program
622 West 168th St.
New York, NY 10032
(212) 694-8013

Cornell University Medical College
IVF Program
515 East 71st St., Second Floor
New York, NY 10032
(212) 472-4693

Mount Sinai Medical Center
In Vitro Fertilization Program
One Gustave Levy Place
Annenberg 20-60
New York, NY 10029
(212) 241-5927

St. Luke's-Roosevelt Hospital Center
IVF-ET Program
1111 Amsterdam Ave.
New York, NY 10025
(212) 870-6603

Wayne H. Decker IVF Program
1430 Second Ave., Suite 103

New York, NY 10021
(212) 744-5500

IVF Australia at United Hospital
406 Boston Post Rd.
Port Chester, NY 10573
(914) 934-7481

*University of Rochester CARE
Program*
University of Rochester Medical
Center
601 Elmwood Ave.
Rochester, NY 14642
(716) 275-2384

NORTH CAROLINA

Chapel Hill Fertility Services
109 Conner Dr., Suite 2104
Chapel Hill, NC 27514
(919) 968-4656

*North Carolina Memorial Hospital**
Fertility Center: IVF Program
Chapel Hill, NC 27514

*University of North Carolina Medical
School*
Fertility Center
Division of Endocrinology and
Infertility
Department of Ob/Gyn: 226H
Chapel Hill, NC 27514
(919) 966-5282

Duke University Medical Center
Department of Ob/Gyn IVF Program
P. O. Box 3143
Durham, NC 27710
(919) 684-5327

OHIO

Akron City Hospital
IVF-ET Program
525 East Market St.
Akron, OH 44309
(216) 375-3585

Jewish Hospital
Department of Ob/Gyn: IVF Program
3120 Burnet Ave., Suite 204
Cincinnati, OH 45229
(513) 221-3062

*University of Cincinnati Medical
Center*
Division of Reproductive
Endocrinology and Infertility
231 Bethesda Ave.
Cincinnati, OH 45267
(513) 872-5046

Cleveland Clinic Foundation
IVF Program
9500 Euclid Ave.
Cleveland, OH 44106
(216) 444-2240

MacDonald Hospital for Women
IVF Program
2105 Adelbert Rd.
Cleveland, OH 44106
(216) 844-1514

*Mount Sinai Medical Center of
Cleveland*
LIFE Program
University Circle
Cleveland, OH 44106
(216) 421-5884

Infertility and Gynecology, Inc.
St. Anthony Hospital

1492 East Broad St.
Columbus, OH 43205
(614) 253-8353

Midwest Reproductive Institute
1409 Hawthorne Ave.
Columbus, OH 43205
(614) 253-0003

University Reproductive Center
Ohio State University Hospitals
410 West Tenth Ave.
Columbus, OH 43210
(614) 421-8937; 421-8511

Miami Valley Hospital
IVF Program
1 Wyoming St.
Dayton, OH 45409
(513) 223-6192, ext. 4066

OKLAHOMA

Henry G. Bennett Fertility Institute
Baptist Medical Center of Oklahoma
3433 N.W. 56th, Suite 200
Oklahoma City, OK 73112
(405) 949-6060

*Oklahoma University Health Sciences
Center*
Section of Reproductive
Endocrinology
P. O. Box 26901, 4SP720
Oklahoma City, OK 73190
(405) 271-8700

Hillcrest Infertility Center
1145 South Utica, Suite 1209
Tulsa, OK 74104
(918) 584-2870

OREGON

*Oregon Health Sciences University
School of Medicine*
Oregon Reproductive Research and
Fertility Program
3181 S.W. Sam Jackson Park Rd.
Portland, OR 97201
(503) 279-8449

PENNSYLVANIA

St. Luke's Hospital
IVF Program
801 Ostrum St.
Bethlehem, PA 18015
(215) 691-7323

Christian Fertility Institute
241 North Thirteenth St.
Easton, PA 18042
(215) 250-9700

*Hospital of the University of
Pennsylvania*
Department of Ob/Gyn: IVF Program
3400 Spruce St., Suite 106
Philadelphia, PA 19104
(215) 662-2981

The Pennsylvania Hospital
IVF-ET Program
Eighth and Spruce St.
Philadelphia, PA 19107
(215) 829-5018

Albert Einstein Medical Center
Department of Ob/Gyn: IVF Program
York and Tabor Rd.
Philadelphia, PA 19141
(215) 456-7990

Magee-Women's Hospital*
IVF Program
Forbes Ave. and Spruce St.
Pittsburgh, PA 15213

Women's Choice Clinic
IVF Program, Suite 385
310 South Seventh Ave.
West Reading, PA 19611-1499
(215) 374-7797

PUERTO RICO

Hospital San Pablo
Edificio Medico Santa Cruz
73 Santa Cruz, Suite 213
Bayamon, PR 00619
(809) 798-0100

RHODE ISLAND

Women's & Infants' Hospital of Rhode Island
IVF Program
Providence, RI 02905
(401) 274-1100

SOUTH CAROLINA

Medical University of South Carolina
Department of Ob/Gyn: IVF Program
171 Ashley Ave.
Charleston, SC 29425
(803) 792-2861

The Southeastern Fertility Center
Trident Regional Medical Center
315 Calhoun St.
Charleston, SC 29401
(803) 722-3294

TENNESSEE

East Tennessee State University
Department of Ob/Gyn
P. O. Box 1957A
Johnson City, TN 37614
(615) 928-6426, ext. 334

East Tennessee Baptist Hospital
Family Life Center
7A Office 715
Box 1788, Blount Ave.
Knoxville, TN 37901
(615) 632-5697

University of Tennessee Memorial Research Center and Hospital
1924 Alcoa Highway
Knoxville, TN 37920
(615) 971-4958

Vanderbilt University
IVF Program
D3200 Medical Center North
Nashville, TN 37232
(615) 322-6576

TEXAS

St. David's Community Hospital
IVF-ET Program
P. O. Box 4039 (1302 East 32nd St.)
Austin, TX 78765
(512) 451-0149

Texas Endocrine and Fertility Institute (formerly Lutheran Medical System North/Texas)
Trinity Medical Center
4323 North Josey Lane, Suite 206
Carrollton, TX 75010
(214) 891-0114

Presbyterian Hospital of Dallas
P. O. Box 17 (8160 Walnut Hill Ave.)
Dallas, TX 75231
(214) 891-2624

University of Texas HSC-SW Medical School
Department of Ob/Gyn: IVF Program
5303 Harry Hines Blvd.
Dallas, TX 75235
(214) 688-2784

Fort Worth Infertility Center-Harris Institute
(formerly Fort Worth Reproductive Center)
1325 Pennsylvania Ave., Suite 750
Fort Worth, TX 76104
(817) 335-0909

University of Texas Medical Branch
Department of Ob/Gyn: IVF Program
Galveston, TX 77550
(409) 761-3985

Baylor College of Medicine
Department of Ob/Gyn: IVF Program
1 Baylor Plaza
Houston, TX 77030
(713) 791-2033

Memorial Reproductive Services
7600 Beechnut
Houston, TX 77074
(713) 776-5514

Texas Women's Hospital
IVF Program
7600 Fannin St.
Houston, TX 77054
(713) 795-7257

The West Houston Infertility Center
(formerly the Sam Houston IVF Center)
Sam Houston Memorial Hospital
1615 Hillendahl Blvd.
P. O. Box 55130
Houston, TX 77055
(713) 932-5600

University of Texas Health Science Center
Department of Reproductive Science
6431 Fannin St., Suite 3270
Houston, TX 77030
(713) 792-5360

Texas Tech University School of Medicine
Department of Ob/Gyn
P. O. Box 4569
Lubbock, TX 79409
(806) 743-2335

Humana Women's Hospital of South Texas
Division of Reproductive Endocrinology
Center for Reproductive Medicine
8109 Fredericksberg Rd.
San Antonio, TX 78229
(512) 692-8971

University of Texas Health Science Center
Department of Ob/Gyn: IVF Program
7703 Floyd Curl Dr.
San Antonio, TX 78284
(512) 567-4955

Texas A & M University
Scott and White Medical Center
Department of Ob/Gyn
Temple, TX 76508

UTAH

University of Utah
Division of Reproductive
Endocrinology
50 Medical Dr. North
Salt Lake City, UT 84132
(801) 581-4837

VERMONT

*University of Vermont College of
Medicine*
Department of Ob/Gyn
Given Building
Burlington, VT 05405
(802) 656-2272

VIRGINIA

University of Virginia Medical Center
Department of Ob/Gyn: IVF Program
Charlottesville, VA 22908
(804) 924-0312

Genetics and IVF Institute
Fairfax Hospital
3020 Javier Rd.
Fairfax, VA 22031
(703) 698-7355

Eastern Virginia Medical School
Jones Institute for Reproductive
Medicine
Hoffheimer Hall, Sixth Floor
Norfolk, VA 23507
(804) 446-8935

IVF Program
Henrico Doctor's Hospital
1602 Skipwith Rd.
Richmond, VA 23229
(804) 289-4315

Medical College of Virginia
IVF Program
Box 34 – MCV Station
Richmond, VA 23298
(804) 786-9638

WASHINGTON

Swedish Hospital Medical Center
Reproductive Genetics
747 Summit Ave.
Seattle, WA 98104
(206) 386-2483

*University of Washington IVF
Program*
Department of Ob/Gyn: RH20
Seattle, WA 98195
(206) 543-0670

Infertility and Reproductive Associates
West 104 Fifth Ave., Room 410
Spokane, WA 99204

Fertility Center of Puget Sound
Third Floor, Puget Sound Hospital
South 36th and Pacific Ave.
Tacoma, WA 98408
(206) 475-5433

Tacoma Fertility Clinic
1811 South K St.
Tacoma, WA 98405
(206) 627-6256

WEST VIRGINIA

West Virginia University
Department of Ob/Gyn
3110 MacCorkle Ave., S.E.
Charleston, WV 25304
(304) 347-1344

WISCONSIN

Appleton Medical Center
Family Fertility Program
1818 Meade St.
Appleton, WI 54911
(414) 731-4101, ext. 3380

University of Wisconsin Clinics
IVF Program
600 Highland Ave., H4/630 CSC
Madison, WI 53792
(608) 263-1217

University of WI-Milwaukee Clinical Campus
Mount Sinai Medical Center
Department of Ob/Gyn
950 North Twelfth St., P. O. Box 342
Milwaukee, WI 53201
(414) 298-8609

Waukesha Memorial Hospital
IVF Program
725 American Ave.
Waukesha, WI 53186
(414) 544-2722

* Indicates clinic not listed in OTA reference

Sources:

U. S. Congress, Office of Technology Assessment, *Infertility: Medical and Social Choices*, OTA-BA-358 (Washington, DC: U. S. Government Printing Office, May 1988), 311-320.

Tilton, Nan and Todd, and Gaylen Moore, *Making Miracles: In Vitro Fertilization* (Garden City, NY: Doubleday & Co., 1985), 161-187.

THIRD-PARTY PREGNANCY (SURROGACY) CONTRACT AGENCIES, CENTERS, AND CLINICS

CENTER FOR REPRODUCTIVE ALTERNATIVES
Bruce Rappaport, Ph.D., Executive Director
3333 Vincent Rd., Suite 222
Pleasant Hill, CA 94523
Established in 1984.

Accepts three to five couples and thirty applicants for third-party pregnancy (TPP) contracts annually; total fee: $25,000 to $30,000; details of contract are negotiable.

CENTER FOR REPRODUCTIVE ALTERNATIVES
Kathryn Wyckoff, Director
727 Via Otono
San Clemente, CA 92672
Established in 1984.

Accepts about fifteen couples and fifteen women for TPP annually; total fee is $18,000+; TPP payment: $6,000, plus $75 monthly cost-of-living allowance; agency fee: $12,000.

CENTER OF SURROGATE PARENTING
William W. Handel, J.D., Director
8383 Wilshire Blvd., Suite 750
Beverly Hills, CA 90211
Established in 1980 through law firm of Sherwyn and Handel, agency created in 1986.
Accepts about twelve couples and fifteen women for TPP annually; total fee is $18,000+; TPP payment: $9,000, plus all related expenses (maternity clothing, life insurance, child care, transportation and supplies); agency fee: $9,000.

HAGAR INSTITUTE
Beth Bacon, Director
1015 Buchanan
Topeka, KS 66604
Established in 1982.
Accepts forty couples and forty women for TPP annually; total fee: $18,500; TPP payment: $8,500; agency fee: $9,500, plus $500 for "home study."

HAGAR INSTITUTE, SAN FRANCISCO FRANCHISE
Beth Bacon, Director
401 Marina Blvd., Suite 125
San Francisco, CA 94080
Established in 1986 as follow-up to Topeka branch.
Statistics not available regarding number of arranged contracts; total fee: about $20,000; TPP payment: $10,000; agency fee: listed above.

INFERTILITY ALTERNATIVES*
Debra A. Patton, Director
P. O. Box 1084
Snellville, GA 30278

INFERTILITY ASSOCIATES INTERNATIONAL
Harriet Blankfeld, Director
5530 Wisconsin Ave.
Chevy Chase, MD 20815
Established in 1980 as the National Center for Surrogate Parenting; name changed in 1985 to Infertility Associates.

Accepts about 100 couples and 125 women for TPP annually; total fee: ranges from $20,000 to $30,000; TPP payment: $10,000, plus up to $8,000 in expenses; agency fee: $12,000.

INFERTILITY CENTER OF NEW YORK

Noel Keane, J.D., Director
14 East Sixtieth St., Suite 1204
New York, NY 10022

Established in 1983 in conjunction with Keane's Michigan center.

Accepts 200 couples and 225 women for TPP annually; fees — see listing under Noel Keane.

NOEL KEANE

930 Mason
Dearborn, MI 48124

Established in 1976 as part of Keane's law practice.

Accepts about 200 couples and 450 women for TPP annually; total fee: about $20,000; TPP payment: $10,000; agency fee: $10,000. Currently shut down due to legislative action implemented in September 1988.

SURROGATE FAMILY SERVICES, INC.

Katie Brophy, J.D., Director
713 West Main St., Suite 400
Louisville, KY 40202

Established in December 1980.

Accepts twelve to fifteen couples annually; negotiable TPP payment; agency fee: $8,000; affected by legislation passed in 1988.

SURROGATE FOUNDATION

Norma Thorsen, Director
P.O. Box 6545
Portland, OR 97206

Established in 1983 as a "service organization."

Accepts about seven couples and twenty women for TPP annually; total fee: $18,000; TPP payment: ranges between $10,000 and $12,000; agency fee: $6,000.

SURROGATE MOTHER PROGRAM*

Betsy Aigen
Suite 3D
640 West End Ave.
New York, NY 10024

SURROGATE MOTHERS, INC.*
Steven Litz, Director
2612 McLeay Dr.
Indianapolis, IN 46220

SURROGATE MOTHERS, INC.*
Juanita Lewis, Director
620 Lander St., Suite 2A
Reno, NV 89509

SURROGATE PARENTING ASSOCIATES
Dr. Richard Levin, M.D., Director
Doctor's Office Building, Suite 222
250 East Liberty
Louisville, KY 40202
Established in 1979.

Receives about 400 inquiries from interested couples and women regarding TPP annually; accepts all couples who can afford to pay and are verifiably infertile; total fee: $20,000+; TPP payment: $10,000 to $12,000; clinic fee: $7,000, plus unspecified expenses. Affected by legislation passed in 1988.

SURROGATE PARENTING PROFESSIONALS
Bernard Sherwyn, J.D., Director
10880 Wilshire Blvd., Suite 614
Los Angeles, CA 90024
Established in 1986.

Accepts about twelve couples and seventeen women for TPP annually; total fee: $22,000 to $25,000; TPP payment: $12,000, plus $75 monthly cost-of-living allowance; agency fee: $10,000.

SURROGATE PREGNANCY CONSULTATION*
Ada D. Greenberg, Director
P. O. Box 52
Jamaica, NY 11415-6052

*Additional information unavailable.

Sources:
U.S. Congress, Office of Technology Assessment, *Infertility: Medical and Social Choices,* OTA-BA-358 (Washington, DC: U.S. Government Printing Office, May 1988), 369-370.

Amy Zuckerman Overvold, *Surrogate Parenting* (New York: Pharos Books, 1988), 205-216.

Glossary

abortifacient: Any drug or substance capable of inducing abortion.

abortion: The spontaneous or deliberate ending of a pregnancy before the developing baby can survive outside the mother's womb.

abortion pill: See *RU486*

abortion rate: The number of abortions during a specific time in relation to the total number of women between the ages of fifteen and forty-four in a given population. (Usually expressed as the number of abortions per 1,000 women ages fifteen to forty-four.)

abortion ratio: The number of abortions during a specific period of time in relation to the total number of live births in a given population. (Usually expressed as the number of abortions per 1,000 live births.)

acrosome: The lead end of the head of a sperm that releases enzymes to dissolve the surface of the ovum.

adhesion: A holding together by new connective tissue of two structures which are normally separate, produced by inflammation, surgery, or injury.

alphafetoprotein [AFP] test: Maternal blood test routinely performed during pregnancy to diagnose neural tube defects such as spina bifida and anencephaly.

American College of Obstetricians and Gynecologists [ACOG]: National organization of certified specialists in obstetrics and gynecology.

amniocentesis: Diagnostic sampling of amniotic fluid during pregnancy, especially for the purpose of genetic analysis. The fluid is obtained by puncturing the mother's abdomen and womb with a special needle.

amnion: The fluid-filled sac or membrane enclosing the developing baby within the womb; also referred to as the "bag of waters."

amniotic fluid: A colorless liquid surrounding the baby within the womb.

amniotomy: The artificial rupture of the amniotic sac by a physician.

anesthesia: The partial or complete loss of sensation with or without loss of consciousness as a result of injury. disease, or the administration of a drug or gas.

anovulation: The absence of ovulation.

antenatal: Occurring before birth.

antepartum: Around the time of birth; a term used to describe the labor and delivery functions and staff of a hospital.

artificial embryonation [AE]: The process by which a human ovum is artificially inseminated within a woman's reproductive tract and then flushed out five to seven days later for transfer to another women's womb; the transfer of an embryo from the womb of a fertile donor to the uterus of an infertile recipient who will attempt to carry the embryo to term. Also called: *in vivo fertilization* and *surrogate embryo transfer* [SET].

artificial insemination [AI]: Semen deposited in the vagina by a mechanical instrument rather than a man's penis.

artificial insemination by donor [AID]: Artificial insemination using sperm obtained from a donor.

artificial insemination by husband [AIH]: Artificial insemination using sperm obtained from one's husband.

artificial placentation: The mechanical provision of nutrients and removal of waste products from a fetus.

artificial placentation system [APS]: A set of interrelated devices that function as an artificial placenta.

artificial womb: A man-made device designed for conducting gestation outside the human body.

aspermia: The absence of sperm and semen.

azoospermia: The absence of sperm in semen.

basal body temperature: The temperature of the body — taken orally, rectally, or vaginally — after at least three hours of sleep, taken before rising.

Basal Body Temperature [BBT] Method of family planning: A method of family planning that relies on identifying the fertile period of a woman's menstrual cycle for the purpose of attempting or avoiding pregnancy.

biopsy: The surgical removal of a sample of tissue for diagnostic purposes.

birth: The process by which a new human being enters the world and begins life outside the mother's body.

birth center: A facility designed to prevent interference in the natural process of childbirth; may be freestanding or connected to a hospital. Many obstetrical departments are now naming redesigned in-hospital units "birthing centers" for consumer appeal. If continuous electronic fetal monitoring, induction of labor, artificial rupture of the membranes, epidural anesthesia, and routine episiotomies are frequently being conducted in a facility using this name, it is *not* a birth center — it is a *hospital.*

birth control: The prevention of birth.

birth mother: A woman who conceives a child as a result of sexual intercourse or artificial insemination and gives up her child by adoption at the time of birth.

birth rate: The number of births during a specific period of time in relation to the total population of a certain area.

blastocyst: The fertilized ovum during its second week of development; name means "many-celled hollow ball."

bonding: The deepening of intimacy over time between two people through emotional, physical, and spiritual interactions. Touch, eye contact, speech, and loving gestures create, sustain, and magnify human bonds within the family.

cannula: A hollow tube or sheath.

catheter: A thin, plastic tube designed to perform invasive medical procedures upon the body.

certified nurse-midwife [C.N.M.]: A registered nurse who is a graduate of an approved training program and who has passed a certification examination.

cervix: The fixed, lower neck-like segment of the uterus that forms the passageway into the vagina.

cesarean section: The surgical removal of a baby through an incision in the mother's abdominal tissue and uterine wall.

chlamydia: A generic term for infection caused by the organism *chlamydia trichomonas*; a sexually transmitted disease characterized by a thick yellow discharge from the cervix which may result in pelvic abscesses, pelvic inflammatory disease, and involuntary sterility. Also called *mucopurulent cervicitis.*

chorion: The outermost membrane covering the developing baby during the first trimester. The chorion encloses the amnion, lies closest to the wall of the uterus, and eventually becomes the placenta.

chorionic villi: Tiny projections extending from the surface of the chorion which secrete human chorionic gonadotropin (HCG).

chorionic villi sampling [CVS]: Diagnostic test using chorionic villi tissue for the purpose of genetic analysis during the first trimester of pregnancy. CVS is performed by a physician using ultrasound as a guide to pass a catheter through the vagina and cervix into the womb to the chorion. A few cells from the chorionic surface are removed by suction and then examined for chromosomal abnormalities, certain genetic conditions, and fetal sex.

chromosome: Thread-like bodies within the nucleus of every cell that make up strands of DNA. These structures contain the genetic material that is passed from parents to their children. Each normal human cell contains forty-six chromosomes arranged in twenty-three pairs from the time of conception.

cilia: Hairlike filaments lining the inner wall of the Fallopian tubes. These filaments beat rhythmically to create a current that takes the egg toward the uterus.

clomiphene citrate [Clomid, Serophene]: A drug used to induce ovulation in anovulatory women. Its precise mechanism of action is unknown.

conception: The fertilization of the egg by a sperm that initiates the growth of a human being and triggers the onset of pregnancy. The American College of Obstetricians and Gynecologists, however, changed the definition of conception in September, 1965: "Fertilization is the *union* of the spermatozoan and ovum; conception is the *implantation* of the fertilized ovum." (ACOG Terminology Bulletin No. 1) This allows birth control methods that prevent implantation of fertilized ova to be called contraceptives rather than contragestives or abortifacients.

conceptus: Fertilized ovum or "pre-embryo"; term used by researchers to dehumanize the earliest stages of human development following conception.

contraception: The act of preventing conception.

contraceptive: Any drug, device, surgery, or method of family planning that prevents conception.

contragestive: Any drug, device, or surgery that interrupts pregnancy and induces an abortion.

corpus luteum: Name means "yellow body;" the temporary gland created within a ruptured ovarian follicle; secretes hormones to protect and maintain pregnancy until the placenta matures and takes over this role.

cryobank: Place where frozen sperm is stored; a commercial business selling frozen sperm.

cryopreservation: The storage of living cells by the use of special chemicals and ultrarapid freezing.

cystic fibrosis: A disease of infants, children, adolescents and young adults affecting the sweat and mucus-secreting glands, resulting in chronic lung disease, pancreatic insufficiency, abnormally salty sweat and, in some cases, liver disease.

DES [diethystilbestrol]: A synthetic estrogen used during the 1950s and 1960s to prevent miscarriage. In 1971, it was found to cause a rare form of vaginal cancer, and vaginal changes were found in a significant number of the daughters born to women who had taken DES during pregnancy.

dilation: The process of opening. In labor, uterine contractions press the baby against the cervix to open the womb. In gynecological procedures, metal rods of increasing size are inserted into the cervix to stretch it open. In either case, cervical dilation is accompanied by a menstrual-like cramping sensation.

dilation and curettage [D&C]: Name literally means "opening, cutting, and scraping." A surgical procedure in which the cervix is forcibly opened and the inside of the uterus is scraped with a sharp, spoonlike instrument called a curette. Used to remove polyps or an overgrowth of uterine tissue, as a way of diagnosing cancer, and after childbirth to remove tissue retained in the womb. Also a method of abortion involving the dismemberment of the developing child by suction and its extraction from the uterus.

dilation and evacuation [D&E]: A surgical procedure used to abort a child during the second trimester of pregnancy requiring crushing of the skull and surgical dismemberment of the baby's body before removal from the womb.

DNA: Deoxyribonucleic acid; a complex molecule carrying genetic information within the nucleus of a cell.

DNA probe: A specific DNA sequence used to identify a like sequence in genetic diagnosis.

donor egg: An egg given up by its biological mother to another woman or couple. The donor's ovum unites with the infertile woman's husband's sperm. The baby is nurtured within the adoptive mother's uterus during pregnancy.

donor embryo: A baby in the earliest stage of human development. It is produced by gametes uniting in a glass dish or within the genetic mother's reproductive tract. The embryo is transferred to a different woman's womb for gestation.

Doppler stethoscope: A device utilizing a form of ultrasound to amplify the heart rate.

dystocia: Slow, prolonged, or difficult labor; often termed "failure to progress." What constitutes a "slow" or "prolonged" labor, however, is a matter of opinion.

ectogenesis: The beginning of life outside the body.

ectopic pregnancy: A pregnancy occurring outside the uterus, usually in a Fallopian tube.

ejaculation: The sudden release of semen from the male urethra.

electrode: A small electrical conductor used to directly pick up and record the baby's heart rate in labor.

electronic fetal monitoring [EFM]: The continuous recording of the baby's heart beat during labor by means of a device attached to the mother's abdomen, telemetry, or electrodes inserted into the baby's scalp.

egg donor: A woman who gives or sells her eggs to another woman.

embryo donor: A woman who gives or sells her embryo to another woman.

embryo: In humans, an unborn child before the eighth week of pregnancy, a period that involves rapid growth, initial development of the major organ systems, and early formation of the main external features.

embryo transfer [ET]: The placement of an embryo into a woman's uterus. The embryo being transferred may have been fertilized *in vitro* (within the laboratory) or *in vivo* (within the reproductive tract of an egg donor).

embryo transplant: The placement of a donated or purchased embryo into a gestational (surrogate) mother's uterus.

endocrine system: The system of glands within the body, including the thymus, pituitary, parathyroid, thyroid, adrenals, ovaries (in females) and testicles (in males).

endocrinologist: A physician specializing in diseases of the endocrine system.

endocrinology/infertility: The branch of obstetrics and gynecology dealing with the hormones, diseases, and conditions that affect fertility.

endometriosis: A growth of endometrial tissue outside the uterus, thought to occur in about 15 percent of women. Women who do not get pregnant until later in life are more likely to acquire this disease, with the average age of diagnosis being thirty-seven. Pregnancy seems to prevent or delay the onset of this problem. The most common symptoms of endometriosis are severe menstrual cramps, painful intercourse, painful bowel movements, and soreness above the pubic bones. Endometriosis is a factor in many cases of female infertility.

endometrium: The inner lining of the uterus.

endorphin: Any one of the substances of the nervous system made by the pituitary gland producing morphine-like effects as a way of reducing pain within the body.

epidemic: A disease spread rapidly throughout the population.

episiotomy: A surgical procedure performed during childbirth in which the opening of the vagina is enlarged with a cut.

estrogen: A hormone secreted by the ovaries that regulates the development of secondary sexual characteristics in women and produces cyclic changes in tissue lining the vagina and the uterus. Natural estrogens include estradiol, estrone, and their metabolic product, estriol. When used therapeutically, estrogens are usually given in a conjugated form, such as ethinyl estradiol, conjugated estrogens (USP), or the synthetic estrogen DES (diethylstilbestrol).

ethics: A system of moral principles or standards governing conduct.

eugenic abortion: The deliberate killing of a preborn child for eugenic reasons.

eugenics: The science which deals with the physical, moral, and intellectual improvement of the human race through genetic control. *Negative eugenics* include those measures which seek to restrict the numbers of offspring with genetically undesirable traits; *positive eugenics* include those measures which seek to bring about an increase in the numbers of offspring of families with genetically desirable traits. Eugenics is based upon Darwinian, or evolutionary, theory.

experimentation: Any research in which the human being represents the object through which or upon which one intends to verify the effect, at present unknown or not sufficiently known, of a given treatment (E.P.G., pharmacological, peratogenic, surgical, etc.).

extracorporeal membrane oxygenation [ECMO]: The mechanical exchange of oxygen, waste products, and nutrients on behalf of a baby incapable of breathing; the artificial accomplishment of placental function outside the mother's body.

evolution: The theory proposed by Charles Darwin that the composition of all living matter is formed in response to environmental conditions. Any changes provoked, however, do not depend solely on the environment but upon the interaction of an organism with its environment. Thus, organisms may or may not respond to the environment by *adaptive genetic change*. This belief concludes that failure to respond positively to the environment may lead to diminution and eventually extinction of a species; successful biologic responses enable the species to survive and expand. Evolution theory leads to three conclusions about the human species: 1) As a species, human beings are in a process of development; therefore, no finished life form exists, including human life. 2) Chance plays a major role in biological change: chance genetic variation leading to diversity within a species and chance environmental changes; natural selection integrates these two components to produce biological change. 3) Competition for survival exists between species and within a species, characterized by a fierce struggle which results in the triumph of the biologically superior over the inferior. These tenets place human identity on a developmental continuum rather than upon an absolute or fixed position of value within nature.

failure to progress: See *dystocia*.

Fallopian tube: The duct that conveys the egg from the ovary to the womb.

family physician: A physician who has completed a three-year residency in family practice medicine.

fertilization: See *conception*.

fertile: Having the ability to conceive and bear offspring; fruitful; not sterile.

fertile mucus: A substance secreted by the cervix that is capable of facilitating the transport of sperm through a woman's reproductive tract.

fertile period: The time during the menstrual cycle in which conception may take place, beginning three to six days before ovulation and ending two to three days afterward.

fetal distress: A term used to describe a shortage of oxygen to the baby resulting in a disrupted heart rate. Obstetrical medications, artificial rupture of membranes, EFM, laying flat on one's back, and maternal stress can contribute to fetal distress in labor.

fetus: The term applied to a developing baby after the eighth week of pregnancy until birth.

fibroid: A noncancerous tumor of the uterus, usually occurring in women thirty to fifty years of age.

fimbria: The fringelike borders of the open ends of the Fallopian tubes.

follicle: A pouchlike recessed structure in the ovary containing an immature ovum called an oocyte and the cells surrounding the oocyte.

follicle-stimulating hormone [FSH]: A hormone secreted by the pituitary gland that is responsible for stimulating the growth of ovarian follicles in women and the development of sperm (spermatogenesis) in men.

forceps: An instrument with two blades and handles designed to forcibly pull the baby, usually by the head, from the vagina.

FSH: See *follicle stimulating hormone.*

gamete: A mature male or female reproductive cell; the spermatozoon or ovum.

gamete intrafallopian transfer [GIFT]: The placement of sperm and oocytes into an unblocked Fallopian tube through a laparoscope for *in vivo* fertilization.

gender: The specific sex of a person; male or female.

gene: The basic unit of heredity in a chromosome that carries characteristics from parent to child.

general anesthesia: Medically induced loss of feeling and sensation, including the loss of memory and consciousness.

generation: The act or process of reproduction; procreation.

genesis: Origin; generation; the act of producing or procreating.

genetic code: A code that fixes amino acids, building blocks of body tissue proteins, into patterns that determine the traits of offspring.

genetic diagnosis: Analysis of an individual's chromosomal makeup for the purpose of identifying a genetic disorder.

genetic engineering: The process of making new DNA molecules.

geneticist: A specialist in genetics.

genetics: The science of heredity and its variations; the study of resemblances and differences of related organisms resulting from the interaction of their genes and the environment.

genic: Of or resembling a gene or genes.

gestation: The period between conception and birth.

gestational mother: See *surrogate mother.*

genome: The complete set of genetic instructions carried within the DNA molecule.

genotype: The unique genetic constitution of a specific person or organism.

gonadotropin: A hormone capable of stimulating the gonads, or primary sex organs.

gonorrhea: A specific, contagious inflammatory infection of the genital mucus membrane, mouth, or anus of either sex transmitted by intimate sexual contact.

gynecologist: A physician who specializes in the problems of the female sexual organs.

gynecology: The branch of medicine dealing with diseases and problems of the female reproductive tract.

gyne-, gyno-: Prefix meaning woman, female.

gynetech: A new form of medicine specializing in the technological control of human reproduction.

hamster-egg penetration assay: Diagnostic test in which sperm are incubated with hamster eggs to test their capability to fertilize ova.

HCG: See *human chorionic gonadotropin.*

HMG: See *human menopausal gonadotropin.*

healing: The process or act in which health is restored to the body, emotions, mind, or spirit.

health: A state of physical, emotional, mental, and spiritual well-being.

heterologous imsemination: See *artificial insemination by donor.*

homologous insemination: See *artificial insemination by husband.*

high-risk pregnancy: Term describing the probability that complications during pregnancy and childbirth may occur.

home birth: Birth taking place at home. As used by those who advocate home birth for healthy childbearing women, the term indicates a planned home birth attended by skilled maternity care providers. As used by those seeking to eliminate home birth, the term is used to indicate all births taking place outside the hospital, including miscarriages, early arrivals during transport, unattended and unplanned home births, and involuntary home births among women too poor to afford hospitalization.

hormone: Chemical substances, produced by ductless glands in one part of the body, that affect an organ or group of cells in another area of the body.

hospital birth: Birth taking place in a hospital.

human chorionic gonadotropin [HCG]: A hormone produced by the chorionic villi; responsible for triggering the release of progesterone and estrogen; measured during a pregnancy test through urine. HCG is extracted from the urine of pregnant women and administered by injection to stimulate ovarian and testicular function.

human menopausal gonadotropin [HMG]: A hormone extracted from the urine of postmenopausal women that can be administered by injection to stimulate the ovaries and testes.

hyster-, hystero-: Prefix: womb; hysteria.

hysterectomy: The surgical removal of the uterus.

hystero-oophorectomy: The surgical removal of the uterus and one or both ovaries.

hysterosalpingogram: X-ray study of the uterus and Fallopian tubes after injecting radiopaque material into these organs; used for diagnosis of infertility or sterility.

hysterosalpingo-oophorectomy: The surgical removal of the uterus, Fallopian tubes, and ovaries.

hysteroscopy: Inspection of the inside of the uterus by means of a lighted instrument called a hysteroscope.

hysterotomy: 1) Incision of the uterus. 2) Cesarean section. 3) A method of induced abortion conducted through incisions in the mother's abdominal wall and uterus.

iatrogenic: Produced or caused by a physician.

idiopathic infertility: Infertility of unknown cause.

implantation: Embedding of the developing baby in the lining of the uterus.

induced abortion: An intentional termination of a pregnancy before an unborn child has developed to the point where he or she can survive outside the uterus.

induction of labor: The artificial production of labor.

infertile: The inability to conceive or produce offspring.

infertility: The state of being infertile or unable to carry a pregnancy. Medically defined as the inability of a couple to conceive after twelve months of intercourse without contraception.

intrauterine contraceptive device [IUCD]: A form of contraception consisting of inserting a bent strip of plastic or copper into the uterus to prevent pregnancy; does not act to prevent ovulation or conception.

IUD: See *intrauterine contraceptive device.*

IVF/ET: See *in vitro fertilization* and *embryo transfer.*

invasive techniques: Any medical procedure that penetrates the boundaries of the body.

in vitro fertilization [IVF]: Conception occurring in laboratory apparatus; name literally means "in glass" fertilization.

in vivo fertilization: Fertilization within the human body.

Kegels: Conscious contractions of pelvic floor muscles done for the purpose of improving muscle tone and sexual response. Named after Dr. Arnold Kegel, a physician whose research proved the value of these exercises in improving the strength of the pelvic floor.

labor: The series of stages during the process of childbirth through which the baby is born and the uterus returns to a normal state; contractions of the uterus that result in the birth of a baby.

lactation: The process by which milk is produced and secreted by the breasts for nourishing an infant.

laminaria: Kelp or seaweed which when dried is capable of absorbing water and expanding with considerable force; used to dilate the cervical canal prior to a surgical abortion.

laparoscopy: Exploration of the pelvic cavity by means of a lighted instrument called a laparascope.

laparotomy: The surgical opening of the abdomen; an abdominal operation.

laser: Acronym for *light amplification by stimulated emission of radiation.*

laser surgery: Any operative procedure which employs a laser rather than a scalpel to excise body tissue.

lay midwife: A birth attendant who has acquired her skills primarily through apprenticeship and experience.

liable: To be legally responsible.

litigate: To seek remedy through a court of law, including the act of carrying on a lawsuit, by means of presenting evidence of damage or harm.

low-risk pregnancy: Term used to describe the probability that pregnancy and childbirth will be normal and uneventful.

luteal: Referring to the corpus luteum, its functions, or its effects.

luteinizing hormone [LH]: A hormone produced by the pituitary gland in both males and females. It stimulates the production of testosterone in men and the secretion of progesterone in women.

malpractice, medical: The failure of a health care professional to render proper services through reprehensible ignorance, negligence, or criminal intent toward a client; bad, wrong, or injudicious treatment resulting in injury, unnecessary suffering, or death; the misconduct or misuse of medicine.

menarche: The onset of menstruation; the beginning of the first menstrual cycle.

menopause: The end of menstruation when the menses stop as a normal result of the decline of monthly hormonal cycles.

menotropin [Pergonal]: See *human menopausal gonadotropin.*

menstrual cycle: The cycle of hormonal changes that begins at puberty and repeats itself on a monthly basis unless interrupted by pregnancy, lactation, medication, or metabolic disorders.

menstruation: The natural process by which the lining of the nonpregnant uterus is cast off, resulting in a discharge of blood and muscosal tissue from the vagina.

menstrual extraction: Removal of the lining of the the uterus by suction before menstruation occurs; also a method of induced abortion. Also called *endometrial aspiration.*

microsurgery: Surgery performed while a physician observes through a microscope.

midwife: A birth attendant who respects nature while supporting and supervising the natural processes of labor during childbirth; a woman who practices the art of midwifery.

midwifery: The traditional practice of providing help and assistance to women during childbirth, characterized by watching and waiting upon nature's design for labor.

miscarriage: The spontaneous loss of a baby before the twenty-eighth week of pregnancy.

monogamy: The practice of marrying only once for life.

morbidity: A state of illness or disease.

morning-after pill: A very large dose of estrogen taken orally within twenty-four to seventy-two hours after intercourse to terminate a pregnancy.

mortality: Death.

mortality rate: The number of deaths during a specific time within a given population. When dealing with fetuses and babies, the rate is based on number of deaths per 1,000 live births; when considering mothers, the rate quoted represents the number of deaths per 100,000 pregnancies.

mucus: The slippery, sticky secretion released by mucous membranes and glands.

natal: Referring to birth.

Natural Family Planning [NFP]: Any method of family planning that does not use drugs or devices to prevent conception.

neonate: A newborn baby; a baby less than twenty-eight days old.

neonatologist: A pediatrician specializing in the care of newborn babies.

neural tube: Tube formed from fusion of the neural folds from which the brain and spinal cord arise.

neural tube defect: A condition resulting from the failure of the neural tube to close during fetal development, resulting in spina bifida or anencephaly.

noninvasive: Referring to any test, treatment, or procedure that does not penetrate the boundaries of the body.

nurse-midwife: See *certified nurse-midwife.*

obstetrics: The branch of medicine dealing with the management of pregnancy and childbirth.

oligogenics: The limitation of offspring through utilizing some form of birth control.

oligospermia: Deficient levels of sperm in seminal fluid; may be temporary or permanent.

oocyte: The early or primitive human egg before it has completed development.

oogenesis: The growth and development of female eggs.

oophorectomy: The surgical removal of an ovary.

oral contraceptive: A steroid drug taken to induce infertility.

orchiectomy: The surgical removal of a testicle.

osteoporosis: Increased porosity of bone tissue; the loss of normal bone density marked by a thinning of bone tissue and the growth of small openings in the bone.

ova: Human eggs; female reproductive or germ cells; a cell which is capable of developing into a new organism of the same species. (Singular: *ovum*.)

ovary: One of the pair of primary sexual organs in females located on each side of the lower abdomen beside the uterus. The ovaries produce the reproductive cell, or ovum, and two known hormones, estrogen and progesterone.

ovariectomy: The removal of an ovary or a portion of the ovary.

oviduct: See *Fallopian tube*.

ovulation: The release of an egg, or ovum, from the ovary after the breaking of a follicle.

Ovulation Method of family planning: A method of family planning that relies on the observation of the type and amount of cervical mucus secreted during the menstrual cycle as a means of predicting fertility.

ovum donor: See *egg donor*.

ovum transfer [OT]: See *embryo transfer*.

pelvic inflammatory disease [PID]: Inflammation of the female reproductive organs in the pelvis, often resulting in scarring, blocked Fallopian tubes, and infertility.

pelvic floor: The muscles and tissues that form the base of the pelvis.

pelvis: The bowl-shaped lower portion of the trunk of the body.

perinatal: The period from the twenty-eighth week of pregnancy to one week after the baby's birth.

perinatologist: A physician who specializes in maternal-fetal medicine.

perineum: The part of the body lying between the inner thighs, with the buttocks to the rear and the genitals to the front.

placenta: A temporary organ created to exchange waste products and carry nutrients between mother and baby during pregnancy; produces hormones to protect and maintain gestation.

polyp: A small, tumorlike growth that protrudes from a mucous membrane surface.

postcoital test: Samples of deposited semen and vaginal-cervical discharge removed from different areas along the length of the cervical canal for diagnostic analysis; the microscopic analysis of vaginal and cervical secretions within several hours of sexual intercourse.

postpartum: After childbirth.

pre-embryo: See *conceptus*.

pregnancy: The growth and development of a new person inside a woman's uterus.

premenstrual syndrome [PMS]: The presence of a set of interrelated symptoms which recur regularly during the same phase of each menstrual cycle.

prenatal: The period before birth.

progesterone: Hormone produced by the corpus luteum and, during pregnancy, the placenta; prepares the uterine lining for implantation and the breasts for lactation; relaxes smooth muscle to prevent uterine contractions and subsequent pregnancy loss.

progestin: Any one of a group of hormones, natural or synthetic, that have progesterone-like effects on the reproductive system.

progestogen: See *progestin*.

prostaglandins: A group of strong hormonelike fatty acids that act on certain body organs. Used as a method of inducing labor and terminating pregnancy.

reproductive endocrinologist: An obstetrician-gynecologist who specializes in diagnosing and treating infertility.

research: Any inductive-deductive process which aims at promoting the systematic observation of a given phenonmenon in the human field or at verifying a hypotheseis arriving at previous observations.

RU486: A drug capable of inducing abortion by inhibiting the secretion of progesterone.

semen: The thick, white-colored fluid released by the male sex organs for the purpose of transporting sperm.

seminal fluid: See *semen*.

sex-linked: A genetic characteristic controlled by genes in sex chromosomes.

sexually transmitted disease [STD]: A contagious disease spread through intimate sexual contact.

sexually transmitted infertility: The inability to conceive or produce children as a result of damage to the reproductive organs due to a sexually transmitted disease.

side effect: A reaction resulting from medical treatment or therapy.

sperm: The male cell of reproduction; also called a *spermatozoa* or *gamete*.

sperm antibody test: Antibodies to sperm may be present in a woman's vaginal secretions; this test examines the sperm-mucus interaction.

sperm bank: See *cryobank*.

sperm count: An estimate of the number of sperm in a given sample of seminal fluid.

sperm donor: A man who produces sperm through masturbation for use in artificial insemination, usually for a fee.

spermatogenesis: The process of sperm production.

spermatozoon: The mature male sex or germ cell formed within the seminiferous tubules of the testes. [Singular: spermatozoa.]

spermicide: Any chemical substance that kills sperm cells.

sperm motility: The rate at which sperm move from one point to another.

sterile: The inability to produce children.

sterilization: An act or process that renders a person incapable of reproduction.

stress: Any factor that requires a response or change on the part of an organism or an individual.

stressor: Anything capable of causing wear and tear on the body's mental, physical, emotional, or spiritual resources.

surrogate embryo transfer [SET]: See *artificial embryonation*.

surrogate mother: A woman who agrees to have another couple's embryo transferred to her uterus for the period of gestation until the time of birth; a woman who bears no genetic relationship to the baby in her womb.

Common usage: a woman who agrees to be artificially inseminated with the sperm of an infertile woman's husband and to carry the baby until birth for a fee.

symptom: Something felt or noticed by an individual that can be used to detect what is going on within the body.

Sympto-Thermal Method of family planning: A method of family planning requiring fertility awareness based on the ovulation and basal body temperature methods of family planning.

syphilis: A sexually transmitted disease caused by an organism called a spirochete.

teaching hospital: A hospital associated with a medical institution in which students train and work with patients.

technician: A person skilled in a particular technique.

technique: The body of specialized procedures and methods used in any particular field.

technological, technology, high-tech: The branch of knowledge that deals with industrial arts, applied science, and engineering; a technological process, invention, method, or the like; in obstetrics and gynecology, medical care characterized by the use of invasive techniques and man-made interventions.

testecotomy: The surgical removal of a testicle. Also called *castration.*

testes: The two male reproductive glands located in the scrotum which produce sperm and the male sex hormone, testosterone. [Singular: testicle or testis.]

testosterone: A naturally secreted hormone in both males and females that is capable of producing masculine secondary sexual characteristics.

therapy: The treatment of an abnormal condition.

thromboembolism: A condition in which a blood vessel is blocked by a clot.

trimester: Period of three months; one of the three phases of pregnancy.

trophoblast: A strand of single cells ringing the blastocyst that will later become the placenta.

tubal cautery: Sterilization of a woman by burning both Fallopian tubes.

tubal ligation: Sterilization of a woman via surgical removal of a small segment of each Fallopian tube.

tubal pregnancy: A pregnancy in which the early embryo implants within the Fallopian tube and cannot develop normally.

ultrasonography: Inaudible high frequency sound waves used to outline the shape of body organs or a developing baby.

ultrasound: See *ultrasonography.*

urethra: The canal that carries urine from the bladder.

urinary stress incontinence: The involuntary passage of urine when coughing, sneezing, or laughing resulting from poor sphincter control of the urethra.

urology: The branch of medicine concerned with the care of the urinary tract in men and women and of the male genital tract.

uterine lavage: Flushing of the uterus performed by use of a catheter inserted into the cervix.

uterus: The thick-walled, hollow, muscular female organ of reproduction.

vacuum aspiration: A method of inducing abortion using a suction machine to remove the developing baby, placenta, and amniotic sac from the uterus.

vacuum extractor: An instrument used as an alternative to forceps that adheres to the baby's scalp and forcibly pulls the baby out of the birth canal.

vagina: The muscular tubelike membrane which forms the passageway between the uterus and genital entrance. It receives the penis during love-making and becomes the canal through which the baby passes during childbirth.

vas deferens: One of a pair of tubes within the male reproductive tract through which sperm pass.

vasectomy: A surgical procedure which produces male sterility by cutting a section out of each vas deferens.

viable: Capable of living, growing, and developing; a baby capable of living outside the uterus.

womb: See *uterus*.

wrongful life action: A lawsuit brought against a physician or health facility because an unwanted child was born.

X-chromosome: The sex-determining chromosome carried by all ova and approximately one-half of sperm.

Y-chromosome: The sex-determining chromosome carried by about one-half of all sperm, never by an egg, that produces a male child.

zygote: The developing egg between the time of fertilization and implantation in the wall of the uterus.

Notes

PREFACE

1. T. S. Eliot, *The Complete Poems and Plays, 1909-1950* (New York: Harcourt, Brace and World, 1958), 96.
2. Lester A. Kirkendall and Michael E. Perry, "The Transition from Sex to Sensuality and Intimacy," in Lester A. Kirkendall and Arthur E. Gravatt, eds., *Marriage and Family in the Year 2020* (New York: Prometheus Books, 1984), 161.
3. Marshall McLuhan and George Leonard, "The Future of Sex," *Look*, 25 July 1967, 56-63. Italics mine.
4. Kirkendall and Gravatt, *op. cit.*, 177. Italics mine.

INTRODUCTION

1. Genesis 49:25

CHAPTER 1: Women and Reproductive Surgery: The Current Crisis

1. George Gilder, *Men and Marriage* (Gretna, LA: Pelican Publishing, 1986), 179-180.
2. Robert S. Mendelsohn, *Male Practice* (Chicago: Contemporary Books, 1982, 1981), p. x.
3. Lloyd Shearer, "Most Frequently Performed Operations," *Parade Magazine*, September 15, 1985, 20. Here are the operations responsible for these alarming statistics: abortion by suction and scraping of the uterine lining (*suction curettage* and *sharp curettage*); surgical removal of the uterus (*hysterectomy*); sterilization by tubal ligation (*bilateral destruction or occlusion of the Fallopian tubes*); diagnostic or therapeutic removal of uterine tissue (*dilation and curettage*); surgical removal of the ovaries and Fallopian tubes with ovaries (*oophorectomy* and *salpingo-oophorectomy*) ; surgically assisted birth of infants by obstetrical instruments (vaginal delivery with *forceps* and *episiotomy*); and surgical birth of infants through an incision of the uterus (abdominal delivery by *cesarean section*).

4. Cary Groner, "Top 25 Most Frequently Performed Surgeries," *HealthWeek*, June 20, 1988, 23. I have added abortion to this total (as I also did in the "top fifteen"). This surgery is not often honestly included in tallies of "most performed surgeries," even though it is the most performed operation on the uterus at 1.6 million annually.
5. James L. Breen, "The Forgotten Half of Our Specialty," *The Female Patient*, 8 (September 1983): 1.
6. American Medical Association Council on Long Range Planning, "The Future of Obstetrics and Gynecology," *Journal of the American Medical Association*, December 25, 1987, 3548.
7. Harry S. Jonas, "The Torch Is Passed," *Journal of the American Medical Association*, December 25, 1987, 3555. Italics mine.
8. Dorothy C. Wertz, "What Birth Has Done for Doctors: A Historical View," *Women & Health* 8 (Spring 1983): 7.
9. National Center for Health Statistics, phone inquiry.
10. Sue Miller, "Physician: Toll of Hysterectomies Underestimated," *Baltimore Evening Sun*, in *Lincoln Sunday Journal Star*, November 13, 1988, 3E. ◆ *Money*, "A Consumer's Guide to Elective Operations" (January/February 1989): 106.

CHAPTER 2: Cesarean Section: Surrendering Childbirth

1. Nancy Wainer Cohen and Lois J. Estner, *Silent Knife: Cesarean Prevention & Vaginal Birth After Cesarean* (South Hadley, MA: Bergin & Garvey, 1983), 1.
2. From the National Center for Health Statistics data on vital statistics as reported by the American College of Obstetricians and Gynecologists, 1985; cited in the American Medical Association Council on Long Range Planning, "The Future of Obstetrics and Gynecology," *Journal of the American Medical Association*, December 25, 1987, 3548.
3. Paul J. Placek, Selma M. Taffel, and Mary Mohen, "1986 C-Sections Rise; VBACs Inch Upward," *American Journal of Public Health* 78 (May 1988): 562. ◆ Patricia H. Shiono, Donald McNellis, and George G. Rhoads, "Reasons for the Rising Cesarean Delivery Rates: 1978-1984," *Obstetrics & Gynecology* 69 (May 1987): 696-700. ◆ Elliot H. Philipson and Mortimer G. Rosen, "Trends in the Frequency of Cesarean Births," *Clinical Obstetrics and Gynecology* 28 (December 1985): 691-696. ◆ NIH Consensus Task Force on Cesarean Childbirth, *Cesarean Childbirth* (Bethesda, MD: U.S. Department of Health and Human Services, October 1981). NIH publication no. 82-2067. ◆ Francis C. Notzon, Paul J. Placek and Selma M. Taffel, "Comparisons of National Cesarean-Section Rates," *New England Journal of Medicine*, February 12, 1987, 386-389.
4. Stephen A. Myers and Norman Gleicher, "A Successful Program to Lower Cesarean-Section Rates," *New England Journal of Medicine*, December 8, 1988, 1511-1516. ◆ Dick Thompson, "Safer Births the Second Time," *Time*, November 7, 1988, 103. ◆ American Hospital Association, "Reducing C-Sections: Third Annual Obstetrical Excellence

Under Fire Teleconference," November 17, 1988, telecast by live satellite. ◆ Brent E. Finley and C. E. Gibbs, "Emergent Cesarean Delivery in Patients Undergoing a Trial of Labor with a Transverse Lower-Segment Scar," *American Journal of Obstetrics and Gynecology* 155 (November 1986): 939-938. ◆ Paul R. Meier and Richard Porreco, "Trial of Labor Following Cesarean Section: A Two-Year Experience," *American Journal of Obstetrics and Gynecology*, November 15, 1982, 671-678. ◆ Paul J. Placek and Selma M. Taffel, "Vaginal Birth After Cesarean (VBAC) in the 1980s," *American Journal of Public Health* 78 (May 1988): 512-515. ◆ Richard P. Porreco, "High Cesarean Section Rate: A New Perspective," *Obstetrics & Gynecology* 65 (March 1985): 307-311.

5. E. Eckholm, "Curbs Sought in Cesarean Deliveries," *New York Times*, August 11, 1986, A10.

6. Paul J. Placek, Selma M. Taffel, and T. Liss, "The Cesarean Future," *American Demographics*, 1987, 46-47.

7. Tim Friend, "Half of All C-Sections May Be Unwarranted," *USA Today*, January 27, 1989, 1D.

8. Helen I. Marieskind, "Cesarean Section," in Diony Young, *Obstetrical Intervention and Technology in the 1980s* (New York: Haworth Press, 1983), 194. Italics mine.

9. Helen I. Marieskind, *An Evaluation of Cesarean Section in the United States* (Washington, DC: U.S. Government Printing Office, 1979).

10. NIH Consensus Task Force on Cesarean Childbirth, *op. cit.* ◆ Mortimer Rosen, "NIH Consensus Development Statement on Cesarean Childbirth," *Obstetrics & Gynecology* 57 (April 1981): 537-545. ◆ Philipson and Rosen, *op. cit.* ◆ Shiono, McNellis and Rhoads, *op. cit.*, ◆ Patricia H. Shiono *et al.*, "Recent Trends in Cesarean Birth and Trial of Labor in the United States," *Journal of the American Medical Association*, January 23/30, 1987, 494-497.

11. Placek and Taffel (1988), op. cit, 514. ◆ Shiono, McNellis, and Rhoads, (1987), op. cit, 696.

12. E. B. Cragin, *New York Journal of Medicine* 104 (1916): 1. ◆ H. E. Schmitz and C. J. Gajewski, "Vaginal Delivery Following Cesarean Section," *American Journal of Obstetrics and Gynecology* 61 (1951): 1232-1241. ◆ J. K. Harris, "Vaginal Delivery Following Cesarean Section," *American Journal of Obstetrics and Gynecology* 66 (1953): 1191-1195. ◆ Paul Pedowitz and Ralph M. Schwartz, "The True Incidence of Silent Rupture of Cesarean Section Scars: A Prospective Analysis of 403 Cases," *American Journal of Obstetrics and Gynecology* 74 (November 1957): 1071-1081.

13. Meyers and Gleicher, *op. cit.*, 1516. ◆ Finley and Gibbs, *op. cit.*, 938. Meier and Porreco, *op. cit.*, 675-677. ◆ Thomas G. Stovall *et al.*, "Trial of Labor in Previous Cesarean Section Patients, Excluding Classical Cesarean Sections," *Obstetrics & Gynecology* 70 (November 1987): 713-717. ◆ Richard H. Paul, Jeffrey P. Phelan and Sze-ya Yeh, "Trial of Labor in the Patient with a Prior Cesarean Birth," *American Journal of Obstetrics and Gynecology*, February 1, 1985, 297-304. ◆ Geoffrey A.

Morewood, Mary J. O'Sullivan and John McConney, "Vaginal Delivery After Cesarean," *Obstetrics & Gynecology 42* (October 1973): 589-595. ◆ Ruth T. Wilf and John B. Franklin, "Six Years' Experience with Vaginal Births After Cesareans at Booth Maternity Center in Philadelphia," *BIRTH* 11 (Spring 1984): 5-9.

14. Beth Shearer, "Cesarean Rate Is a National Scandal," *Genesis* 10 (April/May 1988): 4. C/SEC (*Cesarean Support, Education and Concern*) is a consumer-oriented organization committed to preventing unnecessary cesareans and providing information and support to families who have undergone cesarean birth.

15. Placek and Taffel (1988), *op. cit.*, 512.

16. John R. Evrard and Edwin M. Gold, "Cesarean Section and Maternal Mortality in Rhode Island," *Obstetrics & Gynecology* (November 1977): 594-597.

17. Norbert Gleicher, "Cesarean Section Rates in the United States: The Short-term Failure of the National Consensus Development Conference in 1980," *Journal of the American Medical Association*, December 21, 1982, 3274. ◆ Diana B. Petitti *et al.*, "In-Hospital Maternal Mortality in the United States: Time Trends and Relation to Method of Delivery," *Obstetrics & Gynecology* 59 (1982): 6.

18. Friend, *op. cit.*

19. NIH Consensus Task Force on Cesarean Childbirth, *op. cit.* ◆ Diana B. Petitti, "Maternal Mortality and Morbidity in Cesarean Section," *Clinical Obstetrics and Gynecology* 28 (December 1985): 763-769. ◆ Thorkild F. Nielsen and Klas-Henry Hokegard, "Postoperative Cesarean Section Morbidity: A Prospective Study," *American Journal of Obstetrics and Gynecology*, August 15, 1983, 911-916. ◆ Ben P. Sachs *et al.*, "Cesarean Section: Risks and Benefits for Mother and Fetus," *Journal of the American Medical Association*, October 28, 1983, 2157-2159. ◆ Ralph C. Benson *et al.*, "Fetal Compromise During Elective Cesarean Section," *American Journal of Obstetrics and Gynecology*, March 1, 1965, 645-656.

20. Doris B. Haire, "The Pregnant Patient's Bill of Rights," in *21st Century Obstetrics Now!, Vol. 1*, Lee Stewart and David Stewart, eds. (Chapel Hill, NC: National Association for Parents and Professionals for Safe Alternatives in Childbirth, 1977), 1.

21. Elina Hemminki *et al.*, "Cesarean Section and Subsequent Fertility: Results from the 1982 Survey of Family Growth," *Fertility and Sterility* 43 (April 1985): 520-528. ◆ M. S. Zdeb *et al.*, "Frequency, Spacing, and Outcome of Pregnancies Subsequent to Primary Cesarean Childbirth," *American Journal of Obstetrics and Gynecology* 150 (1984): 205.

22. American College of Obstetricians and Gynecologists, Committee on Obstetrics: Maternal and Fetal Medicine, "Guidelines for Vaginal Birth After a Previous Cesarean," No. 64 (October 1988). ◆ Tim Friend, "New Rules Aim to Reduce C-sections," *USA Today*, October 27, 1988. ◆ Dick Thompson, *op. cit.* ◆ American Hospital Association, *op. cit.*

23. ACOG press release, "Repeat Cesareans No Longer the Norm," October 26, 1988.

24. Gleicher, *op. cit.*, 3273-3276. *Journal of the American Medical*

Association, "Cesarean Section Rates in the United States (Letters)," June 14, 1985, 3247-3249. ◆ Meyers and Gleicher, *op. cit.*, 1516.

25. Friend, *op. cit.*, January 27, 1989.

26. Roberta Haynes de Regt *et al.*, "Relation of Private or Clinic Care to the Cesarean Birth Rate," *New England Journal of Medicine*, September 4, 1986, 619. ◆ Joseph Ahram, "High Cesarean Section Rate," *Obstetrics & Gynecology* 66 (December 1985): 838.

27. Kenneth W. Kizer and Art Ellis, "C-Section Rate Related to Payment Source," *American Journal of Public Health* 78 (January 1988). ◆ Paul J. Placek, Selma M. Taffel, and Mary Mohen, "1986 C-Sections Rise; VBACs Inch Upward," *American Journal of Public Health* 78 (May 1988): 562. ◆ Porreco, *op. cit.*, 308.

28. Gleicher, *op. cit.*, 3274-3275.

29. Marieskind, *op. cit.*, 1979. ◆ Shiono *et al.*, (January 1987), 497. ◆ Bruce A. Harris, "Cesarean Section Rates in the United States (Letter)," *Journal of the American Medical Association*, June 14, 1985, 3247. ◆ Irwin J. Reiner, "Cesarean Section Rates in the United (Letter)," *Journal of the American Medical Association*, June 14, 1985, 3247.

30. Diony Young, "Malpractice," *Childbirth Educator* (Winter 1984/1985). Reprint.

31. John J. Fried, "Too Many Cesarean Births," *Reader's Digest* 118 (March 1981): 100.

32. Emanuel A. Friedman, "The Obstetrician's Dilemma: How Much Fetal Monitoring and Cesarean Section Is Enough?" *New England Journal of Medicine*, September 4, 1986, 642.

33. Lester T. Hibbard, "Changing Trends in Cesarean Section," *American Journal of Obstetrics and Gynecology*, July 15, 1976, 798-804. ◆ O. Hunter Jones, "Cesarean Section in Present-Day Obstetrics," *American Journal of Obstetrics and Gynecology*, November 12, 1976, 521-530. ◆ Ralph C. Benson *et al.*, "Fetal Compromise During Elective Cesarean Section," *American Journal of Obstetrics and Gynecology*, March 1, 1965, 645-656.

34. N. Paneth and R. I. Stark, "Cerebral Palsy and Mental Retardation in Relation to Indicators of Perinatal Asphyxia: An Epidemiologic Overview," *American Journal of Obstetrics and Gynecology* 147 (1983): 960-966. ◆ N. Paneth, "Birth and the Origins of Cerebral Palsy," *New England Journal of Medicine* 315 (1986): 124-126. ◆ Kenneth R. Niswander, "The Obstetrician, Fetal Asphyxia, and Cerebral Palsy," *American Journal of Obstetrics and Gynecology*, February 15, 1979, 358-361. ◆ Douglas Bell *et al.*, "Birth Asphyxia, Trauma, and Mortality in Twins: Has Cesarean Section Improved Outcome?" *American Journal of Obstetrics and Gynecology* 154 (February 1986): 235-239. ◆ S. B. Effer *et al.*, "Effect of Delivery Method on Outcomes in the Very Low-Birth Weight Breech Infant: Is the Improved Survival Rate Related to Cesarean Section or Other Perinatal Care Maneuvers?" *American Journal of Obstetrics and Gynecology*, January 15, 1983, 123-128.

35. Elliot H. Philipson and Mortimer G. Rosen, "Trends in the Frequency of Cesarean Births," *Clinical Obstetrics and Gynecology* 28 (December

1985): 692. ◆ Robin N. Phillips, John Thornton, and Norbert Gleicher, "Physician Bias in Cesarean Sections," *Journal of the American Medical Association*, September 3, 1982, 1083, 1084. ◆ William Fraser *et al.*, "Temporal Variation in Rates of Cesarean Section for Dystocia: Does 'Convenience' Play A Role?" *American Journal of Obstetrics and Gynecology* 156 (February 1987): 300-304. ◆ Gleicher, *op. cit.*, 3274. ◆ Shiono, McNellis and Rhoads, *op. cit.*, 697, 699. ◆ Rosen., *op. cit.* 539. ◆ Marieskind (1983), *op. cit.*, 190.

36. Matt Clark, "Too Many Cesareans?" *Newsweek*, October 6, 1980, 105.

37. Philipson and Rosen, *op. cit.* ◆ Gleicher, *op. cit.* ◆ Shiono, McNellis and Rhoads, *op. cit.* ◆ Rosen, *op. cit.*

38. H. David Banta and Stephen B. Thacker, *Costs and Benefits of Electronic Fetal Monitoring: A Review of the Literature* (Hyattsville, MD: U.S. Department of Health, Education, and Welfare, NCHSR Research Report Series, 1979).

39. Albert D. Haverkamp *et al.*, "The Evaluation of Continuous Fetal Heart Rate Monitoring in High-Risk Pregnancy," *American Journal of Obstetrics and Gynecology*, June 1, 1976, 310-320. ◆ Peter Renou *et al.*, "Controlled Trial of Fetal Intensive Care," *American Journal of Obstetrics and Gynecology* , October 15, 1976, 470-476. ◆ Ian M. Kelso *et al.*, "An Assessment of Continuous Fetal Heart Rate Monitoring in Labor," *American Journal of Obstetrics and Gynecology* 131 (1978): 526-532. ◆ Albert D. Haverkamp *et al.*, "A Controlled Trial of the Differential Effects of Intrapartum Fetal Monitoring," *American Journal of Obstetrics and Gynecology* 134 (1979): 399. ◆ Carl Wood *et al.*, "A Controlled Trial of Fetal Heart Rate Monitoring in a Low-Risk Obstetric Population," *American Journal of Obstetrics and Gynecology*, November 1, 1981, 527-534. ◆ Dermot W. MacDonald *et al.*, "The Dublin Randomized Controlled Trial of Intrapartum Fetal Heart Rate Monitoring," *American Journal of Obstetrics and Gynecology,* July 1, 1985: 524-539. ◆ David A. Luthy *et al.*, "A Randomized Trial of Electronic Fetal Monitoring in Preterm Labor," *Obstetrics & Gynecology* 69 (May 1987): 687-695.

40. Banta and Thacker, *op. cit.*, 13-15.

41. Haverkamp *et al.* (1976), *op. cit.*, 316.

42. Porreco, *op. cit.*, 311. ◆ Meyers and Gleicher, *op. cit.*, 1511-1512 ◆ American Hospital Association, *op. cit.*, teleconference. ◆ T. F. Baskett, "Cesarean Section: What Is an Acceptable Rate?" *Canadian Medical Association Journal*, May 6, 1978, 1019-1020. ◆ Edward Quilligan, "Cesarean Section: Modern Perspective," in J. T. Queenan, ed. *Management of High-Risk Pregnancy*, 2nd ed. (Oradell, NJ: Medical Economics, 1985), 594-600.

43. Herbert Ratner, "The History of the Dehumanization of American Obstetrical Practice," in Stewart and Stewart, *op. cit.*, 120.

CHAPTER 3: Hysterectomy: A Double Standard of a Different Kind

1. Charles B. Inlander, Lowell S. Levin, and Ed Weiner, *Medicine on Trial* (New York: Prentice Hall Press, 1988), 12.

2. Ruth Toumala, "Hysterectomy," *Harvard Medical School Health Letter* 13 (May 1988): 8.
3. Richard C. Dicker *et al.*, "Complications of Abdominal and Vaginal Hysterectomy Among Women of Reproductive Age in the United States, *American Journal of Obstetrics and Gynecology*, December 1, 1982, 841-848.
4. John P. Bunker, "Elective Hysterectomy: Pro and Con," *New England Journal of Medicine*, July 29, 1976, 264.
5. *Journal of the American Medical Association*, "'Legitimacy' of Hysterectomies Remains Subject of Debate," June 28, 1976, 2801-2802. ◆ Tuomala, *op. cit.*, 5.
6. Herbert H. Keyser, *Women Under the Knife* (Philadelphia: George F. Strickley, 1984), 52-53.
7. Sue Miller, "Physician: Toll of Hysterectomies Underestimated," *Baltimore Evening Sun*, reprinted in *Lincoln Sunday Journal Star*, November 13, 1988, 3E.
8. Philip Cole, "Elective Hysterectomy: Pro and Con," *New England Journal of Medicine*, July 29, 1976, 265.
9. Gianfranco Domenighetti *et al.*, "Effect of Information Campaign by the Mass Media on Hysterectomy Rates, " *Lancet*, December 24/31, 1988, 1470.
10. Winnifred B. Cutler, *Hysterectomy: Before and After* (New York: Harper & Row, 1988), 2.
11. *Ibid.* Italics mine.
12. Dicker *et al.*, *op. cit.*, 842.
13. Ralph C. Wright, "Hysterectomy: Past, Present, and Future," *Obstetrics & Gynecology* 33 (April 1969): 562-563.
14. *Ibid.*, 562.
15. *Ibid.*, 267.
16. American Medical Association Council on Long Range Planning, "The Future of Obstetrics and Gynecology," *Journal of the American Medical Association*, December 25, 1987, 3548.
17. "Elective Hysterectomies," *Medical World News* 13 (1972): 37-45.
18. Robert S. Mendelsohn, *Male Practice* (Chicago: Contemporary Books, 1982, 1981), 99.
19. *Ibid.*, 99-100.
20. Malkah T. Notman, "Elective Hysterectomy: Pro and Con," *New England Journal of Medicine*, July 29, 1976, 266.
21. Robert A. Hatcher *et al.*, *Contraceptive Technology, 1988-1989,* 14th rev. ed. (New York: Irvington Publishers, 1988), 420.
22. *Ibid.*
23. *Medical World News*, "Women MDs Join the Fight," October 23, 1970, 24.
24. James C. Doyle, "Unnecessary Ovariectomies," *Journal of the American Medical Association*, March 29, 1952, 1105-1111.
25. *Ibid.*, 1105.
26. *bid.*, 1106.
27. American Cancer Society, "For Men Only: Testicular Cancer and How to Do TSE (A Self Exam)." Pamphlet.

28. *Ob. Gyn. News*, March 1, 1980, 1.
29. Mendelsohn, *op. cit.*, 101.
30. Valentina Clark Donahue *et al.*, "Elective Hysterectomy: Pro and Con," *New England Journal of Medicine* 295 (1976): 264.
31. *Ibid.* ◆ Dicker *et al.*, *op. cit.*, 844. ◆ R. K. Laros and B. A. Work, "Female Sterilization III. Vaginal Hysterectomy," *American Journal of Obstetrics and Gynecology* 122 (1977): 693-697. ◆ Hassan Amirika and T. N. Evans, "Ten-Year Review of Hysterectomies: Trends, Indications, and Risks," *American Journal of Obstetrics and Gynecology* 134 (1979): 431-437.
32. Miller, *op. cit.*
33. Cutler, *op. cit.*, 3-5.
34. Tuomala, *op. cit.*, 8.
35. *Ibid.*, 5.
36. *Ibid.*, 5, 35.
37. *Ibid.*, 35-36

CHAPTER 4: Abortion: Into the Heart of Woman

1. Adelaide Hass and Kurt Haas, *Understanding Sexuality* (St. Louis: Times Mirror/Mosby, 1987), 423.
2. Mary S. Calderone and Eric W. Johnson, *The Family Book About Sexuality* (New York: Bantam, 1983), 109.
3. American College of Obstetricians and Gynecologists, February 1973 and June 1974, quoted in Calderone and Johnson, *Family Book*, 113-114.
4. David C. Reardon, *Aborted Women: Silent No More* (Westchester, IL: Crossway Books, 1987), 89.
5. Mary R. Joyce, "The Sexual Revolution Has Yet to Begin," in Thomas J. Hilgers and Dennis J. Horan, *Abortion and Social Justice* (Thaxton, VA: Sun Life, 1980), 224-225.
6. William B. Ober, "We Should Legalize Abortion," *Saturday Evening Post*, October 8, 1966, 14-16. ◆ Robert H. Williams, "Our Role in the Generation, Modification, and Termination of Life," *Journal of the American Medical Association*, August 11, 1969, 914-917. ◆ Sidney Bolter, "The Psychiatrist's Role in Therapeutic Abortion: The Unwitting Accomplice." Paper read at the 118th annual meeting of The American Psychiatric Association, Toronto, Canada, May 7-11, 1962. *American Journal of Psychiatry* (October 1962): 312, 316. ◆ Phyllis Bailey Thurstone, "Therapeutic Abortion," *Journal of the American Medical Association*, July 14, 1969, 229-231. ◆ Garrett Hardin, "Abortion — or Compulsory Pregnancy?" *Journal of Marriage and the Family* (May 1968): 246-251. ◆ Christopher Tietze and Sarah Lewit, "Abortion," *Scientific American* 220 (January 1969): 21-27. ◆ Harriet F. Pilpel, "The Right of Abortion," *Atlantic Monthly* 223 (June 1969): 69-71.
7. Lester Kinsolving, "What About Therapeutic Abortion?" *Christian Century*, May 13, 1964, 634. Italics mine.
8. *Ibid.*
9. *Ibid.*
10. Ralph J. Gampbell and H. J. Packer, *Stanford Law Review* 2 (May 1959), quoted in Kinsolving, *op. cit.*, 7.

11. Myre Sim, "Abortion: It Is Time for Doctors to Get Off the Fence," *Canadian Medical Journal,* April 15, 1988, 743.

12. Supreme Court of the United States, *Jane Roe et. al. v. Henry Wade.* Supreme Court of the United States, Opinion No. 70-18, January 22, 1973.

13. Supreme Court of the United States, *Doe et. al. v. Bolton.* Attorney of Georgia *et al.* Supreme Court of the United States, Opinion No. 70-40, January 22, 1973.

14. Paul Ramsey, "Protecting the Unborn," *Commonweal,* May 31, 1974, 308-314.

15. Stanley K. Henshaw, "Characteristics of U.S. Women Having Abortions, 1982-1983," *Family Planning Perspectives* 19 (January/February 1987): 5-9. ◆ "Abortion Surveillance: Preliminary Analysis — United States, 1984, 1985," *Journal of the American Medical Association,* December 16, 1988, 3410-3412.

16. Myre Sim, "Abortion: Is It Time for Doctors to Get Off the Fence? (Letters)," *Canadian Medical Journal,* June 15, 1988, 1085.

17. Stanley K. Henshaw, Jaqueline Darroch Forrest, and Jennifer Van Vort, "Abortion Services in the United States, 1984 and 1985," *Family Planning Perspectives* 19 (March/April 1987), 67-68.

18. *Ibid.,* 63.

19. *Ibid.*

20. Henshaw, Forrest, Van Vort, *op. cit.,* 68.

21. *Ibid.,* 68.

22. Robert G. Castadot, "Pregnancy Termination: Techniques, Risks and Complications and Their Management," *Fertility and Sterility* 45 (January 1986): 7.

23. Norma Rosen, "Between Guilt and Gratification: Abortion Doctors Reveal Their Feelings," *New York Times Magazine,* April 17, 1977, 78.

24. Stephen D. Mumford, "Abortion: A National Security Issue," *American Journal of Obstetrics and Gynecology,* April 15, 1982, 951-953.

25. *Ibid.,* 952.

26. Bernard N. Nathanson, "Deeper into Abortion," *New England Journal of Medicine,* November 28, 1974, 1189.

27. *Ibid.*

28. *Ibid.*

29. Castadot, *op. cit.,* 7. ◆ *Journal of the American Medical Association, op. cit.,* 3410.

30. Reardon, *op. cit.,* 94.

31. Castadot, *op. cit.,* 12.

32. H. Trent Mackay, Kenneth F. Schulz, and David A. Grimes, "Safety of Local Versus General Anesthesia for Second-Trimester Dilation and Evacuation Abortion," *Obstetrics & Gynecology* 66 (November 1985): 661-665.

33. Castadot, *op. cit.,* 8-9. ◆ Christopher Tietze, *Induced Abortion, A World Review, 1983* (New York: The Population Council, 1983), 83. ◆ Willard Cates and David A. Grimes, "Deaths from Second Trimester Abortion by Dilation and Evacuation: Causes, Prevention, Facilities," *Obstetrics & Gynecology* 58 (October 1981): 401-408. ◆ Willard Cates, Richard M.

Selik, and Carl W. Tyler, "Behavioral Factors Contributing to Abortion Deaths: A New Approach to Mortality Studies," *Obstetrics & Gynecology* 58 (November 1981): 631. ◆ Christopher R. Harman, David G. Fish, and John E. Tyson, "Factors Influencing Morbidity in Termination of Pregnancy," *American Journal of Obstetrics and Gynecology*, February 1, 1981, 333-337. ◆ Robert A. Hatcher *et al.*, *Contraceptive Technology, 1988-1989*, 2nd ed. (New York: Irvington Publishers, 1988), 394-398.

34. Nancyjo Mann, Foreword, in David C. Reardon, *Aborted Women: Silent No More* (Westchester, IL: Crossway Books, 1987), xxvi.

35. Henshaw, *op. cit.*, 5. ◆ *Journal of the American Medical Association, op. cit.*, 3410.

36. Henshaw, *op. cit.*, 5, 7.

37. *Ibid.*, 7.

38. *Ibid.*, 5, 7.

39. Aida Torres and Jaqueline Darroch Forrest, "Why Do Women Have Abortions?" *Family Planning Perspectives* 20 (July/August 1988): 169-176.

40. Sidney Callahan, "Abortion and the Sexual Agenda: A Case for Pro-Life Feminism," *Commonweal*, April 25, 1986, 235-238.

CHAPTER 5: Egg Harvesting and Embryo Experimentation: Lab-Oriented Conceptions

1. Congressman Ron Wyden, hearing before Subcommittee on Regulation and Business Opportunities, Washington DC, June 1, 1988. In Committee on Small Business, *Consumer Protection Issues Involving In Vitro Fertilization Clinics* (Washington, DC: U.S. Government Printing Office, 1988), 1.

2. C. S. Lewis, *The Screwtape Letters* (New York: Macmillan, 1964), ix.

3. Editorial, "What Comes After Fertilization?" *Nature*, February 15, 1969, 613.

4. For example, see: Landrum Shettles, "Observations on Human Follicular and Tubal Ova," *American Journal of Obstetrics and Gynecology*, 1953, 66(2): 235-247. ◆ Landrum Shettles, "A Morula Stage of Human Ova Developed In Vitro," *Fertility and Sterility*, 1955, 6(4): 287-289. ◆ Landrum Shettles, "Corona Radiata and Zona Pellucida of Living Human Ova," *Fertility and Sterility*, 1958, 9(2): 167-170. ◆ Luigi Mastroianni and Carlos Noriega, "Observations on Human Ova and the Fertilization Process," *American Journal of Obstetrics and Gynecology*, 1970, 107(5): 682-690. ◆ Joseph F. Kennedy and Roger P. Donahue, "Human Oocytes: Maturation in Chemically Defined Media," *Science*, 164 (June 13, 1969): 1292-1293. ◆ P. Liedholm, P. Sundstrom, and H. Wramsky, "A Model for Experimental Studies on Human Egg Transfer, *Archives of Andrology*, 1980, 5(1): 92.

5. Loretta McLaughlin, *The Pill, John Rock and the Church* (Boston: Little, Brown and Company, 1982). ◆ Arthur T. Hertig, "A Fifteen-Year Search for First-Stage Human Ova," *Journal of the American Medical Association*, January 20, 1989, 434-435. ◆ Robert Edwards and Patrick

Steptoe, *A Matter of Life* (New York: William Morrow and Company, 1980).

6. McLaughlin, *op. cit.*, 41.
7. Hertig, *op. cit.*, 434.
8. *Ibid.*
9. McLaughlin, *op. cit.*, 63-64.
10. Hertig, *op. cit.*, 435.
11. McLaughlin, *op. cit.*, 64.
12. James C. Doyle, "Unnecessary Ovariectomies," *Journal of the American Medical Association,* March 29, 1952, 1105-1111.
13. *Ibid.*, 1111.
14. *Ibid.*, 1105.
15. Hertig, *op. cit.*, 434. ◆ McLaughlin, *op. cit.*, 68.
16. Hertig, *op. cit.*, 435.
17. John Rock and Arthur T. Hertig, "Some Aspects of Early Human Development," *American Journal of Obstetrics and Gynecology* 44 (1942): 973-983.
18. Hertig, *op. cit.*, 435.
19. *Ibid.*, 434.
20. John Rock and Miriam F. Menkin, "In Vitro Fertilization and Cleavage of Human Ovarian Eggs," *Science*, August 4, 1944, 105.
21. McLaughlin, *op. cit.*, 78
22. Rock and Menkin, *op. cit.* ◆ Miriam F. Menkin and John Rock, "In Vitro Fertilization and Cleavage of Human Ovarian Eggs," *American Journal of Obstetrics and Gynecology* 55 (March 1948): 440-454.
23. *Ibid.*
24. R. G. Edwards, B. D. Bavister and P. C. Steptoe, "Early Stages of Fertilization In Vitro of Human Oocytes Matured In Vitro," *Nature*, February 15, 1969, 632-635.
25. R. G. Edwards and Patrick Steptoe, *A Matter of Life* (New York: William Morrow and Co., 1980), 42-43.
26. R. G. Edwards, "Maturation In Vitro of Mouse, Sheep, Cow, Pig, Rhesus Monkey and Human Ovarian Oocytes," *Nature*, October 23, 1965, 349-351. ◆ R. G. Edwards, "Maturation In Vitro of Human Ovarian Oocytes," *Lancet*, November 6, 1965, 926-929.
27. *Ibid.*, 349-350.
28. Edwards and Steptoe, *A Matter of Life*, 57.
29. R. G. Edwards, "Chromosomal Abnormalities in Human Embryos," *Nature*, May 26, 1983, 283. ◆ Roslyn R. Angell *et al.*, "Chromosome Abnormalities in Human Embryos After *In Vitro* Fertilization," *Nature*, May 26, 1983, 336-338. ◆ J. L. Watt *et al.*, "Trisomy 1 in an Eight Cell Human Pre-Embryo," *Journal of Medical Genetics* 24 (1987): 60-64. ◆ Gail Vines, "New Insight into Early Embryos," *New Scientist*, July 9, 1987, 22-23.
30. Anne McLaren, "Can We Diagnose Genetic Disease in Pre-Embryos?" *New Scientist*, December 10, 1987, 44-47. ◆ Kathy Johnston, "Sex of New Embryos Known," *Nature*, June 18, 1987, 547.
31. R. G. Edwards, "Mammalian Eggs in the Laboratory, *Scientific American* 215 (August 1966): 81.

32. R. G. Edwards, B. D. Bavister, and P. C. Steptoe, "Early Stages of Fertilization *In Vitro* of Human Oocytes Matured *In Vitro*," *Nature*, February 15, 1969, 632.

33. Edwards and Steptoe, *A Matter of Life*, 186-187.

34. *Ibid.*, 81.

35. *Ibid.*, 82. Italics mine.

36. See Edwards's and Bavister's article and the accompanying editorial in *Nature*, February 15, 1969, 632-635 and 613.

37. Before admission for a diagnostic laparoscopy recently, I asked what would be done with my ovary or ovaries if surgery was deemed absolutely necessary. The site of the procedure was to be a Catholic hospital. They said that ovaries removed from women there are buried, I presume out of respect for women's reproductive dignity and the sanctity of human life. Nevertheless, I decided to include my understanding of this policy on the consent form for my surgery. For any woman undergoing surgery today in which ovarian tissue might be removed, I strongly recommend including a statement such as this: "It is my understanding that it is the policy of this hospital to bury surgically removed ovaries. In the event that an ovariectomy is necessary, I request disposal of all ovarian tissue taken from me by this method, without prior oocyte removal." My gynecologist, who is a woman, fully understood my request. If the hospital had not had this policy, I would have made my own arrangements for the safe disposal of my ova.

CHAPTER 6: Infertility Diagnosis and Treatment: To Catch a Falling Star

1. Richard J. Lilford and Maureen E. Dalton, "Effectiveness of Treatment for Infertility," *British Medical Journal*, July 18, 1987, 155.

2. Committee on Small Business, *Consumer Protection Issues Involving In Vitro Fertilization Clinics* (Washington, DC: U.S. Government Printing Office, 1988), 3.

3. *Ibid.*

4. Committee on Government Operations, *Medical and Social Choices for Infertile Couples and the Federal Role in Prevention and Treatment* (Washington, DC: U.S. Government Printing Office, 1989), 48-49.

5. Sue Halpern, "Infertility: Playing the Odds," *Ms.*, January/February 1989, 148.

6. Diane Harris, "What It Costs to Fight Infertility," *Money*, December 1984, 202.

7. Genesis 30:1.

8. Lewis J. Lord, "Desperately Seeking Baby," *U.S. News & World Report*, October 5, 1987, 58.

9. U.S. Congress, Office of Technology Assessment, *Infertility: Medical and Social Choices*, OTA-BA-358 (Washington, DC: U.S. Government Printing Office, May 1988), 141.

10. *Wisconsin Medical Journal* 87 (March 1988): 63.

11. Sevgi O. Aral and Willard Cates, "The Increasing Concern with Infertility: Why Now?" *Journal of the American Medical Association*, November 4, 1983, 2330.

12. Information obtained by phone from the American College of Obstetricians and Gynecologists.

13. Aral and Cates, *op. cit.*, 2330. Italics mine.

14. Lord, *op. cit.*, 59.

15. Committee on Small Business, *op. cit.*, 16.

16. U.S. Congress, OTA, *op. cit.*, 141. The first dollar figure represents the median fee as determined by a survey of infertility specialists conducted by the Office of Technology Assessment in 1986; the figures in parentheses indicate the range of costs reported in the survey.

17. *Ibid.*, 5.

18. Harris, *op. cit.*, 212.

19. Lord, *op. cit.*, 61.

20. *Ibid.*

21. *Ibid.*, 63.

22. Robert W. Rebar *et al.*, "Are We Exploiting the Infertile Couple?" *Fertility and Sterility* 48 (November 1987): 735.

23. Harris, *op. cit.*, 202.

24. William J. Winslade and Judith Wilson Ross, *Choosing Life or Death: A Guide for Patients, Families, and Professionals* (New York: The Free Press, 1986), 127-128. Italics mine.

25. Harris, *op. cit.*, 206. ◆ U.S. Congress, OTA, *op. cit.*, 141.

26. Medical Economics Co., Inc, *Physician's Desk Reference to Prescription Drugs, 43rd ed., 1989* (Oradell, NJ: Medical Economics, Inc, 1989): 2030-2033. ◆ American Hospital Formulary Service, *Drug Information: 1988* (Bethesda, MD: American Society of Hospital Pharmacists, 1988), 2137-2139. ◆ United States Pharmacopeial Convention, *USP Dispensing Information, 8th ed., 1988* (Rockville, MD: United States Pharmacopeial Convention, 1988), 736-737. ◆ T. Engel *et al.*, "Ovarian Hyperstimulation Syndrome," *American Journal of Obstetrics and Gynecology,* April 15, 1972, 1052-1060. ◆ C. Derom *et al.*, "Increased Monozygotic Twinning Rate After Ovulation Induction," *Lancet,* May 30, 1987, 1236-1238. ◆ Alison MacFarlane *et al.*, "Multiple Pregnancy and Assisted Reproduction," *Lancet,* November 7, 1987, 1090. ◆ Joseph G. Schenker, Shaul Yarkoni, and Menachem Granat, "Multiple Pregnancies Following Induction of Ovulation," *Fertility and Sterility* 35 (February 1981): 105-123.

27. United States Pharmacopeial Convention, *op. cit.*, 736. ◆ Grant E. Schmidt *et al.*, "The Effects of Enclomiphene and Zuclomiphene Citrates on Mouse Embryos Fertilized In Vitro and In Vivo," *American Journal of Obstetrics and Gynecology* 154 (April 1986): 727-736.

28. U.S. Congress, OTA, *op. cit.*, 10.

29. Committee on Small Business, *op. cit.*, 16.

30. U.S. Congress, OTA, *op. cit.*, 131.

31. The Aicardis tell their story in *U.S. News & World Report*, October 5, 1987 on pages 58, 60 and 61.

32. U.S. Congress , OTA, *op. cit.*, 4.

33. Jane Menken, James Trussell, and Ulla Larsen, "Age and Infertility," *Science*, September 26, 1986, 1389-1390. Italics mine.

34. U. S. Congress, OTA, *op. cit.*, 3.

35. Menken, Trussell, and Larsen, *op. cit.*, 1391.

36. John A. Collins *et al.*, "Treatment-Independent Pregnancy Among Infertile Couples," *New England Journal of Medicine*, November 17, 1983, 1201-1205. ◆ See also: Dinu Berstein *et al.*, "Is Conception in Infertile Couples Treatment-related?" *International Journal of Fertility* 24 (1979): 65-67. ◆ J. Jarrell *et al.*, "An In Vitro Fertilization and Embryo Transfer Pilot Study: Treatment-Dependent and Treatment-Independent Pregnancies," *American Journal of Obstetrics and Gynecology* 154 (February 1986): 231-235. ◆ Sung I. Roh *et al.*, "In Vitro Fertilization and Embryo Transfer: Treatment-Dependent versus -Independent Pregnancies," *Fertility and Sterility* 48 (December 1987): 982-986.

37. *Ibid.* Italics mine.

38. Mencken, Trussell, and Larsen, *op. cit.*, 1391. Italics mine.

39. Robert A. Hatcher *et al.*, *Contraceptive Technology 1988-1989*, 14th rev. ed. (New York: Irvington Publishers, 1988), 37-40; 100-102. ◆ A. Eugene Washington, Peter S. Arno, and Marie A. Brooks, "The Economic Cost of Pelvic Inflammatory Disease," *Journal of the American Medical Association*, April 4, 1986, 1735-1738. ◆ Marsha F. Goldsmith, "Sexually Transmitted Diseases May Reverse the 'Revolution,'" *Journal of the American Medical Association*, April 4, 1986, 1665-1672. ◆ Judythe Torrington, "Pelvic Inflammatory Disease," *JOGN Nursing*, Supplement (November/December 1985): 21s-31s. ◆ L. Svensson, P. A. Mardh, and L. Westrom, "Infertility After Acute Salpingitis [PID] with Special Reference to Chlamydia Trachomatis," *Fertility and Sterility* 40 (1983): 322-329.

40. Committee on Small Business, *op. cit.*, 16.

41. Janet R. Daling *et al.*, "Primal Tubal Infertility in Relation to the Use of An Intrauterine Device," *New England Journal of Medicine*, April 11, 1985, 937-941. ◆ Daniel W. Cramer *et al.*, "Tubal Infertility and the Intrauterine Device," *New England Journal of Medicine*, April 11, 1985, 941-947. ◆ William L. Faulkner and Howard W. Ory, "Intrauterine Devices and Acute Pelvic Inflammatory Disease," *Journal of the American Medical Association*, April 26, 1986, 1851-1853. ◆ Katherine Roberts, "The Intrauterine Device as a Health Risk," *Women & Health* 2 (July/August 1977): 21-29. ◆ Y. Hata *et al.*, "The Effect of Long-Term Use of Intrauterine Devices," *International Journal of Fertility* 14 (July-September 1969): 241-249. ◆ Hatcher *et al.*, *op. cit.*, 101. ◆ Sevgi O. Aral, William D. Mosher, and Willard Cates, Jr., "Contraceptive Use, Pelvic Inflammatory Disease, and Fertility Problems Among American Women," *American Journal of Obstetrics and Gynecology* 256 (1987): 59-64. ◆ N. C. Lee, G. L. Rubin, and H. W. Ory, "Type of Intrauterine Device and the Risk of Pelvic Inflammatory Disease," *Obstetrics & Gynecology* 62 (1983): 1-6.

42. Lord, op, cit., 59.

43. Hatcher *et al.*, *op. cit.*, 101.

44. A. Eugene Washington *et al.*, "Oral Contraceptives, Chlamydia Trachomatis Infection, and Pelvic Inflammatory Disease: A Word of

Caution About Protection," *Journal of the American Medical Association*, April 19, 1985, 2246-2250. ◆ Daniel W. Cramer *et al.*, "The Relationship of Tubal Infertility to Barrier Method and Oral Contraceptive Use," *Journal of the American Medical Association*, May 8, 1987, 2446-2450.

45. C. J. Hogue, W. Cates, and C. Tietze, "Effects of Induced Abortion on Subsequent Reproduction," *Epidemiological Review* 4 (1982): 66-94.

46. W. R. Phipps, D. W. Cramer, and I. Schiff, "The Association Between Smoking and Female Infertility as Influenced by the Cause of the Infertility," *Fertility and Sterility* 48 (1987): 377-382. ◆ R. J. Stillman, M. J. Rosenberg, and B. P. Sachs, "Smoking and Reproduction," *Fertility and Sterility* 46 (1986): 545. ◆ A. J. Hartz *et al.*, "The Association of Smoking with Clinical Indicators of Altered Sex Steroids — A Study of 50,145 Women," *Public Health Reports* 102 (1987): 254-259. ◆ Allen Wilcox, Clarice Weinberg, and Donna Baird, "Caffeinated Beverages and Decreased Fertility," *Lancet*, December 24/31, 1988, 1453-1456.

47. James Wyngaarden, "Study Finds Association Between Smoking and Certain Types of Infertility," *Journal of the American Medical Association*, July 8, 1988, 161.

48. Donna Day Baird and Allen J. Wilcox, "Cigarette Smoking with Delayed Conception," *Journal of the American Medical Association*, May 24/31, 1985, 2979-2983.

49. Wilcox, Weinberg, and Baird, op. cit, 1453.

50. U. S. Congress, OTA, *op. cit.*, 63-64. ◆ B. A. Bullen *et al.*, "Induction of Menstrual Disorders by Strenuous Exercise in Untrained Women," *New England Journal of Medicine*, 1985, 1345-1353. ◆ P. T. Ellison and C. Lager, "Moderate Recreational Running Is Associated with Lowered Salivary Progesterone Profiles in Women," *American Journal of Obstetrics and Gynecology* 154 (1986): 1000-1003. ◆ Z. M. Van Der Spuy, "Nutrition and Reproduction," *Clinics in Obstetrics and Gynecology* 12 (1985): 579-604. ◆ R. E. Frisch, "Body Fat, Puberty, and Fertility," *Science* 185 (1984): 949-953. ◆ M. Seibel and M. Taynor, "Emotional Aspects of Infertility," *Fertility and Sterility* 37 (1982): 137-145.

51. Committee on Small Business, *op. cit.*, 16.

52. *Ibid.*, 5.

53. Committee on Small Business, *op. cit.*, 56.

54. Menken, Trussell, and Larsen, *op. cit.*, 1393. Italics mine.

55. Malcolm Potts and David A Grimes, "STDs, IVF, and Barrier Contraception (Letter)," *Journal of the American Medical Association*, October 2, 1987, 1729. Italics mine.

CHAPTER 7: In Vitro Fertilization and Embryo Transfer: Sex in a Dish?

1. Dietrich Bonhoeffer, *Ethics* (New York: Macmillan, 1955 [1975]), 148.

2. Doris Del Zio, "I Was Cheated of My Test-Tube Baby," *Good Housekeeping* (March 1979): 203.

3. *Ibid.*, 135.

4. *Ibid.*, 200.

5. *Ibid.*

6. *Ibid.*

7. *Ibid.*

8. Landrum Shettles, "Observations on Human Follicular and Tubal Ova," *American Journal of Obstetrics and Gynecology*, 1953, 66(2): 235-247. ◆ Landrum Shettles, "A Morula Stage of Human Ova Developed In Vitro," *Fertility and Sterility*, 1955, 6(4): 287-289. ◆ Landrum Shettles, "Corona Radiata and Zona Pellucida of Living Human Ova," *Fertility and Sterility*, 1958, 9(2): 167-170.

9. Del Zio, *op. cit.*, 200.

10. *Ibid.*, 202.

11. U.S. Congress, Office of Technology Assessment, *Infertility: Medical and Social Choices* (Washington, DC: U.S. Government Printing Office, 1988), 36.

12. Leon R. Kass, "Babies by In Vitro Fertilization: Unethical Experiments on the Unborn?" *New England Journal of Medicine*, November 18, 1971, 1176-1178. Italics mine.

13. Robert Edwards and Patrick Steptoe, *A Matter of Life* (New York: William Morrow, 1980), 87. Italics mine.

14. *Ibid.*, 88. Italics mine.

15. Cited in Kass, *op. cit.*, 1178. Italics mine.

16. Edwards and Steptoe, *op. cit.*, 118.

17. *Ibid.*, 90.

18. *Ibid.*

19. *Ibid.*, 90-91.

20. *Ibid.*, 96-97.

21. Edwards is quite vague about the exact dates of IVF experiments in his book. However, in *A Matter of Life*, he says on page 89 that he and Bavister fertilized the first human eggs "last October." He later points out this was during the year before *Nature* published his paper about the experiment (in March 1969). This places the year in which the first human IVF took place as 1968.

22. *Ibid.*, 92.

23. *Ibid.*, 118.

24. Again, Edwards is very careful not to give out exact dates, but one can put the pieces together by other events he provides dates for in his book.

25. R. G. Edwards and Ruth E. Fowler, "Human Embryos in the Laboratory," *Scientific American* 223 (1970): 50.

26. *Ibid.*, 49.

27. The Nuremberg Military Tribunal's decision in the case of *United States v. Karl Brandt et al.* provides a set of clear guidelines for medical experimentation in what is known as the *Nuremberg Code*. In the wake of Nazi war crimes committed during World War II, the Tribunal declared that if treatments of an experimental nature are provided by physicians *the voluntary consent of the subject participating in the research is absolutely essential.*

This means that the person involved should have legal capacity to give consent; should be so situated as to be able to exercise free power of choice, without the intervention of any element of force, fraud, deceit, duress, over-reaching, or other ulterior form of constraint or coercion; and *should have sufficient knowledge and comprehension of the elements of the subject matter involved as to enable him/her to make an understanding and enlightened decision.* This latter element requires that before the acceptance of an affirmative decision by the experimental subject *there should be made known to him/her the nature, duration, and purpose of the experiment; the method and means by which it is to be conducted; all inconveniences and hazards reasonably to be expected; and the effects upon his/her health or person which may possibly come from his/her participation in the experiment . . .*

The experiment should be so designed and based on the results of animal experimentation and a knowledge of the natural history of the disease or other problem (in this case, IVF) under study *that the anticipated results will justify the performance of the experiment.* From Daniel Ch. Overduin and John I. Fleming, *Life in a Test-Tube* (Adelaide, South Australia: Lutheran Publishing House, 1982), 226-227.

The anticipated results could not possibly have been known by Doris Del Zio and Dr. Steptoe's patients: there had been no trials of IVF in higher animals preceding IVF experiments in humans. *The researchers had no idea how effective or successful IVF/ET would be.*

28. Committee on Small Business, *Consumer Protection Issues Involving In Vitro Fertilization Clinics* (Washington, DC: U.S. Government Printing office, 1988), 11, 17.

29. U.S. Congress, Office of Technology Assessment, *op. cit.*, 10.

30. *Ibid.*

31. Medical Research International and the Society of Assisted Reproductive Technology, The American Fertility Society, "In Vitro Fertilization/Embryo Transfer in the United States: 1987 Results from the National IVF-ET Registry," *Fertility and Sterility* 51 (January 1989): 13-19.

32. The U.S House Subcommittee on Regulation, Business Opportunities and Energy released a more recent survey of 146 IVF/ET clinics reporting statistics for 1987-1988. At these clinics 26,332 IVF procedures were performed; 20,483 eggs were recovered at a cost of $4,000 to $7,000 per attempt. There were only 2,463 live births. (The 146 clinics surveyed do not include all IVF/ET clinics in the United States since the number is now over 200.) To get a copy of the survey, write the subcommittee at: Room B-363, Rayburn House Office Building, Washington, DC 20515.

33. See: John D. Biggers, "In Vitro Fertilization and Embryo Transfer in Human Beings," *New England Journal of Medicine*, February 5, 1981, 336-341. ◆ A. Clark *et al.*, "Social and Reproductive Characteristics of the First 100 Couples Treated by In-Vitro Fertilization Programme at National Women's Hospital, Auckland," *New Zealand Medical Journal*, June 24, 1987, 380-382. ◆ *Contemporary OB/GYN*, "Success Rates for IVF and Gift," May 1988, 89-106. ◆ John E. Buster and Mark V. Sauer, "Nonsurgical Donor Ovum Transfer: New Option for Infertile Couples," *Contemporary OB/GYN* August 1986, 39-49. ◆ Ian Craft *et al.*, "Analysis of 1071 GIFT Procedures – The Case for a Flexible Approach to

Treatment," *Lancet*, May 16, 1988, 1094-1097. ◆ Ian Craft *et al.*, "Successful Pregnancies from the Transfer of Pronucleate Embryos in an Outpatient In Vitro Fertilization Program," *Fertility and Sterility* 44 (August 1985): 181-184. ◆ Alan H. DeCherney and Gad Lavy, "Oocyte Recovery Methods in In-Vitro Fertilization," *Clinical Obstetrics and Gynecology* 29 (March 1986): 171-179. ◆ J. Deschacht *et al.*, "In Vitro Fertilization with Husband and Donor Sperm in Patients with Previous Fertilization Failures Using Husband Sperm," *Human Reproduction* 3 (January 1988): 105-108. ◆ Karen S. Edwards, "Reproduction Technology: A Guide to What's Available in Ohio," *OHIO Medicine* (March 1988), 183-190, 193. ◆ Rene Frydman *et al.*, "A New Approach to Follicular Stimulation for In Vitro Fertilization: Programed Oocyte Retrieval," *Fertility and Sterility* 46 (October 1986): 657-659. ◆ Rene Frydman *et al.*, "An Obstetric Assessment of the First 100 Births from the In Vitro Fertilization Program at Clamart, France," *American Journal of Obstetrics and Gynecology* 154 (March 1986): 550-555. ◆ Rene Frydman *et al.*, "Programmed Oocyte Retrieval During Routine Laparoscopy and Embryo Cryopreservation for Later Transfer," *American Journal of Obstetrics and Gynecology* 155 (July 1986): 112-117. ◆ Howard Jones, Jr., *et al.*, "An Analysis of the Obstetric Outcome of 125 Consecutive Pregnancies Conceived In Vitro and Resulting in 100 Deliveries," *American Journal of Obstetrics and Gynecology* 154 (April 1986): 848-854. ◆ Howard Jones, Jr., "The Impact of In Vitro Fertilization on the Practice of Gynecology and Obstetrics," *International Journal of Fertility* 31 (1986): 99-111. ◆ Howard Jones, Jr., Hung-Ching Liu, and Zev Rosenwaks, "The Efficiency of Human Repoduction After In Vitro Fertilization and Embryo Transfer," *Fertility and Sterility* 49 (April 1988): 649-653. ◆ Howard Jones, Jr., *et al.*, "The Program for In Vitro Fertilization at Norfolk," *Fertility and Sterility* 38 (July 1982): 14-20. ◆ Gina Bari Kolata, "In Vitro Fertilization Goes Commercial," *Science* 221 (September 1983): 1160-1161. ◆ John Leeton, Alan Trounson, David Jessup and Carl Wood, "The Technique for Embryo Transfer," *Fertility and Sterility* 38 (August 1982): 156-161. ◆ *Lincoln Journal*, "100 Test-Tube Babies Gather in Baltimore," September 12, 1988, 6. ◆ *Lincoln Sunday Journal-Star*, "In Vitro Clinics Span Globe; Spawn New Treatments," July 24, 1988, 1A, 6A. ◆ Richard P. Marrs, "Human In-Vitro Fertilization," *Clinical Obstetrics and Gynecology* 29 (March 1986): 117. ◆ Richard P. Marrs, "Laboratory Conditions for Human In-Vitro Fertilization Procedures," *Clinical Obstetrics and Gynecology* 29 (March 1986): 180-189. ◆ Medical Research International and the American Fertility Society Special Interest Group, "In Vitro Fertilization/Embryo Transfer in the United States: 1985 and 1986, Results from the National IVF/ET Registry," *Fertility and Sterility* 49 (February 1988): 212-215. ◆ David R. Meldrum *et al.*, "Evolution of a Highly Successful In Vitro Fertilization-Embryo Transfer Program," *Fertility and Sterility* 48 (July 1987): 86-93. ◆ Sylvia Pace-Owens, "In Vitro Fertilization and Embryo Transfer," *JOGN Nursing*, Supplement (November/December 1985): 44S-48S. ◆ Claude Ranoux *et al.*, "A New In Vitro Fertilization Technique: Intravaginal Culture," *Fertility and Sterility* 49 (April 1988): 654-657. ◆ Claude Renoux *et al.*, "Intravaginal Culture and Embryo Transfer. A New Method for the

Fertilization of Human Oocytes," *Review of French Gynecology and Obstetrics* 82 (December 1987): 741-744. ◆ J. M. Rary, et. al., "Techniques of In Vitro Fertilization of Oocytes and Embryo Transfer in Humans," *Archives of Andrology* 5 (1980): 89-90. ◆ Chris Anne Raymond, "IVF Registry Notes More Centers, More Births, Slightly Improved Odds," *Journal of the American Medical Association*, April 1, 1988, 1920-1921. ◆ V. Sharma *et al.*, "An Analysis of Factors Influencing the Establishment of a Clinical Pregnancy in an Ultrasound-Based Ambulatory In Vitro Fertilization Clinic," *Fertility and Sterility* 49 (March 1988): 468-478. ◆ P. H. Wessels *et al.*, "Gamete Intrafallopian Transfer: A Treatment for Long-Standing Infertility," *Journal of In Vitro Fertilization and Embryo Transfer* 4 (October 1987): 256-259. ◆ P. C. Wong *et al.*, "Eighty Consecutive Cases of Gamete Intrafallopian Transfer," *Human Repoduction* 3 (February 1988): 231-233. ◆ Carl Wood *et al.*, "Clinical Features of Eight Pregnancies Resulting from In Vitro Fertilization and Embryo Transfer," *Fertility and Sterility* 38 (July 1982): 22. ◆ Carl Wood *et al.*, "Factors Influencing Pregnancy Rates Following In Vitro Fertilization and Embryo Transfer," *Fertility and Sterility* 43 (1985): 245-250. ◆ John L. Yovich *et al.*, "Place of GIFT in Infertility Services," *Lancet*, February 27, 1988, 470. ◆ John L. Yovich *et al.*, "Pregnancies Following Pronuclear Stage Tubal Transfer," *Fertility and Sterility* 48 (November 1987): 851-857. ◆ John L. Yovich *et al.*, "PROST for Ovum Donation," *Lancet*, May 23, 1987, 1209-1210.

34. Read *Consumer Protection Issues Involving In Vitro Fertilization Clinics* for further insight into the commercialization of human reproduction. It can be obtained by calling or writing to the U.S. Government Printing Office, Washington, DC 20402, and asking for it by title and serial number 100-49.

35. Committee on Small Business, *op. cit.*, 39. Italics mine.

36. *Ibid.*

37. *Ibid.*

38. Medical Research International and The American Fertility Society Special Interest Group, "In Vitro Fertilization/Embryo Transfer in the United States: 1985 and 1986 Results from the National IVF/ET Registry," *Fertility and Sterility* 49 (February 1988): 212-215. ◆ Medical Research International *et al.*, op. cit, 13.

39. Medical Research International *et al.* (January 1989), *op. cit.*, 13.

40. Lisa Gubernick, "Easier Than Selling Soap," *Forbes*, February 9, 1987, 113-114.

41. Committee on Small Business, *op. cit.*, 8.

42. U.S. Congress, OTA, *op. cit.*, 10. As of May 1988, states requiring insurance reimbursement for infertility services included Arkansas, Hawaii, Maryland, Massachusetts, and Texas. Legislation is currently pending in a number of other states. The time to voice concern is *now.*

43. Chris Anne Raymond, "In Vitro Fertilization Enters Stormy Adolescence as Experts Debate the Odds," *Journal of the American Medical Association*, January 22/29, 1988, 464.

44. Madeleine Shearer, "Some Effects of Assisted Reproduction on Perinatal Care," *Birth* 15 (September 1988): 131-132.

45. Howard Jones, Jr. *et al.*, "What Is a Pregnancy? A Question for Programs

of In Vitro Fertilization," *Fertility and Sterility* 40 (December 1983): 728-733. ◆ Arthur F. Haney, "What Is Efficacious Infertility Therapy?" *Fertility and Sterility* 48 (October 1987): 543-545. ◆ Richard J. Lilford and Maureen E. Dalton, "Effectiveness of Treatment for Infertility," *British Medical Journal*, July 18, 1987, 155-156. ◆ Dinu Berstein *et al.*, "Is Conception in Infertile Couples Treatment-related?" *International Journal of Fertility* 24 (1979): 65-67. ◆ J. Jarrell *et al.*, "An In Vitro Fertilization and Embryo Transfer Pilot Study: Treatment Dependent and Treatment-Independent Pregnancies," *American Journal of Obstetrics and Gynecology* 154 (February 1986): 231-235. ◆ Sung I. Roh *et al.*, "In Vitro Fertilization and Embryo Transfer: Treatment-Dependent versus -Independent Pregnancies," *Fertility and Sterility* 48 (December 1987): 982-986.

46. Machelle M. Seibel, "In Vitro Fertilization Success Rates: A Fraction of the Truth," *Obstetrics & Gynecology* 72 (August 1988): 265-266. ◆ Michael R. Soules, "The In Vitro Fertilization Pregnancy Rate: Let's Be Honest with One Another," *Fertility and Sterility* 43 (April 1985): 511-513. ◆ See also: Andrea Bonnicksen, "Some Consumer Aspects of In Vitro Fertilization and Embryo Transfer," *Birth* 15 (September 1988): 148-151. ◆ Andrea L. Bonnicksen and Robert H. Blank, "The Government and In Vitro Fertilization (IVF): Views of IVF Directors," *Fertility and Sterility* 49 (March 1988): 396-398. ◆ *Contemporary OB/GYN*, "Ethical Dilemmas of Infertility," March 1987.

47. Gubernick, *op. cit.*, 113-114. The number of IVF clinics in the U.S. today is more than 200 — and rising.

48. Committee on Small Business, *op. cit.*, 26-27.

49. Alexander Lopata, "Concepts in Human In Vitro Fertilization and Embryo Transfer," *Fertility and Sterility* 40 (September 1983): 289-301. ◆ Ian Craft *et al.*, "How Many Oocytes/Embryos Should Be Transferred?" *Lancet*, July 11, 1987, 109-110.

50. Anders Aberg *et al.*, "Cardiac Puncture of Fetus with Hurler's Disease Avoiding Abortion of Unaffected Co-Twin," *Lancet*, November 4, 1978, 990-991.

51. *Ibid.*, 990.

52. *Ibid.*, 991. ◆ For further reading on the implications of medically promoted eugenic abortion, see Leo Alexander, "Medical Science Under Dictatorship," *New England Journal of Medicine*, July 14, 1949, 39-47. ◆ Frederick Ausubel, Jon Beckwith, and Kaaren Janssen, "The Politics of Genetic Engineering: Who Decides Who's Defective?" *Psychology Today*, June 1974, 31-41. ◆ Lisa Blumberg, "The Right to Live: Disability Is Not a Crime," *The Exceptional Parent*, December 1984, 22-24. ◆ James Bopp, ed. *Human Life and Health Care Ethics* (Frederick, MD: University Publications of America, 1985). ◆ James Burtchaell, *Rachel Weeping*, Chapter Three (New York: Harper & Row, 1982). ◆ Libby G. Cohen, "Selective Abortion and the Diagnosis of Fetal Damage: Issues and Concerns," *Journal of the Association for Persons with Severe Handicaps* 11 (1986): 188-195. ◆ Department of Health and Human Services, "Services and Treatment for Disabled Infants; Interim Model Guidelines

for Health Care Providers to Establish Infant Review Committees," 49 *Federal Register*, No. 238, December 10, 1984, 48170-48173. ◆ Leslie A. Fiedler, "The Tyranny of the Normal," *The Hastings Center Report*, April 1984, 40-42. ◆ Foundation on Economic Trends, *Human Reproductive Technologies, Genetic Screening and Human Genetic Engineering* (Washington, DC, Foundation on Economic Trends, 1988). ◆ Charles Frankel, "The Specter of Eugenics," *Commentary*, March 1974, 25-33. ◆ Mary Johnson, "Life Unworthy of Life," *The Disability Rag* (January/February 1987) 24-26. ◆ Roger R. Lenke and Joanne Nemes, "Wrongful Birth, Wrongful Life: The Doctor Between a Rock and a Hard Place," *Obstetrics & Gynecology* 66 (November 1985) 719-722. ◆ Francis Schaeffer and C. Everett Koop, *Whatever Happened to the Human Race?* (Westchester, IL: Crossway Books, 1983). ◆ George Will, "Discretionary Killing," *Newsweek*, September 20, 1976. ◆ For a sample of readings favoring the eugenic elimination of human beings, see: H. Tristam Engelhardt, "Euthanasia and Children: The Injury of Continued Existence," *Journal of Pediatrics* 83 (July 1973): 170-171. ◆ Joseph Fletcher, "Ethical Aspects of Genetic Controls: Designed Genetic Changes in Man," *New England Journal of Medicine*, September 30, 1971, 776-783. ◆ Bentley Glass, "Science: Endless Horizons or Golden Age?" *Science* , January 8, 1971, 23-29. ◆ Peter Singer, "Sanctity of Life or Quality of Life?" *Pediatrics* 72 (July 1983): 128-129.

53. H. H. H. Kanhai *et al.*, "Selective Termination in Quintuplet Pregnancy During First Trimester," *Lancet*, June 21, 1986, 1447. ◆ Duncan F. Farquharson *et al.*, "Management of Quintuplet Pregnancy by Selective Embryocide," *American Journal of Obstetrics and Gynecology* 158 (February 1988): 413-416. ◆ Mark I. Evans *et al.*, "Selective First Trimester Termination Octuplet and Quadruplet Pregnancies: Clinical and Ethical Issues," *Obstetrics & Gynecology* 71 (March 1988): 289-296. ◆ Richard L. Berkowitz *et al.*, "Selective Reduction of Multifetal Pregnancies in the First Trimester," *New England Journal of Medicine*, April 21, 1988, 1043-1047. ◆ Richard L. Berkowitz *et al.*, "Selective Reduction of Multifetal Pregnancies (Reply)," *New England Journal of Medicine*, October 6, 1988, 950-951. ◆ John M. Lorenz and James S. Terry, "Selective Reduction of Multifetal Pregnancies (Letter)," *New England Journal of Medicine*, October 6, 1988, 949-950. ◆ Seymour L. Romney, "Selective Reduction of Multifetal Pregnancies (Letter)," *New England Journal of Medicine* , October 6, 1988: 949. ◆ Josef Shalev *et al.*, "Selective Reduction of Multifetal Pregnancies (Letter)," *New England Journal of Medicine*, October 6, 1988, 949. ◆ Eugene F. Diamond, "Selective Reduction of Multifetal Pregnancies (Letter)," *New England Journal of Medicine*, October 6, 1988, 950. ◆ David H. James, "Selective Reduction of Multifetal Pregnancies (Letter)," *New England Journal of Medicine*, October 6, 1988, 950. ◆ Ian Craft *et al.*, "Multiple Pregnancy, Selective Reduction, and Flexible Treatment," *Lancet*, November 5, 1988, 1087. ◆ *Lincoln Journal*, "Selective Fetus Destruction Debated," April 21, 1988, 5. ◆ For additional insights on how this subject is being presented in popular women's magazines, see:

Glamour, "Tell Us What You Think: Is It Wrong to Terminate Some Fetuses During a Multiple Pregnancy?" July 1988, 50. ◆ *Glamour*, "This Is What You Thought: 57 Percent Say a Woman Should Have the Right to Terminate Some Fetuses," September 1988, 197. ◆ *Woman's World*, "Choices," January 3, 1989, 44-45.

54. Rene Frydman *et al.*, "Reduction of the Number of Embryos in a Multiple Pregnancy: From Quintuplet to Triplet," *Fertility and Sterility* 48 (August 1987): 326-327.

55. *Ibid.*, 326. Italics mine.

56. *Ibid.*, 326-327. Italics mine.

57. Romney, *op. cit.*, 949.

58. Bruce Hilton, Daniel Callahan, Maureen Harris, Peter Condliffe, and Burton Berkley, *Ethical Issues in Human Genetics* (New York: Plenum Press, 1973), 19.

59. For further information on risks related to advanced reproductive technologies, see: J. Ashkenazi *et al.*, "Abdominal Complications Following Ultrasonically Guided Percutaneous Transvesical Collection of Oocytes for In Vitro Fertilization," *Journal of In Vitro Fertilization and Embryo Transfer* 4 (December 1987): 316-318. ◆ J. Ashkenasi *et al.*, "Multiple Pregnancy After In-Vitro Fertilization and Embryo Transfer: Report of a Quadruplet Pregnancy and Delivery," *Human Reproduction* 2 (August 1987): 511-515. ◆ F. R. Batzer *et al.*, "Multiple Pregnancies with Gamete Intrafallopian Transfer (GIFT): Complications of a New Technique," *Journal of In Vitro Fertilization and Embryo Transfer* 5 (February 1988): 35-37. ◆ Gregory Byrne, "Artificial Insemination Report Prompts Call for Regulation," *Science*, August 19, 1988, 895. ◆ Erwin Chargaff, "Engineering a Molecular Nightmare," *Nature*, May 21, 1987, 199-200. ◆ Helen Bequaert Holmes, "In Vitro Fertilization: Reflections on the State of the Art," *Birth* 15 (September 1988): 134-1144. ◆ Ruth Hubbard with Wendy Sanford, "New Reproductive Technologies," in *The New Our Bodies, Ourselves* by The Boston Women's Health Collective (New York: Simon & Schuster, 1984). ◆ William R. Phipps, Carol B. Benson, and Patricia M. McShane, "Severe Thigh Myositis Following Intramuscular Progesterone Injections in an In Vitro Fertilization Patient," *Fertility and Sterility* 49 (March 1988): 536-537. ◆ Frances V. Price, "The Risk of High Multiparity with IVF/ET," *Birth* 15 (September 1988): 157-163. ◆ James J. Schlesselman, "How Does One Assess the Risk of Abnormalities from Human In Vitro Fertilization?" *American Journal of Obstetrics and Gynecology*, September 1, 1979, 135-148. ◆ David H. Smith *et al.*, "Tubal Pregnancy Occurring After Successful In Vitro Fertilization and Embryo Transfer," *Fertility and Sterility* 38 (July 1982): 105-106. ◆ John L. Yovich, Simon R. Turner, and Anthony J. Murphy, "Embryo Transfer Technique As a Cause of Ectopic Pregnancies in In Vitro Fertilization," *Fertility and Sterility* 44 (September 1985): 318-321.

60. American Fertility Society Committee on Ethics, "Biomedical Research and Respect for the Preembryo," *Fertility and Sterility* 46, Supplement 1 (February 1988): 3S-4S. ◆ American Fertility Society Committee on Ethics, "Research on Preembryos: Justifications and Limitations,"

Fertility and Sterility 46, Supplement 1 (September 1986): 56S-57S. ◆ Virginia Bolton *et al.*, "GIFT in a District Hospital," *Lancet*, January 3, 1987, 50. ◆ Virginia Bolton, Peter Braude, and Stephen Moore, "Ethical Bounds," *Nature*, September 29, 1988, 392. ◆ Virginia Bolton, Peter Braude, and Stephen Moore, "Human Gene Expression First Occurs Between the Four- and Eight-Cell Stages of Preimplantation Development," *Nature*, March 31, 1988, 459-461. ◆ Jeremy Brown, "Research on Human Embryos — A Justification," *Journal of Medical Ethics* 12 (1986): 201-205. ◆ *Current*, "When Life Begins: Embryo Research," May 1987, 9-10. ◆ Steven Dickman, "West German Research Agencies Oppose New Embryo Law," *Nature*, May 7, 1987, 6. ◆ Steven Dickman, "Embryo Research Ban Causes Ructions in West Germany," June 30, 1988, 791. ◆ Steven Dickman, "International Outlook for Embryo Research," June 30, 1988, 6. ◆ H. John Evans and Anne McLaren, "Unborn Children (Protection) Bill," *Nature*, March 14, 1985, 127-128. ◆ Carole B. Fehilly *et al.*, "Cryopreservation of Cleaving Embryos and Expanded Blastocysts in the Human: A Comparative Study," *Fertility and Sterility* 44 (November 1985): 638-644. ◆ *Lancet*, "Research on Human Embryos," December 13, 1986, 1375. ◆ *Lancet*, "Draft Legislation on Infertility Services and Embryo Research," December 5, 1987, 1343. ◆ *Lancet*, "Human Embryo Research: Vote for Progress," December 5, 1987, 1311. ◆ S. E. Lanzendorf *et al.*, "A Preclinical Evaluation of Pronuclear Formation of Human Spermatozoa into Human Oocytes," *Fertility and Sterility* 59 (May 1988): 835-842. ◆ Bruno Lassalle, Jacques Testart, and Jean-Paul Renard, "Human Embryo Features That Influence the Success of Cryopreservation with the Use of 1, 2 Propanediol," *Fertility and Sterility* 44 (November 1985): 64. ◆ Jean L. Marx, "Embryology: Out of the Womb — into the Test Tube," *Science*, November 23, 1973, 811-814. ◆ *Nature*, "Britain Hazards Embryo Research," December 3, 1987, 407. ◆ *Nature*, "More Embryo Research?" May 19, 1988, 194. ◆ *Nature*, "UK Agonizes over Embryo Research," February 7, 1985. ◆ F. Puissant *et al.*, "Embryo Scoring as a Prognostic Tool in IVF Treatments," *Human Repoduction* 2 (November 1987): 705-708. ◆ Jacques Testart *et al.*, "Factors Influencing the Success Rate of Human Embryo Freezing in an In Vitro Fertilization and Embryo Transfer Program," *Fertility and Sterility* 48 (July 1987): 107-112. ◆ Jacques Testart *et al.*, "Human Embryo Viability Related to Freezing and Thawing Procedures," *American Journal of Obstetrics and Gynecology* 157 (June 1987): 168-171. ◆ John Townsend, "Research on Human Embryos," *Lancet*, January 3, 1987, 53. ◆ Alan Trounson *et al.*, "Fertilization of Human Oocytes by Microinjection of a Single Spermatozoon Under the Zona Pellucida," *Fertility and Sterility* 48 (October 1987): 637-642. ◆ Alan Trounson *et al.*, "Tripronuclear Human Oocytes: Altered Cleavage Patterns and Subsequent Karotypic Analysis of Embryos," *Biological Reproduction* 37 (September 1987): 395-401.
61. Leon R. Kass, "New Beginnings in Life," in Michael Hamilton, ed., *The New Genetics and the Future of Man* (Grand Rapids, MI: William B. Eerdman's, 1971), 21, 53, and 54.

CHAPTER 8: Embryo Transplants: The By-products of Manufactured Conception

1. Erwin Chargaff, "Engineering a Molecular Nightmare," *Nature*, May 21, 1987, 199. Professor Chargaff's work in biochemistry during the late 1940s led to the discovery of DNA.
2. Hossam I. Abdalla and Terence Leonard, "Cryopreserved Zygote Intrafallopian Transfer for Anonymous Oocyte Donation," *Lancet*, April 9, 1988, 835. ◆ American Fertility Society Committee on Ethics, "Donor Eggs in In Vitro Fertilization," *Fertility and Sterility* 46, Supplement 1 (September 1986): 42S-44S. ◆ American Fertility Society Committee on Ethics, "Donor Sperm in In Vitro Fertilization," *Fertility and Sterility* 46, Supplement 1 (September 1986): 39S-41S. ◆ American Fertility Society Committee on Ethics, "Surrogate Gestational Mothers: Women Who Gestate a Genetically Unrelated Embryo," *Fertility and Sterility* 46, Supplement 1 (September 1986): 58S-61S. ◆ Lori B. Andrews, "Embryo Technology, *Parent's Magazine* 56 (May 1981): 63-71. ◆ Lori B. Andrews, "Legal and Ethical Aspects of New Reproductive Technologies," *Clinical Obstetrics and Gynecology* 29 (March 1986): 190-204. ◆ Lori B. Andrews, *New Conceptions* (New York: Ballantine Books, 1985). ◆ Lori B. Andrews, "Yours, Mine and Theirs," *Psychology Today* (December 1984), 20-29. ◆ George Annas and John F. Henahan, "Fertilization, Embryo Transfer Procedures Raise Many Questions," *Journal of the American Medical Association*, August 17, 1984, 877-879, 882. ◆ George Annas, "Making Babies Without Sex: The Law and the Profits," *American Journal of Public Health* 74 (December 1984): 1415-1417. ◆ George Annas, "Redefining Parenthood and Protecting Embryos: Why We Need New Laws," *The Hastings Center Report* (October 1984), 50-52. ◆ George Annas and Sherman Elias, "Social Policy Considerations in Noncoital Reproduction," *Journal of the American Medical Association*, January 3, 1986, 62-68. ◆ Paul Bagne, "High-Tech Breeding," *Mother Jones* 8 (August 1983): 23-29, 35. ◆ John E. Buster, "Survey of Attitudes Regarding the Use of Siblings for Gamete Donation," *Fertility and Sterility* 49 (April 1988): 721-722. ◆ J. F. Correy, "Donor Oocyte Pregnancy with Transfer of Deep-Frozen Embryo," *Fertility and Sterility* 49 (March 1988): 534-535. ◆ Ian Craft and John Yovich, "Implications of Embryo Transfer," *Lancet*, September 22, 1979, 642-643. ◆ Ian Craft and Paul F. Serhal, "Ovum Donation—A Simplified Approach," *Fertility and Sterility* 48 (August 1987): 265-269. ◆ Douglas J. Cuisine, "Some Legal Implications of Embryo Transfer," *Lancet*, August 25, 1979, 407-408. ◆ Martin Curie-Cohen, Lesleigh Luttrell, and Sander Shapiro, "Current Practice of Artificial Insemination by Donor in the United States," *New England Journal of Medicine*, March 15, 1979, 585-590. ◆ Richard Fitzhugh, "Where's Poppa?" *US Magazine*, October 22, 1984, 68-69. ◆ *Health Progress*, "What Are the Moral Rights of Frozen Embryos?" (October 1984), 54 and 62. ◆ D. A. Iddenden, H. N. Sallam, and W. P. Collins, "A Prospective Randomized Study Comparing Fresh Semen and Cryopreserved Semen for Artificial Insemination by Donor,"

International Journal of Fertility 30 (1985): 54-56. ◆ Robert P. S. Jansen, "Sperm and Ova as Property," *Journal of Medical Ethics* 11 (1985): 123-126. ◆ Marilyn Johnston, "I Gave Birth to Another Woman's Baby," *Redbook* (May 1984), 44 and 46. ◆ A. M. Junca *et al.*, "Anonymous and Non-Anonymous Oocyte Donation Preliminary Results," *Human Repoduction* 3 (January 1988): 121-123. ◆ Harry D. Krause, "Artificial Conception, Legislative Approaches," *Family Law Quarterly* 19 (Fall 1988): 185-206. ◆ Charles Krauthammer, "The Ethics of Human Manufacture," *The New Republic*, May 4, 1987, 17-21. ◆ John F. Leeton *et al.*, "Donor Oocyte Pregnancy with Transfer of Deep-Frozen Embryo," *Fertility and Sterility* 49 (March 1988): 534-535. ◆ John Leeton *et al.*, "Successful Pregnancy in an Ovulating Recipient Following the Transfer of Two Frozen-Thawed Embryos Obtained from Anonymously Donated Oocytes," *Journal of In Vitro Fertilization and Embryo Transfer* 5 (February 1988): 22-24. ◆ John Leeton and J. Harman, "The Donation of Oocytes to Known Recipients," *Australia and New Zealand Journal of Obstetrics and Gynaecology* 27 (August 1987): 248-250. ◆ *Lincoln Journal*, "Woman Bears Own Grandchild," October 1, 1987, 2. ◆ *Los Angeles Times*, "Babies: No Sale," February 4, 1988. ◆ M. Madhevan, Alan O. Trounson, and John F. Leeton, "Successful Use of Human Semen Cryobanking for In Vitro Fertilization," *Fertility and Sterility* 40 (September 1983): 340-343. ◆ M. C. Michelow, "Mother-Daughter In Vitro Fertilization Triplet Surrogate Pregnancy," *Journal of In Vitro Fertilization and Embryo Transfer* 5 (February 1988): 31-34. ◆ Hermann J. Muller, "Human Evolution by Voluntary Choice of Germ Plasm," *Science*, September 8, 1961, 643-649. ◆ Michael Novak, "Buying & Selling Babies: Limitations on the Marketplace," *Commonweal*, July 17, 1987, 406-407. ◆ Jacques Salat-Baroux *et al.*, "Pregnancies After Replacement of Frozen-Thawed Embryos in a Donation Program," *Fertility and Sterility* 49 (March 1988): 817-821. ◆ R. G. Seed and Rana Weiss, "Embryo Adoption — Technical, Ethical and Legal Aspects," *Archives in Andrology* 5 (1980): 92. ◆ R. Snowden and G. D. Mitchell, *Artificial Reproduction: A Social Investigation* (London: George Allen & Unwin, 1983). ◆ R. Snowden and G. D. Mitchell, *The Artificial Family: A Consideration of Artificial Insemination by Donor* (London: George Allen & Unwin, 1981). ◆ Ronald C. Strickler, David W. Keller, and James C. Warren, "Artificial Insemination with Fresh Donor Semen," *New England Journal of Medicine*, October 23, 1975, 848-853. ◆ John L. Yovich, "Surrogacy," *Lancet*, June 13, 1987, 1374.

3. Barbara Katz Rothman, "How Science Is Redefining Parenthood," *Ms.* (July/August 1982), 154, 156. Italics mine.

4. Gillian Hanscombe, "The Right to Lesbian Parenthood," *Journal of Medical Ethics* 9 (1983): 133-135. ◆ Barbara Kritchevsky, "The Unmarried Woman's Right to Artificial Insemination: A Call for Expanded Definition of Family," *Harvard Women's Law Journal* 4 (1981): 1-42. ◆ Lambda Legal Defense and Education Fund, Inc.; Lesbian Rights Project, San Francisco; Office of Gay and Lesbian Health Concerns, NYC Department of Health; and New York University Women's Center,

Lesbians Choosing Motherhood (New York: Lambda Legal Defense and Education Fund, Inc., 1984). ◆ Lesbian Health Information Project, *Artificial Insemination: An Alternative Conception for the Lesbian and Gay Community* (San Francisco, CA: San Francisco Women's Centers, 1979). ◆ Susan Robinson and H. F. Pizer, *Having a Baby Without a Man* (New York: Simon & Schuster/ Fireside Books, 1987). ◆ Susan Stern, "Lesbian Insemination," *The CoEvolution Quarterly* (Summer 1980), 108-117.

5. Sidney Callahan, "Lovemaking and Babymaking," *Commonweal*, April 24, 1987, 237. ◆ See also Sidney Callahan, "Use of Third-Party Donors Threatens Basic Values," *Health Progress* (March 1987): 26-28.

6. *Ibid.*

7. Leon R. Kass, *Toward a More Natural Science: Biology and Human Affairs* (New York: The Free Press, 1985), 225.

8. Paul Ramsey, "Shall We 'Reproduce'? Part II. Rejoinders and Future Forecast," *Journal of the American Medical Association*, June 12, 1972, 1484-1485. ◆ See also: Paul Ramsey, "Shall We 'Reproduce'? Part I. The Medical Ethics of In Vitro Fertilization," *Journal of the American Medical Association*, June 5, 1972, 1346-1350. ◆ Paul Ramsey, *Fabricated Man* (New Haven, CT: Yale University Press, 1970).

9. Richard G. Seed, Randolph W. Seed, and Donald S. Baker, "Aspects of Bovine Embryo Transplant Directly Applicable to Humans—A Report of Over 300 Procedures," *Fertility and Sterility* 28 (March 1977): 313-314.

10. R. G. Seed and Rana Weiss, op. cit.. ◆ R. G. Seed and R. W. Seed, "Artificial Embryonation—Human Embryo Transplant," *Archives in Andrology* 5 (1980): 90-91. ◆ John E. Buster and Mark V. Sauer, "Nonsurgical Donor Ovum Transfer: New Option for Infertile Couples," *Contemporary OB/GYN* (August 1986): 39-49.

11. Anne Taylor Fleming, "New Frontiers in Conception," *New York Times Magazine*, July 20, 1980, 42.

12. Fern Schumer Chapman, "Going for the Gold in the Baby Business," *Fortune*, September 17, 1984, 41. Curiously, most third-party pregnancy contracts during the same time period called for "surrogate" mothers to be paid exactly the same amount.

13. Buster and Sauer, *op. cit.*, 49.

14. Chapman, *op. cit.*, 46.

15. For an interesting discussion on SET from a lawyer's point of view, see Douglas J. Cuisine, "Some Legal Implications of Embryo Transfer," *Lancet*, August 25, 1979, 407-408.

16. Seed, Seed, and Baker, *op. cit.*

17. *Ibid.*

18. Gena Corea, *The Mother Machine* (New York: Harper & Row/Perennial Library, 1986), 82.

19. *Ibid.*

20. Fleming, *op. cit.*

21. *Ibid.*

22. Seed and Seed, *op. cit.* ◆ John E. Buster, Randolph W. Seed, and Richard G. Seed *et al.*, "Nonsurgical Ovum Transfer As a Treatment in Infertile

Women," *Journal of the American Medical Association*, March 2, 1984, 1171-1173. ◆ Corea, *op. cit.*, 83. ◆ Fleming, *op. cit.*

23. Jacques Ellul, *The Technological Society* (New York: Alfred A Knopf, Vintage Books Edition, 1964), 10.

24. Chapman, *op. cit.* ◆ Buster, Seed, and Seed *et al.*, *op. cit.* ◆ See also: John E. Buster *et al.*, "Survey of Attitudes Regarding the Use of Siblings for Gamete Donation," *Fertility and Sterility* 49 (April 1988): 721-722. ◆ Mark E. Sauer and John E. Buster *et al.*, "An Instrument for the Recovery of Preimplantation Uterine Ova," *Obstetrics & Gynecology* 71 (May 1988): 804-806.

25. Chapman, *op. cit.*, 42.

26. Alan Trounson and Linda Mohr, "Human Pregnancy Following Cryopreservation, Thawing and Transfer of an Eight-Cell Embryo," *Nature*, October 20, 1983, 707-709. ◆ Alan Trounson, "Pregnancy Established in an Infertile Patient After Transfer of a Donated Embryo Fertilised In Vitro," *British Medical Journal*, March 12, 1983, 835-838. ◆ Alan Trounson *et al.*, "Effect of Growth in Culture Medium on the Rate of Mouse Embryo Development and Viability In Vitro," *Journal of In Vitro Fertilization and Embryo Transfer* 4 (October 1987): 265-268. ◆ Alan Trounson, "Preservation of Human Eggs and Embryos," *Fertility and Sterility* 46 (July 1986): 1-11. ◆ Alan Trounson, Anita Peura, and Carol Kirby, "Ultrarapid Freezing: A New Low-Cost and Effective Method of Embryo Cryopreservation," *Fertility and Sterility* 48 (November 1987): 843-850. ◆ Alan Trounson *et al.*, "Ultrarapid Freezing of Early Cleavage Stage Human Embryos and Eight-Cell Mouse Embryos," *Fertility and Sterility* 49 (May 1988): 822-826. ◆ S. Al Hassani *et al.*, "Cryopreservation of Human Oocytes," *Human Repoduction* 2 (November 1987): 695-700.

27. Buster and Sauer, *op. cit.*, 39-40. ◆ Buster, Seed, and Seed *et al.*, *op. cit.*, 1172.

28. Corea, *op. cit.*, 85.

29. Buster, Seed, and Seed *et al.*, *op. cit.*, 1171.

30. Corea, *op. cit.*, 85. ◆ *Ob/Gyn News*, "Ovum Donor Transfer May See Wide Use in Treating Infertility," December 1, 1983, 1.

31. Corea, *op. cit.*, 85.

32. *Ibid.*, 86.

33. Buster, Seed, and Seed *et al.*, *op. cit.*, 1171.

34. John E. Buster, Randolph W. Seed, and Richard G. Seed *et al.*, "Nonsurgical Ovum Transfer of In Vivo Fertilized Donated Ova to Five Infertile Women: Report of Two Pregnancies," *The Lancet*, July 23, 1983, 223-224.

35. Corea, *op. cit.*, 80.

36. Mark V. Sauer and John E. Buster *et al.*, *op. cit.*

37. Buster, Seed, and Seed *et al.*, *Journal of the American Medical Association*, 1171. ◆ Sauer and Buster *et al.*, *op. cit.*

38. Corea, *op. cit.*, 87.

39. Sauer and Buster *et al.*, *op. cit.*, 805.

40. *Ibid.*

41. *Ibid.*
42. *Ibid.*, 806.
43. Mark V. Sauer, Robert E. Anderson, and Richard J. Paulsen, "A Trial of Superovulation in Ovum Donors Undergoing Uterine Lavage," *Fertility and Sterility* 51 (January 1989): 131-134.
44. *Ibid.*, 131. Italics mine.
45. Buster and Sauer, *op. cit.*, 46-47. Italics mine.
46. Ramsey, *op. cit.*, 1485.
47. John T. Noonan, "Christian Tradition and the Control of Reproduction," in *The Death Decision*, ed. Leonard J. Nelson (Ann Arbor, MI: Servant Books, 1984), 14.
48. *Ibid.*, 47. Italics mine.
49. Sauer and Buster *et al.*, *op. cit.*, 806.
50. R. G. Edwards, "Chromosomal Abnormalities in Human Embryos," *Nature*, May 26, 1983, 283. ◆ See also: Roslyn R. Angell *et al.*, "Chromosome Abnormalities in Human Embryos After In Vitro Fertilization," *Nature*, May 26, 1983, 336-338. ◆ Gail Vines, "New Insights into Early Embryos," *New Scientist*, July 9, 1987, 22-23. ◆ J. L. Watt *et al.*, "Trisomy 1 in an Eight Cell Human Pre-Embryo," *Journal of Medical Genetics* 24 (1987): 60-64. ◆ P. M. Summers, J. M. Campbell, and M. W. Miller, "Normal In-Vivo Development of Marmoset Monkey Embryos After Trophectoderm Biopsy," *Human Reproduction* 3 (April 1988): 389-393. ◆ Peter Braude, Virginia Bolton, and Stephen Moore, "Human Gene Expression First Occurs Between the Four- and Eight-Cell Stages of Preimplantation Development," *Nature*, March 31, 1988, 459-461.
51. Robert G. Edwards and David J. Sharpe, "Social Values and Research in Human Embryology," *Nature*, May 14, 1971, 87-88.
52. R. G. Edwards, "Studies in Human Conception," *American Journal of Obstetrics and Gynecology*, November 1, 1973, 587 and 599.
53. R. G. Edwards and M. Puxon, "Parental Consent over Embryos," *Nature*, July 19, 1984, 179.
54. Kathy Johnston, "Sex of New Embryos Known," *Nature*, June 18, 1987, 547.
55. *Ibid.*
56. *Ibid.*
57. Anne McLaren, "Can We Diagnose Genetic Disease in Pre-Embryos," *New Scientist*, December 10, 1987, 44-45.
58. *Ibid.*, 45.
59. *Ibid.*, 46.
60. *Ibid.*
61. *Ibid.*
62. Jean Rostand, *Can Man Be Modified?* (New York: Basic Books, 1959), 82-84; 86-87. Italics mine.

CHAPTER 9: Artificial Wombs: The Final Separation

1. Albert Rosenfeld, *The Second Genesis: The Coming Control of Life* (Englewood Cliffs, NJ: Prentice-Hall, 1969), 120.

2. *Life*, "On the Frontiers of Medicine: Control of Life," September 10, 1965, 60-61. This one is worth checking at your local library.

3. *Ibid.*, 60.

4. For a thorough discussion of abortion-related medical atrocities, see: Suzanne Rini, *Beyond Abortion: A Chronicle of Fetal Experimentation* (Avon-by-the-Sea, NJ: Magnificat Press, 1988).

5. *USA Today*, "Use Science to Help Childless Couples," March 9, 1989, 6A.

6. D. P. Alexander, H. G. Britton, and D. A. Nixon, "Maintenance of Sheep Fetuses by an Extracorporeal Circuit for Periods Up to 24 Hours," *American Journal of Obstetrics and Gynecology*, December 1, 1968, 969-975.

7. Warren M. Zapol *et al.*, "Artificial Placenta: Two Days of Total Extrauterine Support of the Isolated Premature Lamb Fetus," *Science*, October 31, 1969, 617-618.

8. *Ibid.*, 618.

9. University of Nebraska Medical Center, *ECMO Parent Information Manual* (Omaha, NE: UNMC, no publication date listed), 5.

10. A. F. Andrews *et al.*, "Venovenous Extracorporeal Membrane Oxygenation (ECMO) Using a Double-Lumen Cannula," *Artificial Organs* 11 (June 1987): 265-268. ◆ Clyde R. Redmond *et al.*, "Extracorporeal Membrane Oxygenation for Respiratory and Cardiac Failure in Infants and Children," *Journal of Thoracic and Cardiovascular Surgery* 93 (February 1987): 199-204. ◆ Elizabeth Workman and Donna Lentz, "Extracorporeal Membrane Oxygenation," *AORN Journal* 45 (March 1987): 725-739. ◆ Robert H. Bartlett *et al.*, "Extracorporeal Circulation in Neonatal Respiratory Failure: A Prospective Randomized Study," *Pediatrics* 76 (October 1985): 479-487. ◆ Nigel Paneth and Sylvan Wallenstein, "Extracorporeal Membrane Oxygenation and the Play the Winner Rule," *Pediatrics* 76 (October 1986): 622-623. ◆ D. Arnold *et al.*, "Clinical Application of Extracorporeal Membrane Oxygenation (ECMO) in Neonatal Respiratory Failure," *Thoracic and Cardiovascular Surgery* 35 (October 1987): 321-325. ◆ Robert H. Bartlett *et al.*, "Venovenous Perfusion in ECMO for Newborn Respiratory Insufficiency," *Annals in Surgery* 201 (April 1985): 520-526. ◆ R. M. Ortiz, R. E. Cilley, and R. H. Bartlett, "Extracorporeal Membrane Oxygenation in Pediatric Respiratory Failure," *Pediatric Clinics of North America* 34 (February 1987): 39-46.

11. J. M. Toomasian *et al.*, "National Experience with Extracorporeal Membrane Oxygenation for Newborn Respiratory Failure," *ASAIO Transcripts* 34 (April-June 1988): 140-147.

12. Robert T. Francoeur, "Transformations in Human Reproduction," in Lester A. Kirkendall and Arthur E. Gravatt, eds., *Marriage and Family in the Year 2020* (New York: Prometheus Books, 1984), 95.

13. *Ibid.*

14. Margaret Sanger, *Motherhood in Bondage* (New York: Brentano's, 1928), 433.

15. Shulamith Firestone, *The Dialectic of Sex* (New York: William Morrow and Co., 1970), 226.

16. *Ibid.*, 228.
17. Rosenfeld, *op. cit.*, 118.
18. "Doctors Aiding Women Who Want to Abort on Basis of Sex," *Lincoln Journal-Star*, December 25, 1988, 9F. ◆ Blanche P. Alter *et al.*, "Prenatal Diagnosis of Hemoglobinopathies," *New England Journal of Medicine*, December 23, 1976, 1437-1441. ◆ "News (Gene Probes for Prenatal Diagnosis)," *Birth*, 14 (September 1987): 157. ◆ Diane W. Cox and Tammy Mansfield, "Prenatal Diagnosis of Alpha 1 Antitrypsin Deficiency and Estimates of Fetal Risk for Disease," *Journal of Medical Genetics* 24 (1987): 52-59. ◆ Ian Craft *et al.*, "Multiple Pregnancy, Selective Reduction, and Flexible Treatment," *Lancet*, November 5, 1988, 1087. ◆ Dwight P. Cruikshank *et al.*, "Midtrimester Amniocentesis," *American Journal of Obstetrics and Gynecology*, May 15, 1983, 204-211. ◆ F. Daffos *et al.*, "Prenatal Management of 746 Pregnancies at Risk for Toxoplasmosis," *New England Journal of Medicine*, February 4, 1988, 271-275. ◆ Robert G. Edwards, "Chromosomal Abnormalities in Human Embryos," *Nature*, May 26, 1983, 283. ◆ Robert G. Edwards and David J. Sharpe, "Social Values and Research in Human Embryology," *Nature*, May 14, 1971, 87-91. ◆ John Elliott, "Abortion for 'Wrong' Fetal Sex: An Ethical-Legal Dilemma," *Journal of the American Medical Association*, October 5, 1979, 1455-1456. ◆ Ruth R. Faden *et al.*, "Prenatal Screening and Pregnant Women's Attitudes Toward the Abortion of Defective Fetuses," *American Journal of Public Health* 77 (November 1987): 288-290. ◆ M. Ferrari *et al.*, "Termination of Pregnancy by a Dilatation-Evacuation Technique to Obtain Placental Tissue for DNA Analysis," *Prenatal Diagnosis* 8 (March 1988): 235-237. ◆ John C. Fletcher, "Ethics and Amniocentesis for Sex Identification," *The Hastings Center Report* (February 1980), 15-17. ◆ Lyle I. Gardner, "Genetically Expressed Abnormalities in the Fetus," *Clinical Obstetrics and Gynecology* 17 (September 1974): 171-193. ◆ Kenneth L. Garver, Sandra L. Marchese, and Edward G. Boas, "Amniocentesis," *Obstetrics & Gynecology* 49 (January 1977): 127. ◆ Fred Gilbert *et al.*, "Prenatal Diagnostic Options in Cystic Fibrosis," *American Journal of Obstetrics and Gynecology* 158 (April 1988): 947-952. ◆ Mitchell S. Golbus, W. Allen Hogge, and S. A. Schonberg, "Chorionic Villus Sampling: Experience of the First 1000 Cases," *American Journal of Obstetrics and Gynecology* 154 (June 1986): 1249-1252. ◆ Mitchell S. Golbus *et al.*, "Intrauterine Diagnosis of Genetic Defects: Results, Problems, and Follow-Up in a Prenatal Genetic Detection Center," *American Journal of Obstetrics and Gynecology*, April 1, 1974, 897-905. ◆ Jeffrey E. Green *et al.*, "Chorionic Villus Sampling: Experience with an Initial 940 Cases," *Obstetrics & Gynecology* 71 (February 1988): 208-212. ◆ L. Grosset, V. Barrelet, and N. Odartchenko, "Antenatal Fetal Sex Determination from Maternal Blood During Early Pregnancy," *American Journal of Obstetrics and Gynecology*, September 1, 1974, 60-63. ◆ *The Hastings Center Report*, "Prenatal Diagnosis for Sex Choice," February 1980, 20. ◆ Michael R. Hayden *et al.*, "First-Trimester Prenatal Diagnosis for Huntington's Disease with DNA Probes," *Lancet*, June 6, 1987, 1284-

1285. ◆ R. J. Henry and S. Norton, "Prenatal Ultrasound Diagnosis of Fetal Scoliosis with Termination of the Pregnancy: A Case Report," *Prenatal Diagnosis* 7 (November 1987): 663-666. ◆ W. Allen Hogge, "Prenatal Diagnosis Using DNA Probes," *Contemporary OB/GYN*, Technology (1986): 25-31. ◆ Ernest B. Hook and Dina M. Scheinemachers, "Trends in Utilization of Prenatal Cytogenetic Diagnosis by New York State Residents in 1979 and 1980," *American Journal of Public Health* 73 (February 1983): 198-202. ◆ Carl A. Huether, "Projection of Down's Syndrome Births in the United States 1979-2000, and the Potential Effects of Prenatal Diagnosis," *American Journal of Public Health* 73 (October 1983): 1186-1189. ◆ Anthony Johnson and Lynn Goodmilow, "Genetic Amniocentesis at 14 Weeks or Less," *Clinical Obstetrics and Gynecology* 31 (June 1988): 345-352. ◆ John P. Johnson, "Genetic Counseling Using Linked DNA Probes: Cystic Fibrosis as a Prototype," *Journal of Pediatrics* 113 (December 1988): 957-963. ◆ Shirley L. Jones, "Decision Making in Clinical Genetics: Ethical Implications for Perinatal Nursing Practice," *Journal of Perinatal and Neonatal Nursing* 1 (1988): 11-25. ◆ *Lancet*, "Maternal Serum-Alpha-Fetoprotein Measurement in Antenatal Screening for Anencephaly and Spina Bifida in Early Pregnancy," June 25, 1977, 1323-1332. ◆ *Lancet*, "Screening for Fetal and Genetic Abnormality," December 12, 1987, 1408. ◆ *Lancet*, "Screening for Neural-Tube Defects," June 25, 1977, 1345-1346. ◆ N. J. Leschot *et al.*, "Chorionic Villi Sampling: Cytogenetic and Clinical Findings in 500 Pregnancies," *British Medical Journal*, August 15, 1987, 407-410. ◆ James N. Macri *et al.*, "Prenatal Diagnosis for Neural Tube Defects," *Journal of the American Medical Association*, September 13, 1976, 1251-1254. ◆ Michael T. Mennuti and Diane M. Main, "Neural Tube Defects: Issues in Prenatal Diagnosis and Counseling," *Obstetrics & Gynecology* 67 (January 1986): 1-16. ◆ Aubrey Milunsky *et al.*, "Prenatal Diagnosis of Neural Tube Defects," *American Journal of Obstetrics and Gynecology*, April 15, 1982, 1030-1032. ◆ P. Miny and W. Holzgreve, "Chorionic Villi Sampling with an Echogenic Catheter: Experiences of the First 500 Cases," *Journal of Perinatal Medicine* 15 (1987): 244-250. ◆ P. Miny *et al.*, "Safety of Placental Biopsy in the Second and Third Trimesters," *New England Journal of Medicine* 317 (No. 18): 1159. ◆ Bernadete Modell, "Chorionic Villus Sampling," *Lancet*, March 30, 1985, 737-740. ◆ Henry L. Nader and Albert B. Gerbie, "Role of Amniocentesis in the Intrauterine Detection of Genetic Disorders," *New England Journal of Medicine*, March 12, 1970, 596-599. ◆ James V. Neel, "Some Genetic Aspects of Therapeutic Abortion," *Perspectives in Biology and Medicine,* Autumn 1967, 129-135. ◆ *New England Journal of Medicine*, "Determination of Fetal Sex Early in Pregnancy," October 20, 1983, 979-980. ◆ NICHD National Registry for Amniocentesis Study Group, "Midtrimester Amniocentesis for Prenatal Diagnosis," *Journal of the American Medical Association*, September 27, 1976, 1471-1476. ◆ Clark E. Nugent *et al.*, "Prenatal Diagnosis of Cystic Fibrosis by Chorionic Villus Sampling Using 12 Polymorphic Deoxyribonucleic Acid Markers," *Obstetrics &*

Gynecology 71 (February 1988): 213-215. ◆ Harry Ostrer and J. Fielding Hejtmancik, "Prenatal Diagnosis and Carrier Detection of Genetic Diseases by Analysis of Deoxyribonucleic Acid," *Journal of Pediatrics* 112 (May 1988): 679-687. ◆ Glenn E. Palomaki and James E. Haddow, "Maternal Serum Alpha-Fetoprotein, Age, and Down Syndrome Risk," *American Journal of Obstetrics and Gynecology* 156 (February 1987): 460-463. ◆ Marcus Pembrey, "Embryo Transfer in Prevention of Genetic Disease," *Lancet*, October 13, 1979, 802. ◆ B. B. B. K. Pirani et. al., "Amniotic Fluid Testosterone in the Prenatal Determination of Fetal Sex," *American Journal of Obstetrics and Gynecology*, November 1, 1977, 518-520. ◆ Stirling M. Puck and Jeanie Puleston Fleming, *Genetic Environment and Your Baby: A Workbook for Parents to Be* (Sante Fe, NM: Vivagen, Inc., 1986). ◆ O. W. J. Quarrell *et al.*, "Exclusion Testing for Huntington's Disease in Pregnancy with a Closely Linked DNA Marker," *Lancet*, June 6, 1987, 1281-1283. ◆ Samuel A. Rhine *et al.*, "Prenatal Sex Detection with Endocervical Smears: Successful Results Utilizing Y-Body Fluorescence," *American Journal of Obstetrics and Gynecology*, May 15, 1975, 155-160. ◆ Barbara Katz Rothman, *The Tentative Pregnancy: Prenatal Diagnosis and the Future of Motherhood* (New York: Viking/Penguin,1987). ◆ Richard H. Schwarz, "Amniocentesis," *Clinical Obstetrics and Gynecology* 18 (June 1975): 1-22. ◆ Henry F. Selle, Deborah W. Holmes, and Mary Lee Ingbar, "The Growing Demand for Midtrimester Amniocentesis: A Systems Approach to Forecasting the Need for Facilities," *American Journal of Public Health* 69 (June 1979) 574-580. ◆ Mary J. Seller, "Congenital Abnormalities and Selective Abortion," *Journal of Medical Ethics* 2 (1976): 138-141. ◆ Barry Siegel, "The Promise and Problems of Prenatal Testing," *American Baby*, November 1987, 95-101. ◆ Joe Leigh Simpson, Richard L. Berkowitz, James Macri, and Michael Mennuti, "Methods for Detecting Neural Tube Defects," *Contemporary OB/GYN* (January 1986), 202-222. ◆ Nancy E. Simpson *et al.*, "Prenatal Diagnosis of Genetic Disease in Canada: Report of a Collaborative Study," *Canadian Medical Association Journal*, October 23, 1976, 739-746. ◆ David C. Sokal *et al.*, "Prenatal Chromosomal Diagnosis: Racial and Geographic Variation in Older Women in Georgia," *Journal of the American Medical Association*, September 19, 1980, 1355-1357. ◆ M. Super *et al.*, "Clinic Experience of Prenatal Diagnosis of Cystic Fibrosis by Use of Linked DNA Probes," *Lancet*, October 3, 1987, 782-784. ◆ M. S. Verp *et al.*, "Parental Decision Following Prenatal Diagnosis of Fetal Chromosome Abnormality," *American Journal of Medical Genetics* 29 (March 1988): 613-622. ◆ R. J. Wapner and L. Jackson, "Chorionic Villus Sampling," *Clinical Obstetrics and Gynecology* 31 (June 1988): 328-344. ◆ David D. Weaver, "A Survey of Prenatally Diagnosed Disorders," *Clinical Obstetrics and Gynecology* 31 (June 1988): 253-269. ◆ Carl P. Weiner," The Role of Cordocentesis in Fetal Diagnosis," *Clinical Obstetrics and Gynecology* 31 (June 1988): 285-292. ◆ Robert H. Williams, "Our Role in the Generation, Modification, and Termination of Life," *Journal of the American Medical Association*, August 11, 1969, 914-917. ◆ Roger A.

Williamson and Jeffrey C. Murray, "Molecular Analysis of Genetic Disorders," *Clinical Obstetrics and Gynecology* 31 (June 1988): 270-284. ◆ J. W. Wladimiroff *et al.*, "Prenatal Diagnosis of Chromosome Abnormalities in the Presence of Fetal Structural Defects," *American Journal of Medical Genetics* 29 (February 1988); 289-291. ◆ S. Robert Young *et al.*, "The Results of One Thousand Consecutive Prenatal Diagnoses," *American Journal of Obstetrics and Gynecology*, September 15, 1983, 181-188.

19. C. S. Lewis, *The Abolition of Man* (New York: Macmillan, 1965), 63.
20. C. S. Lewis, *That Hideous Strength* (New York: Macmillan, 1965), 172-173. Used by permission of The Estate of C. S. Lewis, London, England.

CHAPTER 10: *Realizations*

1. Quoted in Leon Kass, *Toward a More Natural Science* (New York: The Free Press, 1985), 318.
2. *Christianity Today*, "Reflections," March 17, 1989, 33.
3. *Nature*, "UK Agonizes over Embryo Research," February 7, 1985, 424. ◆ *Nature*, "Warnock Proposals in Trouble," February 7, 1985, 417. ◆ H. John Evans and Anne McLaren, "Unborn Children (Protection) Bill," *Nature*, March 14, 1985, 127-128. ◆ *Nature*, "Britain Hazards Embryo Research," December 3, 1987, 407. ◆ Simon Hadlington, "British Government Hedges Bets on Embryo Research," *Nature*, December 3, 1987, 409. ◆ *Lancet*, "Research on Human Embryos," December 13, 1986, 1375. ◆ *Lancet*, "Draft Legislation on Infertility Services and Embryo Research," December 5, 1987, 1343. ◆ *Lancet*, "Human Embryo Research: Vote for Progress," December 5, 1987, 1311. ◆ John Townsend, "Research on Human Embryos," *Lancet*, January 3, 1987, 53. ◆ *Nature*, "More Embryo Research?" May 19, 1988, 194. ◆ Louis Waller, "In Australia, the Debate Moves to Embryo Experimentation," *The Hastings Center Report*, June 1987, 21-22. ◆ Dittia Bartels, "Regulating IVF," *Nature*, August 18, 1988, 559-560.
4. Diana Brahams, "The Hasty British Ban on Commercial Surrogacy," *The Hastings Center Report*, February 1987, 16-19.
5. Steven Dickman, "West German Research Agencies Oppose New Embryo Law," *Nature*, May 7, 1987, 6. ◆ Steven Dickman, "Embryo Research Ban Causes Ructions in West Germany," *Nature*, June 30, 1988, 791. ◆ Steven Dickman, "International Outlook for Embryo Research," *Nature*, June 30, 1988, 6. ◆ Don Kirk, "West Germany Moving to Make IVF a Crime," *Science*, July 22, 1988, 406.u Rudy Balling *et al.*, "Moratorium Call," *Nature*, August 18, 1988, 560. ◆ Virginia Bolton, Peter Braude, and Stephen Moore, "Ethical Bounds," *Nature*, September 29, 1988, 392.
6. Colin Norman, "IVF Research Moratorium to End?" *Science*, July 22, 1988, 405-406. ◆ Barbara J. Culliton, "Fetal Research Ban Morally 'Acceptable,'" *Science*, September 23, 1988, 1593-1594. ◆ Barbara J. Culliton, "White House Wants Fetal Research Ban," *Science*, September 16, 1988, 1423.
7. Psalm 8:1-5, *New International Version*.

8. Paul Ramsey, *Fabricated Man* (New Haven, CT: Yale University Press, 1970), 39.

9. *Ibid.*, 38-39. Italics used in entire sentence are mine.

10. This term is used by IVF specialist and reproductive endocrinologist Alan DeCherney in his paper, "Doctored Babies," *Fertility and Sterility* 40 (December 1983): 724-727.

11. In summary, the current crisis in women's health is evident because:

● **One in every four mothers in the United States today gives birth by cesarean section.** [Sources: Tim Friend, "New Rules Aim to Reduce C-sections," *USA Today*, October 27, 1988, 1D. ◆ Tim Friend, "Half of All C-sections May Be Unwarranted," *USA Today*, January 27, 1989, 1D. ◆ Dick Thompson, "Safer Births the Second Time," *Time*, November 7, 1988, 103.]

● **Half of all American women experience hysterectomy before they die.** [Sources: Sue Miller, "Physician: Toll of Hysterectomies Underestimated," *Baltimore Evening Sun*, reprinted in *Lincoln Sunday Journal Star*, November 13, 1988, 3E. ◆ Winnifred B. Cutler, *Hysterectomy: Before and After* (New York: Harper & Row, 1988), 2.]

● **Four out of ten women in our country have had at least one surgical abortion.** [Source: *Newsweek*, "The Soviet/U.S. Summit: Data," December 14, 1987, 41.]

● **One in every five cases of infertility is caused by sexually transmitted diseases.** [Sources: Committee on Small Business, *Consumer Protection Issues Involving In Vitro Fertilization Clinics*, (Washington, DC: U.S. Government Printing Office, 1988), 16. ◆ U.S. Congress, Office of Technology Assessment, *Infertility: Medical and Social Choices*, OTA-BA-358 (Washington DC: U.S. Government Printing Office, May 1988), 61. ◆ Edward W. Hook III, Committee on Government Operations, *Medical and Social Choices for Infertile Couples and the Federal Role in Prevention and Treatment* (Washington, DC: U.S. Government Printing Office, 1989), 172.]

● **One third of all reported gonorrhea in American women occurs in women age nineteen or less—70 percent in women age twenty-four or less.** Chlamydia infections are estimated to be twice as common as gonorrhea, causing *three to four million infections annually*. [Source: Committee on Government Operations, *op. cit.*, 172.]

● **Over half of American women have sexual intercourse before age eighteen.** [Source: Robert A. Hatcher *et al.*, *Contraceptive Technology, 1988-1989*, 14th rev. ed. (New York: Irvington, 1988), 51.]

● **One out of every ten women** between the ages of fifteen and nineteen becomes pregnant each year. [Source, Hatcher *et al.*, *op. cit.*, 46.]

　　Public health officials unanimously agree that the infertility rate will rise over the next ten to fifteen years as many of today's adolescents grow older and later discover they are unable to have children.

12. For information on nurse-midwives, contact: American College of Nurse Midwifes, 1012 Fourteenth Street N.W., Suite 801, Washington, DC 20005 (202) 347-5445. For obtaining home birth supplies, herbal remedies, and references for Christian Midwives, write or call: Brenda Matea, Yalad Birthing Supply, 7041 Northview N.E., North Canton, OH

44721 (216) 492-8025. (Yalad is the Old Testament Hebrew word for midwife.) Excellent resources for information on alternatives in maternity care are the *International Childbirth Education Association* (ICEA) and the *National Association of Parents and Professionals for Safe Alternatives in Childbirth* (NAPSAC).

ICEA, P.O. Box 20049, Minneapolis, MN 55420-0048.

NAPSAC, Rte. 1, P.O. Box 646, Marble Hill, MO 63764.

ICEA offers a wide variety of educational materials and programs to assist families in obtaining high-quality, consumer-oriented maternity care. For cesarean prevention information, contact:

Cesarean Support, Education, and Concern (C/SEC), 22 Forest Road, Framingham, MA 10701.

Cesarean Prevention Movement, P.O.Box 152, University Station, Syracuse, NY 13210.

For additional reading, see: Gail Sforza Brewer, *The Very Important Pregnancy Program* (Emmaus, PA: Rodale Press, 1988). ◆ Gail Sforza Brewer and Janice Presser Greene, *Right from the Start* (Emmaus, PA: Rodale Press, 1981). ◆ Debra Evans, *The Complete Book on Childbirth* (Wheaton, IL: Tyndale, 1986). ◆ Alice Gilgoff, *Home Birth*, rev. ed. (Granby, MA: Bergin & Garvey, 1989). ◆ Tracy Hotchner, *Pregnancy & Childbirth: The Complete Guide for a New Life* (New York: Avon, 1984). ◆ Sheila Kitzinger and Penny Simkin, eds., *Episiotomy and the Second Stage of Labor* (Seattle WA: Pennypress, 1986). ◆ Diana Korte and Roberta Scaer, *A Good Birth, A Safe Birth*, 2nd ed. (New York: Bantam, 1984). ◆ Penny Simkin, Janet Whaley, and Ann Keppler, *Pregnancy, Childbirth, and the Newborn* (Deephaven, MN: Meadowbrook Press, 1984). ◆ David Stewart, ed., *The Five Standards for Safe Childbearing* (Marble Hill, MO: NAPSAC Reproductions, 1981). ◆ Charlotte and Fred Ward, *The Home Birth Book* (Garden City, NY: Doubleday/Dolphin Books, 1977). ◆ Diony Young, *Changing Childbirth: Family Birth in the Hospital.* (Rochester, NY: Childbirth Graphics, 1982).

Most of the books under footnotes #12 and #17 may be ordered through ICEA at the above address or by calling the ICEA Bookcenter at 1-800-624-4934.

13. For the name of a lactation consultant or breastfeeding center near you, contact:

International Lactation Consultant Association, P.O. Box 4031, University of Virginia Station, Charlottesville, VA 22903.

La Leche League International, 9616 Minneapolis Ave., Franklin Park, IL 60131.

For additional reading: Marvin Eiger and Sally Wendkos Olds, *The Complete Book of Breastfeeding*, 2nd ed. (New York: Workman, 1987). ◆ Kathleen Huggins, *The Nursing Mother's Companion* (Harvard, MA: Harvard Common Press, 1986). ◆ La Leche League International, *The Womanly Art of Breastfeeding*, 4th ed. (New York: Plume/New American Library, 1987). ◆ Maureen Minchin, *Breastfeeding Matters* (N. Sydney, Australia: George Allen & Unwin, 1985). ◆ Dana Raphael, *The Tender Gift: Breastfeeding* (Englewood Cliffs, NJ: Prentice-Hall, 1973). ◆ Jan

Riordan, *A Practical Guide to Breastfeeding* (St. Louis, MO: C. V. Mosby, 1983). ◆ Candace Woessner, Judith Lauwers, and Barbara Bernard, *Breastfeeding Today: The Mother's Companion* (Wayne, NJ: Avery, 1987).

14. For information on obtaining a natural family planning Home Study Kit (Sympto-Thermal Method), call or write: *The Couple to Couple League*, Dept. 43, P.O. Box 111184, Cincinnati, OH, 45211, (513) 661-7612.

    For information and materials regarding the Ovulation Method of NFP, write Dr. Thomas Hilgers, M.D., Pope Paul VI Institute for the Study of Human Reproduction, 6901 Mercy Road, Suite 200, Omaha, NE 68106.

    For additional reading, see: Sheila and John Kippley, *The Art of Natural Family Planning, 3rd ed.* (Cincinnati: Couple to Couple League, 1984). ◆ Nona Aguilar, *The New, No-Pill, No-Risk Birth Control* (New York: Rawson, 1986). ◆ Debra Evans, *The Mystery of Womanhood* (Westchester, IL: Crossway Books, 1987).

15. For help in the healing process, read: Linda Cochrane, *Women in Ramah: A Post Abortion Bible Study*, 1986. (Printed by and available for $7.00 through PACE, Christian Action Cl Education and Ministries Fund, 701 W. Broad Street, Suite 405, Falls Church, VA 22046. ◆ Teri K. Reisser and Paul C. Reisser, *Help for the Postabortal Woman.* (Printed by and available free through: FOCUS ON THE FAMILY, Pomona, CA 91799.)

16. *When a physician's services are required, shop around before selecting a health care provider.* Call local childbirth education groups and ask for the names of three doctors they are comfortable recommending. Then call the labor and delivery departments of hospitals in your area and ask a nurse to provide the same information. Specifically ask for someone who has a *low cesarean/high VBAC rate, offers a flexible approach to medical treatment, does not routinely use electronic fetal monitoring or I.V.'s, performs a minimum number of labor inductions and episiotomies, lets the mother choose what position to give birth in, and refrains from interfering in the natural process of labor.* Don't rely solely on friends for recommendations; get references from at least four or five different consumer-oriented services. At least one or two names will probably be mentioned by several women you talk to. Arrange for a private consultation with one or two doctors to discuss your health care needs and preferences.

16. For additional reading, see: Yvonne Brackbill, June Rice, and Diony Young, *Birth Trap* (St. Louis, MO: C. V. Mosby, 1984). ◆ Doris Haire, *Cultural Warping of Childbirth* (Minneapolis, MN: ICEA, 1972). ◆ Sally Inch, *Birthrights* (New York: Parthenon, 1984). ◆ Brigitte Jordan, *Birth in Four Cultures* (Toronto: Eden Press, 1983). ◆ Sheila Kitzinger and John A. Davis, eds., *The Place of Birth* (Oxford, England: Oxford University Press, 1978). ◆ Rebecca Rowe Parfitt, *The Birth Primer* (Philadelphia: Running Press, 1977). ◆ David and Lee Stewart, eds., *Compulsory Hospitalization: Freedom of Choice in Childbirth?* (Marble Hill, MO: NAPSAC Reproductions, 1979). ◆ David and Lee Stewart, eds., *Safe Alternatives in Childbirth* (Marble Hill, MO: NAPSAC Reproductions, 1976). ◆ David and Lee Stewart, eds., *21st Century*

Obstetrics Now! Vol. 1 and Vol. 2 (Marble Hill, MO: NAPSAC Reproductions, 1977). ◆ Richard and Dorothy Wertz, *Lying-In: A History of Childbirth in America* (New York: Free Press, 1977).

18. Sheila Kitzinger, *The Midwife Challenge* (London: Pandora Press, 1989), v.

19. Elizabeth Davis, *Heart & Hands: A Midwife's Guide to Pregnancy & Birth* (Berkely, CA: Celestial Arts, 1987), 3.

20. The near-disappearance of the midwife in this country was produced by state health departments working in conjunction with ob/gyns. [See: Dartha Clapper Brack, "Displaced—the Midwife by the Male Physician," *Women & Health* 1 (November/December 1976): 18-23. ◆ Neal Devitt, "The Statistical Case for Elimination of the Midwife: Fact Versus Prejudice, 1890-1935 (Part I)," *Women & Health* 4 (Spring 1979): 81-96. ◆ Neal Devitt, "The Statistical Case for Elimination of the Midwife: Fact Versus Prejudice, 1890-1935 (Part II)," *Women & Health* 4 (Summer 1979): 169-186. ◆ Ann H. Sablosky, "The Power of the Forceps: A Comparative Analysis of the Midwife—Historically and Today," *Women & Health* 1 (January/February 1976): 10-13.]

Articles appearing in the *Journal of the American Medical Association* in 1912 and 1913 provide the evidence for this assertion. Titled "Medical Education and the Midwife Problem in the United States," and "The Elimination of the Midwife," these two papers clearly demonstrate that as a newly emerging profession ob/gyns were directly threatened by their more established, traditional counterparts. [J. Whitridge Williams, "Medical Education and the Midwife Problem in the United States," *Journal of the American Medical Association*, January 6, 1912, 1-7. ◆ Charles Edward Ziegler, "The Elimination of the Midwife," *Journal of the American Medical Association*, January 4, 1913, 32-38.]

"The Elimination of the Midwife," written by Charles Edward Ziegler, a professor of obstetrics at the University of Pittsburgh, begins:

> It is most gratifying to note the interest which has been awakened in the midwife problem during the past few years. The outlook is hopeful and an attempted early solution of the question may be anticipated. The danger lies in too great haste. Either we are going to settle the matter to our credit and future welfare, or we are going to make a serious and perhaps irreparable mistake. My own feeling is that the danger lies in the possibility of attempting to educate the midwife and in licensing her to practice midwifery, giving her thereby a legal status which later cannot perhaps be altered. If she once becomes a fixed element in our social and economic system, as she now is in the British Isles and on the Continent [Europe], *we may never be able to get rid of her*. I agree with Dr. E. P. Davis, that she is a "menace to the health of the community, an unnecessary evil and a nuisance." I am, therefore, unalterably opposed to any plan which seeks to give her a permanent place in the practice of medicine. . . . The argument that large numbers of physicians do

> as poor obstetrics as the midwives is entirely beside the question. We are quite ready to admit this, but to claim for that reason we must retain the midwife, if we retain the physician, is absurd. . . . The fact is, as I shall attempt to point out, we can all get along very nicely without the midwife, whereas all are agreed that the physician is indispensable. It thus seems that the sensible thing to do is to train the physician until he is capable of doing good obstetrics, and then make it financially possible for him to do it, by eliminating the midwife and giving him such other support as may be necessary. [Ziegler, *Ibid.*, 32.]

"Good obstetrics" meant hospitalization for birth and being placed flat on one's back on a delivery table in order to be made unconscious during childbirth. This was primarily to allow doctors to "rescue the baby" from the pressure of the birth canal through the use of metal tongs, called *forceps,* and a cut in the vagina, referred to as *episiotomy.* [J. B. DeLee, "The Prophylactic Forceps Operation," *American Journal of Obstetrics and Gynecology* 1 (1920): 34-44.] The use of such crude, scientifically unproven technology quickly became commonplace.

Dr. Joseph DeLee was largely responsible for normalizing this assault, claiming that 4 to 5 percent of babies died from injuries caused by "natural spontaneous labor." [Richard W. Wertz and Dorothy C. Wertz, *Lying-In: A History of Childbirth in America* (New York: The Free Press, 1977), 142.] DeLee believed that long, hard labors often caused such problems as idiocy, epilepsy, imbecility, and cerebral palsy. Arguing that forceps and episiotomy saved children from this type of brain damage and restored women to "better than new" after they had their babies, DeLee widely promoted "The Prophylactic Forceps Operation" to avoid the devastating effects of natural labor.

After comparing vaginal delivery to the mother's falling on a pitchfork and the baby's head being caught in a door jamb, he says:

> It always strikes physicians as well as laymen as bizarre, to call labor an abnormal function, a disease, and yet it is a decidedly pathological process. Everything, of course, depends on what we define as normal.
>   . . . I have often wondered whether Nature did not deliberately intend women to be used up in the process of reproduction, in a manner analogous to that of the salmon, which dies after spawning. [DeLee, *op. cit.*, 39, 41.]

"By the 1930s, [DeLee's] routine was normative in many hospitals, for his rationale to prevent tears seemed reasonable: Many women delivering in hospitals *were* experiencing tears," write professors Richard and Dorothy Wertz. "But doctors did not ask whether tears resulted from the failings of nature or from hospital practices, which often immobilized [and anesthetized] a woman flat on her back with legs raised in stirrups. DeLee's procedures did not become routine in foreign countries that had a higher proportion of home deliveries and fewer perineal tears. *As late as 1973 doctors were looking for scientific proof of the validity of DeLee's hypothesis that episiotomy and outlet forceps protected the baby's head also."* [Wertz and Wertz, *op. cit.*, 143.] Physicians are still looking for proof today.

21. Lynn Baptisti Richards, "Guest Editorial: Finding the Truth in Birth—A Leap of Faith," *International Journal of Childbirth Education* 4 (February 1989): 20.

22. Proverbs 3:5-8 *New International Version*.

23. See the stories of Sarah (Genesis 11:30; 16:1—17:22; 21:1-20); Rebekah (Genesis 25:21); Rachel (Genesis 29:31—30:24); Samson's mother (Judges 13:1-24); Hannah (1 Samuel 1:1—2:11); the Shunammite woman (2 Kings 4:8-37); and Elizabeth (Luke 1:1-23).

24. Genesis 16:1-16 and 21:8-20; Genesis 30:1-21 and 37:1-36.

25. Galatians 4:21-31.

26. Genesis 35:16-19.

27. John T. Noonan, "Christian Tradition and the Control of Reproduction," in Leonard J. Nelson, ed., *The Death Decision* (Ann Arbor, MI: Servant Books, 1984), 15. Italics mine.

28. 1 Samuel 1:10-18.

29. 1 Samuel 2:6, 9.

30. Adoption resources include: *Adoption Service Info Agency (ASIA)*, 7720 Alaska Avenue N.W., Washington, DC 20012. ◆ *American Adoption Agency*, 1228 M St. N.W., Washington, DC 20005. ◆ *Americans for International Aid and Adoption*, 877 South Adams, Suite 106, Birmingham, MI 48011. ◆ *Catholic Social Services*, 222 North 17th Street, Philadelphia, PA 19103. ◆ *Hand in Hand International Adoption Agency*, 4965 Barnes Road, Colorado Springs, CO 80917. ◆ *Holt International Children's Services*, P.O. Box 2880, Eugene, OR 97402. ◆ *International Concerns Committee for Children*, 911 Cypress Drive, Boulder, CO 80303. ◆ *National Committee for Adoption*, 2025 M Street, N.W., Suite 512, Washington, DC 20036. ◆ *North American Council on Adoptable Children* (NACAC), 810 18th Street, N.W., Suite 703, Washington, DC 20006. ◆ *OURS, INC.* (Organization for United Response), 3307 Highway 100 North, Suite 203, Minneapolis, MN 55422. ◆ *Parents for Private Adoption*, P.O. Box 7, Pawlet, VT 05761. ◆ *Pearl S. Buck Foundation*, Green Hills Farm, Perkasie, PA 18944. ◆ *Welcome House*, P.O. Box 836, Doylestown, PA 18901.

For additional reading, see: Lois Gilam, *The Adoption Resource Book* (New York: Perennial Library/ Harper & Row, 1987). ◆ Charlene Canape, *Adoption: Parenthood Without Pregnancy* (New York: Avon, 1988).

31. Psalm 139:13-14, *New International Version*.

32. Michael Gold, "The Baby Makers," *Science 85* (April 1985): 26-38.

33. Psalm 100:3, *New American Standard Version*

34. Gary D. Hodgen, "Pregnancy Prevention by Intravaginal Delivery of a Progesterone Antagonist: RU486 Tampon for Menstrual Induction and Absorption," *Fertility and Sterility* 44 (August 1985): 263-267.

35. Nan and Todd Tilton with Gaylen Moore, *Making Miracles*. (Garden City NY: Doubleday & Co., 1985), 156.

36. Joseph J. Piccone, "This Kind of Science Is Best Left Unused," *USA*

Today, March 9, 1989, 6A. See also: Brian Goldsmith, "Infertility Giving Birth to New Problems for Doctors and Lawyers," *Canadian Medical Journal* (January 15, 1988), 166-167.

AFTERWORD

1. In reality, reproductive health is more profoundly influenced by monogamy, good nutrition, the three "R's" (rest, relaxation, and recreation), and prayer!
2. Psalm 124:8. *New American Standard Version.*

APPENDIX A

1. Pope John Paul II, Discourse to those taking part in the 81st Congress of the Italian Society of Internal Medicine and the 82nd Congress of the Italian Society of General Surgery, Oct. 27, 1980: AAS 72 (1980) 1126.
2. Pope Paul VI, Discourse to the General Assembly of the United Nations, Oct. 4, 1965: AAS 57 (1965) 878; encyclical *Populorum Progressio*, 13: AAS 59 (1967) 263.
3. Pope Paul VI, Homily during the Mass Closing the Holy Year, Dec. 25, 1975: AAS 68 (1976) 145; Pope John Paul II, encyclical *Dives in Misericordia*, 30: AAS 72 (1980) 1224.
4. Pope John Paul II, Discourse to those taking part in the 35th General Assembly of the World Medical Association, Oct. 29, 1983: AAS 76 (1984) 390.
5. Cf. Declaration *Dignitatis Humanae*, 2.
6. Pastoral constitution *Gaudium et Spes*, 22; Pope John Paul II, encyclical *Redemptor Hominis*, 8: AAS 71 (1979) 270-272.
7. Cf. *Gaudium et Spes*, 35.
8. *Ibid.*,15; cf. also *Populorum Progressio*, 20: AAS 59 (1967) 267; *Redemptor Hominis*, 15: AAS 71 (1979) 286-289; Pope John Paul II, apostolic exhortation *Familiaris Consortio*, 8: AAS 74 (1982) 89.
9. *Familiaris Consortio*, 11: AAS 74 (1982) 92
10. Cf. Pope Paul VI, encyclical *Humanae Vitae*, 10: AAS 60 (1968) 487-488.
11. Pope John Paul II, Discourse to the members of the 35th General Assembly of the World Medical Association, Oct. 29, 1983: AAS 76 (1984) 393.
12. Cf. *Familiaris Consortio*, 11: AAS 74 (1982) 91-92; cf. also *Gaudium et Spes*, 50.
13. Congregation for the Doctrine of the Faith, Declaration on Procured Abortion, 9, AAS 66 (1974) 736-737.
14. Pope John Paul II, Discourse to those taking part in the 35th General Assembly of the World Medical Association, Oct. 29, 1983: AAS 76 (1984) 390.
15. Pope John XXIII, encyclical *Mater et Magistra*, 111: AAS 53 (1961) 447.
16. *Gaudium et Spes*, 24.
17. Cf. Pope Pius XII, encyclical *Humani Generis:* AAS 42 (1950) 575; Pope Paul VI, *Professio Fidei:* AAS 60 (1968) 436.

18. *Mater et Magistra,* III; cf. Pope John Paul II, Discourse to priests participating in a Seminar on "Responsible Procreation," Sept. 17, 1983, *Insegnamenti di Giovanni Paolo II,* VI, 2 (1983) 562: "At the origin of each human person there is a creative act of God: No man comes into existence by chance; he is always the result of the creative love of God."

19. Cf. *Gaudium et Spes,* 24.

20. Cf. Pope Pius XII, Discourse to the St. Luke Medical-Biological Union, Nov. 12, 1944: *Discorsi e Radiomessaggi,* VI (1944-1945) 191-192.

21. Cf, *Gaudium et Spes,* 50.

22. Cf. *Ibid.,* 51: "When it is a question of harmonizing married love with the responsible transmission of life, the moral character of one's behavior does not depend only on the good intention and the evaluation of the motives: The objective criteria must be used, criteria drawn from the nature of the human person and human acts, criteria which respect the total meaning of mutual self-giving and human procreation in the context of true love."

23. *Gaudium et Spes,* 51.

24. Holy See, Charter of the Rights of the Family, 5: *L'Osservatore Romano,* Nov. 25, 1983.

25. Congregation for the Doctrine of the Faith, Declaration on Procured Abortion, 12-13: AAS 66 (1974) 738.

26. Cf. Pope Paul VI, Discourse to participants in the 23rd National Congress of Italian Catholic Jurists, Dec. 9,1972: AAS 64 (1972) 777.

27. The obligation to avoid disproportionate risks involves an authentic respect for human beings and the uprightness of therapeutic intentions. It implies that the doctor "above all . . . must carefully evaluate the possible negative consequences which the necessary use of a particular exploratory technique may have upon the unborn child and avoid recourse to diagnostic procedures which do not offer sufficient guarantees of their honest purpose and substantial harmlessness. And if, as often happens in human choices, a degree of risk must be undertaken, he will take care to assure that it is justified by a truly urgent need for the diagnosis and by the importance of the results that can be achieved by it for the benefit of the unborn child himself" (Pope John Paul II, Discourse to participants in the Pro-Life Movement Congress, Dec. 3, 1982: *Insegnamenti di Giovanni Paolo II,* V, 3 (1982) 1512. This clarification concerning "proportionate risk" is also to be kept in mind in the following sections of the present Instruction, whenever this term appears.

28. Pope John Paul II, Discourse to the participants in the 35th General Assembly of the World Medical Association, Oct. 29, 1983: AAS 76 (1984) 392.

29. Cf. *Ibid.,* Address to a meeting of the Pontifical Academy of Sciences, Oct. 23, 1982: AAS 75 (1983) 37: "I condemn, in the most explicit and formal way, experimental manipulations of the human embryo, since the human being, from conception to death, cannot be exploited for any purpose whatsoever."

30. Charter of the Rights of the Family, 4b. *L'Osservatore Romano,* Nov. 25, 1983.

31. Cf. Pope John Paul II, Address to the participants in the Pro-Life Movement Congress, Dec. 3, 1982: *Insegnamenti di Giovanni Paolo II*, V, 3 (1982) 1511: "Any form of experimentation on the fetus that may damage its integrity or worsen its condition is unacceptable, except in the case of a final effort to save it from death." Congregation for the Doctrine of the Faith, Declaration on Euthanasia, 4: AAS 72 (1980) 550: "In the absence of other sufficient remedies, it is permitted, with the patient's consent, to have recourse to the means provided by the most advanced medical techniques, even if these means are still at the experimental stage and are not without a certain risk."

32. No one, before coming into existence, can claim a subjective right to begin to exist; nevertheless, it is legitimate to affirm the right of the child to have a fully human origin through conception in conformity with the personal nature of the human being. Life is a gift that must be bestowed in a manner worthy both of the subject receiving it and of the subjects transmitting it. This statement is to be borne in mind also for what will be explained concerning artificial human procreation.

33. Cf. Pope John Paul II, Discourse to those taking part in the 35th General Assembly of the World Medical Association, Oct. 29, 1983: AAS 76 (1984) 391.

34. Cf. *Gaudium et Spes*, 50.

35. Cf. *Familiaris Consortio*, 14: AAS 74 (1982) 96.

36. Cf. Pope Pius XII, Discourse to those taking part in the Fourth International Congress of Catholic Doctors, Sept. 29, 1949: AAS 41 (1949) 559. According to the plan of the Creator, "a man leaves his father and his mother and cleaves to his wife, and they become one flesh" (Gn 2:24). The unity of marriage, bound to the order of creation, is a truth accessible to natural reason. The Church's tradition and magisterium frequently make reference to the Book of Genesis, both directly and through the passages of the New Testament that refer to it: Mt 19:4-6; Mk 10:5-8; Eph 5:31. Cf. Athenagoras, *Legatio pro christianis*, 33: PG 6, 965-967; St. Chrysostom, *In Matthaeum homiliae*, LXII, 19, 1: PG 58 597; St. Leo the Great, *Epist. ad Rusticum*, 4: PL 54, 1204; Innocent III, Epist. *Gaudemus in Domino:* DS 778; Council of Lyons II, IV Session: DS 860; Council of Trent, XXIV Session: DS 1798, 1802; Pope Leo XIII, encyclical *Arcanum Divinae Sapientiae:* AAS 12 (1879-1880) 388-391; Pope Pius XI, encyclical Casti Connubii: AAS 22 (1930) 546-547; *Gaudium et Spes*, 48; *Familiaris Consortio*, 19; Code of Canon Law, Canon 1056.

37. Cf. Pope Pius XII, Discourse to those taking part in the Fourth International Congress of Catholic Doctors, Sept. 29,1949 41 (1949) 560; Discourse to those taking part in the Congress of the Italian Catholic Union of Midwives, Oct. 29, 1951: AAS 43 (1951) 850; Code of Canon Law, Canon 1134.

38. *Humanae Vitae*, 12.

39. *Ibid.*

40. Pope Pius XII, Discourse to those taking part in the Second Naples World Congress on Fertility and Human Sterility, May 19, 1956: AAS 48 (1956) 470.

41. Code of Canon Law, Canon 1061. According to this canon, the conjugal act is that by which the marriage is consummated if the couple "have performed (it) between themselves in a human manner."

42. Cf. *Gaudium et Spes,* 14.

43. Cf. Pope John Paul II, General Audience Jan. 16, 1980: *Insegnamenti di Giovanni Paolo II,* III, 1 (1980) 148-152.

44. *Ibid.,* Discourse to those taking part in the 35th General Assembly of the World Medical Association, Oct. 29, 1983: AAS 76 (1984) 393.

45. Cf. *Gaudium et Spes,* 51.

46. *Ibid.,* 50.

47. Cf. Pope Pius XII, Discourse to those taking part in the Fourth International Congress of Catholic Doctors, Oct. 29, 1949: AAS 41 (1949) 560: "It would be erroneous . . . to think that the possibility of resorting to this means (artificial fertilization) might render valid a marriage between persons unable to contract it because of the 'impedimentum impotentiae.'"

48. A similar question was dealt with by Pope Paul VI, *Humanae Vitae,* 14.

49. Cf. supra: I, 1ff.

50. *Familiaris Consortio,* 14: AAS 74 (1982) 96.

51. Cf. Response of the Holy Office, March 17,1897: DS 3323; Pope Pius XII, Discourse to those taking part in the Fourth International Congress of Catholic Doctors, Sept. 29, 1949: AAS 41 (1949) 560; Discourse to the Italian Catholic Union of Midwives, Oct. 29, 1951: AAS 43 (1951) 850; Discourse to those taking part in the Second Naples World Congress on Fertility and Human Sterility, May 19, 1956: AAS, 48 (1956) 471-473; Discourse to those taking part in the Seventh International Congress of the International Society of Hematology, Sept. 1958: AAS 50 (1958) 733; *Mater et Magistra,* III.

52. Pope Pius XII, Discourse to the Italian Catholic Union of Midwives, Oct. 29, 1951: AAS 43 (1951) 850.

53. *Ibid.,* Discourse to those taking part in the Fourth International Congress of Catholic Doctors, Sept. 29,1949: AAS 41(1949) 560.

54. Congregation for the Doctrine of the Faith, Declaration on Certain Questions Concerning Sexual Ethics, 9: AAS 68 (1976) 86, which quotes *Gaudium et Spes,* 51. Cf. Decree of the Holy Office, Aug. 2, 1929: AAS 21 (1929) 490; Pope Pius XII, Discourse to those taking part in the 26th Congress of the Italian Society of Urology, Oct. 8, 1953: AAS 45 (1953) 678.

55. Cf. Pope John XXIII, *Mater et Magistra,* III.

56. Cf. Pope Pius XII, Discourse to those taking part in the Fourth International Congress of Catholic Doctors, Sept. 29, 1949: AAS 41 (1949), 560.

57. Cf. *Ibid.,* Discourse to those taking part in the Second Naples World Congress on Fertility and Human Sterility, May 19, 1956: AAS 48 (1956) 471-473.

59. *Familiaris Consortio,* 14: AAS 74 (1982) 97.

60. Cf. *Dignitatis Humanae,* 7.

Index